About the Author

Alexandra is a mother of two, living in Barcelona, where she writes and rides horses.

The Highwaygirl

Alexandra Spanswick-Smith

The Highwaygirl

Vanguard Press

VANGUARD PAPERBACK

© Copyright 2023
Alexandra Spanswick-Smith

The right of Alexandra Spanswick-Smith to be identified as author of
this work has been asserted by her in accordance with the
Copyright, Designs and Patents Act 1988.

All Rights Reserved

No reproduction, copy or transmission of this publication
may be made without written permission.
No paragraph of this publication may be reproduced,
copied or transmitted save with the written permission of the publisher, or in accordance
with the provisions
of the Copyright Act 1956 (as amended).

Any person who commits any unauthorised act in relation to
this publication may be liable to criminal
prosecution and civil claims for damages.

A CIP catalogue record for this title is
available from the British Library.

ISBN 978 1 83794 060 8

This is a work of fiction. Names, characters, businesses, places, events and incidents are either the product of the author's imagination or used in a fictitious manner. Any resemblance to actual persons, living or dead, or actual events is purely coincidental.

*Vanguard Press is an imprint of
Pegasus Elliot Mackenzie Publishers Ltd.*
www.pegasuspublishers.com

First Published in 2023

**Vanguard Press
Sheraton House Castle Park
Cambridge England**

Printed & Bound in Great Britain

BEATRICE 1799

"FOUR p.m. sharp in the tea room and don't be late, young lady, Earl Staunton has travelled far to meet you!" shouted Lord Seymour to Beatrice as she ran hurriedly out of the kitchens.

"I'm not marrying some fat, old earl!" Beatrice yelled back as she ran towards the horse field and to Asta.

"Then I'll sell Asta. You are eighteen now!" shouted back the Lord. This only made Beatrice run even faster with floods of tears streaming down her face. Once she arrived with Asta, she buried her face and her tears in her beloved horse's neck. Asta and Beatrice were inseparable and utterly devoted.

"Argh!" Beatrice shouted as she stomped her feet in the mud, purposely dirtying them.

"It's not fair, it's horrible, it's… it's…" Beatrice couldn't get the words out through the tears. Asta nuzzled her head into Beatrice, trying to comfort her.

Collecting herself, Beatrice took in a long and deep breath. She then walked to the stables, Asta followed. Beatrice put on her breeches and shirt, threw her skirts and bodice onto the floor and saddled Asta. Like a cannon firing, they bolted out of the barn.

"Come on, girl!" Beatrice shouted with gusto as she raced up the hill and over the fields, freedom running through her blood and the wind blowing through her hair. Beatrice wasn't going to let another argument with her father ruin her ride with Asta. The wind dried her tears as she soon forgot about her worries. Now, all she could think about was the obstacle ahead.

Beatrice cornered the trees tightly as she raced past them, only missing them by a scrape. Mud flew up on her boots. She was in her element. In fact, they both were, Asta was excelling in every daredevil jump and crossing. She too was black with mud. This is what they did best, this was cross-country riding at its best. They rode every obstacle at breakneck speed, literally ripping along and through the woods, pounding upon the ground and crashing through the streams; it was as exhilarating as it was dangerous. It was everything they both lived for and they were champions at it! A fallen tree lay ahead, it was high, it would take a powerful leap to jump it.

"Come on, girl. Let's take it," Beatrice excitedly shouted to Asta. She sped her up as she approached the large tree, and at full power, leapt sky high over the trunk, clearing it by spades. Once over, there was no time to rest as a steep hill lay ahead.

"Let's go!" Beatrice cried.

Beatrice leant forward, high up over Asta's mane, giving her the space to power on up the steep hill. She charged at full speed, her hind legs pushing, pushing and pushing them both to the top of the hill. But again, no time to rest once there.

"Woohoo!" Beatrice shouted out elatedly as they took the curves on the downward hills, twisting and curving with every bend. They crashed through another river enjoying its fresh waters as it splashed and cooled their hot and sweating bodies. This was high-octane, endurance riding and they both didn't want to be doing anything else. There was literally nowhere else Beatrice wanted to be.

Nowhere! But unfortunately, there was somewhere that she had to be. Somewhere she deeply didn't want to go to at all.

Beatrice brought her fine chestnut mare to a slow canter and then to a trot as they emerged from the thick of the woods and into a beautiful English meadow.

"How beautiful spring is, how beautiful is our meadow," Beatrice said aloud to Asta. "If only Christopher were here."

Christopher was Beatrice's cousin and also her best friend. They had grown up together, sharing all their frustrations and joys. But her father had banned her from seeing him as he thought him a bad influence. Her father was also shamed by his family's fall into poverty. So they had to meet and ride together in secret. This was not only her secret meadow it was theirs. They squandered many an hour there, talking and laughing. He always made her laugh. A silly joke, a silly face. She needed his calm demeanour, his tempered balance. She adored her time spent there with Christopher.

She hadn't seen him for a while and missed him dreadfully. But she knew that his life as a criminal would sometimes keep him away for long periods of time. So, for now, she enjoyed the meadow with Asta, letting it give her the refuge she so needed.

Beatrice dropped the reins and Asta lowered her head to graze. Beatrice took her feet out of the stirrups, ungirthed the saddle, letting it fall to the ground and then lay her legs outstretched in front of her as she lay back flat along Asta's back. She put her hands behind her head and looked up into the sky, taking a long deep sigh.

"This place is heaven on Earth," Beatrice whispered out loud. She was amazed at its sheer wonder.

It was mid-April and the meadow was pulsating with the abundance of spring. Life was exploding from every blade of grass, every blossom, every bird song, every flower. It flowed through Beatrice like a live current. She gazed up at the trees as their leaves flickered and danced in the wind. She watched the birds fly back and forth, full of song as they worked. She smelled the pungent perfumes of spring waft through the sweet, gentle air. The bluebells were a carpet of purple.

I love England, Beatrice thought. I hate her rules but I love her birds and trees, smells and colours and meadows and fields. Beatrice daydreamed, lulled by her surroundings and by Asta's soft grazing motion. They both seemed to pulsate on the same vibration. Their relationship bonding and re-bonding over time and through love. A bond only tightened by every new year together. Beatrice and Asta were the best of friends, soulmates of a kind, they were each other's safe place and sanctuary and nothing would part them. Nothing, that is, except for the imminent threat of her impending marriage.

As the sun changed its glorious hue, Beatrice knew that dreaded moment had come. Her stomach sank as she acknowledged what lay ahead. A formal tea is what lay ahead. A formal tea with another potential suitor, a potential husband. Beatrice was filled with nothing but anger at the most abhorrent of thoughts, marriage. Marriage that would rob her of all of her freedoms and joys.

But why did it have to be that way? she thought. Why can I not still enjoy my freedoms and find a love marriage?

Beatrice shuddered at the thought of the ensuing reunion and sat up abruptly in order to stop her thoughts from escalating. Asta instinctively rose her head in response.

"We have to go, girl, it's time for boring teas, boring suitors, boring everything. Boring, boring, boring!" Beatrice moaned. She saddled Asta and climbed up on her back.

"Bye, beautiful meadow, see you very, very soon," Beatrice said to her favourite place as she slowly walked out. She trotted along a sweet and cosy woody path, where the trees had grown tall, overlapping and intertwining with each other creating a beautiful and romantic arch. Beatrice loved this path, it was like a magical tunnel made of trees. Especially today, when the sun flickered and glowed through its leaf tops.

This is where I would like to get married, Beatrice always thought whenever she walked along it. This is my romantic wish if I were to ever have a love marriage. Here in nature's natural chapel arch with the man I love and with Asta by my side. But her heart went heavy, knowing that her romantic dreams would never come true. And so, to shake off her feelings, Beatrice launched into a charging gallop which took them up the green hill behind the estate and straight to the stables.

It was a more secluded path where her male clothes and riding astride could not be seen. Thankfully, the stables and the horse fields lay some distance from the main house which helped with her escapes. Lilly, of course, always knew. Whenever they have their embroidery time together, Beatrice would sneak out. Sometimes she would climb down from her window, other times she would sneak out through the kitchens, stealing some of Mrs Crowley's shortbread as she passed.

Beatrice and Asta stormed up to the stables, coming to a screeching halt as she swung off Asta's back. Beatrice ran into the stables, and in a quick dash, threw off her trousers and threw on her skirts. She was late for her role as the young Lady Seymour-Barclay.

Beatrice unsaddled Asta and walked her to her field.

"See you tomorrow, beautiful girl," Beatrice said as she kissed her mare's neck. She took in a long and slow breath of her potent horse smell. The smell that never ceased to intoxicate. Asta hooked her head around Beatrice in an embrace.

With a big sigh, Beatrice walked quickly back to the house. Lacey Manor was a grand and sprawling Georgian mansion. It was a beautiful home but not a happy one. She preferred to enter through the kitchen entrance. Beatrice felt more comfortable here than in the formal rooms. It was also a good place to soften the transition from country girl to Lady. Beatrice was very fond of Mrs Crowley, the cook, or Betty, as she called her. Betty had more than often soothed Beatrice's frustrations with a warm hearty hug and some shortbread. But today, there was no time for talk, as Beatrice ran straight up to her room where Lilly, her personal maid, was waiting to help her dress for formal tea.

"Urgh! Another tea with another horrible suitor. They're all so ugly and boring and boring and ugly," Beatrice said to Lilly who was holding up two dresses for Beatrice to choose.

"Which dress would you like to wear?" Lilly asked.

"Neither," Beatrice replied angrily as she pointed to the yellow dress.

Lilly helped Beatrice into her dress and then started to comb out her knotted and muddy hair. "How was your ride today?" Lilly asked. Lilly was nineteen-years-old, a year older than Beatrice. They were both two teenage girls but living two very different realities. They liked each other, they had become friends.

"Oh, Lilly, it was wonderful. Asta was going so fast that I nearly lost my seat at one point. If only you liked horses, you could come with me."

They both knew this was a ridiculous statement even though Beatrice would, in fact, love to have a friend to ride with.

"It was quite muddy then?" Lilly said as she combed out some persistent mud. Lilly then braided Beatrice's long and wild hair, and in no time, Beatrice looked like the young Lady Seymour-Barclay she was bred to be.

"You are all ready to meet Earl Staunton," Lilly remarked. She thought about how beautiful Beatrice looked but she didn't envy her. She had seen all the suitors coming to Lacey Manor and she wouldn't want to marry any of them. "You look beautiful," Lilly said trying to cheer Beatrice up.

"Beautiful for nothing!" Beatrice replied sullenly.

"Maybe this one's not so bad. Maybe he's got big ears and a wart on his nose," Lilly said trying to make Beatrice laugh.

"Or a hunchback and a limp," Beatrice added.

"Or some horns and a tail," Lilly retorted. They both laughed out loud at this one. "Or maybe you could escape? Stow away on a ship?" Lilly continued excitedly.

"Yes, Lilly! Maybe I could escape. Stow away on a ship," Beatrice repeated, suddenly inspired by Lilly's flippant joke.

"Or become a pirate?" Lilly added dramatically, continuing the joke.

"Or become a pirate!" Beatrice repeated again taking Lilly's jokes to heart. "I always wanted to see other lands." She was enjoying this conversation about escape and possibilities.

But then, she came to her senses as she realised, "Ahh, but I won't be able to take Asta with me and actually I'm not so keen on ships, so piracy, no."

"What about a highway robber?" Lilly added excitedly enjoying the fun of their scandalous suggestions.

Beatrice hesitated for a moment. A little light bulb went off in her head. She held her breath for a second as she thought to herself. Yes, what about highway robbery?

"Yes, Lilly! A highway robber. I could be a highway robber. Asta and I can be together, no ships involved and I don't have to travel anywhere far. It's the perfect solution," Beatrice answered seriously.

Lilly was, of course, joking, it was a ridiculous idea and she was a little shocked at how seriously Beatrice had taken her light-hearted banter.

"But mistress, highway robbery is a hanging offence and not for young ladies," Lilly felt obliged to state the obvious.

"But maybe I shall be the first woman to be one. Create a scandal, cause a stir! How exciting would that be, Lilly. What a wonderful idea, Lilly. You are a master of brilliant ideas." Beatrice imagined herself on Asta in her highway robber's clothes; she was excited by this sudden turn of thought.

"But mistress, I was only joking," Lilly clarified. She was now a little frightened, maybe she could in some way be blamed if Beatrice was ever caught.

"Yes, yes, yes, of course, you were, Lilly and so am I. It's a preposterous idea. Totally inconceivable and best left here with us in this room," Beatrice affirmed as she came back to her senses. "So what were we joking about?" Beatrice thought it best to bring the conversation back to its light-heartedness. "Something about the Lord having six toes and…"

"…and a crooked nose," Lilly finished Beatrice's sentence, relieved to be back to their original gaiety but she felt something had shifted.

"Well, the time has come, time for tea," Beatrice announced resignedly. "Wish me luck, I'll try not to be too gloomy." Beatrice then leant forward and gave Lilly a big hug. "Thank you for making me laugh."

The tea room was cosy but cold. It was full of rules, etiquette and personal agendas. Beatrice knew the rules and played them well, after all, she had been brought up with an aristocrat's education. She sat with her parents until, finally, Earl Staunton was escorted in. Her heart sank.

Tea was served. Beatrice sipped the finest tea from the finest china tea cups like the finest, well-bred young woman that she was. All of which disguised her simmering disgust. As she sipped, she watched Staunton's mouth moving, spilling out words, an endless stream of boring inconsequential words, of which, she heard almost none.

Her mind drifted away as he continued on and on with his tirade of arrogances and she thought how utterly disgusting he looked; fat, old, ugly, and worst of all, boring. Was her father really going to condemn her to marry him? This thought brought on a rage so engulfing and explosive that the only way to ward it off was to look out of the big grand windows and steal a yearning glance at the beautiful green fields.

The fields called her, they always called her. They beckoned her to come ride her mare across them. To gallop wild and free upon them. They spoke directly to her wild and free spirit.

Beatrice was intriguing, beguiling. People were intoxicated by her. Her beauty blinded them. Long chestnut hair and warm hazel eyes with a hint of green. But there was that something about her that nobody could quite put their finger on. She was different. Not like any of the other debutantes. Her manners were flawless. Her charm seducing. Her conversations well-balanced but there was something else deeper that was bubbling just below the surface. There was something daring, something mysterious, something wild. Something just waiting to explode.

At every social event, Beatrice was the star attraction. The gentlemen swarmed like bees to honey. Beatrice, however, seemed indifferent to their attentions. She looked the part, spoke the part but she was not a part of their world. She came from and breathed from another world. She breathed to the beat of her own drum. Maybe this was the source of all her mystery. The source of her attraction.

And so, as she sat sipping tea and gazing longingly out of the window, she daydreamed of many things.

Maybe it isn't such a bad idea, escaping, stowing away on a ship or, best of them all, highway robbery. Asta would be a fine and fast horse for such a thing. After all, Christopher and I used to play highway robbers, Beatrice thought, laughing to herself as she remembered their games together.

She longed to rip off her corset and throw on her breeches again. The Parisian silk and lace dresses she wore were but a menace and discomfort to her. They smothered a small and dainty but strong and robust figure. She despised their constraints and discomforts and discarded them as often as she could. Of course, this rebellion was always done in secret, along with riding astride. But everybody knew. Her secret rides and disguises were not that secret really. Her parents could do nothing to curtail their wild and reckless daughter.

Beatrice had been riding horses from the age of two. She naturally gravitated to them and Lord and Lady Seymour had admired her enthusiasm. But over the years as she grew older, Beatrice only became more wild, reckless and cavalier with her riding. She was a natural horsewoman. The horses seemed to love her too, even the most spirited ones. The horses felt safe in her hands. They felt heard. And something in Beatrice did hear them. Her father bred horses, and where others failed with their schooling, Beatrice succeeded. This only enraged her father, if only she was a boy, he would think, as a girl her skills were useless to him. But her skills were undeniable and nobody knew from where they came except possibly the horses themselves.

However, her father's frustrations only grew and grew as she got older and older. He had tried everything; banning her from riding, banishing her to her room, banning lunches and dinners, but all to no avail, as Beatrice would always find a way to escape. Father and daughter had been and still were at loggerheads. They were like two stags with their antlers locked. He wanted his heirs and titles, and Beatrice wanted her freedom. So they made a deal and a temporary truce was made. When she reached eighteen years of age, she would marry. When Beatrice was thirteen-years-old, eighteen seemed a lifetime away, so she agreed.

But now, their truce had come to its end. Time was up for Beatrice and Staunton sitting in front of her was the evidence of that.

"Do you like the opera, my dear?" Staunton asked Beatrice in an effort to engage her in some form of conversation.

Beatrice had said nothing so far. Beatrice was about to reply moodily, "No," but her mother interrupted and spoke for her.

"Why, yes, of course. We all love the opera."

"I have a box reserved for the opera Cossi Fan Tutti by Mozart, if you'd care to join me?" Staunton invited.

"Yes, that would be wonderful and a most generous invite," Lady Seymour promptly interrupted again.

"Do you like horses, Earl Staunton?" Beatrice suddenly blurted out, dramatically changing the subject. She said it so sweetly and with eyes so beguiling that Staunton melted for a second. It took him off-guard. He quickly regained his composure and replied curtly,

"No, my dear, I simply loathe them. They are stupid, frightful things. Best kept only as an efficient means of transport."

Of course, she knew he would answer with something like that. She wanted to throw her teacup at him, in fact, she wanted to throw all the cakes and all the shortbreads and all the sandwiches into his fat, ugly face. But she didn't do that, instead she just sweetly said,

"Oh, what a shame, I find them simply enchanting."

Her rage felt insurmountable, and so, to soften its grip, she let her thoughts wander to Christopher. Her beloved cousin and friend. Mousey blond hair, brown eyes, affable and charming, Beatrice's heart lifted just by thinking of him. They were the firmest of friends. He was her only friend and she adored him. He too was a lover of horses, he too, a natural horseman. They both raced cross-country together, egging each other on. She loved how he goaded her, stoking her competitiveness. Christopher was the one person she felt she could be her true self with. No masks, no barriers, no ulterior motives. Just a wonderful feeling of being safe and understood. For Beatrice, her cousin was someone she could open her heart to and receive no judgment. He was fun too and Beatrice thought about all their pranks and the games they played. But most of all, he made her feel calm.

He was cool-headed and she hot-headed. They balanced each other. They were both aristocratic, both handsome, both black sheep.

"How lucky to be a man, to be free to make your own choices," Beatrice would say to him.

She always longed for his visits. Without Christopher, her life would be nothing but doom, gloom, sewing classes, piano and the rudiments of languages. They were both truly grateful to have each other.

"So, we have a night at the opera to look forward to with the Earl, don't we, darling?" Lady Seymour said to Beatrice catapulting her mind back to the room.

"Oh, please call me Edward," said the Earl.

"I am sure Beatrice would much rather a night at the opera than anywhere else. Wouldn't you, darling?" said her father looking daggers at his daughter, threatening her to give the correct reply.

Quite frankly, ladies and gentlemen, I'd much rather be a highway robber than marry this fat, old brute. I would rather risk dying a slow and painful death from a hanging than dying a slow and painful death from a marriage.

This is what Beatrice wanted to say but what she actually said was,

"Yes, a night at the opera would be wonderful. I cannot think of anything more pleasing."

The tea dragged on for a while longer with the typical pleasantries until, finally, the Lord rose to take his leave.

"Lady Seymour, it has been a pleasure," Staunton said as he stood and took a bow in front of Beatrice.

"The pleasure is mine," Beatrice replied. And the pleasure will be mine when I hold you up as a highway robber, she thought as she noticed his fat stomach bulging over his trousers as he bowed. Suddenly, the thought of highway robbery filled her mind. What do I have to lose? she thought, as she sweetly curtsied.

That night, and the next, and the night after that, Beatrice's mind was a flurry of thought. She couldn't stop thinking about highway robbery. In fact, Beatrice couldn't think of anything else. The thought of any impending marriage just seemed totally unimaginable; highway robbery seemed more imaginable.

The day of the opera arrived. Beatrice ran to the field and into the neck of Asta.

"Asta, I just can't bear it any more. I can't bear the thought of seeing him again, let alone marrying him. Father said that Staunton is his preferred suitor," Beatrice said sadly and quietly into Asta's warm neck. Her musky sweet smell gave Beatrice some comfort. She untied her skirts and let them drop, her trousers were already on and she swung herself up on Asta's back, no saddle today, no cross-country today, no joy today. She walked off slowly.

Her heart was heavy. Asta felt it and so too was her walk. Asta felt Beatrice's sorrow and frustration.

Beatrice went into a smooth canter towards the town. She wasn't really thinking about where she was going. She let the path take her.

Should I just ride into town, let everybody see me in trousers and riding bareback? she thought defiantly. She found herself at the big old oak tree at the bend in the road. She walked under its big outstretching branches and sat, slightly hidden. She sat and mused. She sat and thought of the scandal she would create if she went into town now as she was. She thought how ridiculous everybody was with all their rules. She sat and thought of highway robbery. Her heart lifted.

In the distance, a carriage was approaching. Hidden Beatrice could hear its slow approach and she imagined what would be her next move if she actually was a highway robber.

We would wait here and stay hidden and disguised, she thought. We can't be seen at all, hidden by the tree, hidden by the bend. What a perfect place for an ambush!

The carriage got closer. Beatrice waited. Her nerves were steady. In fact, she was excited. The carriage got closer and closer. Its noisy wheels were rattling and the horses' hooves clopping. She could almost feel the carriage as it approached the corner. She felt prickles pulsate along her back as the adrenalin ran through her. She stayed hidden, Asta stayed steady. Neither flinched. The carriage finally clambered round the corner. Beatrice watched it as it trundled along.

Now, was the exact moment when I would jump out in front and stop the carriage. Christopher would go straight to the back. She thought of their future ambush, as the carriage slowly passed. She had time to watch its every move. The driver on top, the people inside, the horses, the road. She noticed the beginnings of a pothole on one side of the road and thought to make it bigger. This would help them in stopping the carriage as well.

Beatrice watched the carriage pass by. She had been totally unnoticed, totally invisible and it felt utterly amazing. This was a completely new feeling for Beatrice. She had always been so entirely visible, so entirely noticed, her beauty shining a light everywhere, but here and now, she was totally invisible. She imagined herself in her highway robbery clothes; hat, scarf and big coat, the young Lady Seymour totally hidden. Beatrice was ecstatic at this new feeling. She suddenly felt in control. The leader of her own destiny. As she watched the carriage noisily go further away down the road, she was filled with a surge of hope, purpose and happiness.

This is it, she thought. This is the solution. She had had time to see the passengers of the carriage, the Duke and Duchess of Clancy. The Duke had been in a meeting with her father that morning. I never liked that man, Beatrice thought. For evicting his tenants harshly from his land.

Beatrice stayed there for a while as the whole idea and plan slowly sunk in. This whole idea of hers was becoming a reality, was taking shape and taking hold. She felt emboldened and courageous and sat a while longer enjoying its feeling. She took out her pocket watch and it was time to go. She had an opera to go to, but instead of her heart sinking at this thought, it lifted. It was filled with hope.

"Mistress, it's time to go. The carriage has arrived," said Lilly to Beatrice as she took out her cape. Beatrice took the cape and dramatically swung it around and over her shoulders.

"Tonight, Lilly, is going to be a wonderful night," Beatrice said with glee.

Lilly was a little taken aback by her mistress's mood; she hadn't seen her so joyous in such a long time.

"But I thought you hated the opera?" Lilly asked a bit confused.

"Yes, Lilly, I do. I simply loathe the opera, all that shouting and singing and it just never seems to end, it goes on and on and on. But tonight, is going to be different, tonight is going to be a night of collecting as much gossip as possible," Beatrice replied enthused by her plan.

"Ooh, I love a little gossip, mistress," Lilly answered.

"Well, I'll tell you all about it tomorrow," Beatrice said.

Beatrice walked down to the main entrance of Lacey Manor where her mother was already waiting. It was a beautiful spring evening with the smell of roses and jasmine filling the air.

"You look beautiful, darling," her mother said as Beatrice arrived. "You sprayed lavender in your hair. How wonderful, darling." Her mother was genuinely touched by Beatrice's effort to look feminine and pretty. It was true, Beatrice did look stunning. She wore a blue silk dress and a cream cape. The dress was embroidered with daisies and real daisies were entwined in her hair. She looked like spring itself, alive and full of life.

The carriage arrived. Her father arrived and they all got in and all travelled to the opera. They were in good time.

On arrival, the Seymour-Barclays were escorted to the earl's box. He was going to be late and had sent his apologies. The three sat and waited until the Earl finally made his entrance.

"My utmost apologies. Do, please, forgive my tardiness, we had a problem with one of the horses. Such a terrible temperamental beast. The coach man had to beat it, but still, it would not calm," Staunton explained.

Beatrice felt her blood boiling. Is there no end to this man's vileness, Beatrice thought, loathing everything about him.

"Lady Seymour, you look simply beautiful. Is there no end to your beauty!" Staunton said as he bowed. Beatrice curtsied politely but said nothing.

Beatrice looked at all the people as they arrived in the theatre, she had an exceptional view from her box. All she could notice though were the jewels draping from the women and the gold coins jangling in the men's pockets. All she could think about was stealing them. About pouncing out from behind the oak tree and stopping their coaches. She needed a pistol though and she had to find a way of lowering her voice. There was still a lot of planning to be done.

"Mother, tell me a bit about the people in the audience," Beatrice asked her mother who looked very surprised at her daughter's sudden curiosity.

"Well, you have the Duke of Marlborough over there in the top box with the Duchess and that is Lord and Lady Grosvenor to the right. The Lord's reputation with gambling and the nightlife somewhat proceeds him; he is the wealthiest man in London."

"Do continue, mama," Beatrice was intrigued. Her ulterior intentions drove her sudden interest. Her mother then proceeded to tell Beatrice all the gossip of the aristocracy that sat before them and there was a lot. In their gossiping, mother and daughter actually had a lovely bonding moment and giggled at some of the stories. It had been a long time since Beatrice had sat and been so friendly with her mother and she liked it. Every now and then, she looked over at her father and Staunton as they sat deep in conversation. So full of themselves, so full of their self-importance, Beatrice cringed. It was hard trying to listen to two different conversations, hers and theirs. Every time Staunton let out one of his big exaggerated laughs, she only felt disgust, especially when a spray of spittle exploded from his mouth. She knew they were plotting her marriage and what gave her comfort was that she was also plotting. Plotting her escape, her crimes, her robberies.

If they can plot, then so can I! she thought. They plot their crimes so I'll plot mine.

If there had been any doubt in Beatrice's mind of actually going ahead with the highway robbery, the opera had only vanquished them. It had only cemented and solidified her determination to be a highway robber.

As she watched the opera, she listened to the voices and it suddenly dawned on her how she can lower her own so as to sound more masculine.

I'll learn to sing, she thought. I′ll have choir lessons and learn to sing tenor. Now, going to church is the most thrilling thing to do, Beatrice thought. I can't wait to go to church this Sunday. Everything now in her life took on a new and purposeful meaning. Everything that was once mundane was now exciting.

Normally, a place of bone-numbing boredom, the opera tonight did nothing but inspire. Finally though, it came to an end.

"Let me escort you all to your carriages," said Staunton.

"It has been an absolute pleasure," said Lady Seymour.

Staunton bowed to Beatrice. "I look forward to our meeting again in a week's time." Beatrice curtsied back but said nothing.

On the way back, mother and daughter sat side by side and held hands. Beatrice felt a warmth and a love for her mother. Their time together at the opera had been lovely. That much was true.

"We have arranged the wedding, daughter," Lord Seymour suddenly said. "It will take place in July. The exact date is still to be confirmed."

Beatrice's heart went cold. She pulled her hand back from her mother's and continued to look out the window. So, she was correct, just as she suspected, they had been planning her future. Laughing and toying with it like it was a mere game. Her rage was insurmountable. Her sorrow overflowing and her defiance dogged. Nothing was going to stop her now, nothing!

I can't wait to see Christopher next week. I can't wait to tell him about my plan, she thought as their carriage took them home.

CHRISTOPHER

CHRISTOPHER was a gentleman, in the truest meaning of the word, he was a gentle man. Whereas Beatrice was a whole mix of contradictions; feisty but soft, dainty but tough, feminine but boyish. Beatrice had inner grit. Christopher had inner refinement. Refined in nature, refined in speech, refined in the words he chose to use and in the tone in which to express them. Refined in his loyalty and his honour. Refined in his ambitions and in his spirit. Beatrice's spirit was wild and free, Christopher's steady and kind and he adored the spirit of his wild cousin. He admired it and followed it. It gave his spirit life, zest and a taste for the wild.

Ever since they were children, he would play her games, follow her up trees, through streams and always, always ride horses with her. The two were bound together since childhood. Their bond only strengthening as they got older together. Over the years, Beatrice grew into her wild spirit, pushing boundaries, bending and breaking the rules, whereas Christopher grew into his refinery. He loved books. Read voraciously and wrote secretly. His passion was the admiration of the beauty of the written word. The unravelling of language and its supreme skill to express, motivate, inspire and emote. The power of the word could move mountains and pillars. Mastering the power of the word was a constant quest for Christopher. For him, writing and its endless array of words was an exquisite tapestry of language, knitted and interlaced together in the pursuit of the highest expression. And it fascinated him. Christopher dreamt of becoming a writer.

Not only did Christopher grow into his flare for using the written word, but he grew into his sweet and affable nature. He had the ability to be able to drink with the unfortunate and the fortunate and make both feel heard. He had the canny ability of smelling out the unworthy and the malignant. And like his cousin, he held within an innate moral code. An innate sense of justice.

His father lost all their wealth due to bad business ventures. His father, unlike his son, was not shrewd in knowing who not to trust and invariably he chose wrong. His mother, on the other hand, would have made an excellent and savvy businesswoman if she had only been allowed to. She had a razor-sharp mind, a natural business acumen and a quick intelligence all of which were wasted on eighteenth century society. And so, she had no other choice but to swallow her frustrations and play the role of Lady Seymour-Rochester, the wife of Lord Seymour-Rochester.

Christopher took after his mother's keen ability to sense out the rat in the room. Christopher by name Christopher by nature, he followed his namesake, Christopher, meaning the Protector, the one who protected and carried Christ across the waters to safety. Maybe that's what his keen ability did, protect those he loved.

His mother died of smallpox when he was fourteen-years-old and his father left soon after to try and salvage some of their wealth in the Caribbean. He never returned.

Christopher's sense of loss and abandonment was all-consuming. He adored his mother. She had flouted the rules of aristocratic mothering and had chosen to feed her baby herself. She was affectionate, warm and loving, and even though at times a little brusque, Christopher understood why, her frustrated heart had to find a vent somehow. He admired her intelligence and he also saw it wasted on tea parties and balls. Mother and son were close, cut from the same cloth and it was always a wrench to leave her when he went back to boarding school.

It was his mother who had introduced him to the world of literature. They shared books together. So, when he got the news of her death, he was devastated. A hole in his heart appeared and only his books could try and fill it. He clung tightly to his education, it was his comfort. Losing himself in literature and Greek mythology, soothed his heart, and spending as much time as possible with Beatrice, enlivened his spirit. The women in Christopher's life had inspired him and he couldn't quite understand why they had to endure such constraints.

Whilst at boarding school, Christopher dreamed of university. It was his 'calling'. He lived and studied for it every moment of every day. He loathed boarding school with every fibre of his being. He found it unjust and patriarchal and downright brutal. He missed the female virtues and sensibilities back at home. Boarding school was grey and he endured it only for the reward of reaching university, Cambridge university. So, when the news came that there was no money left for him to go and no news from his father, Christopher plummeted into a depression. University was all he had lived for. He was going to expand and evolve his mind there. He was going to mix with other intellects and other lovers of the written word. From one day to the next, all his hopes and dreams were shattered. In desperation, he overcame his pride and asked Lord Seymour, his uncle, and Beatrice's father, to financially help him with university, but the Lord declined.

When boarding school was finished, Christopher found himself having to fend for himself in the world. He returned to his home, Oaks Manor, and lived in one of the cottages, alone. He was permitted to stay there only until its sale when all the money would be used to pay off his father's debts. He was quite literally alone in the world, except for Beatrice and his powerful stallion, Moby. He would fight tooth and nail to make sure the creditors would not take Moby and sell him. He'd rather die first. Christopher's loneliness and anger, Beatrice's loneliness and anger, only cemented the cousins' bond and soon they were inseparable. Her grit and his grace, fuelled by their anger were a perfect, plutonic alchemic mix.

Christopher might be a gentle man but he had to survive and he found himself rubbing shoulders with other people also trying to survive. By the age of twenty-one, Christopher had earned himself a trusted reputation with a wide band of smugglers. He had a fast horse and a cool nerve; the smugglers liked that. He would travel back and forth to London, working for different groups. And despite his loathing for his boarding school years, it did, in fact, teach him how to defend himself. After all, he had had to endure some brutal beatings, and so, he had had to learn to fight back.

Christopher played up or played down his aristocratic lineage, using it when needed. He fooled many a king's soldier using his social graces and intellect to outfox them. This, of course, was his asset that benefited the criminals he worked for. Christopher with Moby were uncatchable. They were good for business.

However, Christopher's deep and cultured soul struggled in this world of crime. He didn't belong there. What it did give him was a really wide perspective of this society. Eighty percent of the criminals he knew were only criminals because their poverty put them there, whereas, twenty percent because they were genuinely bad. The hierarchy of society was unfair even though he used to be at the top of it. Now, he was at the bottom of it.

Christopher was a 'batsman' and his job was to keep a look-out for the king's soldiers whilst the other men smuggled the goods. When necessary, he was the bait to lure the soldiers to chase him and not the smugglers. But there had been times when being the bait had nearly gotten him caught.

On the same night that Beatrice went to the opera, was when Christopher had his closest encounter so far. His gang were on the river Thames at Surrey Dock, unloading goods. It was a foggy night. Christopher was on the river bank looking out. Suddenly, he saw two foot soldiers approaching, he gave the smugglers the signal and they scattered. Christopher whistled, catching the soldier's attention, and ran in the opposite direction towards Moby, who was waiting for him as he always did.

"Get him!" shouted one of the soldiers as they ran after Christopher.

Christopher ran fast, straight to where Moby should have been waiting. He 'clicked' for his stallion but Moby didn't come. He couldn't see Moby anywhere.

"Moby, Moby!" Christopher called out in a whispered panic but nothing came back. "Moby, where are you?" He could hear the soldiers approaching and had to make his escape on foot without Moby. He made a quick dash further along the river bank, scrambling over the side where he found a muddy enclave and waited.

Christopher waited and waited and waited. It was an agonising wait as all he could think about was Moby. Soldiers were generally a noisy bunch but he hadn't heard anything for a while so he climbed up from out of his hideout. The fog was lifting but there was still no sign of Moby. Christopher's heart went cold. Where could you be? he thought. Where are you, Moby? Christopher knew something was wrong, it was too unlike his stallion. He smelt mischief and worried for Moby's safety. Staying alert, he sneaked back to the warehouse, and there was Moby, tied to a post. A soldier stood guard.

Christopher hid himself and thought. He didn't rush in. He thought through all the scenarios and finally chose one.

He took off his boots and socks. He knew Moby would sense him long before the soldier would. He sneaked to the back of the warehouse, which was, thankfully, the last one and was surrounded by woodlands. Slowly, Christopher made his approach. Moby's ear flickered in Christopher's direction, Christopher stopped in response. Moby knew it was him. Christopher slowly made his way towards his stallion, finally reaching his back hooves. He was still hidden by the warehouse. Christopher waited. Moby didn't move, didn't nicker; he knew exactly what he had to do.

But just as Christopher was about to make his move to save his horse, the soldier stood up and started to walk towards Moby. Christopher held his breath, Moby held his breath.

The soldier was bored and went up to Moby. He went to stroke his back but that was too close to Christopher, so Moby backed up and offered the soldier his nose. Christopher hardly breathed. He could smell the soldier, he was that close. The damp, muggy smell of his uniform, his sweaty body odour. One tiny move and he would be found. The soldier stroked Moby's nose.

"Boring here, dark and boring. What I'd do to be back at the tavern now," said the soldier to Moby as he stroked him, moving his hand along his back and getting closer to Christopher. Moby instinctively backed up a little more, Christopher held his breath. Moby held his breath. Moby's trick worked and the soldier walked forward to his nose.

"Found a fine girl at the tavern too," the soldier went on. "You're a big horse, ain't ya? The military will make good use of you."

Christopher wanted to jump up and pounce at the soldier when he heard this. But he kept his cool. The King's calvary was not going to take his Moby into the battlefield and to his early slaughter, he thought. Timing and patience were everything and Christopher knew he had to wait to get the best from both.

Finally, the soldier walked back to his perch and went back to some whittling.

Christopher waited some more, and when the soldier finally started to slumber, he silently sneaked up to Moby, took hold of his lead rope and untied it, making sure the metal clasps didn't clang. If the soldier turned his head now he would surely be seen as the light from the warehouse was shining on Moby's head. Stealthily, Christopher loosened the rope, and instead of climbing up on Moby which would have made too much noise, Christopher crept back to the safety of the warehouse. He then took hold of Moby's tail and gently pulled him back, one slow step at a time, careful not to arouse any attention. Moby knew this game well and followed Christopher's feel to perfection until he too was totally behind the warehouse's wall. Moby was a big horse, tall and powerful, but he was also a quiet horse when needed, and tonight, he had performed perfectly.

Hidden by the wall, Christopher then silently swung himself up onto Moby's back and started to walk back to his boots.

"No, you don't!" the other soldier shouted as he pulled Christopher down off Moby, taking him totally by surprise.

As Christopher fell to the ground, he pulled the soldier down with him. It all happened so quickly. There was a bit of a scuffle as the two men wrestled with each other. Moby was shifting his feet trying not to tread on Christopher. Finally, Christopher managed to get the upper hand by grabbing the soldier's pistol as he held him down on the ground

"I'll shoot," Christopher said to the soldier as he stood over him. He could hear the other soldier running towards them, and in a rush of pure adrenalin, Christopher grabbed Moby's mane, swung one leg over the saddle and hung to one side. The same trick Beatrice loved to do whenever they played their trick riding games.

"Go, Moby, go!" Christopher shouted as he clung to the side of Moby. Moby bolted ahead, skidding past the trees in the dark. The other soldier, as he approached, fired his musket. It made such a loud bang, giving both Christopher and Moby a jolt.

Did it hit Moby? Did it hit me? Christopher thought frantically as he held on. No time to check, as they were still not safe. Moby kept his canter. After a little while, Christopher swung himself up on top of Moby. They were still in the woods and still not safe. Christopher checked for any bullet wounds but felt nothing. His heart was racing. That was too close, he thought as he continued cantering ahead. Eventually, after about fifteen minutes, he slowed to a trot and then to a walk. "That was too close, boy. Too close! If he had shot you, I would never have forgiven myself," Christopher said out loud to Moby.

He rode to the neighbouring town, went into the tavern, ordered an ale, and only then, did he let out a long, deep breath. This, he vowed, was his last job as a batsman. From now on, he was not going to be anybody's bait. From now on, he wasn't going to put Moby at such risk. He longed for the sophistication of the arts. He longed for university. He longed to write. He longed for his other life to begin now. But for now, he was stuck and he just couldn't think of a way in which he could achieve his other life.

He loathed mixing with both the lowlifes of smuggling and the highlife of privilege, both fighting and killing for money, either to protect it or to get it. Christopher longed to be somewhere new, somewhere fresh, somewhere not entrenched in tradition. Like his cousin, they both dreamed of escape. He was going to see her soon and he couldn't wait.

THE PROPOSAL

CHRISTOPHER galloped up the field, slowing to a trot as he approached the woodland at the far back of Lacey Manor. This route always kept him out of sight from Lord Seymour. He never did much like his uncle and now, less so, since he had been banned from seeing Beatrice. And there was Beatrice waiting in the woodland as he approached. He couldn't help smiling the minute he saw her, even though today's smile was tinged with worry.

"Cousin, you look dapper as always in your breeches and shirt, but you could do something with that awful hair of yours!" Christopher teased.

Beatrice threw the apple she was eating at him in jest. She instantly noticed Christopher's teasing was not as light as normal. He was smiling and joking but Beatrice sensed something.

"Well, you should see yourself!" Beatrice said with a hint of defensiveness in her voice. "You look like you've been chased by soldiers all night."

"How did you know? Have you been spying on me?" Christopher said with a surprised half smile. How did she guess that? She has the sixth sense of a wolf, Christopher thought.

"Soldiers again!" Beatrice said, as Christopher slowly nodded. "Well, you look awful! Obviously, you got away. Moby is a supreme horse but not as supreme as my Asta, is he, girl? You are the best!" Beatrice said to Asta giving her a warm pat.

"Only just. I only just got away, B! It was far too close," Christopher said seriously, taking a bite of the apple, he was starving.

"Maybe it's time to stop, cousin. Have you thought about working for yourself?"

"And do what? I have half an education and no connections and no money," Christopher replied.

"Well, I have some of Mrs Crowley's best shortbread and sandwiches," Beatrice said.

"Is there no end to your kindness, I'm famished! Mrs Crowley truly does make the best shortbread," Christopher said.

"Let's ride, then we eat and then we talk. I have a proposal for you," Beatrice said, and with that, she galloped off in the direction of their favourite meadow in the woods.

Christopher was curious and dutifully followed.

They bolted at full speed through the woods. The day was sunny and sublime. They crashed through streams and jumped high over fallen trees.

"Too slow!" shouted Christopher as he overtook her in the open field, his mood lifting.

Easily goaded, Beatrice pushed Asta on and then overtook Christopher, giving him a big smile as she passed.

The two cousins couldn't be happier. For now, they both forgot about their worries. All they thought about was the thrill of the ride, the power of their horses and the sun on their backs. Their problems seemed a million miles away.

Beatrice slowed to a canter, coming parallel to Christopher. She gave Christopher the hand signal they used for this trick. They had created a few hand signals when they were children that they used to signal certain horse tricks, it felt like their very own secret. Christopher then immediately held Moby steady, Beatrice then jumped onto the back of Moby and held onto Christopher. Asta kept her canter alongside them both, Christopher then stood up on his saddle, steadied himself and jumped onto Asta.

"Woohoo!" they both shouted, big smiles beaming on their faces. They had been doing this trick for years and never got bored of it.

"Give me back my horse!" Beatrice shouted jokingly. They, once again, steadied their horses and they both jumped back onto their own horses. This time, though, Beatrice slid down the side of her saddle, and holding onto the saddle pommel, rode on the side of Asta. Beatrice loved this trick. She loved the feeling of her hair as it flowed along the ground, she loved to look at Asta's hind legs powering along. She loved the recklessness. With ease, she slid herself back up onto Asta's back and they all galloped on at full speed, until finally slowing as they arrived at the meadow.

It was a magical spring day and the meadow didn't disappointment. It was a rush of life, hues and smells. Butterflies everywhere. They slowly walked to the centre and let their horses graze.

"So, what's really bothering you, cousin?" Beatrice probed.

"You don't miss a trick, literally, whether that's a horse trick or my mood," Christopher replied.

"Well, what is it?" Beatrice probed some more, she knew her cousin well and he definitely seemed preoccupied.

"I have to find a way out of the smuggling. The other night they took Moby and I only just got him back," Christopher confessed. He did indeed feel the weight of the world on his shoulders. He longed to be free from the criminal world but he just couldn't see how.

Beatrice threw him his sandwiches and shortbread. They slid down from their horses and sat in the thick, green grass and bluebells to eat their picnic. It was truly blissful in the meadow. The birds sang, the bees buzzed and hope was in the air, even though neither cousin felt it.

"So, what of your news, B?" Christopher asked.

She lay back on the spongy grass and put her hands behind her head.

"He's a fat, ugly and disgusting old man and the wedding has been arranged for July. But I'm not going to marry him. He's an ogre, the Earl is an ogre," Beatrice said in a quiet voice, as she starred up at the clouds floating by. "Let's just call him the Ogre from now on; Earl is too good a title for him."

"Can't you stall your father any longer, find something, anything," Christopher said helplessly.

"When I reached my eighteenth birthday was…" Beatrice started, but Christopher interrupted.

"…Cousin, I completely forgot," Christopher jumped up and got out a little present from his waistcoat and handed it to Beatrice. "Very belated, I'm sorry. Happy birthday, B."

Beatrice took the little parcel and unwrapped it slowly. It was a beautiful red, silk scarf with her initial B embroidered on it.

"Red is your colour," Christopher said. "Well, do you like it?" Beatrice hadn't said anything, she was stunned actually. It was a wonderful coincidence, a scarf she could wear as a highway robber on the day she was to make her proposal to her cousin to be a highway robber.

"Yes, Christopher. I love it," Beatrice said meaningfully. "Follow me, I have something to show you," and she purposefully swung up on her horse and waited for Christopher to do likewise.

Beatrice rode at a steady canter, until reaching a willow tree, where she stopped. Beatrice then walked through its long and beautiful hanging leaves. It was cosy inside. She waited for Christopher. They had always come to this tree as children to play Robin Hood, hiding within its thick branches. She thought it would be perfectly symbolic for her proposal, made all the more powerful thanks to Christopher's gift. Once inside, she pulled out a hat from her saddle bag and put it on and then tied the red scarf over her nose.

"No, cousin. Are you crazy!" Christopher proclaimed. "No, no, no! It is lunacy!"

"What have I got to lose?" Beatrice replied taking off her scarf.

"But Beatrice, you are not a robber, you are not a criminal, you are an amazing horsewoman but not a thief," Christopher continued in shock.

"Steal from the rich, give to the poor," Beatrice went on. "We've been playing that game for years. Now we can do it for real."

"But you will hang, cousin. They will get you. Just forget all notion of this idea."

"If I have to marry the ogre to save Asta then this will be my last burst of defiance!" Beatrice said seriously.

"Look, what happened to me the other night, I nearly got caught, Moby nearly got shot!" Christopher continued.

"What about your dream? Your writing, your bookshop, your printer? You can keep most of the takings. It is your path to freedom. Finally, you'll have your financial independence." Beatrice enthused.

Beatrice knew she had caught Christopher's attention now, as his breath hesitated for a second. It was a tantalising thought for him. He could finally be free from the criminal life. This could be his way out.

"The criminal life is not for you, cousin," Beatrice continued.

"And it's not for you!" Christopher piped back.

"We only need to do a few robberies and we'll have enough for your bookshop. At least, with me, you take all the bounty and won't be risking so much for so little as you are now for the smugglers. Father has had many visitors recently. Lawyers, dukes, duchesses."

"And you, cousin, what is your gain?" Christopher asked. Suddenly, the thought of his bookshop, his literature, his culture and his writings gave him food for thought.

"Christopher, a life in prison is the same as a life in a loveless marriage. So, before I'm forced to hand over my life to an ogre, I want to have my last outburst of freedom. Look what happened to Duchess Cleveland; the only thing she ever loved were her children and the Duke took them away from her. Where is the humanity in that? The justice? And if I hang, then I will hang having had my last angry rebellion in the name of my beliefs. My marriage is not justice," Beatrice spoke quietly but passionately.

Christopher felt the gravity of her decision and he understood. If he would ever have been torn away from his mother and never allowed to see her again it would've destroyed him, he thought, as he imagined the children of the Duchess being torn from her.

"I'll do it alone if I have to," Beatrice continued. "I do not want your life put at risk. You do this because you want to."

Christopher knew this was to be true, he knew his cousin all too well. She would indeed do this whole escapade by herself and it was exactly this that frightened him the most. She had to be protected. Yes, she would do it by herself but it would be far too dangerous. Besides, he also knew when his cousin's mind was made up there was absolutely no way of changing it.

Christopher's thoughts then changed. It wasn't the bookshop and the printer that were his primary motivations; it was Beatrice's safety. She was headstrong and strong-willed and definitely slightly wild, but deep down, this is what Christopher so admired about her, and deep, deep down, he liked her plan. It was unheard off; a female highway robber, and an aristocratic one at that. She also definitely knew the best people to rob.

"I suppose we have been playing Robin Hood for years," Christopher said in a mild form of agreement. "Steal from the rich and give to the poor," he said, but he still wasn't totally convinced.

"Follow me," Beatrice said as if reading his mind. She walked out from the willow tree and cantered west. Christopher followed her out from behind the long dangling vines. He was intrigued. Where could she be taking him? he thought. They loped for a steady five minutes until Beatrice finally arrived at another willow tree that stood at the top of two stone walls.

Beatrice dismounted, Christopher followed, and she walked Asta through the vines and tied her to a branch. Christopher did the same with Moby. Christopher's curiosity was at fever pitch. He thought he knew every nook and cranny of these fields, but this was something new. Beatrice then crouched down at the base of the willow tree, Christopher crouched next to her and watched as she cleared the rubble and stones to one side revealing a hatch door.

"A tunnel," she proclaimed looking up at Christopher and beaming with a big smile.

"A tunnel?" Christopher said amazed. "How did you find this? This is incredible. How did we not find this before?"

"Follow me," Beatrice said, Christopher happily followed.

Beatrice opened the hatch door and then proceeded to climb the small amount of steps down into the tunnel. The tunnel had a low ceiling so they both had to bend slightly. They walked in the blackness, following the wall with their hands to guide them. It was pretty scary and they couldn't go fast, but eventually, Beatrice felt for the steps at the other end.

"Steady me," she said to Christopher, who did so, and with a huff and puff, she pushed open the other hatch door revealing an explosion of light as it opened.

"The forest. We come out at the forest," Beatrice said, looking at Christopher. "Incredible, no!" Christopher was genuinely amazed. This was incredible and did give some weight to this new criminal venture they could be partaking in. They both climbed out and sat on the forest floor, hidden by two big boulders.

"But how did you find this?" Christopher asked, still amazed.

"I was out riding as always. I had just had another argument with my father and I was inconsolable. The wedding is going to take place this summer, Christopher, this summer! I can't believe I'm being forced to marry this fat, old man!"

"I can't believe it either," Christopher agreed.

"Anyway, I was sitting in the field just aways from the willow tree hatch, I had let Asta loose to graze and she wondered afar, so was out of sight. Then I saw Michael, the stable boy. He sneaked up silently to the tree. I can't believe he didn't see me. I sneaked up to the wall and peeked over to see what he was doing. I could just about see him as he rummaged on the ground and that was when I saw him lift the hatch and disappear down the tunnel. I too couldn't believe it. I too thought the same; how did I not know about a secret tunnel at Lacey Manor. I had so many questions, but my first feeling was, what an incredible coincidence. I had been thinking that very morning about escaping or highway robbery, anything, and then I miraculously discover Michael and his secret tunnel. So, on the same day my father tells me my wedding is on July 22nd I find myself an escape route! As you know, cousin, I'm not the religious type, but this felt like some divine intervention."

"But why is there a tunnel here?" Christopher asked.

"The Roundheads. It was for the Roundheads. Lacey Manor supported Cromwell. Of course, I know Lacey's history, but I never knew about a tunnel!" Beatrice answered.

"And Michael?"

"Oh, yes, so, I waited a few seconds and then followed him down the tunnel. He had a light so I could see him and shouted his name. He was absolutely shocked and could hardly breathe but I assured him I would keep his secret, if he would keep mine. We exchanged secrets and made a gentlewoman's oath together. I trust him."

"You trust him!" Christopher wasn't sure.

"I trust him," Beatrice replied giving a very solid and confident nod.

"But why does he use the tunnel?"

"It's a short cut to the village and he goes to see his sweetheart from which he is banned and to give some food to his family, whenever he can. We will give him some of the bounty too."

"So you've actually thought this out?"

"Yes, I have, and yes, I am serious. This is not a girl's playful fancy. This is a girl's fight for her life."

"But B, you won't have a life if they hang you."

"But at least it is mine to choose. This is my life, Christopher. It was given to me and to nobody else and I'm not giving it away to a fat Earl without a fight," Beatrice replied with anger and rebellion in her voice. A powerful combination.

"Come with me," Beatrice said to Christopher. She stood up and reached out her hand for Christopher to take. He took hold of it and stood up. It was easy to follow her, and this was the problem. There was something about her that Christopher just couldn't help himself from following. Was it her confidence? Her conviction? Whatever it was, he always followed.

"I want to show you something," Beatrice said, as she opened the hatch, letting Christopher pass back down. She then climbed down herself, lowering the hatch and covering it as best she could. Christopher followed her back through the tunnel and then back out the other side, under the camouflage of the willow tree where Moby and Asta were still standing. It was an enormous willow tree, centuries old and easily able to hide the two horses inside its long branches that swept across the floor. The cousins mounted their horses and Beatrice led the way out. She then cantered back towards Lacey Manor, but this time, heading towards the main road that lead to London. She stopped at the big, old, oak tree.

"This is where we can stop the carriages. It's just after the bend so they won't see us waiting, but we'll be able to hear them coming."

"And how do you propose to do the stealing? Cousin, you are not a thief, you are a lady…"

"…I will jump out on Asta to the front of the carriage and you to the back," Beatrice said interrupting Christopher, she knew exactly where his train of thought was going. "And yes, I know I'm a lady and not a man and…"

"…And not very threatening," Christopher continued.

"I am when holding a pistol in my hand. Doesn't matter if it's a lady's or a man's finger on the trigger," Beatrice piped back.

"And where will you get a pistol from?" Christopher questioned.

"You," she replied simply.

And again, Christopher was inwardly completely floored. How does she know I have one? Christopher thought. He was, again, amazed at her sixth sense.

"You've definitely been spying on me?" Christopher said as he pulled out the pistol he had taken and kept from the soldier the other night.

Beatrice just smiled in response. A weighted silence now hung over them. It was filled with Christopher's amazement, Beatrice's knowing, and the reality of this new venture.

"And so, you become a highway robber and steal from the rich, give to the poor, and you don't get caught, then what? What will you do?"

Christopher asked brushing off his amazement over the pistol and bringing their conversation back to its original tone.

"I'll be a countess with a devilish secret. A secret that will keep me entertained for many years. A secret I'll tell only my children. I have nothing to lose, cousin, and only to gain," Beatrice answered confidently. Christopher smiled at this. "So, what do you say, cousin? You too have nothing to lose, only to gain."

"You've definitely been busy thinking this through," Christopher said smiling, even though he was taken aback by the whole proposal.

"Yes, I have been busy thinking this through," Beatrice replied confirming Christopher's words.

"I only want to rob the maligned," Christopher said in another soft form of consent.

"Exactly! Only the corrupt associates of my father's. I will send you word when I know who'll be visiting. Think about it, Christopher. It's a step up from what you are doing now. We stick to this road. We don't compete with the other robbers and we don't get greedy. We stop when we have enough money for your printer's shop. This is your way out."

"And the horses?" Christopher questioned.

"They can stay hidden in the willow tree, and if we don't come back, they'll return to Lacey."

"You've got it all planned out."

"I'm determined." Beatrice gave her cousin a look of determination to match her words.

"You're stubborn and mad!" Christopher replied.

"That is my offer to you, darling cousin. Join me as a highway robber. I have nothing to lose. You have nothing to lose." Beatrice was utterly convincing.

"Okay, I'll do it," Christopher said.

Beatrice lowered her head in a serious gesture of agreement and put out her hand for a handshake. "We are in this together, cousin," Beatrice said, as they shook hands firmly.

"Together!" Christopher confirmed.

They both let the weight of the moment settle, before Beatrice released her hand, and then, in a jovial tone, said, "One last rick before we depart!"

Beatrice gave Christopher a cheeky smile, changing their serious moods in a flash.

Beatrice swung Asta's head around and galloped off in the opposite direction. Christopher knew what she was about to do. He smiled and his mood lifted instantly. She was beguiling and very funny to watch. She was entertaining. Beatrice then cantered towards the oak tree and to Christopher, and as she approached the big, outstretched branch, she grabbed hold of it and swung herself up onto it. Asta cantered on underneath the branch, coming to a halt further along.

"So, now, your turn, cousin, come on!" Beatrice shouted down to Christopher from up in the branch, where she now sat.

Christopher couldn't resist and took the bait. He sharply turned Moby and did exactly the same as Beatrice, joining her up on the branch of the oak tree. They sat with their legs dangling.

"Partners, finally, cousin," Beatrice said taking a deep breath.

"But in crime, cousin," Christopher added.

"Yes, partners in crime. Partners in crime, it has a good ring to it, do you not think?" Beatrice said smiling. She was excited.

"Yes, it does actually," Christopher had to agree.

"Feels right too, don't you think?" Beatrice said.

"Yes, it does actually," again he had to agree. It did feel right, he thought to himself, however strange that might be.

"Well, then, stop being so serious, Kit," Beatrice said thumping Christopher's arm in a gesture of comradery.

Christopher was always taken aback when Beatrice called him Kit, it was her special name for him and she always knew the most poignant of moments to use it that would make the deepest of impacts on his sentimental heart. Christopher felt a rush of love for his wild cousin and thumped her back on the shoulder.

"Ow!" Beatrice said in feigned hurt.

"Last one back to Lacey is a squashed tomato!" Beatrice shouted as she whistled for Asta to come for her. Christopher laughed at this. Here, they were about to embark on a serious venture of highway robbery and his cousin was using their childhood expressions of goading. As usual, he fell for it and whistled for Moby.

Beatrice was the first to swing down from the tree trunk and onto Asta's back. She galloped off. "Too slow, cousin, too slow!" Beatrice shouted back.

Christopher swung down from the tree onto Moby's back and raced to catch up with her. Beatrice threw her arms up into the air as she cantered. She revelled in the wind blowing through her hair and raised her face to the sky.

"Partners in crime, Kit, partners in crime!"

Christopher raised his arms and felt the freedom run through his veins. He actually felt happy.

THE TRAINING

IT was cold and rainy the morning Beatrice woke for their first day of training. She woke with zest and zeal and Beatrice didn't see any obstacle in front of her, not even the dire weather. Her new venture was to begin today and nothing was going to stop that. Feeling brazen, she went down to the kitchens in her breeches and shirt, she knew her parents would be sleeping. The kitchens were warm and cosy and full of the hearty, yeasty smell of freshly-baked bread.

"There's no stopping you, young lady," said Betty.

"Can I have some sandwiches to take with me, Betty?" Beatrice asked.

"But it's raining, child, you'll catch a chill," Betty said as she handed Beatrice some shortbread. "I'll just make you up a bundle whilst I warm up a cup of tea."

Betty poured Beatrice a cup of tea who drank it slowly, steeling a fried egg next to her as she drank. "Fingers off, young lady, that's mine," Betty snapped. "I'll make you a fresh one."

Beatrice loved Betty. Betty had been the cook at Lacey all her life. She was big-hearted, warm and loving; all the ingredients that she put into her food which is probably why her food always tasted wonderful. Hearts lifted when they ate Betty's food.

"You are a stubborn girl. Always have been. There's no stopping you, that's for sure, so no point trying. I'll have a hot broth waiting for you for when you get back. Can't you wait for the rain to stop, at least?" Betty handed Beatrice the freshly-made sandwiches.

Warmed through and with an impatience to get going, Beatrice jumped up.

"Thank you, Betty," Beatrice said running out the door and straight to the stables to greet Asta. The stables were warm, full of the smell and heat of the horses, the rain hit hard against the barn roof. Asta neighed and raised her head the minute Beatrice walked in; she knew it was her. Asta walked to Beatrice, they both tilted their heads together for a morning embrace. Asta knew instantly Beatrice was happy this morning. A happiness that was also deadly serious.

"Come on, girl, this is our first day of training," Beatrice quietly spoke as she stroked her mare's left eye. "Today is an important day."

Beatrice quickly saddled her up and walked out of the stables. She continued on to the woodland nearest to the stables and there was Christopher waiting. The rain had eased off a bit now, raindrops were falling off his hat, his jacket was pretty wet.

"You picked a fine morning for our first day of training," Christopher berated with a smile.

"No rest for the wicked," Beatrice piped back with an even bigger smile.

"I plan on being cunning not wicked."

"You look a little wet, cousin. Here are some sandwiches," Beatrice threw Christopher Betty's best. "First, we ride the route. Oak tree, the hold up, meadow, and lastly, the tunnel. I brought a candle for the tunnel," Beatrice said holding it up for Christopher to see.

"I think we should practice the tunnel without light, get to know every nook and cranny," Christopher said, Beatrice nodded in agreement.

"And then, repeat the whole route backwards. Tunnel, meadow, hold up, oak tree," Beatrice added. The cousins loped off towards the oak tree. The rain sprayed on her face and it felt good. Cold, bracing and enlivening. The rain started to come down a bit harder; perfect weather for a practice, as there was nobody about.

They reached the oak tree and stopped behind it's outstretched branches; they stood hidden. Beatrice got out her red initialled scarf and wrapped it around her face. Christopher did likewise.

"When the carriage peaks out from the bend, I'll leap forward and hold my position and my pistol strong," Beatrice said; she was deadly serious. Christopher nodded. "Then you jump out to cover the rear. Let's go," she said as she placed her hat on her head.

Beatrice walked Asta to the end of the large branch so she was ready to make her entrance stepping out in front of the carriage. Christopher thought how amazing Beatrice was as he stood listening to her commands. She seemed so utterly primed for such a thing, he thought. So totally unfazed and so totally at ease with it all. The whole thing seems incredibly natural to her, like her whole life so far had been waiting for this moment. Christopher, on the other hand, was not feeling so at ease. But was going to ride on her wave of confidence.

Beatrice made her calm entrance forward. She definitely commanded her space. She seemed to grow in stature, expand in aura, even Asta seemed to take on her role as a horse larger than life.

Christopher took his cue and leapt out from the other side of the oak tree and took his position at the rear of their imaginary carriage. He held his position strong but felt vulnerable without a pistol. I must somehow get another pistol, he thought.

"Hand over your valuables! " Beatrice calmly said in a low and firm voice. She had presence, she had weight. Any hint of her tiny frame or vulnerability were lost.

As she stood in front of the imaginary carriage with the rain dripping from her hat and off her coat, Beatrice imagined the carriage to be Earl Staunton's. She hoped to hold up his carriage. What a delight that would be. She imagined his pathetic demeanour as she held her pistol directly in front of him; how utterly satisfying that would be.

She envisioned all the operas she had seen, the acting, the dramatics, and with all these theatrics taken to heart, she now took on her new role, as the 'Highwaygirl' and she loved it. She sat tall and strong and empowered on the majestic Asta and thought how utterly natural this felt. Beatrice then lowered her pistol, gestured with a wave of her head to Christopher and the cousins galloped off straight to the meadow.

"Beatrice, you have to lower your voice some more," Christopher said as they galloped.

They soon arrived at the meadow.

"Christopher, I have to lower my voice some more," Beatrice repeated back in both irritation and agreement. She hated being told what to do but she totally agreed with her cousin and this, after all, was serious. "I've started my choir lessons, I need a bit more time to perfect it."

"Are you sure you don't want me to go out front."

"Absolutely not. I want to do this," Beatrice was utterly serious as she said this. Christopher knew this tone and this look too well.

They stood silent for a while, taking it all in and listening to the rain as it hit the leaves and their hats.

"So, the plan is, we go straight to the meadow and hide here for a while. We leave our robber's masks and scarfs here," Beatrice walked to a tree with a hollow in it. "We hide our things in here. Only in an emergency do we use the tunnel."

"Let's go to the tunnel," Christopher said. "For our practice run."

They both cantered off in the direction of the tunnel. Once at the willow tree, they walked through the draping vines and dismounted. It was cosy and dryer within the long willow vines. They could hear the rain hitting and sliding off its leaves.

"We'll leave them untied in case they need to make their way back," Beatrice said.

Beatrice then went to the hatch door of the tunnel, cleared the leaves and opened it. Beatrice climbed down. Inside the tunnel, everything was wet and pungent. The spring rains had made it thick with smells. Christopher followed her down and closed the hatch door, being careful to cover it as best as possible. It was pitch black, damp and dank. They could hear little creepy crawly sounds as they hugged tight to the cold stone wall, following it with their hands. Beatrice led and they both went slowly.

"We must come and practice walking this tunnel often so we know it well and become faster," Christopher whispered.

"Is this what it's like for blind people?" Beatrice wondered out loud.

They continued on for only a little longer, and finally, came to the hatch door on the other side. Beatrice found the handle and pushed it open, plunging a warm and glorious light into the tunnel. They climbed out and slumped on the floor by the two large boulders.

"You can always back out, cousin, if this is not for you," Beatrice said.

"Are you crazy! I don't want you having all the fun," Christopher added turning his head and giving her a smile.

"I want to hold up Staunton so when I walk down the church aisle looking as sweet as sugar, highway robbery will be my sweetest secret."

"And mine," Christopher replied as he stood up and held out his hand for Beatrice to take.

"I'm wet through. Sneak into the kitchens when we get back and dry off. I'll get Betty to cook you up something," Beatrice said as she took Christopher's hand and jumped up.

The cousins went back along the tunnel and back to their waiting horses. They rode back, silent in their thoughts. Once back at Lacey, Beatrice went into the kitchens first and checked with the staff if her parents were busy. Her father had gone to London and her mother was resting. Beatrice got Imogen to go get Christopher from the woodland, his hiding place.

Betty liked Christopher and felt for him, all alone and abandoned by his family. He was always courteous and affable, shared a joke or two and got the staff laughing so it was a pleasure to feed him up.

"Come here, lad, give us ya coat and hat, let's get you warm and dry," Betty said as she took his coat and hat, gave it to William, the boy in charge of stoking the fire, and handed him some hot bread and butter. "This'll warm you up in no time."

Christopher sat himself at the big wooden table and inwardly collapsed, his gratefulness taking hold of him, outwardly though he was more reserved and gave Betty a big smile and said, "thank you, Betty."

Beatrice had gone to quickly change her wet clothes. She returned to the cosy kitchen and joined Christopher at the table. They both ate in silence. They were lulled by the hearty broth and the hustle and bustle of the staff as they worked around them.

"You know you could stay tonight, father is staying in London," Beatrice offered as they ate.

"I've got some cakes for afters, if I can tempt you," Betty offered to Christopher. "William, mind that shovel there, somebody might fall," Betty shouted out over to William.

"I don't need to be tempted, Betty. Your cakes are the best. You are going to make me fat!" Christopher answered.

"That's the idea, young man, you lookin' too scrawny," Betty said handing him some tea cakes.

"I would love to stay, B, but I think it best I head back home."

"How about a game of Whist before you go?"

"Splendid."

Betty poured the cousins some tea as Beatrice dealt out the cards for their game. Betty loved having the cousins spending time in the kitchens. It was like family, and even though she knew all too well the societal boundaries, she enjoyed the informality she could have with them. Beatrice, in a way, was like her daughter; she had known her all her life and loved her. It had broken her heart whenever she saw her upset and she loved being able to give her a big warm hug to soothe away her tears. Betty sympathised with Beatrice's frustrations but she didn't envy her; for all her wealth, she had so little freedom to enjoy it, a cruel irony, she thought.

"I don't know why I bother playing cards with you, B, you always win," Christopher cried as he threw down his hand playfully.

"Sore loser!" Beatrice loved winning, her competitive spirit thrived.

"Well, I best be going," Christopher stood up and went to get his now dry clothes.

Betty handed Christopher a small bundle of goodies, "for the journey," she said.

"Much obliged, Betty" Christopher answered warmly.

At the door, Beatrice signed with her hands 'meadow,' and whispered, "at eight a.m." They enjoyed using their secret language. They then hugged goodbye.

The next day it wasn't raining, it was a bright and beautiful spring day. The chill of yesterday had gone. Beatrice rose early, enthused. Her new mission fuelling her with energy. A quick stop at the kitchens for some of Betty's bread and she was off.

It was a glorious morning full of hope. Yesterday was full of determination, today hope. The air was warm and alive and Beatrice was soon at the meadow where Christopher was already waiting. He was sitting on the ground leaning back on the tree with the hollow.

"Feels like you've been here a while? Would I be correct in my assumption?" Beatrice said. She was curious as to Christopher's mood.

"Well, I've been busy talking to the inhabitants of this hollow, the Humming Fairies, who have been trying to help me," Christopher said playfully.

Beatrice was used to Christopher's moments of playful storytelling but her impatience would usually get the better of her and she'd invariably interrupt, especially if Christopher started to go on a bit with the story.

"You see the giant arrived, that's me, of course," Christopher explained, feeling the need to clarify, Beatrice felt her impatience rising; they didn't have time for stories but only for training.

"…arrived at the secret meadow," Christopher continued, "and sang his song on his recorder, asking permission to have a parley with the Queen of the beautiful Humming Fairies. A parley was arranged…"

"…and the moral of the story is?" Beatrice's impatience got the better of her.

"The moral of the story is to know people in low places that could give me this," and he pulled out a pistol. "We need another one. I can't be defending you from the rear without a pistol. You interrupted my story!"

"That is incredible, Christopher. I went to bed worried about that very thing and thought to maybe steal one from father but that would be too obvious," Beatrice said overriding Christopher's earlier comment.

"We practice riding the horses back and forth from the meadow to Lacey, Lacey to the meadow, so the direct route is ingrained just in case they'll need to return to Lacey by themselves," Beatrice commanded.

Christopher jumped to his feet and swung up on Moby and they both cantered purposefully back to Lacey. They repeated this journey four times and then rode to the tunnel and practised walking the tunnel. Back and forth, back and forth. It was slow in the tunnel at first, but by the third time, they were getting faster. Beatrice always led and she could now recognise from touch the little nooks and crannies along the wall and on the floor. A slight indentation in one of the bricks just by the hatch on the forest side intrigued her. I must see these marks with a light, she thought.

Returning from their fourth practice run, they left the tunnel and went back to the horses waiting at the willow tree, Beatrice felt confident.

"The tunnel walk felt solid, don't you think, we walked fast. I think we can walk it faster though, we need more practice," Beatrice spoke excitedly, she was happy so far with the training.

"What now?" Christopher asked.

"Pistol training," Beatrice stated.

"I only have a little bit of gun powder so you will have to learn quick," Christopher kindly but assertively said.

"Learning quickly is my forte." Christopher knew this, oh, so well.

"Let's practice in the barren field on the far, far side, we shouldn't be heard there," Beatrice said.

They cantered fast to the field, stopped, dismounted and went straight to work. Christopher got out his pouch with the ammunition inside.

"So, you push the lead ball down the barrel, then pour some powder into the flintlock," Christopher instructed.

Beatrice followed his instructions. Christopher then walked forward and put an apple on top of a log.

"There's your aim. Hold the pistol strong but relaxed, breathe, take aim, focus and pull the trigger with your intention."

Beatrice listened and followed his instructions. She focused on the apple, let out her breath as she fired and bang! Smoke filled the air with the smell of gun powder. She hit it. She looked at Christopher and smiled a calm and confident smile. She was a natural. And she loved it.

"I told you I was a quick learner," Beatrice conficently stated.

"Well, I don't think we need to waste any more gun powder on you practicing," Christopher said. As always, he was impressed.

"Tomorrow, we meet at the tunnel,"

"Father is away for the night, do you want to sneak in again? Can I tempt you to another game of Whist?"

"I have to meet someone at the tavern tonight. Whist tomorrow?" The cousins swung up on their horses and said their goodbyes.

Beatrice hated saying her goodbyes, but with their new mission together already in action, she didn't feel her normal sadness. They were partners in crime, they were a team and this feeling gave her both purpose and comfort.

For the next ten days, the cousins trained their horses to make the journey from the tunnel to the meadow. The signal was, when they were hidden in the willow tree and about to go down the tunnel, they would slap their horses on their rears and that would mean for them to go to the meadow.

Beatrice did it first. Christopher slapped Moby on his rear, and with Beatrice riding Asta, rode alongside Moby and straight to the meadow. The next time they swapped riders, so Beatrice stayed back at the willow tree and slapped Asta, whilst Christopher guided them to the meadow. They did this over and over and over again until they tried it where they both slapped their horses and let them ride alone to the meadow. The cousins then, on foot, walked to the meadow to see if their faithful steeds had been able to get to the meadow by themselves. They arrived after their long walk and were elated to see their beautiful horses grazing; their training had worked.

"You are both mighty and beautiful and clever," Christopher lovingly said to their horses.

"All four of us are in this together. We couldn't be doing this without them," Beatrice proudly said.

"I am feeling more confident about the whole venture. I think we've trained well," Christopher said.

"Yes, I do too. I think we are ready for our first robbery. I'll let you know when I have news of our first customer."

The cousins stayed in the meadow for a while longer, stroking their horses and letting the weight of their endeavour sink in. It was, as always, beautiful in the meadow. Butterflies filled the air, birds were a chorus of song. As they stood, a beautiful white butterfly came close to Beatrice, fluttered around her face and settled on Asta's rump.

"A good luck omen?" Beatrice said.

"I don't believe in all that," Christopher replied with a big smile.

"Well, I'll take it as one."

The cousins said their goodbyes and headed in their opposite directions.

That night, Beatrice couldn't sleep as she was excited with her new venture; she absolutely thrived on it. The scandal, the secrecy, the escapism, the role playing, the adrenalin, the training, the team work, the disguise, the purpose. For the first time in her life, she felt truly alive.

Two days later, the cousins met in the meadow and Beatrice came with news.

"Next Tuesday, a judge is meeting with father. I know from overhearing their conversations that he is ruthless and unforgiving. Many a poor soul has been hung for their innocence. He does not possess mercy in a single bone but he does possess a lot of money on his person. I can hear his coins chinking in his pockets," Beatrice explained as they stood hidden in the willow tree.

"Sounds like he will be ripe for our picking," Christopher replied.

"The meeting starts at eleven. The Judge usually lunches so I think we should be at the oak tree already waiting at two o'clock."

The cousins then practiced one more time their walk along the tunnel. They walked in the dark and were fast and precise; they knew the tunnel well by now. Near the exit hatch, Beatrice stopped at the markings in the wall.

"Stop!" I want to see what's on the wall. I've been wondering what these markings could be," Beatrice said as she got out a candle. She lit it with some tinder she brought.

The tunnel lit up and instantly became alive. It was the first time they had seen the tunnel lit up. Beatrice envisioned all the soldiers making their escapes. The clanking noise of their weapons, their heavy breathing as they ran, their panic and relief. The tunnel had seen a lot, neutral in its observations, strong in its salvation. Beatrice put the candle up close to the markings. Beatrice and Christopher leant forward to get a closer look.

"Lux libertas," they both quietly read the Latin out loud as Beatrice softly passed her fingertips over the engraved writing.

"Light and liberty," Beatrice translated out loud and looked at Christopher.

The weight and meaning of the words were not lost on the cousins. It held meaning for both of them albeit in slightly different ways. It was a beautifully poetic finding just before their first robbery. A meaningful silence hung for a while until Beatrice gave Christopher the candle and opened the hatch door. The light of the forest flooded in.

"Light and Liberty, what an incredible thing to find," Beatrice said as she sat amazed by the moment.

"I wonder what soldier wrote it? I wonder what became of him?" Christopher said.

They ate their sandwiches leaning back against the big boulders. The birds were busy with song. The forest, like Beatrice, was happy. They headed back through the tunnel and then back on their horses and galloped back to the meadow.

"See you at the oak tree at two o'clock next Tuesday," Beatrice stated seriously.

"Two o'clock," Christopher replied with the same seriousness.

"Partners in crime," Beatrice said.

"Partners in crime," Christopher replied.

"Light and Liberty," Beatrice added.

The cousins galloped off in their separate directions. Beatrice was excited, and to be honest, a little nervous.

For the next few days, Beatrice was busy with her aristocratic life but really she was just going through the motions and counting the days and hours until next Tuesday. At night she found it hard to sleep she was so excited. The thought of her own silent revenge upon a judge incapable of mercy was tantalising. She whiled away some of her time sitting on the hay next to Asta in her stable box. Asta would sit too; she felt the imminence of something.

Monday came and went. Over dinner with her parents, Beatrice could hardly contain herself knowing her secret.

"Earl Staunton is paying a visit next week. He looks forward to your company," Beatrice's father announced.

Instead of rage and sadness engulfing Beatrice, she felt emboldened and defiant full of the knowledge of her secret life to be. The sound of Earl Staunton's name being said now only brought on feelings of excitement instead of horror. There wasn't anything more thrilling and liberating to her now in this moment than knowing that, tomorrow morning, she would put on her highway robber's disguise, and start her secret clandestine venture as a highwaygirl.

ROBBERY 1

BEATRICE couldn't sleep. She woke early despite having to wait the whole morning until her rendezvous with Christopher. Lilly came late morning with a snack.

"As requested, mistress," Lilly said putting the tray down on the table. "Would you like anything else?"

"No, thank you, Lilly. Actually, yes, could you find out if my father's luncheon is to time," Beatrice asked.

"Yes, mistress," Lilly replied. She noticed a slight distraction about Beatrice but brushed it off, thinking it to be nothing important.

In no time Lilly returned.

"Yes, they are about to lunch now, anything you'd like me to relay?" Lilly asked.

"No, thank you, Lilly, that'll be all for now," Beatrice replied.

When Lilly left, Beatrice opened her wardrobe and got out her already-prepared bag. This was it. Showtime. Beatrice walked out and went straight to the kitchens and then headed straight to the stables and to Asta. Beatrice calmly saddled her, put on her breeches and coat and walked out of the stables. Beatrice walked straight to the woodland. Once there, she cantered straight to the oak tree and waited for Christopher. Beatrice took out her pocket watch, she was early. After a short while, she heard hooves clopping, she knew that gait. Christopher and Moby appeared a few minutes later. He was early. They smiled at each other.

"You're early," he said as he parked himself behind the big outstretched branch.

"You're early," Beatrice replied.

They stood in an anticipated silence, no need for talk, they both knew what they had to do. It was an overcast spring day but warm. They could hear the sheep's bells ringing in the next field. Their horses grazed and shook off the flies. They waited to hear the carriage approach but nothing.

They could hear their leather saddles creaking, the horses' bits clinking. They heard hooves of a horse approaching but the sound disappeared as it took a turn for the fields. The air stood still. But still no sound of a carriage. Until, finally, they heard the clanking of wheels, a carriage was approaching in the distance. But was it their carriage?

"The Judge's carriage is black with red lines," Beatrice said quietly and calmly. "When you see it, give me the nod."

Christopher stood to the side of the tree that was the nearest to the bend so he had first sight of anything approaching.

Beatrice tied on her red scarf, put her mask on. Her hair was already tied back and hidden under her hat, her tiny frame hidden under her big coat.

"Ready your pistol," Christopher said.

The sound of hooves and rattling wheels got closer. Christopher sneaked out of his cover to take a look at the carriage. Beatrice looked at him and waited, was it theirs? Was this the moment of no return? Her heart pumped, adrenalin pumped through her. Christopher turned to Beatrice and nodded, no need for words.

This was it. Showtime. No going back. Everything they had rehearsed and trained for was now going to be put into play. Christopher took his position back hidden and Beatrice gave an extra tie to hold down her hat. The carriage was approaching. The sound of hooves was getting louder and louder. Christopher readied his pistol. He was slightly nervous but knew he had a job to do. The horses finally came to the crest of the bend and turned it. Beatrice took her cue. No turning back now. Beatrice strode out from behind her hiding place and stood powerfully in the middle of the road, commanding all of its space and raised her pistol. The Highwaygirl was born. Christopher, on the other hand, quietly stepped out and took his place at the rear. The surprised carriage horses neighed, the coach driver immediately pulled on the reigns bringing his horses to a stop. The horses were fidgety and nervous, Beatrice and Asta were not. They stood their ground. It all went a lot slower than Beatrice imagined. She had time to think. Beatrice saw the coach driver moving his hand to his side in an attempt to get his pistol. Beatrice took a dramatic leap forward, reared Asta high on her hind legs. The carriage horses jostled and made small rears which put the driver off-balance, his pistol dropped to the floor. Beatrice then calmly walked up to the side of the coach driver, and pointing her pistol directly at him, shook her head. She then stepped back, making room for him to step down.

"Down," Beatrice ordered.

The coach driver stepped down from his seat. Beatrice, then using Asta, pushed him forward to stand next to the coach's door With her pistol, she pointed it to the Judge who was looking ahead and not at Beatrice. Beatrice kicked the side of the carriage to get the judges attention. He startled and looked at her, she got the attention she wanted. She then motioned using her pistol for the judge to get out.

"Out," she ordered.

The Judge turned the coach door handle and stepped down, closing the door behind him. Everything seemed to go in slow motion.

"Valuables," Beatrice said. She held her pistol directly at them both, strong and solid without a single quiver. She was in her power.

Christopher held the fort from behind. He stood observant and steady with Moby, checking for any surprises.

"Gold," Beatrice demanded in her lowered voice.

"But I travel empty-handed," the judge stammered in a feigned attempt of defence.

Beatrice was thankful for all those boring tea parties. She knew for a fact that the Judge and the guests never travelled empty-handed.

Beatrice took a menacingly big step forward. Pointed her pistol even closer to the Judge. Asta nudged and prodded him with her head. And with this extra menace, he put his hand inside his coat looking for his money pouch. Whilst he fumbled, Beatrice thought of the poor young girl the Judge had sentenced to hang for a petty handkerchief crime. He found his pouch and threw it up to Beatrice, she caught it, it felt heavy. Beatrice then gestured to Christopher to come forward. She gave him one of their hand signals. On cue, Christopher sidled Moby up to stand alongside the two men, keeping them caught between the carriage and him. Beatrice then went to the carriage horses, and in a flash, unbridled the two of them. She then turned, nodded to Christopher and they both galloped off, racing at full speed straight to the meadow.

Once there, they circled their horses as adrenalin was high. Beatrice pulled down her scarf and flipped her hat back to hang round her neck and let out a deep breath.

"Ahh, what a performance, what a show, a scandal. Did you see his grovelling, his trembling. Now he knows how it feels for every boy, girl, woman and man he's had hanged," Beatrice was exultant. She enjoyed, relished and felt justified for its every moment. Christopher was quiet. "Cousin you have nothing to say?"

"Yes, B, quite the show," Christopher was also exultant but inwardly so. He was, however and most of all, amazed at his cousin. She was, as she had been in their training, a natural, more so come the real event. She was both intimidating and commanding. He also felt safe in her leadership. She had, after all, improvised the whole hold-up. She was calm and composed. A master. She had become, in an instant, the Highwaygirl.

"And I enjoyed it, cousin! What outrage, what rebellion, what freedom! I will surely hang but hang happy indeed," Beatrice was still feeling alive from the robbery. "Here, this is all yours, you have earned it, cousin," Beatrice said as she threw Christopher the bag of coins.

"Don't you want any of the reward?" Christopher questioned.

"Oh, Kit, my reward was seeing that arrogant man's grovelling face. "Give me back one coin for Michael though, as promised."

They both slowly calmed and slid down from their horses. It still wasn't safe to leave their secret meadow. They let their horses graze, standing close to them in case of any sudden escapes. Everything was quiet. Only the buzzing sounds of the meadow. Despite his reserve, Christopher was very happy with how it went. This highway robbery did go well but what about the others? He understood his cousin's justifications; she had nothing to lose with the prospect of her doomed wedding laying ahead of her. But he, however, did have something to lose. Her. He could lose her if they were ever caught. He couldn't bear the thought of losing his darling cousin, his only remaining family. He couldn't bear the thought of losing her to the hangman's noose. He looked at her dainty neck and imagined the hangman's noose around it and his blood curdled. There and then, he vowed he had to protect her.

"So let's count the prize?" Beatrice said excitedly.

Christopher got out the pouch, it felt heavy and wonderful in the palm of his hand. He gave Beatrice a big smile.

"It's all yours," Beatrice said once again gleefully. "Just think of your bookshop."

"Are you sure you don't want some of the prize?" Christopher questioned.

"No, it's yours. As I said, my prize was seeing the Judge's face as he handed over his money,"

"The horses were formidable, weren't they?" Christopher commended. He was proud of them, they stood strong and powerful, they knew what was needed of them and they delivered at every gesture, breath, silence or gallop.

"We all make a gallant team," Beatrice too gave Asta her love and appreciation. She had delivered beyond measure and Beatrice could do none of this if it wasn't with her. Becoming the Highwaygirl was made possible only with Asta. They too were now partners in crime.

The cousins now sat, time had passed. Christopher counted the money. "Three pounds and four shillings," Christopher said smiling.

"Ahh, Kit, what a marvel. Your printer's shop is not so far away!" Beatrice jumped up with joy.

Christopher jumped up too, her joy was totally contagious. Beatrice took his hands and swung around him. Spinning and laughing. Christopher laughed. She was totally beguiling. This felt good, he thought. They made a perfect team. In tune and in synch.

Time enough had passed. If Beatrice was away any longer, she would be missed. She had her piano class to attend to and everything must continue as normal.

"I must go. I think it is safe now. I will send you word, cousin." Beatrice said. "We only need to do a couple more robberies and we will have enough."

"Partners in crime," Christopher said beaming a smile.

"Partners in crime."

The cousins embraced a hearty and deep embrace. They had both shared a monumental moment together and they knew it. They mounted their horses and galloped off in their separate directions.

Back at the stables, Beatrice put on her skirts and walked purposefully back to the house. She walked through the kitchens.

"No time for lunch today, Betty."

Beatrice went straight to the piano room and to her waiting tutor. The piano sat proudly by the bay windows. Beatrice's cheeks were rosy and full of life. Mr Rochester noticed her to be in a completely different mood. Normally, she entered heavy and despondent but not today, he was taken by surprise.

"Good day, Mr Rochester," Beatrice said with a happy smile. "Beethoven or Bach today?" Mr Rochester was somewhat speechless.

"Beethoven," he replied.

Mr Rochester was taken aback at the lightness and joy that came from the piano today. It was like a different person playing, he thought, and he wasn't that far from the truth. Beatrice had opened up a whole new side of herself, a side that had been lying dormant for years, a side that had been waiting for just this moment. It felt liberating. Finally, Beatrice felt she could breathe. As Beatrice continued to play, she just kept smiling to herself that, only a few hours ago, she held the Judge at gunpoint and stole his money. Only a few hours ago she had become her alter ego, the Highwaygirl. She couldn't wait for her next opportunity.

ROBBERY 2

BEATRICE was ready for the ball, Earl Staunton's annual spring ball. Normally, the prospect of this ball would send shivers down her spine, but today, it was going to be her new source of information. Who she would be robbing next. It had only been a few days since their first robbery and Beatrice wanted to send word to Christopher of another. And this ball would do just that.

"Mistress, that dress is the perfect choice of gown," Lilly said as she weaved some wild flowers into her hair.

Beatrice had purposefully picked some corncockles, ramsons and columbines to put in her hair, the wildest of the wildflowers, she thought.

"You look beautiful, mistress," Lilly genuinely thought how beautiful Beatrice looked.

"Thank you, Lilly," Beatrice politely replied.

Lilly had noticed how light of person Beatrice seemed of late. She had a bounce in her step. She seemed happy. Lilly was suspicious.

"I hope you'll have a wonderful time, mistress," Lilly said.

"I'll tell you all the gossip," Beatrice replied as she took her cape and left to get the carriage.

The Seymour-Barclays arrived at the grand and overly ostentatious Georgian house of Earl Staunton in good time. There were already a number of carriages in front of them as they arrived. Staunton's spring ball was a calendar event and most of society's best and worst were there. Staunton's wealth came from sugar plantations in the Caribbean and various other business ventures. Today, he masqueraded around his vast ballroom like an overweight peacock. Beatrice would normally be inconsolable at having to be at this event and anywhere near his company but she held her Highwaygirl secret close to her heart and it, not only gave her strength, but also an added mysterious aura. She looked glowing and effervescent and she caught everybody's attention. Unfortunately, Staunton was the first to make sure that everybody knew who Beatrice Seymour-Barclay was soon going to marry. He flaunted himself upon her sickeningly.

"Beatrice, you have surpassed yourself. You simply glow," Staunton gushed as he bowed a long and slow bow, wanting everybody to look. And everybody did look. Everybody was both amazed and intrigued at the impending wedding of Earl Staunton to Beatrice.

"And Edward, you have surpassed yourself. This year seems your grandest ball yet," Lord Seymour replied.

"I have a lot to feel grand about," the Earl said directly to Beatrice as he made another bow. "I am the happiest gentleman in this room. Please, will you take my arm, as I introduce you to some of my guests."

Staunton put his arm out for Beatrice to take. She felt herself physically recoil as she gave Staunton her arm. She created as much space as she could between them as Staunton lead her straight through the middle of the ballroom. He was showing off his future bride for all in society to see. The orchestra played as Beatrice was paraded like a beautiful puppet. If it weren't for her highwaygirl secret life, Beatrice felt she would've collapsed. It was a little ironic, she thought, that, just as she had found her invisible persona, it was at the same time as being made to feel so visible. Two polar extremes.

It took an agonising three minutes to cross the room. Time seemed to have stood still. Hundreds of eyes were on her and it felt horrific. Beatrice froze inwardly, and when Staunton put his hand on top of her arm, she went cold. Was this really happening? She thought. Am I really going to be marrying this sixty-year-old man who repulses me? I can't believe he's even touching me! she thought. Staunton's pomp and joy were in stark contrast to her loathing. But as she imagined her next robbery, her spirits lifted, her demeanour changed and she then walked across the ballroom as the Highwaygirl disguised as a debutante. On finally reaching the other side, Staunton stopped at a small group.

"May I introduce you to the Duke and Duchess of Marlborough," Staunton said, Beatrice curtsied.

"You look incandescent, my dear," the Duke flattered. "You are a very lucky gentleman," Marlborough said as he looked at the Earl.

Beatrice could only notice the jewels. They sparkled and flickered in the luminous light of the ballroom's enormous chandeliers. She nodded and smiled and spoke only when spoken to, which was perfect for her as it allowed her mind to wander, to imagine her next robbery. As the people chatted, she let her mind wander to their first robbery. She analysed it, breaking it down moment by moment and finding places where it could improve. She laughed inwardly as she remembered the Judge and his pitiful face as he tried to withhold giving his money. Beatrice was brought back from her reverie when Staunton requested she take his arm once again. They said their goodbyes and Staunton led Beatrice to another group. Her parents quickly joined them.

"Congratulations to the happy couple," Countess Richmond said. "You will soon be a countess yourself. How wonderful and exciting to have such an innocent to join our few. I'm afraid though, my dear, your youth and beauty won't protect you from many of its difficulties." The expression cloak and daggers came to Beatrice's mind. There was nothing kind in her words or her tone. In fact there was nothing kind about the woman at all Beatrice thought.

The thought of being a countess was as exciting to Beatrice as were her Latin classes. Beatrice instantly disliked the Countess; she was spiteful, arrogant, and although beautiful on the outside, was ugly on the inside. Beatrice, however, found herself goaded by her, and if the occasion allowed, Beatrice would've enjoyed some verbal sparring. The Countess, no doubt, would probably win, her tongue as sharp as knives but Beatrice would've enjoyed the game. But instead Beatrice courteously flattered her.

"Your earrings her simply beautiful. Sapphires, are they not?"

"Sapphires indeed. You have a keen eye, young girl. My darling Earl Richmond gifted them to me as a celebration of acquiring our fourth tobacco plantation in Virginia," the Countess replied arrogantly.

"Do excuse me, there is someone I have to welcome," Staunton said. He bowed to Beatrice and made his leave. Beatrice let out an inward sigh of relief.

"The price has risen, business is better than ever. The slaves cheaper too," Lord Seymour said speaking directly to the Earl of Richmond.

"Yes, better than ever. A boom. I hear the same is for you in the Caribbean," the Earl of Richmond said.

"Indeed," Beatrice's father replied.

Their voices faded away into the distance as Beatrice couldn't bear to listen to their conversation any longer, her stomach literally curdled at every boast and cruelty, she had to block them out, so she focused on the room around her. Her eyes wandered and all that grabbed her attention were the jewels and riches flaunted everywhere, riches she wanted to steal.

"Next Wednesday, we have a quartet performing for Lady Seymour's birthday, it would be a pleasure to have your company," Seymour said to the Earl and Countess of Richmond. Seymour then spoke directly to the Earl, "I also have a business proposition I'd like to share with you."

Beatrice was instantly bolted back to their conversation. Next Wednesday they would be at Lacey Manor. Next Wednesday is going to be our next robbery, Beatrice proclaimed to herself. I can't think of a better person to rob other than Countess Richmond, she thought.

Now that Beatrice had the information she wanted, the rest of the evening was painful. Pretty young debutantes gossiping and talking of nothing but triviality. Her feet ached and more so her waist, she yearned to take off her corset and let out her stomach. The music, she had to admit, was wonderful; the cello reaching directly to her senses. But the hardest of all, more than anything she could've imagined, was the one dance she had to have with Staunton. They danced the Cotillon where, thankfully, the dance was shared with another couple. Staunton took her hand and guided her to the floor. He smiled at her and took her demure demeanour as innocence. He didn't, for one instance, take her demureness as utter repugnance. And Beatrice knew this which made her loathing all the fouler. Once again, time seemed to travel painfully slowly as she held his sweaty hands and endured every step. It was a strange and incomprehensible thought that, in only a few months, she would be married to this stranger. Finally, the ordeal came to an end.

"Excuse me, your grace, but I have to go see my mother," Beatrice said making her escape.

"It is time we leave my dear. Our carriage is being prepared," Lady Seymour said as Beatrice approached.

Just as lady Seymour and Beatrice were walking towards the exit, the Judge walked in, unfashionably late. Beatrice held her breath. What a scandal, what joy!

"Good evening, Walter," Staunton said as he greeted his friend.

"Oh, apologies, my friend, for my tardiness, I had problems with the horses. I really must acquire some new ones," the Judge replied. "But I wouldn't miss this event for anything."

Beatrice was standing to one side with her mother, and on overhearing the Judge, she absolutely reeled with joy that she had actually threatened this man, held a pistol to him.

"I'm so sorry to hear about your incident with the robbers the other day. What a heinous crime and one committed on such a noble person of character and standing," said a gentleman as he approached the Judge specifically to express his sympathies.

"Yes, awful it was. I defended myself well but the attackers were bullies and blaggards and I had no choice but to surrender my valuables. I intend with all the powers vested in me to find the men and have them hanged."

Beatrice, instead of trembling with fear, found hearing this news utterly exciting. Here she was, the very blaggard mentioned, and nobody upon nobody would ever suspect it to be her as she stood a picture of demureness and harmlessness. Her thoughts, however, raced to Christopher. He, of course, would not find this interaction as light-hearted and humorous as she did but she longed to share it with him.

"I will support you with whatever you need to catch these terrible people. They are of no value to society and deserve to be hanged." Beatrice turned her head as her father spoke these words. Her moment of joy was suddenly dampened. The thought of Christopher coming to any harm, let alone a hanging, she could and would not bear. They had to be vigilant and she promised herself that they would only do four highway robberies. Enough for Christopher's printer's shop and publishing house.

The next day, Beatrice sent word to Christopher. Michael always delivered her letters. Next Wednesday was their next robbery. They had to meet at the oak tree at six o'clock. Michael gave Beatrice her reply letter from Christopher. It was arranged. Next Wednesday at six at the oak tree.

The next few days, Beatrice rode out with Asta, went through the motions with all her classes, all so utterly mundane. More importantly, Beatrice went through all the details of the robbery. She played out different scenarios and visualised its smooth running. She couldn't wait to become the Highwaygirl once again.

Wednesday arrived. It rained all day. Sweet, spring rain. It was April and surprisingly hot and muggy. The air was thick with anticipation as Beatrice trotted up to the oak tree.

"You're early," said Beatrice as she arrived, Christopher was already there. She was so pleased to see him that she went straight up to him on his horse and leant over to hug him.

"You're early," he said smiling. "I'm pleased to see you too,"

The rain was dripping off their hats, falling in front of their faces and onto their shoulders. They liked it when it rained, it worked in their favour; harder to see them. They both took their positions behind the oak tree and waited.

"Your pistol is dry, isn't it? Remember I told you to always keep it dry."

"It's dry," Beatrice replied tapping it safely hidden under her coat.

"Remember it's a red and white carriage with two coachmen; one at the front and one at the back."

They waited. The rain stopped. Six o'clock came and went. Beatrice took out her pocket watch. It was twenty-past-six.

"They must be running late," she said.

"Do you think they'll be coming?"

"Absolutely,"

They waited a while longer. There was no need for any conversation. They both knew what they had to do. Finally, they heard the carriage approaching in the distance. The cousins looked at each other. Beatrice pulled up her red scarf and tightened it, her mask was already on, she was unrecognisable as the young Lady Seymour-Barclay. Christopher did likewise with his black scarf and mask. They waited, they prepared themselves. The sound of the pounding hooves got closer. Christopher left his position to go and take his peek round the bend, he looked at Beatrice and nodded. Beatrice took her pistol out and got herself in her position and in character. The hooves got louder. The crack of the whip could be heard. The carriage came to the bend and turned at its peak. The Highwaygirl strode out with her pistol outstretched and took her place, the road was hers. She held her ground as the carriage approached. The horses flustered, so did the driver but they didn't stop. The Highwaygirl held her ground. The driver tried to stop the horses but they weren't stopping. The Highwaygirl held her ground. They got closer. Christopher jumped out from the back.

The rear coachman fumbled to hold on as the carriage became unsteady. And still, the Highwaygirl held her ground as the carriage got closer and closer and close to colliding. At the last minute, Beatrice reared Asta high up onto her hind legs. They both looked intimidating which made the carriage horses finally stop. The coach driver instantly dropped the reins and put his arms up. He had no interest in fighting. The horses were riled though and flustered. Stomping and snorting

"Down," Beatrice said.

The driver climbed down. Beatrice walked round to the coach door and put the tip of the pistol through the window and gestured for the inhabitants to get out. The Earl and Countess of Richmond stepped down and stood up quivering against the carriage. They genuinely looked scared. Beatrice towered above them, menacingly. She felt no pity whatsoever, in fact she enjoyed seeing them belittled, they deserved it she thought, brought to heel for once in their petulant lives.

"Valuables," Beatrice said authoritatively. But what she really wanted to say was… from one Countess to another, I ask you to hand over your jewels. But she restrained herself.

Without any resistance, the Earl threw up his money pouch, and the countess, hers. Beatrice thought of their high and mighty conversation when at the ball and now they stood not so high and mighty at all. Beatrice enjoyed bringing them down a peg or two.

With her pistol and her focus still held straight at the Earl, the countess and their driver, Beatrice stepped backwards and towards the horses. With one hand, she deftly untied the two halters on the horses and let them drop to the ground. She then gave the cue to Christopher, nodding for them to make their escape. They then galloped off at a tumultuous speed towards the meadow, leaving their victims stunned and motionless.

The mud splattered up onto the legs of their horses as the cousins galloped to the meadow. Once there, Beatrice, in an explosion of adrenalin, swung off Asta and jumped to the ground.

"Ahh, cousin, what a triumph! Did you see their faces! Oh, what a revelation, what joy to see them so belittled. At the ball they were so pompous and self-righteous," Beatrice quietly roared.

Christopher swung down from Moby, as always, a little less enthused but jubilant nonetheless. "I can imagine. I wasn't at the ball but I can imagine, I have been to enough," Christopher said agreeing with Beatrice.

Beatrice sat on the ground, Christopher joined her. The early spring evening was sublime as was their success. Beatrice slowly calmed and handed Christopher the pouches.

"Yours to open," Beatrice said.

Christopher opened the Earl's pouch revealing a few coins.

"No wonder he handed it over so easily, not much here," Christopher said.

He then proceeded to open the Countess's silk pouch that revealed some jewels. "That's more like it," Christopher said.

"The sapphires," Beatrice knowingly said. "The Countess boasted about these earrings at the ball as I commented on their beauty. They are beautiful, aren't they?" Beatrice had to acknowledge their beauty. The gems had travelled a long way from where they were mined, Beatrice thought, as she held them in her hands admiring them.

"We should only do two more robberies. That should be enough for what we need, and I suppose by then, my rebellion will be satisfied," Beatrice said. "I think also that maybe we should change roads, be less predictable. At the ball, everybody was talking about the Judge's attack."

"I agree, two more robberies," Christopher said. "I will find our next carriage to rob." Beatrice nodded and handed Christopher some of Betty's sandwiches.

"It makes me hungry being the Highwaygirl. I'm sure the actors at the opera have their food after their performances," Beatrice said.

"Well, you just did your own very good performance as the Highwaygirl."

"A performance that must end soon, unfortunately." Beatrice then slapped Christopher jovially on the back, "You are the best rear man I could ever possibly want. It's a pleasure being in business with you."

They both smiled.

It was time to leave and the cousins hugged and went their separate ways.

Back at Lacey, Beatrice went straight to her room and dressed for bed. She was tired. As she lay in bed she recounted the robbery step by step. She relished every single moment. She thought of the dance she had with Staunton at the ball, holding his hands and suddenly went cold and so quickly returned to her and Christopher as highway robbers and her heart lifted again. But relying on Christopher to find their next robbery was frustrating. All she could do was wait. And waiting Beatrice did not like to do.

MONTIFIORRE AND ROBBERY THREE

Mıchael gave Beatrice a note, she eagerly opened it. Christopher had sent word. 'Next Thursday we meet at the woodland behind the pond at four o'clock in Newbury. I'll explain everything there. Come prepared.'

Beatrice counted the days until next Thursday. Thursday finally arrived and she had to feign a stomach upset to get out of her piano lesson.

"Lilly, can you give word to Mr Rochester that I am unwell and unable to do my lesson," Beatrice said in a weakened voice.

"Of course, mistress," Lilly replied leaving straight away.

Beatrice jumped out of bed. She went straight to get her prepared bag, and just as she was about to open her door to leave, her mother walked into her room.

Taken by surprise, Beatrice immediately threw her bag to one side, where it fortunately, was hidden by the long curtains. She then flung herself back onto the bed.

"Darling, I hear you are not feeling well? Can I read to you?"

"Oh, Mother, thank you but I prefer to sleep, I'm very tired. Beatrice replied.

"I thought it good to take this opportunity to talk about the wedding and the Earl. You know, darling..."

Beatrice's mind switched off. All she could think about was getting to Christopher in time and going ahead with their robbery. She heard something about 'you'll get used to the Earl in good time' but Beatrice's mind was elsewhere. The time was ticking and she would surely be late. Beatrice felt the anxiety rising as every slow word of her mother's was spoken. Christopher would be wondering where she was. And on and on her mother spoke. I can't let Christopher down, Beatrice thought. Desperate Beatrice closed her eyes pretending she was asleep. Her mother continued for a bit longer and then finally stopped talking. Thinking Beatrice was asleep, Lady Seymour stroked Beatrice's hair and kissed her forehead.

"I love you, darling," Lady Seymour whispered. She got up and quietly opened the door and left. Beatrice didn't have time to ponder that sentimental moment but it did touch her and a pang of love for her mother ran through her. Beatrice then leapt out of bed, grabbed her bag and sneaked out of her door. Everything seemed quiet. She sneaked safely down to the kitchens. The minute she entered she 'shh'd' the staff and tip-toed past them. They weren't surprised as Beatrice had done this many times before, but what they didn't know, was that today she was creeping out to go be the Highwaygirl.

Beatrice ran to Asta, and in time, had her saddled and bolting out of the stables. She raced her as fast as she could to get to the pond. The journey felt like agony, it was too slow. If only I could go faster, Beatrice thought.

"Come on, girl," Beatrice said urging Asta to go faster.

Beatrice slowed as she approached the pond. She saw Christopher in the woodland behind it and trotted to him.

"You're early," Beatrice said out of breath, she was breathing heavily.

"You're late!" Christopher said, emphasising 'late'.

"Yes, sorry about that. Mother wanted a talk just as I was about to escape. Are we too late?"

"No."

Beatrice calmed and caught her breath.

"We will be holding up a merchant, who hasn't paid his labourers for months. Not a nice fellow. Heard him drunk and boasting in the tavern a few times. His small carriage is black with a white emblem and he has one coachman."

The pond was a little ways out from Newbury town; the woodland gave them some cover but they hadn't rehearsed here and it all felt new.

"Here he comes," Christopher said.

Beatrice pulled up her scarf over her face, readied her pistol and prepared herself. The carriage trundled along until, finally, it reached the pond. Beatrice, as the Highwaygirl, stepped out.

The hold-up was over in a dash. The merchant had surrendered his coins easily and without any resistance from either him or his coachman. Beatrice and Christopher fled from the robbery at a tremendous gallop, straight to the meadow but from a completely different direction.

They had to gallop across a big open field which they didn't like to do so, despite the muddy field, they went as fast as they could. Christopher was slightly ahead when Beatrice felt the money drop to the ground, she instantly brought Asta to a crashing stop. Hearing the commotion from behind, Christopher turned and Beatrice signalled for him to continue and so he did. She couldn't see the pouch anywhere. I must have trampled it in the mud, she thought, as she frantically searched for it in in the mud, but on hearing the sound of a horse in pursuit, Beatrice abandoned her search, swung up on Asta and galloped away as fast as she could. The woodland to her estate was just in front of her, and once there, she would be safe.

Beatrice careered into the woodland, and just as she entered, she nearly crashed into another horse and rider cantering at speed from the other direction. Asta reared up in shock, Beatrice held her seat but only just, her hat slid to one side revealing her feminine chestnut hair. Both Beatrice and Asta were in such a rush that they had failed to notice this other rider as it came careering along the tiny woodland path. What in almighty heaven was another rider doing out here! She thought. Beatrice was utterly taken by surprise and totally infuriated. Asta landed on her feet, the other rider came to an emergency stop reining in his horse. All parties collected themselves and their spooked horses. As Beatrice looked up, she instantly locked eyes with the rider in front of her. A spark was ignited. Time stood still. The two horses panted, they were still jittery, shuffling their feet. It was but a second but it felt like an hour, in fact, it felt timeless. Catapulted back to the present, Beatrice pulled herself away from the stranger and sprang into a canter straight towards the meadow.

As she cantered on she felt rattled. Who was that stranger? How handsome he was. What on earth was he doing on that woodland path? What was he doing riding so fast? Was my identity revealed? Should I tell Christopher? Beatrice's thoughts raced.

Beatrice cantered fast straight into the meadow, screeching to a halt and swinging down off Asta, landing dramatically in front of Christopher.

"What happened?" Christopher asked. "I've been worried waiting here. Did anyone follow? Did anyone see you?"

"Nobody," Beatrice instantly lied.

"What happened?"

"I dropped the pouch, it had gotten trampled in the mud and I couldn't find it. Hearing a horse from behind, I decided to take the woodland path."

"And you are sure nobody saw you?" Christopher questioned again.

"Yes," Beatrice said looking down slightly.

"B, you are lying, I know when you are lying! What happened?" Christopher pushed.

"I collided with another horseman on the woodland path. It was but a second. Who, for heaven's sake, rides down that path? Who was he?" Beatrice was both angry and intrigued.

"Did he notice you? Your face I mean,"

"No," Beatrice simply replied but she wasn't that sure, her hat had slid to one side, could the stranger have noticed anything from that? She kept this thought to herself.

They stood in silence for a while, recovering from the whole affair.

"We stick to the main road out to London. I don't like that open field," Beatrice said.

After much time in the wood and shaking off the events of the collision with the stranger on horseback, it was time for the cousins to leave. They hugged as always and went their separate ways. But as Beatrice trotted back, she couldn't quite shake off the collision with the handsome stranger. Who was he? What on earth was he doing on that road? Beatrice thought. But most troubling of all, were her feelings. Feelings she had never felt before. Stirrings and feelings coming from a strong source, feelings of an attraction. Her heart pumped stronger and butterflies fluttered in her stomach. It was a glorious feeling to her and a new one. Could she trust these feelings? Would these feelings trust her? Beatrice trotted on and put those new and mysterious feelings to one side. Her mind told her it was a chanced and fleeting moment, never to be repeated. But that's not what her instincts told her. Her instincts told her that she would be meeting that stranger again. But when would that be? Beatrice could hardly wait.

Beatrice did not have to wait long to find out when that would be. She returned to Lacey and left Asta in her field. They had their sweet goodbye embrace and Beatrice walked back to the house in her skirts and corsets. She went and sat in the kitchens and ate some lunch when, out the window, she saw the mystery horse and rider walking down the main driveway. Her heart fluttered and stammered but her speech stayed calm.

"Who was the visitor?" Beatrice asked Betty casually.

"I'm not sure. He came to do business with your father, they lunched together," Betty replied.

Later that evening over dinner, Beatrice wanted to find out about the young gentleman.

"I noticed your guest today had a beautiful horse," Beatrice said to her parents at the table.

"Yes, a beautiful horse indeed, sired from Miles Stapleton's Godolphin Arabian," Lady Seymour replied.

"That is not far from here. But I've never seen that horse or its rider here before," Beatrice continued as she subtly tried to pry out any information.

"No, the owner was visiting me on business, he's normally away on business," Lord Seymour said. "I liked his acumen, I think we could do some positive business ventures together. He was here on his father's behalf."

"Of Italian descent, no?" Lady Seymour queried.

"Joseph Montifiorre. The family are Venetian," the Lord clarified.

Beatrice was mightily intrigued now. Pedigree horse, Venetian, business man, traveller; he sounded exotic. But for now, Beatrice had to put her heart's desires to one side, she had to find their next robbery.

Beatrice gave word to Christopher for their next robbery. Next Friday at twelve noon. A lawyer would be visiting. Beatrice wasn't able to discover much information about him so was a bit doubtful as to whether to go ahead with the robbery but decided, yes. His carriage was green and red, that she definitely knew.

Friday arrived. It was an overcast day. As planned, Christopher rode up to the oak tree, Beatrice was already standing there.

"You're early," Christopher said smiling.

"You're early," Beatrice returned the smile.

"Is the Highwaygirl ready?"

"Couldn't be readier."

They heard wheels and hooves. Christopher checked to see if it was their carriage, he nodded. It was driving fast, he thought. They were both, by now, very smooth and slick with their roles. Each knowing exactly what to do and when to do it. They had complete confidence in each other's abilities.

"It's fast," Christopher called over.

Beatrice got into position, the carriage got louder, and very soon, made its turn on the bend. As the horses' heads appeared from the bend, the Highwaygirl stepped out. The coach driver was completely taken by surprise. They were driving fast and in a rush. He pulled up the reins, the horses tried to stop but were in a race with each other and they didn't slow, they just kept going at full speed. As they got too close, much like their robbery before, Beatrice once again reared Asta high up on her hind legs, making a striking and dramatic pose. The carriage horses reared themselves, the carriage swerved, hit the pothole to its left hard and the wheel fell off. The carriage dropped heavily to the ground making a big thud as it fell in the pothole. Thankfully, the driver managed to hang on. Christopher at the rear looked on to check all was safe. There was a lot of commotion as the horses snorted and blew out, stomped and jittered, spooked by everything. The coach door banged wide open and its inhabitants, huffing and puffing, tried not to fall out. Unperturbed by the commotion, Beatrice held her pistol outstretched, signalling the driver to get down. He obediently did. Beatrice then motioned for the inhabitants, who were half falling out anyway, to do likewise.

On seeing two passengers get out of the carriage Beatrice was taken by surprise, she was only expecting the lawyer. The lawyer stepped out, a bit shaken but all in one piece. Then the other passenger stepped out. Beatrice held her pistol strong and outstretched. There was nothing that could've prepared her for who she saw. The directness of her pistol belied her inner shock, her heart pumped and her stomach fluttered with butterflies as Montifiorre stood before her. She stood her ground, she played her part, she didn't flinch, despite being completely blown off-kilter.

"Valuables," Beatrice said in the deepest of voices that she could muster.

The lawyer happily handed over his. Then she pointed her pistol to Montifiorre motioning for his too. Their eyes locked. Despite all her efforts, she couldn't leave their hold. Montifiorre broke the spell by throwing his leather pouch up to Beatrice.

"From one gentleman to another," he said.

Beatrice was so shocked she could've fallen off Asta. Asta, of course, felt her every quiver, she felt her sudden nerves and disturbance and so she held her weight lower, stronger.

Beatrice took the pouch, tipped her hat, nodded to Christopher and they both galloped off to the meadow.

Beatrice rode faster today; she was driven and fired up. Christopher wondered what had happened. They screeched to a halt once at the meadow. Beatrice threw her hat off, pulled down her scarf and ripped off her mask. She made repetitive fast circles.

"Cousin, what is going on? What happened back there?" Christopher asked impatiently.

"You asked the other day whether I had been seen, well, I lied, I had."

"I knew it, you are the most terrible liar, to me, that is. Well, he didn't recognise you, did he?"

"No, how could he? He has only seen me in my disguise."

"Well, then, we have nothing to worry about," Christopher calmly said. He was, however, a little surprised at her reaction; she seemed unusually stressed.

"Here, see how much we got." Beatrice threw the pouches to Christopher, and now calmer, slid down from Asta.

"Today, all the honour is yours," Christopher threw back the pouches. Beatrice opened the black one first.

"Well, that's a hearty amount," she said and threw it back to Christopher. "It's yours. Well, actually, give me some back to give to Lilly and Michael."

Beatrice took some coins back from Christopher and put them in her pocket. She then opened the next pouch. It had a lot of coins; it also had a piece of paper wrapped up very small. She unfolded it and read it. Her breath stood still, her heart skipped a beat. She handed it to Christopher to read out loud.

"Your secret is safe with me," Christopher read out. "Two of the coins are for the mother and her child begging by the wishing well. I trust you will give them to her."

They both looked at each other.

"One more and we stop," Beatrice said.

"What I really want to know is how he knows it is you?" Christopher queried, his mind was trying to put any pieces together. "Unless, of course, you're not telling me something?"

"Well, when we collided, my hat slipped and some of my hair came lose. Maybe that lead to something?"

"Maybe, but he hasn't seen you in person. I mean he now knows you are a girl but what girl he doesn't know. Unless maybe he saw your portrait at Lacey? But even so, I can't imagine him recognising you."

They stood in silence for a while, lost in their own thoughts.

"Are you sure you want to risk another robbery?" Christopher asked.

"Of course, I do," Beatrice said annoyed. "I'm not worried about Montifiorre and my identity, how ridiculous! I'm worried about my feelings about Montifiorre. Feelings I've never had before. Is it love? Did you have that with Sophie? What was it like?"

"When did that happen? When you collided?"

"When we locked eyes together. When time froze."

"Well, I can't say really if love can be ignited from just a look. I suppose so. Sophie and I knew each other for a while. You are to be wed in July. I would leave it all behind you and take it as a fleeting moment."

"I don't want to talk about it any more," Beatrice was rattled and uncomfortable. "I'll give word for our next robbery."

The cousins hurriedly hugged and said their goodbyes, and then rode their separate ways.

Back home and back in her skirts, Beatrice hid her highway robber's clothes and went down to the tea room to join her parents for tea. She was still rattled, Beatrice couldn't shake off the robbery and her feelings.

"Scandalous, absolutely scandalous! Highway robbers here on our stretch of road to London! Scandalous! Who would have thought. All three of my guests here at Lacey have been robbed. Nobody will want to visit us at Lacey, this has to be stopped. This has to be stopped." Lord Seymour said enraged.

"They have already become quite infamous. Everybody is talking about them. The papers have described the leader as medium height and that he hardly speaks. Don't worry, dear, it won't take long before they find them," Lady Seymour said.

"Look!" The Lord was aghast as he held up one of the broadsheets that had a caricature of the highway robbers. Beatrice laughed inside. If they only knew, she thought.

"All the wedding arrangements are nearly complete. Edward has arranged a couple of outings for you both, which I expect you to enjoy, so you can both get to know each other better before the wedding," Seymour told Beatrice in his rather patronising tone which only infuriated Beatrice more.

"It plans to be a wonderful ceremony. The whole of society are looking forward to it," Lady Seymour encouragingly said having seen Beatrice's sullen face. "You will get used to him, darling."

All these words were too painful to hear so Beatrice thought only of her highwaygirl secret life. She enjoyed this new infamy, her name was in the papers, her secret had become famous. It gave her strength and joy. She longed for the next one. But still, she felt rattled. She couldn't believe that she had held a pistol to the man that was giving her these feelings of love. She couldn't really believe what had just happened. Their highway robberies had taken a different turn.

"Next Friday, Staunton is coming for a private meeting with me for business and to talk about the wedding. His sister will be joining us too. Lord Staunton wants you to meet her. We will all have tea together after our meeting," the Lord announced.

Beatrice was overjoyed. There was her next robbery and her last. She knew it was a risk to rob her future husband but it was too much of a temptation. She'd end her scandalous escapade on a high note. A crescendo, the finale of the opera. But would it end a tragedy?

The next day, Beatrice rode Asta into the village. The mother and her child were begging by the wishing well as Montifiorre had said in his note. Beatrice slid down from Asta and gave the mother two silver coins from Montifiorre's pouch.

"Ahh, miss, that's awful generous…" The mother stopped talking when she realised what she had been given. Tears welled up in her eyes.

"I don't know what to say, miss," the woman was in shock.

"Nothing to say," Beatrice replied as she swung back up on Asta.

As she rode back, she thought of Montifiorre. The stranger that made her heart beat faster. That made her feel things she had never felt before.

The stranger who knew her secret. Already they shared something together. But can I trust him? Beatrice thought as she walked back. He was definitely handsome and generous but it could all be some cunning ploy. Beatrice let her thoughts wander as she hoped that she would, one day, meet Montifiorre again.

THE LAST ROBBERY

"I hear there has been another highway robbery along the main road here to London. What awful beasts. The culprits will be found and hanged," Mary Staunton said with much vitriol.

Beatrice looked at her as she sat on the sofa and sipped her tea. Beatrice hated her. She was pompous and conceited. Beatrice had to admit, however, that she was annoyingly quite pretty but the words that left her mouth were nothing but ugly.

"I prided myself on the safety of this part of Surrey, but now not so. These foul people have sullied it. They are like vermin, of no use to society and thus better off hanged," Mary Staunton continued.

Am I really being condemned to join this family? Beatrice thought, shocked rather than her usual anger. Is this really going to be my destiny? Am I really going to be forced to have this grotesque man's children?

"Maybe if they were not so poor there would be no need to rob," Beatrice added provokingly. She just couldn't help herself.

"Maybe, my dear, if they worked harder and complained less, then they would earn more money," Mary replied caustically.

"Here, here!" Earl Staunton agreed.

"A few years ago, my brother discovered a thief red-handed amongst our staff, and I'm happy to report, that he had him instantly removed and instantly hanged. His wife begged for his freedom, for their children. But no crime can go unpunished. A lesson has to be taught and an example made that theft is punishable by hanging," Mary said proudly.

Could I detest a family more? Beatrice thought. There was absolutely no use in attempting to reply or indulge in any conversation with the Stauntons. I'll leave everything I have to say to them at the time of our robbery.

Beatrice looked over at the clock on the fireplace. It was time to make her leave.

"Do excuse me, everybody, but I'm feeling dreadfully faint. I think it must be the sudden heat. I apologise enormously but I must take my leave," Beatrice stood up, feigned her sudden weakness, curtsied and left the room.

She walked with haste directly to the kitchens. She knew both her parents would be occupied for quite some time with the Stauntons so wouldn't be coming to check on her.

With haste, Beatrice sneaked across to the stables. Once inside, she saddled Asta. Michael was there, as always, mucking out the stables. They greeted each other, but that was all. Beatrice dropped a silver coin in the hay for him as she saddled Asta, nodded to let him know it was there and then trotted out and straight to the oak tree, Christopher was already there. The horses greeted each other.

"You're early," Beatrice said with a smile as she took her position.

"You're late," Christopher replied.

"This is our last and final robbery. I'm going to make it mean something, go out with a bang. You don't get many chances to hold a pistol to the man who's going to steal your freedom, so I'm going to steal something of his," Beatrice was quietly angry.

"Well, I'm right there behind you, holding up the rear," Christopher added.

The cousins waited. Beatrice prepared herself with mask, hat and scarf. Her thick hair was tied back in a queue and tucked into the back of her coat; she wore its collar high. She put on her man's leather gloves to disguise her petite female hands and was ready. She looked absolutely nothing like her aristocratic self and even further away from being a countess in a few months. Christopher too prepared himself. He raised his scarf, put on his mask, lowered his hat and raised his coat collars. His mousey blonde hair was also tied in a queue. He readied his pistols.

Finally, they heard a coach and it's horses approaching.

Christopher went to check if it was black with a green insignia. It was. He nodded. Beatrice had never been so ready. She couldn't wait to step out in front of the Ogre as the Highwaygirl.

Just as the horses' heads came round the corner, the Highwaygirl stepped out, pistol outstretched. This was it. She reared Asta high up making her dramatic entrance. It worked, the carriage's horses jolted and came to a sudden stop. Christopher stood strong from the rear.

"Down," Beatrice said to the driver pointing her pistol strong at him.

As the driver climbed down, he sneakily got a small pistol out from the inside of his boots. Beatrice saw his movements, and coming up close to the man, reared Asta again so that her hooves were only centimetres from his face. He instantly dropped the pistol as he fell down onto the floor. Christopher pulled out his second pistol and pointed it directly to the rear coach groom. Beatrice then gestured for the driver to move along the side of the carriage, and with her foot, banged the door hard.

"Out!" she said.

Staunton opened the door, as he lowered his head to get out of the carriage, he knocked his wig backwards revealing his bald head. How pitiful, Beatrice thought.

"Valuables," Beatrice demanded.

She pointed her pistol directly at Staunton. He was sweating, drips rolled down his face,

Mary stood tall but she didn't look up; she either looked at the ground or looked away, but to look directly at her assailant was too much.

"We shall hand over nothing," Staunton said in an attempt at defiance but it wasn't very convincing and only made him look more pathetic.

Beatrice calmly walked straight to Staunton. She towered above him, thanks to Asta's powerful height. Pointing her pistol a few centimetres from Staunton's head, Beatrice repeated,

"Valuables."

There was no rush, she was going to enjoy this moment. It had to last for a long time, for a whole marriage. So Beatrice savoured it. She too was sweating; it was a hot May day. What joy this was for Beatrice. After weeks of having to put up with everything the Earl had put her through, his flagrant disregard for her happiness, his conceitedness and gloating, and his joy in stealing her personal sovereignty, Beatrice now enjoyed watching his discomfort, she enjoyed stealing some of his sovereignty.

"Move to the front," Christopher said to the groom he had guarded from the back. The man moved alongside the carriage and stood next to Mary.

The two horses pinned the group to the carriage, there was nowhere to go. They were all huddled together, and despite fearing for her valuables, Mary was disgusted to be rubbing shoulders with the groom man. They were all the same now, no hierarchy, as they stood pinned to the side of the carriage.

Beatrice moved Asta one crucial step forward, she was nearly on top of Staunton, she held the pistol to his head.

"You scoundrels, you will all not get away with this," Staunton said quietly in an attempt at defence.

"I repeat, hand over your valuables," Christopher demanded.

Christopher menacingly pointed his pistol at Mary. Christopher, when needed, was intimidating. He was quite tall and sturdily built so, when sitting on top of the mighty Moby, he too became quite the threatening character. It was the first time he had seen the Earl and he now realised all that Beatrice had been telling him. Poor Beatrice, he thought. What an ogre, he thought, a repellent ogre. So, with his pistol held strong, he too enjoyed every moment of watching their intimidation. He stood proudly next to his cousin, the Highwaygirl. The two cousins stood side by side, their two horses stood side by side, they were all partners in crime.

The Earl looked at his sister and nodded, Mary fumbled in her skirt pockets. Staunton looked up at the highway robbers. There was something familiar about the one to his right, the leader, he thought. He couldn't quite put his finger on it exactly but just something about him. He might be an ogre but a cunning one.

Mary finally retrieved a small green silk pouch and reluctantly threw it up to Christopher.

Beatrice pushed Asta into Staunton purposefully, treading on his foot. She took one step backwards and off his foot.

"Argh," Staunton inwardly cried.

Beatrice then motioned for Asta to rub her head up and down in Staunton's face. She snorted and blew out on him, covering him in horse's breath and snot. His head knocked back and hit the carriage. Staunton was loathing every second. This was sheer hell for him, especially as a man hating and fearing horses. He was literally trembling now, and instantly, went for his pouch in his coat pocket. With Asta still rubbing his face, he held up his pouch with his one hand. Beatrice pulled back Asta's head. Staunton threw the pouch up to Beatrice who gave it to Christopher.

Beatrice nodded to Christopher, She then reversed and untied the halters of the horses. Beatrice then turned, and in doing so, purposefully hit

Staunton's face with Asta's rear, she then reversed one step back so Asta's bottom was completely in his face. Then she turned to face them.

"Gentleman," Beatrice said as she tipped her hat.

The cousins then flew off at a hard gallop in the direction of the meadow. The show was over. Or so they thought. Christopher was slightly behind Beatrice and soon heard a horse galloping in fast pursuit. He turned to look and saw, to his surprise, a horseman galloping hard towards them.

"Beatrice the tunnel! And fast!" Christopher shouted, his heartbeat jumped.

Beatrice pushed Asta on and Christopher too with Moby. The horses felt the serious urgency and dug down to get more speed, which worked, as it gave the cousins the distance they needed in order to arrive at the willow tree. They flew through the willow tree's draping vines , screeched to a stop and swung down from their horses.

"Let the horses go now," Beatrice said urgently.

They both slapped their horses who leapt out of the willow tree, and as trained, headed straight back at lightning speed to the meadow.

No time to breathe, they went straight into their training mode. Beatrice cleared the hatch door, opened it and they both climbed down, being careful to close it with its rubble on top. They moved as quickly as possible. They were grateful for all the rehearsals they had done, as it now really paid off. Adrenalin moved them faster than expected down the tunnel, their hearts were pumping hard. It was pitch black, no light whatsoever but they walked sure-footed and their hands guided them along the wall. Beatrice felt the Latin engravings and knew they had arrived at the exit hatch. 'Light and Liberty,' she said to herself. She fumbled for the handle, found it and pushed it open, the light flooded in. They climbed out and into the forest, closed and covered the hatch. As fast as they could, they climbed up the hill, and at a deeply overgrown section, pushed through the wild bracken and crawled in. Now, it was a waiting game.

Meanwhile, their pursuer, the coach driver had had the two cousins in sight. He was actually gaining on them. But then suddenly, they seemed to disappear. He veered to the right but saw nothing. He then veered to the left to see if they had gone down the hill towards the river, but nothing there either.

"Argh!" He yelled out loud, infuriated.

"Go get them now!" Staunton had yelled when they were all back at the carriage. The cousins had bolted off, Mary was in tears and Staunton screamed again, "Go get them now! Dead, if need be! You will be rewarded. Now go!"

The coach driver had leapt into action and hadn't bothered to re-halter the nearest horse; he simply untied its coach harness, threw a rope around its neck, swung on top and bolted off in the direction of their attackers. But now, after having had them in sight, they seemed to have disappeared into thin air.

"Where the hell are they?" he said out loud bemused.

He circled the surrounding area, went up and down but nothing, not a clue. He went as far back to the carriage as he could without Staunton seeing him and retraced his steps at a walk to see if he could find something. And find something he did. A twinkle of silver caught his eye. He stopped, slid down from his horse and picked it up. It was a lady's silver bracelet. He looked it over and noticed it had the initials BSB. He thought it was probably some of the stolen jewellery that they had dropped. He also thought, should I keep it, or should I give it to Staunton?

The coach driver rode back at a trot.

"They disappeared, sir," the coach driver loyally informed his boss.

"Scoundrels, scoundrels!" Staunton shouted, kicking the mud up as he yelled.

"I found this on the ground. They must have dropped it." The coach driver handed Staunton the bracelet. He was hoping to be rewarded for his loyalty by asking for a position for his nephew.

Staunton took it and looked at the initials BSB.

"Go back and scour the area, see if they have come out of their hiding. It's getting dark now so maybe they'll start moving," Staunton said. "But go quietly."

The coach driver haltered his horse this time and walked on slowly. He was determined to find them.

"B, I think it best if you go back to Lacey. It'll look suspicious if you are gone for the night. I'll walk you back. It's nearly dark now anyway," Christopher said.

"We'll walk by way of the woodlands. When it's dark we'll head off," Beatrice said agreeing.

The May night was warm and the forest was full of life. Beatrice took off her gloves and wrapped her hands around her knees. Sitting quietly in their hideout, a rabbit, a hedgehog and some wild mice all paid them a visit. They sat in silence, listening for any pursuers. As Beatrice sat, she suddenly noticed that her silver bracelet was not on her wrist.

"Christopher! My bracelet, my silver bracelet. It must have dropped!" Beatrice said panicked as she looked upon her now bare wrist.

"Are you sure you had it on?" Christopher asked.

"Yes, I did. Mother had specifically asked me to wear it to the tea with Staunton. Normally I would never have worn it," Beatrice explained. "In the rush, I forgot to take it off. Argh, I'm so angry with myself."

"Let's not panic yet. Early in the morning, I'll go and look for it,"

They waited a while longer. The night and the forest was quiet. They were both hungry.

"Fifty-fifty this time, a fair split for our last robbery," Christopher said handing Beatrice Mary Staunton's silk pouch.

"Let's go," Beatrice suddenly said. "Yes, I think it is safe now."

They walked down the hill to the hatch entrance. Lifted it, stepped down, closed it and started their walk back. On the way back, Beatrice stroked the Latin words, 'light and liberty' on the wall as a touch of encouragement. They walked steadily, soon arriving at the other side.

"As slow as possible, open it, as slow as possible, maybe someone is waiting," Christopher whispered, almost mouthed.

Beatrice moved like a cat, slow and stealthily. Was the coach driver waiting outside? Staunton? She peered her eyes just through the crack to see if she saw anything. She saw nothing. It could be an ambush, she thought. Beatrice took a deep breath and opened the hatch fully, swinging her head quickly to both sides to see if anyone was waiting, nobody was.

"It's clear. Let's go!" she whispered.

They both clambered out, covered the hatch well and sneaked out of the willow tree. To get to their first woodland, they had to cross an open field so they ran as fast as they could across it. Beatrice was thankful her corsets weren't on; she could never run as fast if she was wearing them. They saw their first woodland in front of them at the bottom of the field. The run seemed endless as they charged towards it. Safely there, they walked a fast walk.

The coach driver trotted up the hill to the willow tree, he had failed to see the cousins at the bottom of the hill to his left and they had failed to see him on their right. He walked around the tree, along the brick walls and back around again but found nothing. He decided to look further to the east.

The cousins didn't speak much, they just wanted to arrive back at the meadow and to their horses, they hoped they were still there. They crossed a stream and then had to run across another small open field to get to another little woodland, which then took them straight to the meadow.

"Asta!" Beatrice called out quietly running straight to her. "You're safe, you're safe. I've been so worried. You both waited for us. Christopher, what faithful horses we've been blessed with." Beatrice was jubilant as she hugged her mare.

"Blessed indeed," Christopher said as he gave Moby a strong hug.

Without wasting any more time, they swung up on their horses and cantered back straight to Lacey, making sure they moved slowly as they approached from the woodland at the rear of the stables.

"Let's not meet for a while," Christopher said staying back in the woodland.

Beatrice nodded and gave him her hand signal for 'I love you' and then walked out of the woodland and into the stables.

Meanwhile, the coach driver was still on the hunt. He had taken the hold-up personally and wanted to find his attackers. It was dark and he scoured the area but found nobody and nothing. But something in him didn't want to give up.

Michael was in the stables when Beatrice walked in, he was alone, she looked out of breath and frazzled.

"We had to use the tunnel. Staunton's man chased us," Beatrice whispered.

"I'll put Asta away, you go on up to the house," Michael said.

Beatrice quickly changed back into her skirts. She handed the bag of her highway clothes and the loot to Michael.

"Hide it here. I won't need it for a while," Beatrice said to Michael.

Beatrice then walked at speed back to Lacey. She sailed past all the kitchen staff, not saying a word and straight up to her room. She collapsed on her bed, and for the first time in hours, took a deep breath. Even though the chase was serious and scary, Beatrice enjoyed every minute of it. The excitement, the realness of it all, the adrenalin. As she lay on her bed, she felt both glee and trepidation.

She went over the details of the robbery; Staunton's face, his wig falling, his sister, the chase, the tunnel, the forest, their beloved horses, and felt alive as she thought. We certainly ended our escapade as highway robbers on a dramatic note, she thought.

Lady Seymour climbed the steps and crossed the long corridor that took her to Beatrice's rooms. She had checked on her earlier and was a bit surprised in not seeing her in her bed. Maybe she had gone out for a walk, Lady Seymour had thought. This wasn't too uncommon as Beatrice preferred the fresh air when she didn't feel too well. I'll check on her later, she thought, as she closed her daughter's bedroom door.

Later, once all her other guests had left, Lady Seymour dined alone in her rooms, and then, after dinner and later that night, she went to check on Beatrice. She sneaked her door open and there she was slumped on her bed completely asleep and still in her clothes. Even though Lady Seymour was used to her daughter's wayward ways, there was something about tonight that made her feel a little suspicious. Something felt different this time.

THE ARRESTS

BEATRICE woke the next morning with an eery feeling. Christopher was the first thing that came to her mind. Was he all right? She thought. Had he found the bracelet? She also woke with her heart as heavy as a rock. All the light and hope now left her. Despite the day being sunny and bright, all she saw was darkness. She now had no more Highwaygirl adventures to lift her heart. All she had ahead of her was a wedding to the Ogre. In a way, she hoped Christopher hadn't found her bracelet. I'd prefer to get caught, Beatrice thought. The thought of her life rotting in a jail was a more appealing option than her life rotting in a loveless marriage. She thought of her dream wedding, riding on top of Asta, walking along the tunnel of trees by the meadow, to a man she loved. Montifiorre flew into her mind, her heart fluttered as she thought of his dark chocolate eyes and European flare. She imagined walking through the tree tunnel with him. But suddenly, her door flew open and all thoughts of Montifiorre were immediately dashed from her mind.

"Lilly has been removed from service, mistress," said Violet in a stream of tears. "Sorry, miss, I know I shouldn't be crying but I was told to come and tell you but I know she wouldn't have done such a thing!" Violet was Lilly's fourteen-year-old sister.

"Done what, Violet, what!" Beatrice insisted.

"Stolen the lady's jewels, miss," Violet said through her sobs.

Beatrice flew out the room and raced downstairs to the kitchens, where she saw both the Lord and Lady enraged, the Lord was shouting to all the staff.

"She will go to prison for this! You're all the same, thieving and untrustworthy!" the Lord shouted.

"But Father, Lilly would never have done such a thing!" Beatrice interjected trying to defend her friend.

"Shut-up! What the hell do you know about anything! You're a worthless example of a daughter. I'm nothing but ashamed of you, galivanting in trousers on that bloody horse. You think you're so clever but you're nothing but a fool! I only tolerate you because I want my heirs."

The Lord was utterly enraged and so was Beatrice. She was glad she had become a highwaygirl, she was glad her bracelet had dropped, she wanted to be caught, she wanted him shamed. Beatrice turned calmly and walked out of the room; she wasn't going to give him any satisfaction as to her feelings. No anger, no tears, nothing. But once back in her room, she fell face down on her bed and sobbed.

The morning after the robbery, Christopher had risen early at dawn, he saddled Moby and headed out in search of Beatrice's bracelet. He retraced their steps but always making sure not to seem suspicious. He rode slowly, as he scoured the ground. He searched the willow tree, the hill up in the open field, the main road even. He didn't want to but thought it best to go to the hatch and see if she had lost it whilst opening the door. I never heard anything drop, Christopher thought, as he went over every detail of the robbery. He approached the willow tree, looked around cautiously, and on seeing nobody, he dismounted, and let Moby graze free. Christopher then bent down alongside the stone wall to see if it had fallen there when, suddenly, two men jumped over the wall and pinned Christopher down.

"Got ya!" the coach driver cried.

"Thought ya could get away with it, stealing from the Earl," the other said.

Christopher was completely taken by surprise. How would they have recognised him or even known he was one of the highway robbers?

Christopher grappled with the two men, trying his best to free himself. He kicked one of the men in the crotch which only made the coach driver punch him in the face, Christopher fell to the floor, the other man was up on his feet and then kicked Christopher in the stomach. They then held him up against the stone wall.

"I'm not the highway robber," Christopher breathlessly said.

"I recognise that horse anywhere, the same horse that did rob us yesterday," the coach driver said. Both men then started searching Christopher for anything he may have. Christopher then knew his luck had run out. He had decided to keep Staunton's pouch in his pocket despite thinking it best not to, as he wanted to give some coins to some folk in need in the village.

"There you go, caught red-handed. That's the Earl's money pouch and there are his initials. You're gonna hang for what ya done and I'm gonna get your horse as a reward," said the coach driver.

Christopher struggled with the men. His heart jumped out of his chest when he heard that Moby would be given to this lowlife.

"Big horse you got, heavy. Left his tracks everywhere, easy to spot. Your secret tunnel ain't no secret any more," the coach driver said.

The men tied Christopher's arms together and dragged him towards Moby. His arms were tied in front of him, and as he reached his horse, he slapped him hard on his rear. Moby sped off at full speed straight to the meadow. All the men could do was look on as Moby ran down the hill. One of them suddenly turned and punched Christopher in the face.

"That's for slapping your horse," the man said.

Christopher's bleeding lip was hurting now. His mind was racing. So maybe they did find the bracelet. What about Beatrice? Had they found her? He felt so helpless. This is exactly what I didn't want to happen. I was the one meant to be protecting Beatrice, Christopher thought.

Meanwhile, back at Lacey, Beatrice was inconsolable, and as always, she ran to her safe place, Asta. Asta was in her box when she arrived and Beatrice went straight and buried her head in her neck and just sobbed. The smell of Asta was such a comfort to Beatrice that it lifted her spirits even if only a little. Beatrice then flopped down on the floor, on the hay and slumped her back against the wooden wall. She was exhausted, utterly exhausted, the accumulation of the last days, weeks and even years had finally caught up with her and she was utterly spent. Lulled by the smell of horse, wood and hay, Beatrice's eyes slowly got heavy and she fell asleep sitting up against the wall. Asta lowered her heavy weight to the ground and sat next to Beatrice, lowering her head so it rested just by her feet. Sensing Asta next to her, Beatrice woke a little and moved so that she was lying on Asta's side. Despite all the traumas, it was a beautiful picture of harmony and contentment. The sun was dreamlike and hot and streamed through the big window, the birds were singing loudly and the lulling sound of voices in the far distance made for a perfect English spring morning. It was a shame a storm was approaching though, both in life and in the weather.

Beatrice woke after just a short time and went to find Michael. "Where's my bag?" she whispered quietly.

Michael gestured for Beatrice to follow him. The head groom was out so it was perfect timing. Michael led Beatrice to the tack room, a brick room. He then moved some saddles and halters, and behind them, jiggled a brick near the floor and pulled it away revealing a secret hole. They both bent down and Michael reached for the bag and handed it to Beatrice. She opened it in front of him and handed him the pistol.

"Can you hide this?" she asked.

Michael put the pistol back in its hiding place. She then got out her scarf and mask and put it in her skirt pocket.

"For memory's sake," she said.

Beatrice then got out the silk pouch she stole from Mary Staunton with the intention of giving something to Michael. She opened it and was utterly shocked at what she found. It literally took her breath away. She couldn't speak for a few seconds.

"Miss, what is it?" Michael asked in a whisper.

"These are Mother's jewels. Look! Her precious diamond ring and her gold and emerald ring, this is her treasured family heirloom." Beatrice was genuinely astounded. "Michael, I can't believe this, that rotten, evil snake, the sister, Mary Staunton. I can't believe it. She stole Mother's jewels!"

They heard the head groom's voice in the distance as he approached, and quickly, they stuffed everything including the jewels back into the bag and then back in the brick wall. Michael placed the brick back in its place and then all the tack.

"I'll leave everything here for now but will come back for the jewels later. I must return them to Mother," Beatrice said in a rushed whisper.

The head groom walked in. "Ma'am," he said politely.

"Yes, I was looking at Asta's saddle and I think it needs another clean. Would you look at her left shin, I thought I noticed something," Beatrice asked.

"Of course, ma'am," the groom said. "Excuse me, ma'am, but I need Michael back in the field."

"Of course," and everybody departed.

Beatrice made her way back to the manor in a shocked daze. She was still processing what she had discovered. I just can't believe it, she kept repeating in her head. But it was important to not act hastily.

"Ma'am, they've asked for your company in the tea room. Early morning tea has been announced," Betty said as Beatrice walked into the kitchens.

Beatrice went straight to the tea room, opened the door and for the second time that morning her heart stopped.

"Why, darling, what a wonderful and unexpected visit we have once again from the Earl," Lady Seymour said.

Beatrice wanted to run up to him and tear off his wig and punch him in the face, but instead, she curtsied and said nothing.

"The Earl came specifically and in great haste as he says he has a gift especially for you," Lady Seymour continued.

"Something I had personalised for you. Something I think you will be in great need of," the Earl added.

Beatrice's instincts were alerted and she knew what was coming.

One of the servants came in and set the tea on the table. Everybody took their seats.

"Why, Mistress Seymour, you once again look simply ravishing today," said the Earl with a subtle provocative tone.

Beatrice waited, she had no choice but to let the Earl relish at this moment.

"It is my pleasure in life to shower you with gifts; scarfs and hats and bracelets," the Earl continued.

Beatrice went cold, her instincts were correct. But she wasn't going to give him any satisfaction by revealing any emotion. She maintained her composure. Kept her head high. Her mother, however, sensed a change in the atmosphere.

"My dear Lady Seymour, I'm afraid I have some terrible news to impart upon you" said the Earl.

"Oh, what could that possibly be?" Beatrice's mother was slightly afraid now as to what this news may be. "Nothing too dramatic I hope?"

"Well, dramatic is one word that could describe it," the Earl tormentingly went on.

Beatrice loathed him. He was enjoying every little moment of his revenge. Little did he know that Beatrice was inwardly relieved, happy even. She looked squarely at Staunton. Frightened, she was not. She faced him directly, bold and brazen in her look, defiance glared from her eyes. She wasn't going to cower in front of him, she wasn't going to give him that satisfaction.

"This, I believe, is yours?" the Earl said as he held up Beatrice's bracelet.

"Oh, darling, this is your birth bracelet. Oh, Edward, how wonderful of you for returning it to us. It's such a precious item. Beatrice, will you thank the Earl?"

"Thank you," Beatrice said as she went to take it back, staring directly at Staunton who kept hold of the bracelet.

"But where did you find it?" Lady Seymour questioned suspiciously, not liking Staunton's reaction.

"Well, Felicity, that is where the 'dramatic' comes in," Staunton arrogantly stated as his crowning moment was about to come, his moment of triumph. Beatrice could feel him almost salivating with anticipation.

"Lady Seymour, your daughter is the infamous Highwaygirl, and today, I am here to arrest her." And there it was, the Earl's triumphant moment, Beatrice's relief and Lady Seymour's fall from grace.

"Guards!" the Earl shouted.

Lady Seymour, despite her utter shock, stood up in an attempt to protect her daughter as the guards walked in.

"Take her away!" Staunton commanded.

"Edward, you cannot do this! I demand you release Beatrice! You have no proof! Release her immediately!" Beatrice's mother protested.

"I understand this may seem utterly incredulous to you, my Lady, but your daughter has been living a clandestine and scandalous double life and I am afraid she will pay deeply for it. Highway robbery is treason and must be punished!" Staunton replied, utterly triumphant.

"And what authority do you have? Just wait until Robert gets back, he will have your guts for garters!"

Staunton motioned with his head for the guards to take Beatrice away. They walked her out of the room.

"Beatrice!" her mother yelled running after her. "You cannot do this! Edward, what are you doing!"

And before she knew it, Beatrice and Staunton were out the door and in the carriage.

"You beast, Edward, you beast! You will not get away with this, when Robert returns a war will erupt!" the Lady shouted from the doorway.

"Tell Robert the wedding, as of now, is off. Oh, and he may wage a war, but my dear, your daughter will hang! I'll make sure of that!"

And on that heavy note, Staunton thumped the carriage roof and it rode off. Lady Seymour then slumped down on the front steps too shocked to even cry.

All the staff had come out to see the commotion. They too were shocked even though they had their gossip and suspicions. But all the staff liked Beatrice and were heartbroken at seeing her taken so violently away and by such a despicable person.

The lady continued to sit. I must at once save Beatrice from hanging. I must at once use any power, she thought. But can I forgive her? I've defended and tolerated all of her rebellions but this has exceeded them all. She has now brought unutterable shame to the family name. All that we have done to secure her future and the future of our heirs. What has she done? She's destroyed us all with one of her childish games, the lady thought, as she remained on the steps.

"Mi'lady, can I get you anything?" said the head butler.

"Get Michael, with one of our fastest horses, to go and send a message to the Lord," she said.

Lady Seymour then went to her rooms and scrawled an urgent letter to her husband who was now in Parliament. He would now use his influence in the House of Lords to get Beatrice freed. At least, that is what Lady Seymour hoped.

The guards dragged Beatrice down a dark and damp corridor.

"You know you don't need to hold me so hard, I'm not going to run away," Beatrice calmly said.

"Beatrice!" shouted Christopher from his cell.

"Christopher!" shouted Beatrice.

The guards threw her into a cold and foreboding cell and left. Christopher's cell was two down. "Christopher, they caught you too! Oh, Cristopher, I'm truly sorry for what I've put you through."

"We made a deal, remember. Partners in crime."

"Partners in crime," Beatrice said agreeing but without its usual enthusiasm.

"Christopher, she stole mother's jewels, can you believe it! What a terrible person and to let Lilly take the blame and be dismissed along with her younger sister."

Christopher didn't reply. It didn't surprise him and it only made him feel sad, truly sad. It was all really rather sad. Beatrice's fight for her freedom, his fight for survival, Staunton's fight for revenge and the list goes on. Christopher didn't mind if he was hanged, life for him over the years had lost its art, it's beauty. It had just become one big slog and battle for survival. Beatrice, however, must not hang.

The two cousins fell into silence. There was nothing to be said, their fates were sealed. Prison was ghastly they both had to admit. It was cold and miserable. Both cells had but a tiny window where some light entered. Beatrice quietly sobbed. She sobbed for Christopher and Asta. What will they do to the most important loved ones in her life? Beatrice thought. She watched the window as the light changed to late afternoon. A blackbird suddenly appeared on the thick stone ledge and sat for a while. Nature, as always, was her companion in times of desperation. Asta would be worried, sensing something had gone wrong. She would be wondering why she wouldn't be coming to see her. Her heart broke at the thought of her being left inside her box for weeks. Michael would put her out into the field, I'm sure, she thought. She said a prayer for Michael that he wouldn't be caught. She said a prayer for Christopher, Asta, herself, Lilly, her sister and for her mother. The blackbird then flew off. She had read somewhere that blackbirds were good omens. A symbol of hope and transformation. At least, I won't be marrying that brute, she thought. But I have been selfish and put Christopher in danger, her thoughts rambled on. It was cold now and darkness fell in the cell. The true reality of her actions were now falling heavily upon her shoulders.

"Christopher, Christopher, you awake?" Beatrice called out quietly.

"Yes."

"I'm so sorry, Christopher, for what I've done to you."

"I made my own choice B."

"I will do everything I can so you don't hang. I got you into this, I will get you out. I promise, Kit."

"As I said, I made my own choice to join you, remember, 'partners in crime'."

He sounded tired and dejected. Her heart wrenched.

"Maybe the printer's shop just has to wait a while," Beatrice tried to sound hopeful. Now was the time where she'd need to dig deep and find her real strength.

"Maybe, cousin."

For the next three days, the cousins stayed in the local jail. On the third day, the jailer unbolted Beatrice's big iron door and came in, put irons on her wrists and escorted her out.

"Where are we going? Christopher?" Beatrice called out.

"I'm here, cousin," he replied as another guard did the same to him.

The two cousins were then taken outside and told to get up in the prisoners' carriage. "Where are we going?" Beatrice demanded.

"London," said the guard.

"Does my father know about this. He's a very powerful man," Beatrice asserted.

"I'm sure he is but not powerful enough to stop the hanging of the century. The whole country want you both dead, especially you, the Highwaygirl. You caused a right storm, you did," the guard said with a hint of relish in his voice.

It was true. Her arrest had spread like wildfire. When the nation discovered that the highwayman was, in fact, a highwaygirl, the public exploded into an uproar. It was this unbelievable revelation, and that the Highwaygirl was also an aristocrat, a debutante, that had sent the nation into a frenzy.

Beatrice was still in her lace dress that she wore for the tea. She looked pretty and dainty and nothing like her highway robber alter ego; it was incongruous and exactly the reason why it had captured the nation.

The journey was long and bumpy but it was glorious to smell the fresh air again full of the early summer. Beatrice raised her head to the sun in prayer and let its rays warm her through.

Everybody looked and stared, some threw tomatoes, some booed and some cheered. The convicts were meant to be on show. To be paraded and humiliated. And it worked. As they approached London, more people came out to see the Highwaygirl.

By the time they reached Newgate Prison, there was a large crowd of people following their carriage. London stank, was dirty and noisy. Beatrice hated it.

They were unloaded from the carriage and the crowd shouted and goaded itself into a frenzy. "Hang! Hang!" it shouted. "The Highwaygirl hang!"

Some pulled Beatrice's hair, she yelped. Others pulled at her dress wanting something of the Highwaygirl. Christopher jumped in and tried to shield her but it was only when they went through the big main gates was the crowd put at bay.

They were taken straight to their different cells. Silence fell upon them like a boulder dropping. Beatrice was utterly shocked by the vitriol of the crowd.

In a short while, Beatrice heard footsteps. Footsteps she knew too well. Footsteps she had heard many a year pounding down a very different corridor. Her father was approaching. Beatrice prepared herself.

He entered the cell with a bundle of clothes in his arms, and without a word, through them at her. Out of nowhere a sharp and hard slap came swiping across her face.

"You incorrigible wench. You've ruined our family. You've destroyed your mother. She is inconsolable. You are now disowned. You are no longer my daughter. You are a black and disgusting stain upon our good name. I care not if you hang. Change into these clothes and I will see you in court," Lord Seymour said with utter rage searing through him. He then stormed out.

Beatrice just sat there alone, in a cold damp cell. It is true, she thought, I have brought this upon myself, but do I regret it? I only regret getting Christopher intwined in my rebellion. Hanging was always my preferred choice over marriage but Christopher... she blocked her thoughts. She couldn't bear to think of her only true friend going to the gallows. And Mother? Beatrice thought, yes, I regret hurting Mother, poor Mother. And what about Asta? Beatrice burst into uncontrollable tears. It was all too much to bear.

Days passed. It was cold and dingy in the cell. Rats were everywhere, her bed was made of wicker and the food was meagre. Beatrice was a long, long way away from Lacey Manor and all its privileges.

Her thoughts went back to Christopher. She didn't know where Christopher was. Her heart was heavy and lonely. No blackbirds would come to this cell. Her mind raced, thinking of a way to save her cousin. She had one idea, the only idea, but would it work?

Beatrice was woken early the next morning with the sound of her door bolt opening. To her surprise, a very debonair-looking young man walked in, with a briefcase and a cane.

"My name is Sir Benjamin Radcliffe, a lawyer at Palmer, Dukes and Partners and I am here to defend you."

SIR BENJAMIN RADCLIFF

RADCLIFF was brought up and educated by his duchess mother whom he adored and admired. She was formidable and unconventional and had money to support both those attributes. She was an innate rebel, smart and progressive. She didn't disguise her intellect or her femininity. As a mother, she defied convention and didn't use wet nurses; she was warm, exuberant and captivating. Radcliff observed and learnt from her. Cambridge University was her university of choice for her son and law her choice of career. Radcliff agreed. Radcliff and the Duchess were followers of the Enlightenment movement. Their sharp intellects believing in slowly trying to change the protocols of society. So, when Radcliff heard about Beatrice's arrest, he couldn't resist the chance in defending her. He must defend her at all costs and he must win. She was everything that inspired him. Beatrice defied the status quo and rocked the institution. She was a woman willing to hang for her beliefs and her actions. She was utterly brazen and he couldn't wait to meet her.

So, when he walked into her cell, he wasn't disappointed.

He was, however, amazed at how petite she was and would have loved to have seen her as the Highwaygirl. He had to admit he was a little star-struck on meeting her. She was small in stature but large in character.

"You are here to defend me? I'm sorry to disappoint you but I don't possess the funds for your defence," Beatrice said. "My family has disowned me."

"May I?" Radcliff asked as he gestured for himself to sit next to her on her wicker bed. Beatrice nodded and Radcliff then proceeded to place his leather work satchel neatly on his lap.

Beatrice thought he was going to get out a pile of papers or something, but instead, he got out a big meat sandwich.

"You have become quite the celebrity, a larger-than-life character, thanks to your highway robbery persona. You look hungry. You must be famished?" Radcliff said handing Beatrice the sandwich.

She ate it with all her graces and manners still intact. Hunger hadn't yet robbed her of her refinements.

"No need to worry about funds, my dear. I will defend you for free. Your beliefs are your funds and I intend to defend them and win. I am, I must warn you, brazenly optimistic and stupendously confident and that I have the weight of the law on my side if I can manipulate it well enough. How's your sandwich?"

Beatrice nodded. It tasted like hope itself. No blackbirds came to visit her here at this jail but one of her prayers had been answered. Whoever this flamboyant gentleman was that came gallantly into her jail, she was exceedingly happy about it. As he talked, Beatrice listened to him, watched him, wondered and guessed about him. He was definitely confident and she definitely had nothing to lose by accepting his offer; she only hoped he was genuine and not just after the celebrity.

"Do you know where my cousin is?"

"No, but I'll find him and tell you tomorrow. Your trial starts in a week so there's not much time for preparation. But I like a challenge."

He is very cavalier, Beatrice thought, but I like him. She's very aloof, Radcliff thought, but I like her. Maybe he's the blackbird, Beatrice thought, after all he is wearing all black and a yellow waistcoat, the colours of a blackbird. Beatrice took heart.

"Could you free Christopher as well? He is the most loyal and most devoted of people I know. He wants to write books; he only became a highway robber to protect me. He doesn't deserve to hang. And Asta, my beloved mare. Can you save her too. Father, I'm sure, will kill her."

"Christopher we shall save. And your Asta. You don't ask for much, do you?" Radcliff said with a smile. "But on a serious note, my dear. I may like winning at all costs but so do your opponents. They have the force of the institution on their side. Nepotism is rife."

DAY ONE

TUESDAY

DRESSED in the fresh clothes her father had brought her, Beatrice was escorted up to the court house. She may have looked more of a lady but she certainly didn't smell like one. Prison life was dirty and degrading.

Once in the courtroom, she was escorted to go to Radcliff. They smiled at each other and sat. The courtroom was filled with the seriousness of the trial, the seriousness of condemning lives. Once sat, Radcliff squeezed Beatrice's hand. How informal, she thought, I hardly know him. But how nice and reassuring.

"Christopher is in Bristol jail, Asta and Moby are in hiding, they can't be used as evidence. So far so good," Radcliff said encouragingly.

Beatrice sighed an inward sigh. Her heart lifted. Maybe he will free us all?

Beatrice could not believe the number of people in the courtroom. It was bulging with people. Little did she know how much this trial had captivated the country. It was in every newspaper, in everybody's conversations; from the slums to high society. An aristocratic young lady dressed as a man, riding a horse like a man, wielding a pistol like a man and then stealing like a man was irresistible news. Beatrice was infamous.

The government, the people, and especially, Staunton wanted their pound of flesh. They wanted their hanging. They wanted to see the first ever highwaygirl hanged. A few of them loved her for it, most hated her for it. Her face adorned every newspaper, and even though her mother could hide within the safety of her estate, her father had to face the world. Thanks to Beatrice, his family had fallen cataclysmically from society. From the highs of their imminent society wedding, to the lows in a matter of a few days. The fall was absolute.

"All rise," the court clerk said as the Judge walked in.

The smell of wigs and men and the law filled the room. Judge Walker walked in and took his seat. The audience was spellbound.

"The plaintiff has been accused of five counts of highway treason. How does your client plead?" Walker spoke to Radcliff.

"Not guilty," he said. The courtroom gasped.

Radcliff, of course, knew Judge Walker. He, like every lawman in the courtroom, were of the establishment. There was nothing enlightened or of the enlightenment about him. Radcliff stood alone but defiant.

"The courtroom calls the Earl of Staunton."

Staunton limped into the court. Puffed up and arrogant. He took his seat and said his vows upon the Bible.

"Is this the highway robber that stopped and molested you and your sister, Mary Staunton on May 15th 1799?" stated the prosecution.

"Yes, indeed, that is the lady. She held a pistol to my head, she molested and injured me with her horse. My foot is permanently injured."

"And did she not steal off your person?" the prosecution continued.

"Yes, she most violently did. My poor sister was accosted too. Her jewels of great sentiment stolen."

Beatrice gasped. Her jewels! That scoundrel just lied under oath, Beatrice thought.

Beatrice sat composed and looked every bit the lady. At first, she listened to the attacks thrown at her character, but after a while, she allowed her mind to wander, to daydream. The countryside and it's rivers and woodlands and meadows and birds seemed a very long way away. With all her heart, she hoped Christopher was strong and that Asta wasn't missing her.

The public got their entertainment as their tuts, gasps and heckles filled the courtroom. It was time for Radcliff to stand before Staunton.

"Good morning, sir. So the basis of your accusations is on the findings of a silver bracelet. Are they not?" Radcliff went immediately for his argument.

"Yes. The BSB, Beatrice Seymour-Barclay are engraved on it," Staunton replied.

"Lady Seymour could have lost that bracelet at any given time of the year. She rides the acreages of her estate regularly."

The courtroom tutted and stirred. Radcliff noticed the minutest of flickers cross Staunton's eyes. Radcliff liked it whenever this happened. A chink in the Earl's armour had been made. A re-addressing of power and Staunton didn't like it.

"Is that all you have as evidence?" Radcliff came back with.

"I recognise her. I looked into her eyes. And that is the strongest evidence there is. Lady Seymour-Barclay is the highway robber!" Staunton said desperately, feeling suddenly weakened, and pointed his finger directly at Beatrice.

"Hang! Hang!" the courtroom exploded into a frenzy.

"Silence!" Walker demanded as he thumped his hammer.

Beatrice's fate seemed sealed. There didn't seem anything Radcliff could do now. Other witnesses were brought to testify against Beatrice. The Duchess and her stolen sapphires, the Judge; all wanted their revenge. There seemed little hope.

The hours slipped by and day one was finally over. The guard came to escort Beatrice back to her cell, accompanied by Radcliff.

"Here, my dear, I brought you a coat, a blanket and some sandwiches," Radcliff kindly gave them to Beatrice.

"You know Staunton lied. His lies filled the courtroom," Beatrice commented. "Of course, only the naive tell the truth. Mary Staunton stole the jewels. My mother's treasured jewels. She stole my mother's jewels and then, unknowingly, I stole them back from her."

"There is a lot of stealing going on. Stealing the truth, stealing jewels, stealing lives. But why didn't you tell me this before? I can use this information," Radcliff said, encouraged.

"I was hoping to return them to mother somehow."

"Beatrice this is your get-out-of-jail-card, your card to both your life and Christopher's." Radcliff had omitted to tell Beatrice that Christopher was due to hang this Sunday.

"But will you expose Mary Staunton's thievery in court?"

"No, of course not. I'll use this information as bribery. Old fashioned tactics are often the most effective. Where are they?"

"Michael, the stable boy hid them, the pistol and my clothes in the tack room. He will give them to you if I write a note asking him to. Please protect him and make sure he doesn't get incriminated."

"We have no time to lose. I will arrange a meeting with Staunton immediately."

Radcliff was instantly enthused. If he was honest with himself he wasn't sure if he could win the case for this young aristocrat. Everything was against her. The public wanted to see her hang and the government wanted to make her their show of an example. But if he could get hold of the jewels, he could save both Beatrice and Christopher. It would be a race against time.

DAY TWO

WEDNESDAY

RADCLIFF leapt into action. He immediately sent a message to Earl Staunton and then another to Lord Seymour, requesting meetings. He needed these individual meetings for his plan to work.

Other witnesses were brought in to testify against Beatrice. There seemed little hope.

Radcliff went through the motions as all he was waiting for was his letters to arrive confirming his meetings with Lord Seymour and Staunton. Finally they arrived, at the end of the day. Today was Wednesday, the meeting with Seymour Thursday early afternoon, the meeting with Staunton late afternoon, get the jewels Thursday, have a meeting with Judge Walker Friday, Christopher hangs Sunday in Bristol, time is of the essence, Radcliff thought, as he arranged the order of events in his head.

Court was ended for the day and Beatrice was guided back down to her cell. Radcliff followed her. "Is Christopher all right? How is he faring?" Beatrice asked.

"Dear, I have some news that I should have shared with you before. Christopher has been sentenced to hang this Sunday coming. But with the evidence we have, I am sure we will get him released."

Beatrice put her hands up over her face and sobbed a deep sob. Her worst fears and her unimaginable regret had come true.

"I will beg my father for his life," Beatrice asked through her tears.

"It's a very good thing you never returned those jewels to your mother, they are our best weapon now. Chin up. As I said, I always win."

Radcliff was cool, calm and collected. His confidence came from his profound belief that he had the greater good on his side.

DAY THREE

THURSDAY

BEATRICE was brought up to the courtroom. And then asked to walk up to the witness box. She was so tired and hungry and despondent. This is what the court had been waiting for. To hear, see and witness the Highwaygirl, to hear her speak. She stood in the box in front of the entire courtroom, the air was full of anticipation, the tension palpitating.

I have a life to live, a cousin to save, a horse to save, today I stand tall, Beatrice thought to herself, as she looked directly at Staunton.

"Do you, Lady Beatrice Annabelle Seymour-Barclay, swear to tell the truth, the whole truth and nothing but the truth?"

"I do."

The court held its breath, the atmosphere was electric. "This belongs to you, does it not?" the prosecution stated.

"Yes," replied Beatrice.

"And it was found moments after the robbery. When were you aware that your bracelet went missing?"

"I don't recall," Beatrice replied, not lying but not revealing the truth.

"The Duchess, the Judge and the Earl, all people of standing and reputation, all state that you are the highway robber. They clearly recognise your voice. The prosecutor continued.

"Is there anything you would like to add, Sir Radcliff?" Judge Walker asked.

"No, mi'lord," Radcliff replied. He was biding his time until tomorrow. Beatrice's life now hinged, not with her defence, but on those jewels and on Radcliff getting them.

Beatrice was taken back below to await her fate. Radcliff sat with her. Beatrice was alone with her thoughts. Thoughts that only travelled to Christopher and the saving of his life. It was cold, she was hungry and her will and desire to live rose to the fore. She wanted to live, she wanted to fight another fight, she chose life, of course, but would the jury.

"Well, mi'lady, personally, I hope you get off but I'm afraid I don't think you will, sorry to be the bearer of bad news. Oh, well. Heaven could do with a feisty one. They never hanged a highwaygirl before so the crowd will be wanting their show," said the guard in a weird joviality.

Beatrice sat in her cell feeling very alone, and despite her normal stoic exterior, she was very, very scared.

Beatrice heard footsteps approaching and they weren't footsteps she was familiar with. They were slow and tempered, calm and steady. Who could it be? Beatrice wondered.

"Good day, young lady. I'm Benjamin's mother, Duchess Radcliff," the Duchess said as she stood before Beatrice.

"Good day, your grace," Beatrice curtsied.

"No need for formalities, my dear, hardly the place or the occasion. Call me Henrietta." The Duchess smiled.

Beatrice smiled back and was instantly taken by the Duchess's awe. She had grace, power, intellect and kindness all rolled into one. It was a package to be respected. She seemed to simply tower above everybody both in stature and presence. Beatrice now understood why Benjamin had so much admiration for his mother.

"I want you to have this. My gift for you."

The Duchess handed a book, The Vindication of the Rights of Women, to Beatrice.

"I think you might find it interesting. Strike a chord, as they say. One strong woman to another."

"I do not think I'll be able to read this where I'm going, your grace, I mean, Henrietta."

"I think you'll have time, don't you worry. Kindred spirits have to be protected. And women should be more kindred with each other. You created quite a stir, Lady Seymour, and I admire that."

"Thank you for your gift."

"Oh, no, my dear, thank you for your gift. Your spirit within is your greatest gift. Mine is just paper."

The Duchess then came forward and gave Beatrice a hug. It was heartfelt, warm and encouraging. It was the loveliest thing a person could have done at that moment. Tears welled up in Beatrice's eyes as she received all its love and kindness, but most of all, all its understanding. For the first time, Beatrice didn't feel so utterly alone. The hug was imbued with all the solidarity and solace Beatrice needed. Beatrice all her life had felt completely alone, alone taking on the world, fighting its boundaries and limits. But today, the Duchess made Beatrice feel included, a heroine.

The Duchess walked out and left Beatrice in the haze of her aura. She looked at the book and wondered if the Duchess was right. Would I live to actually read it?

THE SENTENCE

THURSDAY

BEATRICE didn't have to wait long. Once again, Beatrice was led into court, once again, she faced her audience. The whole room was against her. She stood tall. Today no invisibility. No highway robber's costume, no mask, no red scarf. She had committed crimes, this was true, but her accusers had committed far worse.

"All rise," the clerk announced.

The courtroom rose and its wood creaked. The Judge walked in.

Beatrice thought how puffed up he looked, full of his own importance and power. He wore his Judge's cloaks and wig and it could easily be like a costume for the opera. This whole affair seemed like its own opera, but this opera was with real lives in real-time. Judge Walker banged his hammer and the courtroom sat, in silence.

"Beatrice Annabelle Clementine Seymour-Barclay, I do sentence you for the heinous crimes of highway robbery death by hanging."

And that was it. Her life would end at eighteen years of age. In less than ten seconds, her life had been decided upon. The court exploded into a rapture of gasps and screams.

"Hang! Hang!" they cried. They had got what they wanted. The crowd was jubilant, with one person in particular exultant. Staunton was triumphant, he looked at the Judge and tipped his hat, their friendship had paid its due. Staunton's humiliation was now exonerated as he watched with glee the Highwaygirl receiving her sentence.

Beatrice stood motionless. Frozen. She thought about how many times she had said to herself, I would prefer to hang than marry, but now that that moment had come, she didn't feel like dying. She wanted to live. She wanted her life. And somehow, somewhat bizarrely, she felt that is exactly what would happen.

The guard came and took Beatrice back to her cell. Radcliff followed.

"Well, I said they'd do it, didn't I? Give you a hanging. They usually do, the crowd love a hanging," he said.

He said it so matter-of-factly that he could've been talking about the weather and not someone's life.

"We have our last card to play. There is no time to spare. Chin up," Radcliff said to Beatrice, and at speed, he walked out of the cell; there was not a moment to lose.

Radcliff jumped into his gig and raced to Lacey Manor for his meeting with Seymour. He arrived in good time.

Radcliff stepped down from his gig, calmly walked to the front door and prepared himself for his meeting. He rang the bell, waited and heard footsteps approaching. The head butler opened the door.

"Good afternoon, sir. Please follow me. The Lord is expecting you," the butler formally said. Radcliff was then escorted to the Lord's private study.

"'Afternoon, sir," Radcliff said as he walked straight to the Lord and put his hand out; the two gentlemen shook hands.

"As you know, sentence has been passed and I'm sure you've already been duly informed," Radcliff continued.

"Yes. She deserves it. Shaming me, shaming this family. Parading as a man and robbing from the respected. What was she thinking, along with that rogue of a cousin of hers? I never want to see her again," Seymour blurted.

"Well, sir, you won't be," Radcliff said with just a subtle hint of sarcasm. He wanted to keep this meeting as neutral as possible but he couldn't help himself, what an awful man, he thought.

"She has requested one thing before her hanging. That I deliver for her a letter to Michael, the stable boy," Radcliff requested, returning to neutrality.

"And what was she doing conversing and spending so much time with the staff, it was an abomination the way she cavorted. I'll have O'Riley, the butler, deliver it."

"Sir, she specifically requested that I deliver it."

"What in God's name! No! O'Riley will deliver it. That's how it's done and that's how it will be. These are the rules, goddam it! Why does she constantly have the need to break the rules!"

"Sir, I do ask you to call upon your sensibilities at this most sensitive of times and permit your daughter's last request. The only request she has asked for before she will leave this earth forever!" Radcliff felt the need and the emergency to tug at Seymour's extremely hardened heart.

"All right. I'll get O'Riley to escort you there."

"That is most gracious of you, sir. Your daughter, I'm sure, will appreciate her last and final wish having been granted."

Seymour rang his bell. Radcliff felt a murmur of a feeling pass over the Lord. Surely, he must have some forgiveness in his heart, Radcliff was shocked at the coldness of the man.

O'Riley walked in.

"Good evening, sir," Radcliff said and followed O'Riley out of the room. O'Riley escorted Radcliff out of the house and they walked towards the stables.

"Michael isn't here," O'Riley simply said.

"Where is he?" for the first time Radcliff stammered inwardly. Everything and two lives hinged on Michael and these jewels. Radcliff kept his composure.

"I don't know, sir. I can take you to the head groom, maybe he knows something."

"Yes, immediately," Radcliff said dryly.

They both arrived at the stables. "Mack!" O'Riley called out. "Mack!"

They waited. Radcliff was starting to get tense. He was now too personally involved with saving the life of the Highwaygirl. He had become fond of her and his passion for saving her life had gone far beyond just winning a case.

"Mack! I'll go outside to see if he's there," O'Riley informed him.

His relaxed and leisurely pace was in complete contrast to Radcliff's inner speed, time was of the essence and here the butler was walking like nobody's life depended on it.

After an agonising wait, Mack walked in. "What can I do you for?" Mack asked casually.

"The young Lady Seymour has requested that I deliver a personal note to Michael," Radcliff informed.

"He's not here. Gone away for a few days."

"Do you know where. This is of the utmost importance and urgency," Radcliff questioned.

"No, sorry, I don't, go ask Betty, the cook, they were friends."

Radcliff's heart was beginning to race. Michael not being here had raised the stakes to an unbearable level.

O'Riley and Radcliff walked to the kitchens. Betty was taking a tea,

"Madam, my name is Benjamin Radcliff and it is of great urgency that I get in contact with Michael. Do you know where he is?"

"Went to his mother's in the village of Ripley, a couple of miles from here. 10 Oakly Street, Ripley." Betty replied. "Terrible news, just terrible. We here at Lacey are heartbroken, to the core, heartbroken."

"Thank you, Betty, if you don't mind me calling you so." Radcliff tipped his hat and walked out purposefully to his gig driver.

"As fast as you can, John, here's something to help you ride faster," Radcliff gave John some coins. Radcliff then returned to the kitchens and waited, inwardly anxious, outwardly composed. Betty, however, noticed him nervously rubbing his little finger and thumb together.

"I hope you got something up that posh sleeve of yas. Something that'll save 'em," Betty said as she handed him some shortbread. "The best in all of Surrey, recipe handed down from my Scottish grandma."

"Thank you, Betty."

John sped off. He raced as fast as he could, and in about fifteen minutes, he arrived in Ripley. He went straight to the tavern. John jumped down and walked at speed straight inside.

"Oakly Street? Good sir." John asked the landlord as he walked up to the bar.

"Two down on the right," the landlord said.

John tipped his hat and walked straight out.

He set off, the village was small so, in a second, he arrived. John, once again, jumped down, walked quickly to the house and knocked on the very humble door of the tiny cottage. He could hear the sounds of children playing, crying, running, laughing; it was a full house, full of life. Nobody came so John knocked once again. He heard footsteps and shouting coming towards the door. The footsteps stopped and the door was opened by a tall young woman.

"What you be wanting?" said the young lady.

"Good afternoon. My name is John and I come on behalf of Benjamin Radcliff and I urgently need to speak to Michael. I'm sent on the request of Lady Beatrice Seymour," John spoke fast and formally.

"Oh, poor lass, her, she don't deserve to hang though, yes, come right in, Michael's out back with the little 'uns.

The house was painfully rundown and packed to the rafters with people. Kids ran past, dogs ran past barking as they played with the children. There must be at a least four families living here in three rooms, thought John, not far from his own upbringing. He tipped his hat to the adults as he walked past.

"Hello, lad," John said as he fondly touched the head of a child running past him chasing the dog. "You got a lot a mouths to feed, ain't ya,"

"Yup, it don't stop round here. Poor blighters, never enough food for 'em," said the young woman. "Michael, someone's here to see you," the young woman said as they reached the yard at the back,

Michael was sitting on a stool whittling.

"I've been sent by Lady Seymour's lawyer, he wants to see you back at the Manor immediately. It's mighty important, lad," John said urgently.

Michael stood up the minute he heard Beatrice's name.

"So they gonna hang her then," Michael said sadly.

"Let's go immediately, we have no time to lose," John said waving his hand to leave. Michael grabbed his hat and sprang into action. The men walked hastily down the corridor.

"I'll see you later, Maggie," Michael shouted back behind him as he closed the door.

The men leapt into the gig and John slapped the horses to go, he rode them as fast as he could.

Meanwhile back at Lacey, Radcliff's nerves were spent. As a lawyer, he had learnt to disguise every emotion, especially anxiety. Anxiety, more than anger, showed a weak state of being. But despite his composure, every waiting second tore at his nerves. He had two lives to save, it was a tremendous responsibility. At least the busy life of the kitchen staff kept him somewhat distracted. Finally, he heard the sound of horses galloping up the driveway. He stood up instantly and saw John with another man. That must be Michael, Radcliff thought. He let a wave of relief run through him, he still had a long way to go though and a few more obstacles left until he saved those lives.

The two men walked into the kitchens, looking windswept and hasty. "Michael, sir," John said to Radcliff. "Delivered as requested."

"Good man, John. Michael, may I talk with you in private?" Radcliff said. "Let us take a walk." Radcliff lead Michael back out the kitchen door.

"I am Benjamin Radcliff, I am Lady Seymour's lawyer and I have been sent at her request. Michael, Beatrice is due to be hanged along with her cousin. She says you have her bag of robber's clothes and the silk pouch of Mary Staunton's with Lady Seymour's jewels inside. You must give them to me as I need to use them as bargaining power to free the cousins. Beatrice wanted me to give you this." Radcliff spoke very quietly and walked slowly, he handed Michael the note. Michael took it, opened it, looked it over and handed it straight back to Radcliff. Radcliff nodded on understanding Michael's actions, Michael couldn't read.

"Of course," Radcliff said warmly.

Dear Michael

I hope you are now standing in the company of my lawyer and friend, Sir Benjamin Radcliff, he's one of the good ones! You will also know by now that I am, along with Christopher, due to be hanged. Please give the jewels to Benjamin, you can trust him, he is going to try and use them as a way of saving our lives, if not mine, then Christopher's.

Michael, if I don't see you again I want to say thank you for being my friend and thank you for keeping my secret, but most of all, thank you for looking after Asta. I miss her terribly and our rides across the country.

Yours, most affectionately, Beatrice.

"I'll show you where they are," Michael instantly said. His heart was deeply touched. He loved the young Lady Seymour in a way; they had made a connection and she had been both loyal and generous to him. A lump hardened in his throat as he listened to her words being read out loud before him. He could even imagine her standing in front of him in her breeches saying those words herself. "Follow me."

Michael led Radcliff to the tack room, and with great haste, he went to the brick wall behind the stacked saddles and pulled out the lose brick. He rummaged for the linen bag and handed it to Radcliff.

"You will save her, wont ya?" Michael said.

"With this, my boy, you will save her! Good man, Michael." Radcliff said patting Michael on the back.

They both raced back to Radcliff's gig, John was waiting. Radcliff tipped his hat to Michael, and at lightning speed, they both sped off straight for London and to meet Staunton.

The gigs were made to be fast and this one was. It was imperative that Radcliff arrived on time. Their meeting was made for six o'clock, and at five-thirty p.m. they rode into London. It really was a race against time. Staunton would not meet with Radcliff if he was late.

John pushed through the crowds. It was a busy Thursday afternoon on the streets. They had just past St James' park and rode into Berkeley Street, when they came across a road block, a carriage that had lost its wheel. It had created quite the hold-up. It was now five-fifty p.m.

"I'll have to walk it, John. Meet me at Staunton's when you get through the traffic," Radcliff said.

"Will do, sir."

It was at least a fifteen minute walk to Staunton's so Radcliff had to run. His rowing at Cambridge had served him well. He ran fast and all the way. He looked at his pocket watch. Five-fifty-six p.m. He put his foot down and bolted down Cork Street. He was sweaty and breathless. Finally, he reached Bruton Street, and at exactly six o'clock, Radcliff rang Staunton's doorbell. He quickly wiped the sweat off his face, rearranged his hair, hat, jacket and waistcoat. He was thankful the butler was slow to come and open the door; it gave him just the amount of time he needed to catch his breath.

"The Earl is expecting you, please follow me to his study," the butler said on opening the door.

"So, what brings you here, young man? There's nothing more to be shared. The girl and that young man got what they deserved. You said this meeting is of the gravest of importance that would benefit me greatly. What in God's name could you bring that could benefit me? I won, didn't I!" Staunton spoke in his usual brusque manner.

"Yes, indeed you did, sir. Quite the victory," Radcliff calmly replied.

"Get on with it, I don't have much time."

"Neither do I," Radcliff replied making sure to keep the status quo.

Staunton looked up and gave Radcliff a sharp look, he was not expecting such a curt reply.

"I do believe I could bring you something that could benefit you greatly, indirectly so that is," Radcliff continued.

Radcliff proceeded to take out from his coat pocket Mary Staunton's silk pouch, her name visibly embroidered across the front.

"She wasn't very discreet in her kleptomaniac thieving, was she? We wouldn't want her to hang too, would we? Or be sent to the colonies or, worse still be sent just round the corner to the asylum. I don't think I need to show you Lady Seymour's precious jewels inside, as you already know what they are." Radcliff paused for dramatic effect.

"Sir, drop all charges for the cousins, and I won't say a word. By doing so you will be seen as pious and merciful. A man progressive of thought and a man forgiving of heart, not wanting a young girl to hang. Your eleventh-hour moment will be seen as the knight in shining armour. My very close friends at the press will make sure you look like a hero. They could also ruin you. The choice, sir, is yours."

Without a word, Staunton sat down to his desk, got out his ink and quill and wrote a letter to Judge Walker and to Judge Weymouth in Bristol.

As he wrote, the silence was heavy and impatient. The scribbling sounds of his quill across the paper seemed to go on for an age and a day. Finally, Staunton finished his writing and was about to seal the letters, when Radcliff interrupted.

"Would you mind if I check the wording, sir, I wouldn't want any misunderstandings with the executioner," Radcliff then read the letters and handed them back to Staunton to be sealed.

"Thank you, sir." Radcliff said formally as he took the letters off Staunton.

"I will be returning these to their rightful owner," Radcliff said as he held up the purse full of the jewels. "And without further ado, I'll see myself out. Sir." Radcliff swung round and left.

Once outside, John was there waiting for him. "Good man!" Radcliff said as he jumped in.

"Tomorrow morning, we'll go to the Judge and get his official pardon then straight to Bristol. It's audacious but we have come this far, I won't let a judge stand in my way. But John, I fear that time will be our enemy, not the judge."

Radcliff woke early the next morning and went straight to his gig and a waiting John. "The Judge's residence, John," Radcliff urged.

They travelled as fast as they could along the already busy London streets and arrived at the Judge's London residence. Radcliff charged up the steps, banged on the door, and in his finest of manners, demanded to see the Judge.

"Sir Walker is out at present," said his butler.

"Where is he?" demanded Radcliff.

"Who might you be?"

"Sir Benjamin Radcliff and it is of the utmost of importance. Imperative that I give this letter to Sir Walker.

"He's at the Billings Gentleman's Club on Savile Row."

"Obliged to you," and Radcliff flew back down the stairs and to his gig. "Saville Row!" Radcliff instructed John.

It didn't take long to arrive at the gentleman's club. Once again, Radcliff demanded to see Sir Walker and he was led into the dimly-lit room, full of men sipping their whiskeys and port; it smelt musky. The smell of cigars and spirits hit Radcliff like a bomb as he walked in. He tipped his hat as he entered.

"Gentlemen," he said as he walked past them all, making quite the entrance until he reached Walker at the end of the room sitting by the fireplace.

"Sir, may I speak in private? I come sent by Earl Staunton."

Walker stood up and walked straight away back down the room and led Radcliff into another wood-panelled, musky room, albeit much smaller. Once inside, Radcliff handed Walker the envelope. Walker opened it slowly and read it even slower.

"Sly young fox, you are. You will go far. After all, this is exactly how the world is run, doing our deals in dimly-lit back rooms." The Judge then sat down, got out his quill and slowly wrote a letter, and gave it to Radcliff.

"The King and the country want her punished. She will have to be punished."

"May I?" Radcliff asked to read the letter and duly satisfied, he returned it for its official seal.

One life has been saved, he thought, another one to go. "Sir," Radcliff said tipping his hat and walked out.

CHRISTOPHER'S HANGING

Death did not scare Christopher, the dying did. Was it painful? Long? Frightening? But after all his days in jail, in the cold and damp and with the constant hunger, he had now accepted the inevitable. Heaven awaited. He knew he had done wrong. Stealing from another was bad even if those he stole from had money and morals to spare. But he regretted none of it. In fact, he loved every moment of it. Life was truly an adventure when with his cousin.

One of Christopher's jailers was a younger man, not much younger than himself, his name was Samuel. Christopher persuaded him to bring him a pen and some paper and it was a true godsend that he could offload many of his fears onto the paper. He also wrote about some of Samuel's stories, he had been an orphan living on the streets. It would make for a good book, one he would now not have the chance to write, Christopher thought.

Christopher knew nothing of his cousin; his stomach wrenched every time he thought of her. Where was she? What was her fate? Had she been suffering? Had she been saved? And what about Moby? He thought. Had his captors taken him? Whatever became of him? It was just too painful to think about the most important beings in his life so he tried not to. He had so many questions and no answers. All he knew was that tomorrow he will be hanged, that was the only answer he knew. Today was going to be his last day on this earth so he wrote. Poems, thoughts, ramblings, anything that distracted his mind and eased his heart.

Beatrice, meanwhile, could hardly think, eat or do anything other than pace up and down her cell. She was beside herself with anxiety. Would her plan work? Would Radcliff get the jewels? Jewels she had had a feeling would be useful. Would Staunton take the bait? Would he reach Christopher in time? Time, she thought, was the saving and the ruining of lives. Time, time, time, it never stopped, it ticked, it tocked and it just kept going, relentlessly, argh! Time, stop, please, stop, just for a second, just enough to save Christopher's life, Beatrice thought as the frustrations and heartbreak spiralled.

Radcliff and John rode as fast as they could to Newgate prison. They were going to release Beatrice from jail, her hanging was planned for Tuesday morning so they were in good time in the saving of her life; it was the saving of Christopher's that was of the essence.

They arrived at the prison. Radcliff jumped down from the gig and walked with speed to the entrance banging on the door.

"Open the doors immediately, I have a pardon!"

Radcliff heard footsteps approach. Radcliff waited. A little shutter opened.

"My name is Sir Benjamin Radcliff and I have a letter of pardon for Lady Seymour-Barclay." The big and heavy prison doors opened.

"It's all who you know, ain't it?" said the guard as he led Radcliff down the corridor and to Beatrice's cell.

"I have the pardons. I have the pardons!" Radcliff said overjoyed but impatient.

"Let me see that before I let anyone go," the guard said.

Radcliff handed him the letter, he knew the guard couldn't read and the guard knew Radcliff knew but he went through the motions of reading the pardon as if he did, asserting the little power he had. He did see the seal which he knew was Judge Walker's. The guard handed back the letter and then went and got his big bundle of keys. The beautiful sound of keys unlocking someone to their freedom echoed through the jail house.

"Ain't you a lucky girl. The public ain't gonna see the famous Highwaygirl hang after all, more's the pity," the guard said. "But I ain't letting anyone out till the Governor sees this letter and he ain't here. You'll have to wait till the morning.

"May I?" Radcliff asked the guard to let him in Beatrice's cell.

"I told you I'd win," Radcliff confidently said with a smile as he walked up to Beatrice. "By any means possible, no?"

Beatrice walked forward and wrapped her arms around Radcliff. "Christopher? What about Christopher?"

"Free too but I have to reach Bristol in time before his hanging. I have no time to spare. Christopher's hanging is Sunday morning, John is waiting outside for me. It worked Beatrice. The jewels worked! Good job, girl."

"I'll be seeing you in three days for the release of Lady Seymour," Radcliff said to the jailer. Radcliff then bid his farewells and flew out of the prison and straight to his waiting gig. "To Bristol," Radcliff commanded.

The journey to Bristol was going painfully slowly for such dire circumstances, even though the gig was the fastest means of travel, it wasn't fast enough. The roads were bumpy and potholed and they had to slow to a walk for some parts.

At first, Radcliff kept his cool. He refused to look at his watch; it made the journey seem slower. His mind wandered as the journey slogged on. Time, he thought, is a human's construct, well, the clock is a human construct, breaking time up into tiny little pieces. Mother nature's time was an irrefutable motion and impossible to fight against, her clock was also relentless, but more spacious, less exact. His mind wandered some more. He thought about the cousins. He had certainly taken this case to heart. These two aristocratic cousins challenging their stereotypes, defying the institution. But after one pothole too many, Radcliff just couldn't help himself and looked at his pocket watch. It was eleven o'clock. They were travelling too slowly. At this speed, they would never reach Christopher in time. He would surely hang.

"We are too slow travelling like this. I'll take one of the horses and travel alone," Radcliff said. At the next stage coach tavern, Radcliff jumped down from the gig. John unharnessed one of the horses.

"She's the fastest, sir," John said handing Radcliff the horse.

"Wait for me here, I will meet you back here," Radcliff ordered.

Radcliff swung up on the horse. He put the precious letter of pardon safely in his inner pocket. It was more precious than any jewel, more precious than money; it held the precious power of saving a life.

Radcliff flew into motion and galloped ahead, he simply must reach Christopher, he thought. Both, not just one cousin, have to be saved.

Radcliff travelled through most of the night, stopping around three a.m. at a tavern to rest the horse, sleep some hours himself and eat some food.

At the crack of dawn, Radcliff was up on his horse and out on the road. It was a beautiful and hot day. He felt the sun's warmth on his back as it rose. Radcliff didn't stop, he travelled at a steady but solid canter. It was relentless riding. His horse was tiring so he stopped by the roadside for her to graze. He was a quarter of the way there. Still a lot more journey left but he would make it in good time to save Christopher, he thought. The sun rose higher, and as lunch neared, Radcliff stopped again for his horse to rest. This time at a tavern. He ate, he was hungry but too anxious to eat much. He looked at his watch. I should make it there with time to spare, he thought. His hanging is not until seven p.m.

Having rested his horse well, it was now fresh and fast. He let his mind wander. With his eyes constantly focused on the road, he thought of the Romans and their masterful engineering. He imagined all the soldiers soldiering away in the rain and cold to build this road he now rode on. Had humanity progressed since then? Not enough, he thought. I'm hoping the Age of Enlightenment will push us all forward. He looked at his watch; he was making good time. The afternoon sun heated his back, finally, he could see Bristol in the distance.

"Where's the prison, please?" Radcliff asked a stranger as he entered the city.

"Left, down West Street and then right on Winchester. You going to the hanging?"

"Whose hanging?" Radcliff asked fearing the worst.

"That highway robbery lad," the man casually said.

Without taking another breath, Radcliff bolted off. He galloped over the cobbled streets and was ruthless in his shouting at the pedestrians.

"Get out of my way! Move!" Radcliff yelled.

He took a wrong turn and had to go back on himself. "Argh!" he said aloud, enraged with himself. That mistake could've cost Christopher his life, he thought. He careered around the corners, coming to a dramatic stop once at the prison gates.

"Open the doors immediately! I have a pardon!" he shouted. Finally, a guard came to the doors.

"Christopher Seymour-Barclay! Where is Sir Christopher Seymour-Barclay?"

"They already took him. He's probably hanged by now. They took him early," the guard said.

If his heart could have stopped beating then this was that moment. He climbed up on his horse and bolted straight to the square where all the hangings took place.

Oh, no! It's too late! It can't be! Radcliff felt desperate as he rode up to the square. It's all too late. It has all been for nothing, after everything we've done! Just as he had given up all hope, he suddenly saw from the other side of the square, Christopher and two other prisoners being walked towards the scaffold and up the stairs. Radcliff's sigh of relief was immeasurable. He then tied his horse, and on foot, pushed through the waiting mob until he reached the scaffold.

"Release this man immediately! My name is Sir Benjamin Radcliff and I have a letter of pardon for this man's release," Radcliff shouted up to the executioner. Christopher looked just like his artist's painting, Radcliff thought. It was the first time he had seen him.

"From whom?" the executioner said as he stood checking the nooses. "This crowd want their hanging. They're going to be disappointed, and a disappointed crowd is a dangerous crowd."

"From the Governor," Radcliff claimed as he walked up the stairs and onto the scaffold.

This was a lie. He still had to deliver Judge Walker's letter to the Judge who sentenced Christopher in Bristol, they needed his signature of approval but Radcliff just wanted Christopher off that scaffold and in his protection before he worried about practicalities.

"Release this man," Radcliff repeated handing the letter to the executioner.

The executioner nodded to the guard to release Christopher without bothering to take the letter. He didn't want to embarrass himself in front of the swelling crowd with his illiteracy.

The guard, as ordered, untied Christopher who, at this moment, was in an absolute daze and shock at the turn of events.

"I'll take him with me," Radcliff said authoritatively to the guard.

Radcliff then took Christopher's arm gently, and in that smallest of movements, the changeover of power was made. And there it was; Christopher was now free. Christopher had his life. Christopher, having been so prepared for death, now needed some time to prepare himself for life again. He needed some time to adjust.

The crowd started to boo and hiss, they were eager for the hanging of the highway robber, the Highwaygirl's assistant. They were disappointed and started to throw tomatoes and stones.

"Why was your hanging brought forward? It was meant to be in two hours' time?" Radcliff asked as he speedily led Christopher away from the angry mob.

"Said they were behind and had four other executions to do," Christopher replied, he was in shock, he couldn't believe he was walking back to the prison alive and not dead.

"Beatrice?" Christopher asked holding his breath for the reply.

"Pardoned but indentured, as with you, my friend. I come gaining your life but the King requires your punishment. You'll both be sent to America. I'm afraid the Highwaygirl and her accomplice had to be punished. Don't worry, I have contacts in America. I will get to that soon."

Christopher was lost for words. He didn't know how he felt. He was obviously elated but he had so prepared himself for his death that he was now in shock.

Back at the prison, Christopher was put back in his cell. They waited for the Governor.

Loud steps came pounding down the corridor. The governor must be a big man, thought Radcliff.

"What's the meaning of this! A pardon?" bellowed the Governor who was indeed a big man. Six foot four and a stomach seemingly just as big.

Radcliff prepared himself, stood up, pulled down his waistcoat and tidied his coat. He was not intimidated by the man, he had after all justice on his side.

"What's the meaning of this? I want this man hanged! Who are you?" shouted the Governor.

"Sir Benjamin Radcliff," he handed the Governor the letter. The Governor opened it and read it. It made him angry.

"He'll stay here in my charge until his ship is ready for sail," he commanded, he was angry this young vagabond hadn't been hanged. He then stormed out, stomping his way back down the stone corridor. Radcliff and Christopher let the Governor's footsteps disappear completely before they spoke.

"Nice to meet you, Christopher," Radcliff said tipping his hat.

"Nice to meet you, Radcliff, it was Radcliff, no?" Christopher replied.

"Yes, indeed. Benjamin Radcliff. Beatrice's lawyer."

"One day, I will find the appropriate words of gratitude, but now at this precise moment, I'm a little lost for words," Christopher humbly replied.

"All in good time."

"Moby?" Christopher was frightened to ask but ask he had to too.

"Safe, in hiding. I didn't want the horses used as evidence in the court trial," Radcliff explained.

"Would you...?" Christopher started to say.

"Yes, I will keep both Moby and Asta in my care for now," Radcliff said interrupting Christopher, reading his thoughts. "You will travel directly from here to your ship for America in Plymouth, where you will be reunited with Beatrice. I'm sorry, Christopher, nothing I could do to avoid the servitude. King's orders."

Radcliff talked a while longer but soon made his leave. The two men said their farewells. Christopher then sat in silence once again alone with his thoughts. Thoughts that were now very much different from just a moment ago. He needed to slowly take in what had just happened. Once outside Radcliff started his journey back to the stage-coach stop to meet John, who was still waiting.

Radcliff took an easier canter back towards John. He had won, he thought. He was happy. The cousins were free. It had all been worth it. Their infamy, however, had created too much of a stir so they had to be punished. Radcliff accepted this. The King and country had demanded this. He had saved their lives, he had won, the rest he could manage in good time. Radcliff had friends in America and he would somehow try and find a suitable residence for their indentureship.

He reached the tavern, dismounted, gave his horse to the livery, saw his gig and went into the tavern to find John.

"Good man, John, good man!" Radcliff said as he slowly sipped his ale, nothing could have tasted better in the whole world than the ale he was sipping. Sweet and warm from the taste of winning. The cousins were free and America was a new horizon. He liked Christopher, he thought. Handsome and charming, a gentleman. America could do with another one of those, he thought. He was different from Beatrice, he thought. Her fire jumped right out of her, his quietness jumped right out of him. Radcliff was happy they lived. He was happy he had won. He was happy he had saved them both.

"Good man, John, we made it!" Radcliff said taking a very long sigh. "But we must leave in the morning for Newgate. Beatrice must be ragged with nerves wondering if we had made it time."

Meanwhile, back at Newgate prison, Beatrice hadn't slept. She sang songs to ease her beating heart. Was Christopher dead? Did Radcliff reach him in time? She prayed a lot and played her counting game; counting from one to one hundred repeatedly, anything to keep her mind off the waiting. The waiting was excruciating. The sitting still agony. Nowhere to run, ride or escape to. She felt pent up and manic. She hadn't felt her hunger, hadn't smelt the foul stench, the dank walls, the cold, heard the other prisoners' grim noises, she hadn't paid attention to any of it; all she could do was think about Christopher's life being saved.

Sleep finally took her in the early hours of Monday morning. She was exhausted. Footsteps she recognised came towards her cell. This was the moment of truth, was Christopher dead or alive? She could hardly breathe as she waited for Radcliff's steps to reach her cell. They stopped. She didn't look at him. She couldn't bear it in case his face revealed the horrible truth. She waited.

"Alive," Radcliff said.

Beatrice dropped her head in silent relief. A relief coursed through her body, through every vein and every cell. She collected herself and turned to Radcliff.

"Thank you," is all she said but it was laden with all the emotion that words sometimes fail to describe.

"Oh, I believe these are yours," Radcliff said handing Beatrice her mother's jewels.

"Benjamin, could you do me one last kindness?"

"Of course."

"Would you mind giving them back to my mother?"

"Of course."

Radcliff then told Beatrice in the kindest of words that she and Christopher would be sent to America to serve seven years of indentured servitude. Beatrice sat quietly. This was a blessing. Her cousin's life had been saved. Her life had been saved. Beatrice only felt gratitude as she listened to Radcliff explain all the details. She would have to stay in prison until her ship was to set sail.

"Asta?" Beatrice asked.

"Still in hiding. Safe," Radcliff reassured.

"Would you...?" Beatrice started to say but was interrupted by Radcliff.

"Yes, I will look after her for you. Chin up, dear. I have lots of friends in America and I will find a residency fit for a rebel and a rogue and an ex-highwaygirl," Radcliff said warmly. "And don't worry, Asta will be fine."

Radcliff's heart wrenched a bit as he spoke. He had invested so much in this case both emotionally and physically. He had become attached to the cousins and would, in a strange way, miss them. America seemed very, very far away.

"I will keep an eye on you. I'll come and visit before you go," Radcliff said warmly. Beatrice leant forward and gave Radcliff a hug.

"Thank you," Beatrice said quietly and lovingly. "I will never forget what you have done, never."

The next day, back at home and over breakfast, Radcliff opened The Times broadsheets to see the headlines.

The Highwaygirl and Accomplice Walk Free.

Radcliff was pleased that his friends at The Times had kept to their word and painted Staunton as the hero. He was nothing but merciful and forgiving in his saving of the lives of the highway robbers. Staunton's image was portrayed just as Radcliff said it would be.

Radcliff folded the paper and rang the bell for his head groom to prepare his carriage. He had to pay an important visit to Lady Seymour-Barclay at Lacey Manor. He had some jewels to return to their rightful owner.

STORMBOY

RADCLIFF had sent word to Beatrice and Christopher that their ship to America had been postponed due to bad weather. The cousins were being sent to Virginia. Whilst they waited for the weather to turn for the better, they were sent to different places to start their time as indentured servants. Christopher was sent to Oxford and Beatrice to Merseyside.

Beatrice was taken to Lord Derby's estate, Knowsley Hall, by one of her prison guards. On arrival, she was taken to the matron, Mrs Leaver, and shown to her room. There was no fuss, no fanfare; Beatrice was put straight to work. All the staff knew who she was and felt she needed no special attention. She was here to work, to pay for her crimes.

"These are yours," Mrs Leaver said handing Beatrice her uniform. "Wash and tidy yourself up and be ready to start work in the kitchens in an hour. Don't think because you got off from a hanging, that you'll get off lightly here. You won't know what hard work is."

Beatrice just nodded and took her uniform from Mrs Leaver. She then went and filled her jug up with water and took it back to her room so she could wash. The cold, fresh water cleaned away the dirt, the grime, the tears, the sleepless nights, the worry. Christopher was alive, Christopher was alive, what a miracle, she kept thinking. What about Asta though? Beatrice thought, her heart wrenched every time she thought about it.

She combed and tidied her hair. There was no Lilly now to dress and groom her. There were no silk dresses or flowers entwined in hair. No embroidery and no piano lessons here; this she was at least thankful for. Being here as one of the staff, was the place she least thought she would be. She was a long, long way away from her luxury and privilege. Beatrice didn't rush, neither did she linger, and when ready, she walked out of her simple room and stepped into the new episode of her life.

All the staff were excited to see the Highwaygirl; she was a mild celebrity. Some were angry she hadn't hanged, infuriated that her privilege had saved her, that wouldn't have been the same if it had been one of them. The odd few were happy she was released and admired her rebellion. Whichever side you were on, Beatrice's arrival was the highlight of the year and they all couldn't believe she was once a debutante, a lady, an aristocrat and now she was a scullery maid.

Being the scullery maid was the hardest work Beatrice had ever known, it was back-breaking and utterly exhausting, She cleaned ovens, scrubbed floors, washed clothes, plucked chickens, scaled fish and served all the staff; it was hard to imagine that only a few months ago she was Lady Seymour-Barclay and didn't know how to scrub a plate, let alone a floor. It was hard to believe that, only a few months ago, Beatrice was wearing silk gowns and had flowers woven in her hair but now was wearing a coarse cotton uniform that constantly scratched. For the first time in Beatrice's life, she really realised the work all the staff had done at Lacey. She suddenly missed them; Lilly, Betty, Michael. At night, Beatrice honestly did not care what bed she slept in; she was so exhausted that any bed was better than her prior prison bed. She thought of Christopher often. How was his work? Were the people kind to him? What was his home like? She longed to be able to write at least.

Lord Derby was passionate about horses and about racing them. But most of all, he was passionate about winning with them. Beatrice was asked one day to deliver a hamper to the head groom at the stables. It was a beautiful May day. England was bursting with an approaching summer. The air was sweet and bright and wanton. Beatrice walked slowly, she didn't care if she would be scolded for taking too long. It had been a while since she breathed in the fresh air. She stopped, leant back against a brick wall, and with her face raised to the sun, let it soak within. Oh, what a feeling of utter healing, she thought. After all the tensions, this sweet little moment against the wall was totally rejuvenating, she thought.

She carried on across the sprawling gardens and then onto the stables. The minute she approached the stables she gasped. It was the smell that hit her first. That horse smell that completely intoxicates. Then she saw them all lined up in their boxes, heads out and curious to know who the intruder was. The sight of them all was like a blissful and warm blanket had fallen upon her. She went up to them one by one.

"Shame you aren't all in the field together," Beatrice whispered to one as its warm sweet breath nuzzled her curiously.

Then she walked up to a chestnut colt. Stroked its nose, stroked its forelock. There was a look in its eye that jumped straight to her heart. It rocked its head up and down and kicked the stable door.

"You want to get out, don't you? I know the feeling, I've been locked up for a while too. I wish I could let you all out. What's your name?" Beatrice asked as she looked down at the stable door. "Stormboy," Oh, that seems about right, she thought.

Stormboy nuzzled his head into her head.

"I know, Stormboy, you're asking me to let you out but I can't."

Beatrice pulled herself away from Stormboy and walked out the other side of the stables where she saw a small race track. She stopped instantly, hid herself slightly behind a tree and watched enthralled at the spectacle she saw before her. Beatrice had never seen a horse race before so, when she saw a horse and it's rider bolt around the track, she was utterly enthralled, goosebumps erupted. The pounding of the horse's gallop, the thudding sound of its hooves hitting the grass. The jockey low and intent. The careering around the corners. Beatrice was completely exhilarated and was instantly blinded by her desire to race that track.

Beatrice shook herself back to reality, and holding the hamper, walked up to the race track. The jockey slowed as he too approached the head groom and trainer. As Beatrice reached the head groom, Lord Derby also came walking towards the little group.

"This is for a Mr Boorman," Beatrice said confidently.

"Ahh, that's for us, thank you;" said Boorman.

"Good afternoon, all. How was the last lap? Not much time until the Derby. Let's do one round again and time it," said the Lord who took a quick glance at Beatrice.

"That'll be all," said Boorman irritably, he had noticed the Lord's glance. She had overstayed her welcome for a maid and he had failed to tell her to leave sooner.

Beatrice turned and walked away. On her way back, she could feel her rebellious spirit rising again. She thought of Stormboy, she thought of racing.

She went back to her scrubbing and washing and cleaning and stoking, and despite its arduousness, it did nothing to tire the rising force of her rebellion. Beatrice had something now that occupied her mind, gave her mundane work purpose. As she worked, she planned a way in which to ride Stormboy.

A few nights later was a full moon. Beatrice couldn't sleep and neither could her rebellious spirit. She dressed and opened her door. She thankfully slept alone and thankfully was on the ground floor. At five, she would have to be back to start the morning fires so everything would have to go to plan.

The night was fresh and silent. The moon took her breath away when she first saw it. Big and low. It almost felt like she could touch it, it felt like it was goading her on. It gave her the light she needed to sneak her way straight to the stables. The stable boy slept in the hay barn next to the horses so she would have to be extra quiet with Stormboy.

So far so good, Beatrice thought, as she approached the stables. Nobody was seen or heard. All she could hear was the banging of hooves on a stable door and she knew exactly who those hooves belonged to.

As she sneaked in, all the horses' heads rose, some nickered quietly, Stormboy shook his head impatiently. It was like he knew she was coming, Beatrice thought.

Beatrice crept up to Stormboy. His saddle and halter were stored in front of his box. She grabbed them and opened his door as quietly as humanly possible. Stormboy was like a mouse and obediently let Beatrice saddle and halter him. She walked him out. She could feel his excitement, Beatrice was excited too, her adrenalin was pumping fast, this was the most daring she had been, she thought. Very different from the Highwaygirl. But something in her thrived on the adrenalin and the excitement. Something bigger than her takes a hold and Beatrice is beholden to it.

The moon lit up the race track like a big stage light. Beatrice walked Stormboy onto the track, she climbed up on top and sat. Oh, the feeling to be back on a horse, there was nothing like it in the whole world, she thought. She thought of Asta, she missed her, felt a twinge of betrayal. Stormboy was itching to go which pulled Beatrice back from her thoughts. She walked him a little bit first to warm him up and to get a feel of him. As he walked, he felt electric, just waiting to run, waiting for Beatrice's signal. Beatrice too felt alive. The feelings running between them were mutual. She walked some more and then, at the furthest corner from the stables, she raised her energy for a gallop and Stormboy just exploded from her. Even for Beatrice, it was a surprise. She held her connection and kept herself high up off his back and just let him run.

Beatrice had never experienced anything like it. It was utterly thrilling, utter adrenalin. He just loved to run, he excelled at it and that's exactly what she let him do. She hardly touched the reins, it was all Stormboy. He belted round the track, and if anybody could have seen this image from the outside, the moon bulbous, sitting low, horse and rider storming round the track under its glow, they would have recognised its magnificence. But there was someone who had seen this sight and he did think it magnificent.

The stable boy, Simon, had woken as he heard hooves. So he went out to check and was simply amazed by what he saw. He was in shock. Somebody was riding Stormboy. Nobody can ride Stormboy, was his first thought and then to see that it was a girl riding Stormboy, a girl! He was aghast. A young girl with her skirts wrapped up, riding laps around the track having taken one of the Lord's horses. It was incredulous. What do I do? He thought. I'll have to tell Mr Boorman, he thought. He couldn't help himself from watching. Nobody can ride Stormboy, he's impossible to ride, he thought. I will definitely have to tell Mr Boorman. I've never seen him ridden so fast.

Beatrice slowed Stormboy up and gradually came to a trot and then a walk. Both rider and horse were buzzing with life. Stormboy hadn't been happier. They both needed exactly what had occurred. Both had been pent up and contained. The race track was their vent. They both walked, Beatrice was happy, so happy, so incredibly happy, that she lay over his neck and just kept thanking him.

But Beatrice was aware that time was ticking and fires had to be started. She quickly returned and unsaddled Stormboy.

"I'll come back soon, boy," she whispered.

With speed, she ran back to the kitchens and started the fires. Her mind was in a whirl. She had done it and it was staggering. Stormboy had given her back her vitality and energy and purpose.

In the following days, Beatrice's work felt half its weight in hardship. All she thought about was riding Stormboy again. The need to ride him again was great. It might not be a full moon, but the following week,

Beatrice planned to escape for her night ride again. She had been stuck inside all week, the days were bright and beautiful but it pained her to be trapped inside.

Friday, early morning, the same time, four o'clock, Beatrice woke, dressed and creeped out. She crossed the gardens by way of the tall brick wall and then reached the stables easily. She could hear Stormboy kicking his door. As she approached, he shook his head.

"You've been waiting for me, haven't you? I've been waiting for you!" Beatrice whispered.

With ease, Beatrice saddled Stormboy and walked him out to the track. Simon had heard, he had been waiting every night to see if they would ride again. He quickly put his breeches on and crept to watch. Once again, it was a sight to see. Riding at night at the most incredible speed. The stillness of the night was in stark contrast to the speed of the race.

Throwing her arms in the air, Beatrice let out the longest sigh.

"What an incredible ride, Stormboy. I've never ridden a horse so fast."

Beatrice was elated as she walked to calm Stormboy, but as she came to the gate, all her senses of joy dropped.

"Pretty fast, eh?" Simon said.

"Yes, he's fast indeed," Beatrice cautiously replied, disguising her shock.

"You that Highwaygirl, ain't ya?"

"Yes."

"Nobody can ride that horse, he's crazy. That was fast what you just rode."

"He's incredible to ride," Beatrice replied, still cautious as to where this conversation was going to go.

"The Lord will be mighty angry if he finds out."

"If he finds out," Beatrice came back with emphasising the 'if.'

"Well, that's where I'm a bit confused. My name is Simon, by the way."

"Beatrice."

"Do I tell Boorman or do I not?"

"Oh, get on with it," Beatrice said impatiently as she slid down from Stormboy. "I've got to get back to the fires, otherwise I'll be in real trouble. Are you going to tell or not?"

"Well, with you on his back, that's the fastest horse the Lord's got. So maybe I should and maybe you should show 'em," Simon said. "Shame to keep that horse in a box all day, kicking and squirming about. I tell you what, I'll tell Boorman and you ride Stormboy like you did just now. Boorman's my uncle, you see, and he, like me, loves a fast horse. Could win some pennies at the Derby, we could."

Beatrice loved the plan. Loved it! But how could they get past the prejudices? A scullery maid, a girl and a criminal; it was a lot to get past. But if money was involved then maybe they could.

"Next Friday?" Beatrice said.

"Next Friday," Simon confirmed. "At the same time."

"At the same time," Beatrice confirmed.

All week Beatrice couldn't wait. She was nervous about how it would go but impatient for Friday to arrive.

Friday arrived and Beatrice, as planned, crept down to the stables. Stormboy knew, he couldn't wait to start running. Beatrice walked out onto the race track and walked Stormboy. No sight of Simon or Boorman. Maybe it was all a trap. She continued as planned. Stormboy was raring to go, but since their rides together, Beatrice had centred him, grounded him, which, in turn, made him run faster; he had focus now, not so wild, not so pent up. He was being allowed to run and run in his way. Beatrice gave him free reign, he appreciated that so he gave her speed and she loved that. Stormboy liked her. Beatrice liked Stormboy. Their feelings, once again, were mutual.

They walked and then they ran. They both flew around the track in total harmony. It was like nothing Simon or Boorman had ever seen. They watched as they walked towards the track.

"Could win us quite a bit," Simon said.

"Could indeed. They're fast indeed, lad, fast indeed," Boorman replied. "You was right." Boorman kept his reserve, not to show too much excitement but inwardly he couldn't believe it. It was the fastest he'd seen a horse run since Diomed in 1790. That was an incredible horse, Boorman thought. He was angry it was a girl on Stormboy but had to admit it was quite a feat seeing her ride him, no other jockey had got as far as this. Stormboy would just about let them get on him.

"She was the Highwaygirl, no? A lady, no?" Boorman asked as he was busily thinking, the thought of money motivating him.

"Yes."

"Well, we could put her in man's clothes again, the same as the jockeys, and no one would be the wiser. For the race, that is; somehow we'd have to convince the Lord."

They stood in silence chewing over their thoughts as they watched Beatrice walk Stormboy around the track.

"He would be coming in as an outsider. Nobody would be expecting him to win. The Lord would make a fortune and he'd like that, for sure. We'll get her to ride in front of the Lord dressed in man's clothes and see how he reacts.

"But how will we get her away from her duties during the day?" Simon questioned.

"Oh, I'll see to that, don't worry. I'll get her to do some errands for us."

They reached the gate as Beatrice was coming out. "Not bad," Boorman said. "For a girl," he added.

Beatrice nodded. She stayed impartial. She wanted to ride. She wanted to ride the Derby but she also wasn't going to bootlick to get it. She was still a lady. And anyway' she knew money usually did override most people's prejudices. This is what she hoped would happen for her for the Derby.

"The fastest ride you will get out of him," Beatrice confidently replied, she knew her talents.

"You're confident as well," Boorman replied. "Girls aren't allowed to ride at the Derby."

"Not even the fast ones? Why don't you put one of your other boys on Stormboy and then see for yourself how much faster I am?" Beatrice gambled.

Boorman didn't answer, he was slightly taken aback at her forthrightness but then reminded himself she was/is a lady, a debutante, not too long ago. Beatrice was happy, Boorman's silence was evidence that she had planted a seed.

"Mmm," Boorman grumbled. He was peeved to be talked to like that by a girl but he couldn't resist the temptation of winning a lot of money.

Beatrice returned Stormboy and went back to her duties. Two days passed and she still hadn't heard anything. The waiting was agony. Would Boorman want her to ride? Would he play along with the subterfuge, the game and the disguise? Or would he simply report her to the Lord and have her either jailed or dismissed? It felt like a day and an age for Beatrice as she toiled away at her jobs. Again, she had her own little secret going on. Her own secret life that nobody except Boorman and Simon knew about. Beatrice liked this. It felt adventurous and not boring. Beatrice hated boring more than anything. She also hated waiting.

The staff were used to Beatrice by now, her celebrity had worn off. They were still slightly fascinated with the fact that a lady was working alongside them but not enough to make any leniencies, so there was always a bit of a distance between them all. But Beatrice did, however, realise how hard they all worked and that this hard work wasn't just for a few years of servitude, it was for their lifetimes.

"Beatrice, you've been called on an errand at the stables. They want a hamper sent down and they asked for you. Beats me why they asked for you," Margaret the cook said as she handed the hamper to Beatrice. "I only let them have you for an hour, so don't dilly-dally."

Beatrice's heart skipped a beat. This was the moment. They want her to race. Her stomach filled with butterflies. She couldn't wait to show them all, her and Stormboy riding together.

Beatrice calmly walked down to the stables. She was met by Simon who guided her to Stormboy's box. Stormboy, as always, was kicking, but on seeing Beatrice he calmed, he knew he was about to go running. Simon handed her a bag.

"Change into these."

Beatrice changed and led Stormboy out. She tied her hair up in her riding cap and tied the cap down hard.

Beatrice walked slowly with Simon at her side. Beatrice was nervous, Simon was nervous, Stormboy was biting at the bit raring to go. Stormboy's energy was rising so Beatrice turned off her nerves, she needed Stormboy calm and centred, so she had to be calm and centred herself.

They reached the race track and Beatrice began her warm-up walk. This was the cue for Boorman to lead Derby down to the track. Boorman had asked the Lord to come and see about a lame horse; this was actually true in a way. Stormboy had been lame with being unrideable; Boorman used it perfectly for his subterfuge.

Just as they arrived, Beatrice asked Stormboy to run and run he did, as if he knew it was the moment to impress and impress he did.

"Why, is that not Stormboy? I thought we had given up on him?" Derby said bemused rather than angry. "What an incredible speed!"

Simon let Beatrice's and Stormboy's running do all the talking. Derby watched in amazement. He was not expecting to see this, especially from Stormboy. They both stood in silence as they ran. As they approached the final line, Beatrice asked for more and Stormboy gave it, flying past their important spectators at a breakneck speed.

"Well, I never! I thought that horse was unrideable. What happened? I haven't seen a horse run as fast since Diomed in 1790."

"Only with that rider can he ride that fast. That is the key," Boorman replied.

"Mmm." Derby was intrigued.

"Sir, there is a lot of money to be won with that horse," Boorman felt this was the perfect timing for his proposal.

"Mmm." Derby was thinking.

"If he went in as the outsider, you're assured to make a fortune, sir."

"I want to meet the rider. Find out how he did it."

Banking on this, he had a solution up his sleeve and it was all thanks to Beatrice. He was a man of instinct and had a good relationship with the Lord and felt the idea would work.

"Yes, of course, sir. But I'd like you to see something before I make the introductions," Boorman replied.

Boorman then waved across the track to Beatrice. This was the signal for her to make the changeover. Beatrice got down from Stormboy and another rider got up on him. The new rider then walked the track.

"Sir, I'd like you to choose which rider you prefer," Boorman said. He was confident his strategy of tapping into Derby's ego would work.

The jockey then put Stormboy into a gallop. They shot off but it was scattered, laboured and without grace. It lacked the all-important element, the element that would make them a lot of money, it lacked speed. Stormboy just didn't perform with another rider and everybody watching could see it.

"We put on the first rider. We have ourselves a winner," Derby said.

Boorman had gambled right. Derby was a competitive man. Competitive in business as well as sport. His good friend and fellow cofounder of the Epsom Derby, Charles Bunbury, were in constant competition with each other, especially when it came to horses. Derby was thirsty for a win and Boorman knew it. Bunbury's horses had won the last two Derbies and Lord Derby wanted to beat his friend.

"I want to meet the rider," Derby said enthused about the prospect of a win with this new horse and rider combination.

"I think an open mind is due, sir. The rider is a little out of the ordinary," Boorman said.

This was the moment of truth; would Derby play in with the subterfuge or would he be outraged? After all, women were absolutely prohibited to race, Derby's rules. But would he be willing to break his own rules? Or at least bend them? Boorman thought. Boorman could lose his job for this, so he was banking on his instincts to be right.

Boorman nodded to Simon who walked over to Beatrice and told her to come and meet the Lord. Beatrice climbed up on Stormboy. They looked good together. A perfect match, a good team. Stormboy was happy to have his rider back. They walked towards the Lord, in silence.

"Nice to meet you, sir," Beatrice bent down and gave Derby her hand,

Derby was taken aback and didn't know what to do. A girl rider! Shaking hands! There was a moment's hesitation until, finally, he raised his arm and gave Beatrice his hand for a soft shake.

"Lady Seymour-Barclay, scullery maid and Highwaygirl, now at your service," Beatrice said tipping her hat. She felt suddenly emboldened and thought she had nothing to lose and that, by using her title, it would actually appeal to his snobbery as well as his competitiveness. Derby tipped his hat. He was never lost for words but today was his first.

"I can win the Epsom Derby for you, sir." Beatrice confidently said. "If winning is what you want?"

"Mmm," Derby replied.

The Lord's mind was racing. A girl racing the Derby, that's too outlandish, he thought. I don't think I could get away with it. What if we were caught, it's too great a risk.

"Tomorrow we race Stormboy and Mr T and I'll decide then. Same time," Derby said and walked away.

Beatrice slid down from the horse.

"Well, at least we weren't all dismissed," she said.

They all walked back in silence and returned to their jobs.

Beatrice went back inside and carried on scrubbing, plucking and washing. She missed not being outside, breathing in the beautiful fresh air. She could still feel and smell Stormboy on her and could still feel the wind on her face as they ran. She thought of Asta and begged that she was all right, still alive and being looked after. She ran differently, she seemed earthed and grounded. Older and wiser, a leader, a horse of the fields and the woodlands. Beatrice missed her. Stormboy, on the other hand, was a rogue, cocky and mischievous, a horse made for competition. She thought of Christopher. He would probably be shocked by her Stormboy escapades, her risks. Beatrice could see his smile in her mind's eye, a smile that expressed his silent admiration for her risks.

The next day came. It was warm. Beatrice and Stormboy were waiting. Along came Mr T and his rider, Mark Johnson. Beatrice was excited to run, to race. She was also nervous. It would be her first race and she would have to make an overwhelming impression, big enough to convince Lord Derby.

The riders entered the track and warmed up their horses as Derby approached with Boorman. They were talking.

Beatrice stayed calm, she thought of nothing else but beating Mr T. She focused on the finish line. She imagined herself and Stormboy as the clear winners running through it.

"Take your positions," Boorman said as he reached the race track and got out his pocket watch. The horses got in line. Boorman blew his whistle and they were off. They stormed off. The ground thundered from their speed. Mr T kept the pressure on as he hung to the side of Stormboy. Then, as if showing off, Stormboy pushed past effortlessly and took the lead. With ease, he gained half a lap and glided to the end. It was effortless. Beatrice hardly did a thing, she just sat high, gave him the reins and let him run. Stormboy was an utter joy to ride, he was the rare mix of power and lightness as if a divine speed flowed through him, and it showed on the track. Beatrice couldn't wait to ride in the Derby to show off Stormboy in all his glory. But being a girl would probably stop this. It would need a very open-minded Derby for her to ride. Or the prospect of lots of money.

"Tempting indeed, Boorman. Incredible. Shame she's a girl," Derby said.

"I told you we were fast," Beatrice said confidently as she approached the men.

"Very fast," Derby had to admit.

He was well aware of the various cheatings that had gone on at the Derby. Whether it was lying about the horse's age or dying horses to change their identity, so why not change the identity of a rider; a boy to a girl. She was petite, and in man's clothes, could easily pass as a jockey. I'll have a hat made especially, a bit bigger, to fully cover her hair, or, better still, she could cut it, Derby's mind was racing.

"Nowhere does it say women can't ride. It's just presumed, so, technically, I'm not breaking the Epsom Derby rules, just etiquette's rules," the Lord said thinking aloud.

Beatrice swung down from Stormboy, she walked alongside Derby and Boorman, presuming her equal position, her scullery maid position seemed non-existent.

"I'll have to pass you through undetected somehow and keep you away from the other jockeys." Derby said.

"I'm good at disguising myself," Beatrice said.

"Are you good at cutting your hair?" Derby said.

Beatrice hesitated a moment and then, without a moment's doubt, said, "Yes, very good."

"The race is next week and we have much to do," Derby said. "Tomorrow you train with Stormboy again, same time. I will speak to Mrs Leaver to make sure you are available, but otherwise, you continue as normal."

The next day, when Beatrice trained, she was on fire. There would be nothing to stop her and Stormboy. It would be their secret. The only thing that worried her was whether her ship would be ready to sail. She could get notice any day. She crossed her fingers and kept her mind on the race.

The next day, Boorman and Derby arrived with a different energy. They were focused on training and winning.

"At the start-up, find your space quickly, they will try and push you out and pull you down. It's violent and shameless. You will need to keep your wits," Boorman advised.

Beatrice and Stormboy ran even faster. Derby and Boorman were feeling more confident. The next day, faster. It absolutely amazed them.

Derby, in particular, had completely given up on his horse, but now, he couldn't wait to show him off at the races and then, against all odds, win. There could always be something to prevent a win and guarantee a loss, after all, he knew too well about losing. But this year, his confidence was booming and his excitement rising as he watched this precocious young girl and this precocious young horse, run. He couldn't believe how utterly brazen she was and inwardly couldn't help himself admiring her. She defied all protocol; she too had cheated in her role as Lady Seymour. So they became cheats together; he was starting to like this.

On the second and third day, Beatrice practised some exercises assimilating the starting line with Stormboy. She walked him into some tight and claustrophobic places. In between tight buildings, bales of hay, bumped and banged him against trailers and barns, all trying to mimic the melee of the start-off. Stormboy wasn't as confident here as he was on the track.

On the fourth day, there was still no word from her ship. She sighed a sigh of relief.

On the fifth day, still no word. I'll cut my hair on the morning of the race, Beatrice decided.

On the sixth day, Stormboy ran his fastest time. They were all feeling confident but nervous about their subterfuge. Derby had been busy laying his plans, planting his seeds. But would it work on the day?

THE EPSOM DERBY

THE day had finally come. Derby day. Beatrice hadn't slept most of the night; she was nervous but bursting with excitement. Once again, she was a part of a secret, an enormous secret, and she loved it. She thought of herself and Christopher and their secret, their secret that was revealed to the world, but would this secret stay a secret?

Beatrice took her scissors out, and without any ceremony, cut her hair. She tied her hair into a small and neat man's queue. She then put her jockey hat on and looked at herself in the mirror. A male jockey she truly looked. Ah, what a wonderful feeling, she thought. I feel so light. Beatrice picked up the long dark brown hair from the floor and put it in a little bag. She would give it away to Emily, one of the other maids, who could sell it.

As planned, Beatrice went straight to the stables and there Boorman was waiting. They then, along with Simon, loaded everything they needed and travelled to Epsom. Beatrice was so excited she could hardly contain herself. She just couldn't wait to get on that rack and show the world how two underdogs win, even if it was only for herself and Derby to know. She wanted this secret to be kept a secret. Stormboy had been taken the night before so he could rest properly.

Once they arrived, it was mayhem. People everywhere. Tents mounted, horses resting. People knocking shoulders from all backgrounds, the rich and the poor, money being their common denominator. They all wanted to win.

Beatrice loved the energy and atmosphere. She loved being on 'the other side' and not in one of the boxes, sitting pretty and looking on. She was exactly where she wanted to be, thick in the middle of it all.

Their plan of squeezing her in undetected had been rehearsed. They had another jockey that would be the front man, and then at the last minute, change just before the race on the pretence of changing Stormboy's saddle.

It was four-ten p.m. and time to leave. The race was at four-thirty p.m. The energy was rising, the nerves were escalating. The atmosphere among the tents was starting to palpitate. Nobody took any notice of Beatrice as she waited hidden in Derby's tent.

"Time to leave, Mack," Boorman said to their cover-up jockey.

Mack, Stormboy and Boorman walked down to the track. Beatrice waited. They could easily not come back for her. Anything could happen to prevent this, she thought nervously. Beatrice was more nervous about not racing than about being caught. She waited to hear Stormboy's footsteps. Nothing.

Lord Derby stood at the track with his friends. He was full of cheer and celebration.

"James, I thought you were entering Mr T, strange choice entering Stormboy," said Lord Walford.

"Mr T is lame and I didn't want to miss my favourite race, so I've entered Stormboy, just for the fun of it. Good sportsmanship, old boy," Derby replied.

Derby was cool and confident, laughing and joking, nobody knew that, behind the scenes, he was planning the deception of his lifetime.

Beatrice waited in the tent, still nothing. Disappointment started to raise until, finally, she heard Stormboy approaching.

"Quick! We're late," said Boorman. "Change into these."

Beatrice went behind the screen, and in a flash, stepped out as the jockey. Yet again, she put on another character, another role.

"Let's go, let's go!" Boorman spoke urgently.

Beatrice found the composure inside, her focus was absolute. Once at the starting point, everybody was too distracted with the imminence of the race to notice Beatrice slide in with the other horses and jump on top of Stormboy.

The atmosphere was electric. Derby, by now, couldn't quite contain himself and he stood by the fence with his heart racing, he had a lot hinging on this race, the girl just had to win, he thought.

Boorman and Simon waited by the sides.

"So far so good, boy, so far so good. She's just got to win, she's got to win," Boorman said, the tension could break a glass.

Stormboy was restless. This was his first time in the melee amongst so many other horses and he was jumpy. Beatrice put him in circles trying to calm him. He was bursting with adrenalin, he was bursting to run. Beatrice kept him steady, channelling his adrenalin. The other horses were skittish too. The anticipation was hard to contain until, finally, the steward shouted for all the horses to get on the starting line. They all bumped and jolted with each other, heads rearing and mouths frothing. Stormboy didn't like being trapped here, he was getting too heated up. Beatrice kept her cool. Finally, the steward dropped the flag and the horses exploded from the starting line. Stormboy was third in from the outside. From the start off, Beatrice and Stormboy were caught in a melee with two other riders, jostling for their positions. Beatrice held Stormboy tight on the reins, he listened to her as she guided him in the fight. One of the jockeys kicked her, the other tried to push her off. There was a lot of kicking and shoving. Turf and sweat were flying everywhere. Beatrice kept her hold, kept Stormboy steady. It was brutal. I am not going to lose this race because of two other brutes, Beatrice thought. Against all instinct, she pulled on the reins pulling Stormboy back a bit, just enough for the others to gallop on ahead. Beatrice then steered Stormboy to the outside and then gave him the cue to go, go, go! It was the cue Stormboy had been waiting for and he flew out of the fight and into the clear on the outside. He had trusted her completely and let her guide him, now it was his turn to take the lead. They were behind, but with his free rein and open space, Stormboy did what he did best, run. But they were behind and had a lot of distance to cover in order to close the gap.

"James, just as well you're here for the fun of it," Lord Murry, another friend said shouting over the noise.

Derby wasn't listening to anybody, he was absolutely at a fever pitch of tension. Every nerve in his body was wired. Boorman and Simon could hardly breathe as they watched from the sides.

"She's got to win!" Boorman breathed under his breath.

"Not looking good, uncle," Simon said.

It wasn't looking good. Beatrice and Stormboy had lost some valuable distance from their starting line jostle.

Beatrice sat high, let the reins free and whispered, "Run! Stormboy, run!

And he did, he did just that. He flew. He hit the first corner and sped round it. He was angry he had lost time and distance. He wanted to beat the other horses. He wanted to win. Beatrice wanted him to win, Derby, Boorman, Simon all wanted him to win. The whole grounds were electric. Everybody was screaming for their horses, but as Stormboy overtook from the outside one horse after another, the crowd started to scream for Stormboy. Beatrice sat high and goaded Stormboy.

"Come on, boy, win, come on, boy!"

Stormboy then approached the group of horses in the lead. He came alongside. The crowd exploded. Derby could hardly contain himself. Beatrice guided him wide so as not to get caught up in any jostling. She knew he had a lot more speed in him. And he did. It was as if he had copious amounts of speed waiting to be harnessed, to be let free. Stormboy knew what he had to do, Beatrice just guided him to the side and he belted past the horses at an incredible speed, pounding the turf as he past. It was utterly exhilarating, the whole crowd exploded into a cheer, jumping up and down. Stormboy caught up with the lead horse and stayed neck and neck with him as if just to tease him, as if to create more tension for the crowd. Then he took his moment, his crowning glorious moment and galloped past him. The crowd went berserk, they hadn't seen anything like it, it was riveting! Beatrice felt all the other horses slip away and fall behind and then into the distance. She felt the air and space between them and the track ahead of them was empty, it was all theirs for the taking and they took it all. They stormed down the last lap taking all the glory and victory. Every cell in her being was exultant. Joy and freedom flooded over her. She threw her arms up in the air. Nothing in her life so far had come close to this feeling of sheer joy.

Derby was beside himself cheering. Boorman and Simon jumped up and down, embracing and screaming for joy. They had done it.

"That bloody girl did it," Boorman cried quietly.

"We just won us a lot of money," Simon said.

"We won, boy, we won, you did it," Beatrice said to Stormboy as they did a slow canter round the lap to warm down.

The crowd were in an uproar. They started to rush forward from the back wanting to run onto the track. Beatrice saw this and immediately trotted away and to the tent. None of them had planned for this. They didn't expect the crowd to come storming onto the track in celebration. Beatrice got out quickly just as the crowd was now on the track looking for the victors and looking for Stormboy. As quickly as possible, Beatrice found her tent, found Boorman and Simon and immediately slid down and handed them Stormboy and ran inside to change and hide. Mack then knew it was his time to get up on Stormboy and immediately trotted away from their tent. The crowd, however, saw them and ran up to them in a flood of joy and emotion. The subterfuge only just made it. If Beatrice had been found out not only as a girl but as the Highwaygirl, their euphoria would have turned to outrage.

Mack and Derby took all the glory. The winner's wreath was placed around Stormboy's neck and the victory was pure and glorious. There was no better feeling in the world than what Derby felt now, he thought. He lapped up the attention and the euphoria, it was intoxicating.

"We won, boy, we won," he said quietly to Stormboy.

Stormboy was a magnet for attention, he too lapped up all its intoxication.

James rejoiced with his pals in the gentleman's exclusive tent. He didn't care that he had bent the rules, he didn't care it was a woman rider, he didn't care about any of it. His outsider horse against all the odds had won at the Epson Derby. He was jubilant. He also won a lot of money, a lot.

Beatrice sat in the tent alone. She was ecstatic, overflowing with joy and retribution. She silently jumped up and down. It was the most thrilling thing she had ever done. It was scandalous, outrageous, and against all the odds, she had won. She only wished Christopher was there to celebrate with her. She hoped he wasn't suffering.

Back at the estate, Beatrice was put back to work. It was a comedown but she had prepared herself for this reality. Riding on her euphoric victory, her work seemed lighter, and easier.

The next day Beatrice got word that her ship was now ready to set sail in four days. She had just made the race in time. Destiny had given her her wish. She was both sad and excited by this news. Sad to leave Stormboy, broken-hearted, in fact, and excited to see Christopher, but then, scared of travelling on a ship going all the way to America. What would Christopher think of her short hair? She thought. Beatrice had two errands to do before she left.

That night, Beatrice sneaked up to Emily's room. And knocked on her door.

"This is for you," Beatrice said taking her bonnet off and handing her the bag of her cut hair. "Sell it, it could get quite a bit. No use to me."

"Oh, Beatrice! Your hair! It's gone, you cut it off, oh my goodness!" Emily was totally shocked. "I can't take your hair from you. All your beautiful hair."

"Take it, I have absolutely no use for it where I'm going."

Emily took the bundle. She opened it and had to admit it was a beautiful mound of hair and she would get a pretty penny for it.

"Thank you," is all Emily could say.

Beatrice then walked back down, and when the cook wasn't looking, sneaked out of the kitchen and ran down to the stables.

Her heart skipped a bit and tears welled in her eyes the minute she saw Stormboy.

"We did it, boy, we did. I'll miss you. I hope they treat you well. You gave me the best run of my life, Stormboy. Now I know why they gave you that name."

Beatrice nuzzled into his neck and stayed there for a while. She wanted to absorb him for as long as she could, it was going to have to last a long, long time.

"I'll probably never see you again, so run fast, just keep running fast, for me, you were born to run." Stormboy understood the moment, he felt it. He was sad too, he would miss her, he would never forget her, she had, after all, given him his freedom.

Beatrice walked out of the stables with tears rolling down her face. Why did it all have to be so hard? She thought.

AMERICA

THE guards came early for Beatrice. She packed what few belongings she had and was waiting in the kitchens. She had thought that Lord Derby would come and say goodbye but it was Simon and Emily who did.

"I hope the journey is not too harsh," said Emily sweetly. She couldn't think of anything more horrendous than sailing to America.

Beatrice was led outside, Simon approached. He handed her her racing hat. "Don't tell the Lord I gave it to you. Boorman don't like goodbyes so he sent me."

"Thank you," Beatrice quietly said. "Look after Stormboy for me, let him run."

"Maybe, in the future, they'll find out our secret," Simon said leaning into her ear.

"Probably not. But I had fun all the same."

The guards then took Beatrice away. She was taken in a prisoners' carriage. She watched Knowsley Hall fall into the distance as her carriage slowly made its way out and towards Plymouth.

She had lots of time to think during her journey. She couldn't believe she was going on a ship and sailing to America. What was America going to be like? The people? What was their home going to be like? The owners? The staff? Was she going to be safe? The journey on the ship? The native people, what were they like? Will Christopher and I be on the same estates? So many questions spun around in her head. The day was cloudy and the journey slow; Beatrice was exhausted, bone-numbing exhaustion. She couldn't wait to see Christopher, she hoped he was going to be well and healthy.

Finally, after four days journeying, they approached the port. There was a small crowd gathered. They wanted to see the Highwaygirl leave, they wanted to see her fulfil her punishment.

"Hang! Hang!" some people heckled.

It saddened her when she heard such things. Such hatred flying in her direction. She just sat and weathered their verbal blows. Her carriage stopped. The guards came to get her. She saw newspaper men quickly sketching her image, the Highwaygirl sailing to America, she imagined the headlines. Then she saw what she wasn't expecting to see in a thousand years. Beatrice stopped in her tracks and froze. Her mother stood waiting on the corner of the tiny cobbled street that led down to the quayside.

"Guards, I wish to have a word with my daughter," Lady Seymour assertively demanded.

The guards walked to one side to respect the lady's wishes. Mother and daughter dived into each other's arms.

"I have been so worried about you, darling. You look thin," Lady Seymour said.

"I'm sorry, Mother, about the wedding," Beatrice said, she found it hard to talk, the lump in her throat was so hard.

"He would have happily seen you hang, not much of a future husband. His sister is not very nice either. I am so sorry, darling, about everything, I am sorry I didn't protect you more. I was weak and confused. I'm proud of you. I wish I had an ounce of your bravery."

Both mother and daughter fought to hold back the tears. This would probably be the last time they would ever see each other.

"We've got to go, the ship is preparing to leave," said the guard.

"Beatrice, I want you to have this," Lady Seymour spoke now with more urgency and handed her the gold and emerald crusader ring.

"It will protect you, darling. At least now, you will be protected, it is the least I can do. I love you, Beatrice. Please look after yourself. You know the world just isn't ready for you. You were born before your time."

Beatrice couldn't hold back the tears and sobbed uncontrollably into her mother's shoulders. "I love you, Mother."

"I love you, Beatrice. And remember, if you marry, marry the man you love. I wish I had."

"Got to go," the guard said pulling Beatrice away. "They're calling for us."

"Write to me," Lady Seymour shouted as she watched her daughter being taken away.

Beatrice couldn't look back, the tears were rolling down her face. I didn't even ask about Asta, she thought.

They reached their ship, The Fortune. Beatrice's heart was so heavy she felt it would collapse, but then, the one thing that could bring some light stood waiting on the deck, Christopher. A smile crossed her face the minute she saw him. All the heckles from the crowd faded into the distance, she heard none of them. Christopher smiled back, he was so excited to see his cousin. They both ran into each other's arms and embraced, a long and grateful embrace. They hadn't seen each other since nearly losing their lives. They embraced each other and felt the power of life itself run through them.

"You can untie her now, she is in my charge," Captain Cooper said. "Follow me," Cooper ordered.

Cooper was neither warm, nor cold. Neither too firm nor too lax. After years of living on the sea, navigating its precarious waters, commanding men and living under the weight of heavy responsibility, he had found a neutral state of being. He was tall and imposing and let his stature do most of the talking.

Cooper gestured for Christopher to follow. Christopher joined them but nothing between the cousins was spoken, they waited.

"You both can stay untied and not in the brig, but you'll have to work. Christopher, you'll be under the first mate's charge and you, young lady, can help the cook. I will escort you both safely to Virginia and then hand you over to the governor's guards there. Christopher, you can sleep with the sailors and you can sleep in the brig," Cooper instructed the cousins and then walked out.

"You're early," Beatrice said, pulling herself back from the sadness of her mother.

"You're late," Christopher replied smiling.

"You're looking gaunt, cousin, did they work you hard?"

"Goodness! Did they cut your hair, cousin?"

"No. I cut my hair."

"Were you back in men's clothing again, cousin?" Christopher asked dubious of what she had been up to,

"Christopher, I have so much to tell you."

"Did they feed you well? You don't look like you've been eating enough."

"I miss Betty's shortbread and sandwiches."

"And stews and pies," Christopher added.

"I miss Asta."

"I miss Moby."

"You! Up on deck now!" The first mate, Robson, called down to Christopher.

Beatrice went and found the gulley and sat as the ship creaked and rocked. Voices and commands were flying back and forth on the top deck. She heard ropes being dropped and sails being heaved. She instinctively ran to the port hole to take a look.

"Can I take one last look at England?" Beatrice politely asked McGregor the cook.

"Up you go but don't get in anyone's way. Just a peak and then back down again."

Beatrice did just that. She went to the top of the stairs, crouched down and peaked out. There was the sight of England fading away as their ship slowly sailed out of the Pool of London. Beatrice watched the sailors' busy feet and all the commotion of sailing and couldn't quite believe this was all happening.

Sailing didn't quite agree with Beatrice. It took a while for her stomach to adjust. The wind in her hair was the only gratification for what was mainly one discomfort after another. It was the constant movement that troubled Beatrice the most. No ground beneath her, nothing solid, no stillness, just a constant swaying and rolling, it never stopped, day in and day out. The journey so far, however, was relatively calm. The ship in itself felt alive, as it creaked and moaned under the weight of ocean and wind. Was it going to bring fortune as its name so proudly stated? Beatrice wondered. Would it take them to some fortune in America? Or to their terrible fate?

Beatrice worked all day in the gulley. McGregor was small and forever busy. He'd met enough people to not be too interested in a Lady Seymour-Barclay, ex-Highwaygirl, but despite his stern indifference, he couldn't help himself from being slightly interested.

"Yous dropped a long way. Not so high and mighty now, are yers?" McGregor said in his thick Scottish accent.

"Depends how high one was in the first place, but yes, I am a long way from Lady Seymour."

"Well, you certainly aren't no ordinary lady, what with your man's clothes, short hair and robbing. I give you that."

Christopher was busy with the sailors. He had to scrub and haul and learn very quickly how to sail. The men were tough and direct, there wasn't any time to mince words or use too many. Decisions had to be quickly made, lives depended on it.

The cousins were so grateful to have each other on board. They didn't see each other much even though the ship was small, but when they did, it gave them the strength they needed.

"Can't wait to get on a horse, feel the land beneath my feet, even if it's American land," Beatrice said.

"Yes, just to be on dry land. Hard, immovable and reliable," Christopher replied, he too wasn't fond of sailing.

They were both too exhausted for conversation.

Halfway across the Atlantic, they hit a big storm. Both Beatrice and Christopher had never experienced anything like it, it was utterly harrowing. Beatrice was happy to be down below, even though she was thrown about all over the gulley. The storm was relentless. There was no give in its bombardment. It was utterly unforgiving and totally harrowing. The Fortune moaned and groaned under the ocean's constant attacks. Beatrice was amazed that this little hunk of put-together wood managed to withstand such attacks or, at least for now, it did. Beatrice feared for Christopher above on top deck. It must be deplorable up there, she thought. She was amazed at McGregor. Anybody would think he was at a tea party the way he carried himself. Completely ambivalent.

"Argh!" Beatrice cried when she took another hit and flung to one side of the gulley.

"Had a mate once back in Glasgow who used to knit jumpers for me whilst at sea, sweet lad, died fighting the French somewhere. I prefer to be on the merchant ships, me."

Beatrice could not partake in any form of small talk and was literally sick to her stomach with worry and sea sickness. The storm seemed never-ending, wave after wave after wave pounding The Fortune, hour after hour, after hour.

Christopher was soaked to the bone. He too hadn't experienced anything like this. He missed the land and the solid heartbeat of the land. He felt unhinged on a boat, he didn't like it.

The waves were literally as tall as buildings, black, grey and absolutely deadly. There really must be angels of the sea that kept them from not capsizing as he just couldn't believe they were still afloat. It was the most harrowing and imposing thing he'd ever confronted, the sea in a storm. The sailors shouted at him an endless amount of orders, there was no time to think, just do as they say and do it exactly.

Finally, the storm abated. It softened its grip and the ship settled. Everybody was exhausted except, of course, McGregor. He seemed to still be talking about some old friend or another.

The rest of the journey was easy enough. Anything was easy after that storm, Beatrice thought.

"We're approaching Virginia soon. I can feel the American coast, the wind has a feel about it," McGregor said.

Beatrice couldn't wait to get her feet on solid ground. She was allowed up on top deck to see their approach into Virginia. Christopher came up to join her. They didn't speak, it was all too much to process. The enormous land of America lay ahead. What lay within? What other-world creatures, people, beliefs, landscapes lay within it? All the time Beatrice had been busy living her rebellious life back in England, this land before her was busy living its life and rebellions too. And here she was, about to embark with her cousin on a completely new journey. The coin had completely flipped to the other side. Would it bring her fortune?

The Fortune pulled into port. Ropes were tied, and for the first time in five weeks, Beatrice and Christopher stopped moving. Christopher was ordered to help with the unloading of goods, Beatrice was told to wait.

"Bring the prisoners forward," Cooper ordered after some time. Beatrice and Christopher came forward.

"You did well, lad, you'd make a good sailor. I'll be handing you over to the governor's guards. Lady Seymour, good luck in Virginia," Cooper said without ceremony and went straight back to work. He had to get the ship unloaded and ready for its return sail.

And that was it. Beatrice and Christopher were led down the plank and onto American soil. Their feet landed on solid soil, American soil, for the first time in what felt like an age. They both swayed as their land sickness was strong. They were then led to the governor's office.

Beatrice was overwhelmed with the sights and sounds. It was a port much like any English port. It was busy and bustling but it was not any port; it was a port in Virginia, America and not England. It was a lot to absorb.

So this was the new world, thought Beatrice. This is what all the fighting was about.

They arrived at the governor's office. Both Beatrice and Christopher looked at each other. There was a notice on the wall outside, an artist's picture of a Highwaygirl. Both cousins couldn't believe her notoriety had reached here.

"Yes, we already know about you here, my dear," said Governor Singleton as they walked in.

"You have a long journey ahead of you both to Kentucky where your indentured servitude will start. You are going to Alexander Riley's Stud Estate. You will be escorted just in case any of you think it might be a good idea to escape. Believe me, it's not a good idea, what with the Indians and the bears and wolves and foxes and snakes, oh, and did I forget to mention the outlaws? Oh, but then you are both familiar with outlaws. Well, good day to you both. This will be the last I hear of you both," said Singleton.

Singleton then stood up and the guards came back.

"You created quite a storm back home, young lady. No wonder they want to get rid of you. You let down the side, ol' girl. You let down our class, and quite frankly, they should have had you hanged," Singleton added.

They were then taken out to their horses.

"Ahh, sweet animal, what bliss, what joy!" Beatrice couldn't help herself as she flung herself onto her horse's neck. For the entire sea journey, she had dreamed of just this. To be back on land, to be back on a horse. It was her only source of grounding. A horse was her safe place and her constant. Christopher had his books, Beatrice had her horses.

They started to walk and made their first steps on their journey through America. As they walked through the town of Jamestown, they also saw a few more of those Highwaygirl posters proclaiming her arrival. Beatrice and Christopher looked at each other. How incredible and how very odd to have her reputation arrive here before she did.

'The Famous English Highwaygirl Graces our Shore,' she read on one poster.

This was totally shocking to her. She thought at least by coming here she would be able to leave her scandalous reputation behind her but it actually got here first.

The sky was big and the sun was hot; it was now July. Here the sun sat higher, and felt more potent. The people all looked the same but felt different. The buildings were mixed brick and wood and in the colonial style. Beatrice's mind was in a boggle trying to absorb it all. England, Lacey Manor and her life as a debutante seemed to be another planet away. Am I really here? Beatrice thought.

Before long, they were on the outskirts of Jamestown and heading into the country. Now, was when Beatrice and Christopher saw an even bigger sky. Everything was bigger, the trees, the grass, the heat, the mountains in the distance, big, big, big. How big was man's ambition to have come here in the first place? That was the biggest thing of all, man's ambition.

Beatrice and Christopher were so relieved to be riding on horseback, back in the countryside and not on ships, or in jails or prison carriages, that they slowly started to decompress. Everything so far had happened so quickly, all the different events rolling and tumbling over each other that there had hardly been any time to think. For the first time, they gradually let out slow deep breaths and began to relax into their new chapter. It was so strange being here in this new land, where everything was new and different that they couldn't completely relax yet. Their uncertain future gave reason for their anticipation, along with the wolves and the bears.

Beatrice still had her bag with her full of her small amount of possessions. Her highway robber clothes, the book, her red and white jockey hat, and a pouch with some of their guineas stolen, and of course, the jewels.

"You still have your money from the robberies, don't you? Beatrice whispered to Christopher in the quietest whisper she could muster. They rode closely next to each other.

Christopher nodded and then pointed to the inside of his waistcoat. Beatrice nodded. He had sewn the money inside his waistcoat. Beatrice was relieved and amazed it had survived so far.

Their guards were nice enough, they had their jobs to do. They knew where they were going, they knew the land well; they were mountain men. They stopped for the night. One of the guards made a fire.

"You that Highwaygirl, ain't ya?" one of the guards said. Beatrice couldn't pinpoint his accent. Was he an American or English? "You a lady or something?" said the other guard.

"Yes, my name is Lady Beatrice Seymour. Call me Beatrice. Are you English or American?" she couldn't resist asking.

"Lancashire, been here a while though, fought with the confederates, so am used to taking prisoners here and there," the first guard said.

The conversation went on a little while longer, but in truth, all parties were hesitant. Nobody wanted to get too friendly and nobody was ready to completely trust each other.

The next day, they rose with the light and carried on with their journey. Beatrice was grateful that it was summer, the night under the stars wasn't too cold, wasn't too uncomfortable. She was also grateful to be outside and with the horses. The air was full of the smells of pine trees and cedars. The woodpeckers were loud and the birds a constant chorus. As they rode out of the woodlands, they walked into the wide sweeping hills. The air was rich and clean and Beatrice could do nothing but admit it was breathtakingly beautiful. There was a similarity to England; rolling green fields but it stopped there. It had its differences but Beatrice couldn't yet define them.

Christopher, alone with his thoughts, was overawed by what was around him. He didn't know what lay ahead of him in terms of servitude but he was happy with what was behind him, because it was what had gotten him here. He liked it. It was wild and untamed and he liked it. It was new and it was exactly that that he liked. The animals at night sounded different, the birds, the air.

They travelled on for two more days until, finally, they rode into Kentucky. "Half a day's more riding, then we'll be there," said the Lancashire guard.

Rolling hills of the greenest grass unfolded endlessly around them as they continued on.

They all stopped by a river to fill up their water canisters and let the horses drink. It was hot, they were tired. Beatrice sat on a rock and listened to the soothing trickling sounds of the river, it was hypnotic, and where they had stopped, was simply beautiful. It felt utterly pristine, man and his influence seemed very far away. Beatrice let her mind wander. What will my new bosses be like? What will the household be like? Will the staff be friendly? When, suddenly, Beatrice skipped a heartbeat!

"Christopher, look slowly to your right, very slowly," Beatrice said.

Christopher turned and fell silent inwardly and outwardly. Time stood still as he watched a mother black bear and her cubs come out of the woodland and go for a drink in the river. Everybody stopped what they were doing just to watch. They took their time, the mother obviously knew they were there, but didn't seem too anxious. When they had finished they simply walked back into the woods.

"You don't see that in England," said the Lancashire guard.

"It was worth the journey," Christopher said.

"And the hardships," Beatrice added.

"They must've already eaten and the mother seemed pretty relaxed about her cubs. They can get quite angry," said the other guard.

"Time to move on," the Lancashire guard said.

They all stood up, grabbed their horses from their grazing and continued with their journey. In no time, they entered some white gates.

"This is it, Mr Alexander and Mrs Elizabeth Rileys' estate, The White House," said the Lancashire guard.

"So this is it, B," Christopher said quietly. "For the next five years, cousin."

"Partners in crime," Christopher said.

"Partners in crime," Beatrice said looking at her cousin trepidatiously.

THE WHITE HOUSE

Perfectly cut green lawns sprawled out from behind perfect white fencing. The driveway to the house was long. But most wonderful of all, was that those lawns were full of horses grazing. Stormboy would love it here, was Beatrice's first thought. Maybe being here might not feel so strange after all, thought Beatrice. Surrounded by horses was the familiarity she needed.

The white fences along the fields seemed to go on for ages. Where was the house? Beatrice thought. Finally, they saw it. A big white colonial house with tall white pillars and verandas all the way around. It was definitely grand and imposing. Beatrice and Christopher looked at each other.

"Very different from Lacey Manor," Beatrice quietly said.

"And from Three Oaks," Christopher replied.

They all walked on down the imposing path until, finally, reaching the side of the house, the staff quarters.

They dismounted, a young groom boy took the horses and the Lancashire guard took them to the door. The butler, Mr Shaw, opened the door.

"Here, the two new conv… workers have finally arrived," he said, he was about to say convicts but caught himself and said workers.

"We've been expecting you both, come in," said the butler in his American accent.

Beatrice and Christopher walked in, everything was so new to them.

"This came for you two days ago," Shaw handed Beatrice a letter. "Read it later, I'll get you both straight to work. There is the summer ball tomorrow and there is a lot to do," said Mr Shaw very business-like, he was preoccupied with getting everything done for the ball.

"Change into these," Shaw continued, handing the cousins their uniforms. "Christopher, you will go with the horses, and Beatrice, you will stay in the kitchens under Mrs Watson's charge."

And that was it, they were put to work in their new residence, in their new country, in their new lives, having travelled thousands of miles to get there.

Christopher waved to Beatrice as he followed Mr Shaw.

"So, lass, a long way from home, hey! I've been a long time away from my Scotland, twenty years now, you'll get used to it. Now, you get to work. Start by cleaning the roasting pots and then go get those table linens and scrub them white clean, then I'll show you your room, you'll be sharing with Ann," said Mrs Watson.

"Yes, Mrs Watson," Beatrice politely replied.

"Must be strange being a maid now, you having been a lady and all," Watson questioned.

"Well, I'm still a lady, that part hasn't changed, just my circumstances."

"And that short hair of yers must have created quite a stir back in England. Was that what yers wore for the highway robberies?"

Beatrice was a little stunned that her infamy had travelled so far. She would never have expected it to be such a sensation.

"Caused quite a sensation yer did, lass. Everybody loves the story of a lady fallen from grace," Watson continued.

Beatrice thought how chatty and forthright she was. It was true, Beatrice had to admit, everybody loves the story of somebody falling from the high levels of the aristocracy.

Watson was nothing like Betty and Beatrice suddenly had an overwhelming longing to be sitting in her kitchen, next to the fire, eating Betty's shortbread and playing cards with Christopher. That world and all those people in it seemed so far away. Had it gone forever? Beatrice wondered. Will I ever see them again? How is Asta? And Michael? How was mother? Beatrice cut her thoughts off as she felt herself being sentimental which was of no help to her now.

There was much work to do and the house was enormous. Lacey Manor had more nooks and crannies and was not so grand and ostentatious in style. That night, Beatrice went straight to her room, she was exhausted. As she lay in bed, she thought of that mummy bear and her cubs, what a beautiful and serene sight. Would I have any children one day? Beatrice thought. Beatrice was just about to read her letter when Ann came bursting through the door.

"So yer my new roommate then? Yer that Highwaygirl, ain't yer? What was that like? Robbing all those rich folk? Did yer cut yer hair for the occasion? You do look like a boy, not much like a lady. Not bad that short hair, much easier to handle, I'd say, and cooler in the summer. You've got to tell me all about the highway robberies."

Ann was a ball of energy and extremely talkative and Beatrice liked her. She was refreshing and joyful and was very glad she was her roommate.

"Ann, I'd love to tell you all about it but I just have to read this letter," Beatrice said.

"Oh, don't mind me, you go ahead."

Beatrice opened the letter, she already knew it was from Radcliff from the stamp and forwarding address.

Dear Beatrice.

I hope Kentucky finds you well. I hope too that you hadn't suffered too much on your journey. I regret enormously not being able to say goodbye at the port but I had to be in York for an important legal case.

You might be wondering why you were sent to Riley's estate, well, it was all my mother's doing, the Duchess. She so admired your zest for life that she thought The White House stud farm, and especially, Mrs Riley herself would appreciate such zest and your love of horses. Mrs Riley and the Duchess are firm friends and firm believers in the Age of Enlightenment and its contribution to the rights of women, so I think you will fit in at The White House.

I am sorry, dear, but there was nothing I could do to annul your servitude. The King himself insisted on your punishment. So this was the best that we could do.

I will pray for your good health and strong spirit and hope that, not too far in the near future, we will be able to meet again and under more favourable circumstances.

Yours most fondly, Benjamin Radcliff.

"So who's yer letter from? A lover? A suitor? I want to know all the secrets," Ann said excitedly.

"Oh, definitely not a lover or a suitor but definitely a friend."

Talking of love, sparked Beatrice's mind instantly to think of Montifiorre and their dramatic meeting. All hopes of any romance, Beatrice had erased from her being on the day she was arrested. Montifiorre had, of course, entered her mind and triggered her heart a few times, especially when she was in jail, but she didn't allow her heart to linger long on such thoughts now that her life had taken such a diversion. And now, being a million miles away had made any hope of love with Montifiorre die forever.

Beatrice's work didn't stop. She was up and down stairs, in and out of cupboards. She was scrubbing and carrying and stoking and washing. All the staff were busy careering around, as the Rileys' annual spring ball got into full swing. Beatrice was actually curious as to what an American ball would be like. She had gone to so many in her life and found them utterly boring but maybe an American ball would be different. From the kitchen she did see the line of carriages and guests arriving. She was bemused as to where they arrived from, the land around the The White House seemed wild and uninhabited. The ball was definitely glamorous and more informal but Beatrice thought it much like all the other balls; people parading themselves and gossiping. It was also the first time she had observed the rich at play from the other side. It was definitely hot. Hotter than England which made her work a much sweatier affair. Beatrice thought of Christopher and wondered how he was doing with all the horses and carriages. It would be so lovely to sneak over to him and have a game of Whist, she thought.

That night after the ball, Beatrice collapsed in her bed. Even the ever bubbly Ann fell into bed without saying a word. They were both exhausted.

The next day, Mrs Riley walked into the kitchens.

"Good morning, Mrs Watson. I'm looking for the new girl. Do you know where she is?"

"I sent her to the chicken coup, ma'am," Watson replied.

"Could you send her up to my study when she comes back, please."

"Yes, of course, ma'am."

Beatrice collected her eggs. She could see the stables just down the path. Should I run down and see if I can say hello to Christopher? she thought, her rebellious spirit starting to rise again. But she thought better of it as she didn't want to get Christopher into trouble. So she walked back to the kitchens with her basket of eggs over her arm.

"Mrs Riley has asked to see you. You better tidy yourself up a bit and somehow make that hair of yours decent," Mrs Watson ordered Beatrice the minute she walked through the door.

Beatrice was intrigued. She made her way up to Mrs Riley's study and politely knocked on the door.

"Come in," Mrs Riley said.

Beatrice walked in. She didn't curtsy. Mrs Riley liked that.

Mrs Riley's smallish stature and fair hair surprised Beatrice; she had expected to meet a tall woman with dark hair, but in fact, Mrs Riley was the opposite. Her maiden name was Benezet and she came from a long line of American-born Quakers. Mrs Riley, not only inherited a vast amount of money on her father's death, she also inherited the Quaker belief in equality amongst all men, including between men and women.

"So, the Highwaygirl has travelled far. I've heard a lot about you. A girl dressed as a boy, a girl riding like a boy or, should I say, a lady dressed and riding like a boy, how brazen. What rebellion."

"Well, I was angry about having to marry an earl I didn't love," Beatrice replied candidly. She was surprised at her own more informal tone.

"Well, that's no excuse for stealing but I can understand your frustrations; a loveless marriage can be quite despairing. After all, a marriage is for a long time so the preferred choice is to be in love for its duration."

"Please sit, Lady Seymour," Mrs Riley said without any hint of sarcasm in reference to Beatrice's title.

Beatrice sat confidently on the sofa in front of Mrs Riley. Beatrice noticed the quality of the furniture in her room. There were some Chippendale pieces, her writing desk for example, and some Hepplewhite pieces. The room was cosy, lavish and practical.

"I have a proposition for you, my dear. I hear you are a talented horse woman. Would you say that was a correct opinion?"

"Yes, I am a very capable horse woman," Beatrice replied succinctly. She couldn't wait to hear what Mrs Riley was about to propose.

"I like to partake in the odd bit of gambling, horses being my choice of preference. Next week, we have an informal race taking place here at The White House between some of the nearby estates and I'd like you to be our rider, represent The White House."

"Yes, I'll ride," Beatrice replied dryly trying to contain her excitement.

"Next week's race is just a fun race, a warm-up, shall we say, for a bigger race we are holding next month. It's not quite the Epsom Derby by any stretch but it will be a lot of fun."

Beatrice thought, how does she know about the Epsom Derby? Surely not! She felt it best not to say anything"

"I'll have to train with the horse as soon as possible."

"That's why tomorrow you'll go down to the stables and choose the horse you think will be the best. I'll send Thomas, the groom boy, to come and fetch you at nine o'clock."

"Yes, ma'am. I won't ride in my skirts," Beatrice added.

"Of course not. There's nothing more ridiculous than racing in a skirt. We won't say anything yet about you racing, you'll ride dressed as a boy, as a jockey. For now, just myself, you and the trainer will know. I'll see you on the track tomorrow."

Mrs Riley didn't want to create a storm yet. She wanted to tread slowly. Breaking beliefs had to be done softly sometimes, even surreptitiously. She thought it best to gauge the first fun race with Beatrice as a male jockey, and then if the circumstances were right, she would let Beatrice ride as the proud girl that she was.

Beatrice, even though now an indentured servant, was obviously still comfortable in the company of nobility and wealth. Mrs Riley wasn't from the nobility but she was from wealth. Beatrice hadn't lost any of her graces and looked at ease sitting on the sofa, albeit in her servant's clothing, talking with Mrs Riley. Beatrice had already played many a role; a debutante, a lady, a highwaygirl, a jockey and a maid. What could her next role be? Wife? Mother? she wondered as she talked with Mrs Riley. Beatrice hated boring and by no means was her life so far boring.

"Well, young lady, that will be all," Mrs Riley said bringing the conversation to a close. Beatrice stood up to see herself out.

"Ma'am," she said.

"Oh, and dear, I would read that book if I were you. Very enlightening," Mrs Riley emphasized the word enlightening.

"I'll try and find the time," Beatrice replied.

So the Duchess and Mrs Riley had already been talking, it was probably the Duchess's idea I ride, thought Beatrice. Well, I won't disappoint. But how did she know about the Epsom Derby?

THE RACE

AT nine o'clock, Beatrice was down at the stables. She took a deep breath in of the smell of horses. It was a beautiful summer day in Kentucky, it was hot and humid, Beatrice was already sweating. The staff back in the house were not too pleased to have Beatrice sent down to the stables, they needed her for the morning rush.

For the first time, Beatrice and Christopher saw each other. They gave each other big smiles but it wasn't the moment for embracing. He looked well, Beatrice thought. Thomas led her to the horses. The trainer came to join them.

"Barrow, William Barrow," the trainer introduced himself dryly.

"Miss Seymour," Beatrice replied, she instantly noted Barrow's reticence. "Mrs Riley has told me to find myself a horse. I'm just going to go to the field."

"I know what Mrs Riley has told you," Barrow replied curtly.

Beatrice then looked over at Christopher, smiled and walked out into the field where some horses grazed.

"Who does she think she is?" said Barrow, infuriated as he stayed back at the stables. "Most ridiculous thing I've ever heard. So she's going to race in man's clothes. What farce is Riley playing at?"

Beatrice walked into the field and went up to each horse one by one. They were all beautiful horses.

"You can't have a girl racing. A girl can't race. Just because she was some sort of lady or something in England," Barrow continued. "Well, out here that don't sit well. Look at her, look how she thinks she knows about horses."

Barrow was utterly indignant as he spoke to Thomas.

There was one horse that caught Beatrice's eye. Its head was the first to bob up when Beatrice approached, and whilst Beatrice was stroking a horse, she watched the mare pushing the rest of the horses around the field. She was the boss and Beatrice liked her.

"Feel like running in a race?" Beatrice said as she approached the mare.

The horse pushed her head into Beatrice's hands, playfully. Beatrice then had the sudden urge to swing right up on her back that very moment. She stroked her neck and then her withers, and in one swing, was up on her back. The mare stayed still and was totally willing. She was very playful Beatrice thought. She was small and seemingly unremarkable but Beatrice felt that playful spirit would make her fast on the track.

"Oh, in heaven's name, what is she doing?" Barrow said watching.

Beatrice had a little ride in the field, slid off and walked back to the stables. "What's her name?" Beatrice asked; she felt Barrow's anger.

"Girls don't ride horses, is her name," Barrow replied sarcastically.

"And her other name?" Beatrice asked looking directly at Barrow.

"Two socks," Thomas answered.

"I'd like to ride her on the track."

"I'll get her ready," Thomas said.

"No, I can do that if you like. Get to know her better if I do," Beatrice said. Beatrice walked off towards the stables, Thomas followed.

"She's trying to take our jobs too," Barrow whispered under his breath which was just as well as Mrs Riley walked into the stables.

"Good morning, to you all. How's she doing? Chosen a horse yet?" Mrs Riley was excited.

"Yes, ma'am. I don't think a girl riding is right, ma'am," said Barrow.

"That's for me to decide, Barrow," Mrs Riley replied curtly.

Thomas was showing Beatrice the tack for Two Socks when Christopher walked in.

"She looks fun," Christopher said, and when Thomas wasn't looking, rolled his eyes in reference to Barrow

Beatrice gestured back, she got it. It was so nice having him here, she thought. Christopher then got out a pack of cards from his pocket and waved them to her. Beatrice smiled and got that too. They must find a time to play.

Beatrice then changed into her breeches and walked out and onto the track. Mrs Riley and Barrow were already there. When she saw Beatrice in her breeches, Mrs Riley was inwardly triumphant. Beatrice warmed up Two Socks and then trotted her. At the starting line, she went into a full gallop and skidded around the track. It was a crude track, the corners were tight but it was fun and fast to ride, Beatrice thought. It would be a lot more precarious to ride when full of riders.

"She's fast, Barrow," Mrs Riley said closing her watch. "I must get Alexander to come and watch her on another day."

Barrow didn't reply. He was utterly enraged and detested the whole charade. Women don't jockey and they don't race and that's how it has always been done, he thought. Mrs Riley, of course, was thrilled.

"So, it's true," Mrs Riley continued. "This Highwaygirl is an excellent rider. We should have some fun next Sunday, Barrow, that's for sure."

Beatrice slowed and cooled down Two Socks and walked back to the stables and to Mrs Riley.

"Every day at the same time you practice. That was a good run but I think you can do it faster," said Riley.

"Yes, much faster. She's a little scattered but I presume she hasn't been ridden that much, has she?" Beatrice said looking at Barrow. "I'll get her riding lighter in no time."

"You've got to hit her harder on the bends and pull more on the inside rein," Barrow said asserting his position.

"That wouldn't be my approach, sir," Beatrice replied aware not to antagonise too much but still maintaining her status.

"Well, back to work, my dear," Mrs Riley said sensing the tension.

Beatrice went back to work. The gossip had gone round that she'd be riding in the fun race which mostly brought a good reaction. Her Highwaygirl reputation brought mainly admiration here in America. Beatrice didn't feel so vilified except by Mr Barrow. In fact, she felt celebrated here, which she did like.

Every day, Beatrice practiced at the track with Two Socks, and every day, Mrs Riley was there. Beatrice had become her muse, her symbol for female independence and she was enjoying every minute of it. Having Beatrice riding said more than words. Action spoke louder than words, Mrs Riley thought.

Mrs Riley actually thought against inviting Alexander to the practices and wanted to surprise him on the day. The expectation for Beatrice to win was enormous and tantamount to Mrs Riley's beliefs that women are as equal as men in certain endeavours. She shared her excitement with the

Duchess in her letters and only wished she was here to celebrate with her. She also shared her excitement, albeit a lot more reservedly so, with Beatrice. Mrs Riley adored both her and her abilities.

The day before the race, Beatrice clocked her fastest lap. Two Socks had channelled all her playfulness into the track and into her coordination, thanks to Beatrice's guidance. Having run the Epsom Derby, she was a little more experienced with the start-off and practised with Two Socks at the starting line. Beatrice repeated and repeated the start. She had two choices; either the fastest to leave the start line or the slowest. Beatrice knew Two Socks was fast enough to catch up if she was slow at the start and she knew she could hold her speed if she was the fastest out, but what Beatrice wasn't so sure about was how both of them would be in the melee.

Barrow, however, knew exactly where he wanted Beatrice and Two Socks to be and he talked to two other jockeys racing to make sure she would get knocked off. She was not going to win under his watch.

"Just get her off that horse. Do what you've got to do," Barrow said to Johnson, one of the jockeys.

"We'll do our best but I'm here to win as well, not get waylaid trying to get her down," said Johnson.

"Just do what you can. Where's Thomson? I need to speak to him too. You owe me, Johnson," Barrow replied threateningly.

Sunday morning arrived. Race day. The night before, Beatrice had hardly slept. She went through every scenario and visualised the race in detail in her mind's eye. Beatrice was so excited about the racing that she would have loved to have shared her secret with Ann, but for now, Beatrice racing was only between Mrs Riley, herself, Barrow and Thomas.

"Aren't you going to let it grow? All pretty and long. It's very boyish like that," Ann said curiously as they both woke in the morning-

"It's a lot more practical like this and cooler in the summer. Under my bonnet, you can't see much of it anyway."

Mrs Riley, the night before, could hardly sleep either. Personally, she had so much hinged on this race. Her beliefs for the most.

The other riders had all arrived early and had collected themselves around the track. Mrs Riley and Alexander were at the centre of the hub as it was their event. There was much pandemonium. Horses, carriages, people and grooms, no public, just friends and associates. The Rileys' stud breeding farm was one of the most respected in Kentucky and they supplied horses, not only to the army all over America, but to the most prestigious of the elite. For all the other estates, it was an opportunity to show their horses and themselves amongst Kentucky's wealthy society.

As the clock ticked, the anticipation rose. Beatrice had decided to use the tactic of getting first out of the starting line and avoid the melee. All the horses made their way down to the track. The hot summer air was thick with humidity and tension. The horses were getting nervous, the small, private crowd too, but most of all, was Mrs Riley. She stood under her summer umbrella with Alexander and waited, gripped with tension.

"I'm sure you are going to love your surprise. You remember the filly I gave you on your birthday, Two Socks, well, I think you are going to be very proud of her," Elizabeth Riley said excitedly.

Christopher raced down to the tracks. He just finished his last job in time. He wasn't going to miss this for anything.

"Come on, cousin, you can do this," he said to himself quietly.

It was hot and tense down by the track and it was getting a little fraught. The head steward shouted for everybody to get into their positions. Beatrice and Two Socks walked in to join the horse melee but went directly to the outer side, Johnson followed her and then, approached from behind, and with a stick, prodded Two Socks giving her a jolt that made her rear, she jumped and spooked to the side and into another horse, which then created a ripple effect along the line. Chaos ensued. Another jockey came in and did the same. They were now all over the shop, pushing and shoving, banging and bumping into each other, every rider trying to settle their horse. Beatrice had been taken totally by surprise, but instead of cowering, she was utterly enraged. She knew what Barrow was trying to do and she wasn't going to let it faze her. Two Socks was not so cool and was totally nerved by the whole thing. She had never raced before so such jostling completely rattled her. She was all over the place, rearing and bucking. Beatrice then decided to change her tactic.

"We're going to pull back, girl," Beatrice said in a soothing voice. "Sshh, everything is fine. We'll win, don't worry."

Beatrice calmly turned Two Socks as if walking away completely from the race.

"What is she doing," Mrs Riley was beside herself with tension. "What on earth is she doing?" Beatrice saw the steward approaching with his foghorn, and just as he put it to his mouth, she turned Two Socks back around to face the race. He blew loud and Beatrice bolted Two Socks into the race. Beatrice was last, but in the race. Those few seconds of walking away was enough to have calmed and collected Two Socks a little but it was not enough, she was still too scattered and emotional.

Christopher was incensed by what he had just seen. He knew instantly it was skulduggery and knew exactly who he thought was the culprit.

"Come on, B, come on, B. Get her more focused. Yes. Yes, that's it," Christopher encouraged from afar.

Elizabeth was beside herself with tension.

"Come on, Two Socks!" she shouted. "Come on, girls!" Alexander looked at Elizabeth.

"Oops. Just slipped out," she said with a cheeky smile. Elizabeth and Alexander's marriage was a love marriage.

Beatrice, by the first bend, finally collected all of Two Socks spooked energy and let the reins loose and her seat high and let her run.

"Run, girl, run!" Beatrice shouted.

Beatrice was absolutely hell-bent on not being defeated. She was utterly enraged by her saboteurs and would rather die than let them get the better of her. Two Socks felt this determined focus and she found that extra power that pushed them past the first group of horses by the second bend. But she had a lot of distance to close and not much track. Both Beatrice and Two Socks had a lot of grit left in them though.

"Come on, girl, you can do it, come on! This is fun!" Beatrice laughed as she said this.

This was exactly the trigger Two Socks needed. Beatrice harnessed her playful spirit and Two Socks galloped the hardest she could, she was slowly making ground, the lead pack were closing. The crowd was raucous and Beatrice could hear their shouts over the pounding of the horses.

Elizabeth couldn't shout any more, it was all too much. She just lowered herself, and quietly said, "Come on, Lady Seymour, come on."

As Beatrice came close to the rear of the lead horses, her hat fell off and her short hair fell lose. Only Elizabeth took in a small and hidden gasp.

"What game are you playing, Elizabeth?" Alexander said quietly.

"The game of equality, my darling. My favourite game of all," Elizabeth replied quietly but then couldn't help herself and shouted at the top of her voice. "Come on, come on!"

Beatrice swung Two Socks to the outside. The final line was in sight. Beatrice pushed on Two Socks and made the almighty leap forward and past the pack and into second position. The lead rider had gained his lead with a yard in front. Beatrice dug deep, Two Socks deeper. It was brutal riding. She could smell the other horse as she got closer. The jockey looked round and pushed his horse on. Beatrice was neck and neck, the sweat was flying and the final line was nearing.

"Argh! Come on!" Beatrice shouted as she pushed over the line. The other rider won by a nose.

"Yeah!, Yeah!" shouted Elizabeth. "Spectacular, spectacular. Did you see how she came from the back. Spectacular riding!"

"But she didn't win," Alexander said dryly.

"Oh, but she did. She proved her metal before and during the race. She came straight from the back, overtaking the lot of them. Incredible riding, Alec, and you know it and you can congratulate both horse and rider later," Elizabeth said confidently.

"How are you going to get round the whole girl riding in man's clothes?"

"Oh, I have an idea. See you back at the house."

Elizabeth then hurried to the stables to congratulate Beatrice.

"Scoundrels, ma'am. Two of the jockeys tried to get me bucked off before the race. I would have won," Beatrice said as she slid down from Two Socks, enraged at the skulduggery.

"I know you would've won, that's why I want you to race as the Highwaygirl in next month's race. Then you'll win. And we'll charge an entrance fee. And people can pay to come see the Highwaygirl race. It will be a big event. Oh, and please call me Elizabeth."

Christopher came bounding in.

"Cousin, what a race. All the way from the back," Christopher cheered with glee.

"But I didn't win."

"Oh, but you did. You didn't let them get to you. And anyway, sometimes, cousin, it's not always about the winning. You got Two Socks together and then pulled her up from the back."

"Excuse me, ma'am. In the excitement, I completely forgot my manners," Christopher said to Mrs Riley lowering his head in a soft bow. "Fine run, fine horse."

"Fine indeed. It will be even finer for our next race," Elizabeth excitedly said and left. Beatrice praised Two Socks, she had performed with her heart and with passion.

"Johnson and another jockey poked her with a stick at the beginning, just before the start, got her really riled. So much for a gentleman's sport," Beatrice said.

"Barrow was behind it, I know, but I'll keep an ear out and try to find some evidence," Christopher said.

Beatrice and Christopher walked Two Socks out of their camp and back up to the stables, when two women came running up to Beatrice.

"It's the Highwaygirl from England!" said one of the women. Other people then turned to look at the Highwaygirl.

"It was a girl riding!" said another.

"You best get back to the house. I'll take Two Socks back to her stables," Christopher said. Beatrice made a quick exit, changed quickly back into her maid's uniform and went straight back to work as normal. No fanfare, no ceremony, after all, she still was an indentured servant.

Elizabeth was jubilant and started immediately to plan their big annual summer horse race. It would still be between the neighbouring estates but those from much further afield would be invited. It would be double the size and on a much grander scale. But this year, it was going to be different for three reasons. Firstly, Mrs Riley will be charging an entrance fee, secondly, the Highwaygirl would be racing, and thirdly, this time, she would win.

THE HIGHWAYGIRL RIDES AGAIN

Eᴌɪᴢᴀʙᴇᴛʜ promoted this year's annual race to its full potential using Beatrice's infamy. Beatrice was surprised to find out that, here in America, her notoriety was not her downfall, it was, in fact, her salvation. Her celebrity had travelled far and everybody was curious about the English Highwaygirl. It was too tantalising for them to miss.

"You won't be getting any special treatment now that you're racing in the summer races, lassy," Mrs Watson said the day after her last race. The secret of her riding in the race hadn't lasted long and all the staff knew Beatrice had raced.

And it was true, Beatrice had to continue with her work as normal. It was hard and sweaty work. There was no time to miss Asta, her mother or read her book. She worked and she trained. She trained and she worked. There wasn't even time to have a game of cards with Christopher. No sneaking down to the stables at night for a game of Whist in the stables on a bale of hay.

But despite Mrs Watson's words, there had been a slight shift in attention towards Beatrice. The staff admired her; thought her both eccentric and brave. Most of all, they were amazed to watch the Highwaygirl in action. They knew she was going to ride as the Highwaygirl in the summer race so some of them managed a sneak a peek at her training. Some had even started laying bets on the race. But in the meantime, it was work, work, work for everyone. Beatrice did, however, get one or two secret pats on the back as she passed with the buckets of water or with the linens. Ann was the only one who was outward with her joy.

"Girl, you ride like a boy. I've never seen anything like it. You're a crazy one, Miss Seymour," Ann said laughing.

Meanwhile, Christopher was busy trying to find out anything about any looming skulduggery but he heard nothing. He too was busy. One night, Christopher was working late cleaning all the leather saddles. He had fallen asleep in one of the barns and woke to the whispering voices of some men. He stayed very quiet.

"Drug the horse two hours before the race. Put it in its food."

"But what if it goes wrong; too much or something?" said the other man.

"Just half a bottle, that will be enough to put her out for the day, it won't kill her, don't worry." Christopher knew that voice. It was Barrow's voice. Christopher couldn't believe it but was also not surprised. Barrow must really hate Beatrice racing, so much so, that he was willing to maybe kill a horse if too much of the drug was given, Christopher thought. The other voice, however, he didn't recognise. Christopher would have to stay vigilant.

Christopher worked not only as one of the stable grooms but also as one of the carriage drivers. He now held a pistol next to his lap. He now knew what it was like to be on the receiving end of a possible highway robbery. Thankfully, he hadn't had to use it, having never been stopped.

Christopher also got to know a lot of the guests that visited The White House, having to take them up and down, back and forth. He frequented the taverns and stage stops with his work and hoped to maybe recognise the voice of the other man Barrow was talking to. So far, no luck.

Beatrice kept her focus and kept working and training. She was excited to race and counted the days but was also nervous. The energy building up before this race was greater. The pressure for her to win, more intense. Beatrice would have to muster greater discipline to keep her nerves steady.

Beatrice trained Two Socks with every inevitability in mind. She practised the jostling with other horses but it wasn't really the same as the real thing. She was, however, glad for her trick riding years with Asta, as it gave her the strength to withstand some of the blows coming from other horses or riders. She practised the start, the moment when the starting rope dropped and the moment she pushed Two Socks forward as fast as she could, away from any potential fight in the melee. This track was fast and wild. The corners were tight and short and it had a fast downhill. After much training, Beatrice finally felt ready. Beatrice felt defiant.

One day coming back from her morning training, Barrow casually walked up to her. "This is a man's race, lassy, you'll be down on the first bend,"

"Is that so," Beatrice replied, remaining neutral.

"Think you're so high and mighty. You just watch your back because a lot of people don't want you to race."

If he was trying to intimidate her it didn't work. It only made her more resolute. I am going to win, this time I'm going to win, Beatrice thought.

The night before the race was rather raucous in the town. It was all full of people wanting to see the Highwaygirl run, wanting to see a girl dressed as a boy riding in a race. The taverns and boarding houses were full of people, packed to the rafters, celebrating and putting down their own bets. It was bubbling with excitement. Elizabeth hadn't needed to do much promotion as Beatrice's notoriety had done that for her as word of the race had spread like wildfire.

The White House was also full of guests. Elizabeth and Alexander had their friends with their horses staying at the house. Beatrice, along with all the staff, were run off their feet. Back and forth, up and down. Plates dropped and tempers rose, the whole household was prickly with anticipation. Beatrice overheard some of the staff making their own bets, just like last time. She couldn't quite believe it really. Why! So much fuss and excitement! She went to bed very late and was very exhausted.

Christopher still hadn't seen or heard of anything suspicious. He had been so busy, however, that he couldn't stay as vigilant as he wanted. He had asked the stable boy, Peter, to listen out for anything untoward.

On the morning of the race, Christopher tried to make sure his work was centred around the stables. Mid-morning, he was told to prepare Alexander's carriage, putting Christopher in a good place to eavesdrop on anything.

Christopher walked into the stables. He heard some rustling that suddenly stopped the minute he entered the big room. Christopher walked slowly down the corridor when, suddenly, a man ran out of a horse box on the left. Christopher dropped his things and ran after him, grabbed him and pulled him down. The man rolled over, got up and swung at Christopher, missing him. Christopher then tried to pin him up against the wall, the man, once again, lashed out and hit Christopher bang on the lip which bled instantly. Christopher hit back and they both fell to the ground in a tight and suffocating grapple. Christopher got a good look at his face, he looked nasty and definitely didn't look like anybody from around here. He had marks on his face. The man got himself out of their hold and kicked Christopher in the stomach a few times, Christopher couldn't help but coil inwards as a reflex, letting the man get away. He ran out of the stables leaving Christopher on the floor. The other horses were neighing and moving. Christopher got up and ran into Two Socks' box. She seemed all right but it was impossible to tell now if she had been drugged. He would have to wait until nearer the race. Christopher rubbed his bleeding lip and felt his bruised eye. He picked up the dropped halter and went straight back to Alexander's carriage. I'll have to check on Two Socks in an hour, Christopher thought as he ran, he was late.

Meanwhile, Beatrice woke early. She was keen for the race to get started. Her adrenalin was rising. She went straight to work.

"We're all betting on you, lass," said Mrs Watson. "Do yer best in winning, would ya, I could do with the extra pennies."

"Oh, I'll win," Beatrice said confidently.

The pressure was mounting on Beatrice. I could have easily said no to riding this race, Beatrice thought. But I just can't help myself.

"Off you go then," Mrs Watson said at eleven o'clock. "Here's something to make you run faster, some rum biscuits," Mrs Watson smiled and handed Beatrice the biscuits.

"Thank you, Mrs Watson. I'm sure these will do the trick. I'll make sure to have just the one before I run."

Beatrice then headed down to the stables, she was surprised to see Christopher and Peter. "What happened to you?" Beatrice was alarmed at Christopher's face.

"Took a hit from some intruder. Nasty looking man. He came running out of Two Socks' box."

"Two Socks?" Beatrice held her breath.

"Two Socks is absolutely fine, thanks to Peter," Christopher said and then turned to the next box showing her Scout.

"Oh, my goodness! What happened?" Beatrice was alarmed to see Scout on the floor. "Asleep or dead?"

"Asleep, thank the Lord!" said Christopher. "Peter changed their boxes. The perpetrator thought he was poisoning Two Socks. He's obviously not from here as he doesn't know the horses by sight."

This whole episode gave a strange feeling to the imminent race but Beatrice didn't have time to ponder. She went straight to saddle Two Socks and warm her up in the grounds behind the stables and away from the crowds.

The crowds were increasing. Elizabeth watched from her window as the fields around the track filled up with people and commotion. This would be an exciting day. This would be a memorable day. A day that would be written in local history. Elizabeth hoped, for the best reasons and not for the worst.

"Alexander, look! The Highwaygirl has brought quite a crowd. Never the like have we seen this before at The White House," Elizabeth was excited and nervous.

"Elizabeth, you will go down in history as the most outlandish woman I've known," Alexander said as he joined Elizabeth at the window.

"It will certainly be an entertaining race," said Elizabeth.

"Did you put enough stewards on at the entrance?" Alexander asked.

"I did. What were your bets? For her to win or to lose? Mine are to win, of course."

"I'll let you know after the race."

Everybody did all their betting amongst themselves, nothing official. This was, after all, still an informal and fun race, thoroughbred against thoroughbred, estate against estate. Elizabeth obviously wanted The White House estate to win but what she really wanted was for Beatrice to win and create a chink in people's rigid beliefs. A girl jockey winning a horse race.

The tension all over the grounds was palpitating. It was fever pitch amongst the different riders and their trainers and horses. It was nothing like the Derby though, Beatrice thought, it was chaotic, it was wild. Every estate had brought their best thoroughbreds with their best jockeys who were either servants or slaves. It was organised pandemonium.

It was time for Beatrice to walk down to the track. But she held back, her tactic was to arrive late and miss any confrontations. Beatrice was going to take advantage of the loose, if any, rules.

The horses were nervous and jumpy as the atmosphere got more charged.

Elizabeth and Alexander were down by the tracks. They had a private section cornered off.

"Where is she?" Elizabeth asked. She was getting nervous.

Christopher was by the starting line, he stood on a box so he could see better and higher. "Where is she?" he said to Peter.

All the staff were there. Nobody was going to miss the race of the century, literally the last race of the eighteenth century, July 15th 1799.

Still no sign of Beatrice. All the horses were on the starting line, spitting and anxious, raring to go. The waiting was agony for everybody and every horse.

Beatrice held Two Socks back, just by one of the tents. She held her calm, she held her focussed. Could Beatrice pull this off? She had to time it perfectly otherwise she'd fall too far behind. Beatrice watched the steward walk to the starting rope. Beatrice moved in a bit closer. Two Socks was calm.

"Where, in God's name, is she!" Elizabeth cried. "Alexander, I'm going to throttle her if she doesn't ride!"

The steward got hold of his flag, the tension was at fever pitch. The adrenalin of every rider and every horse was pumped to the full. Beatrice moved closer. The steward waved his flag down, Beatrice slowly cantered towards the starting line, still keeping her distance, holding Two Socks back. The horses were frothing to go, the tension was explosive, finally, the line dropped to the ground and all the horses exploded onto the track.

The crowd too exploded into a chorus of cheer. The horses pounded along the ground. From her position in the rear, Beatrice quickly caught up to the pack of horses. Her strategy had lost her three precious seconds but seconds she knew she could easily regain. She stormed ahead on the outside making sure to stay as far away from the horses as possible. But one of the riders came to her side and crashed into her, pulled her arm and tried to get her to fall. Beatrice tried pushing him off, she was losing time. Get off me, get off me, she thought. I'm losing time. Two Socks kept her gallop, kept her focus as Beatrice and the man grappled. This was wild, reckless and a free-for-all, this was brutal. Two other horses caught up with her, and from the outside, collided with Beatrice. Two Socks slid in the collision. Beatrice couldn't see a way out of this melee, she was trapped. They all took the tight bend, mud was flying up in the air. Feeling trapped and enraged Beatrice, took her hat off and swiped it across one of the rider's faces, he wavered a bit, just enough to give Beatrice the impetus she needed to bolt forward and out of the scramble.

"Come on, girl! Come on!" Beatrice cried as she pushed on Two Socks.

Now free from any foul play, Two Socks was in her element, she rode in her full glory and collected power. Beatrice had kept her safe and Two Socks now wanted to play.

"Come on, Highwaygirl, come on!" the crowd was ecstatic, screaming and shouting. Elizabeth could hardly contain herself, her whole being was electric.

Turf was flying up from the ground as the horses pounded up to the second bend. Beatrice, instead of taking it wide, decided to go in tight. She huddled up to the rear of the pack, it was a charging mass of horses and jockeys, sweat and adrenalin. She skidded around the bend but couldn't quite get past them all.

"Come on, come on, come on!" Elizabeth shouted, it was too much to bear.

"Come on, girl!" Alexander shouted, his cool demeanour finally cracked under the excitement exposing who he had secretly betted on. Elizabeth smiled.

"Come on, cousin!" Christopher shouted.

As they cornered the bend, Beatrice suddenly let go of all her desire of winning, let go of all her desire to prove herself and Two Socks felt it, it was as if she had become lighter, like a feather on her back. With this new energy, Two Socks glided past the lead pack, and as if galloping on air, stormed down the final straight. It was electrifying and the crowd went berserk.

Beatrice then took her lead. She owned it. She pounded down the straight. Beatrice sat high and glorious and let Two Socks gallop into the glory of the finish line. She burst over the line, the clear and victorious winner.

The crowd exploded into an almighty cheer. It could be heard from miles away.

"She did it, she did it!" Christopher shouted as he and Peter jumped.

"She did it, she did it!" Elizabeth screamed as she pushed her way out of her enclosure and straight through the crowds to get to Beatrice.

"We did it, Two Socks, we did it," Beatrice said letting out the longest and deepest of breaths. Everybody was euphoric; Beatrice, Two Socks, Christopher, Elizabeth, Alexander, the crowd, the list went on. The only person not celebrating was Barrow. He had watched the race in a pool of disgust. A woman rider and so brazen, it was utterly abhorrent to him.

The crowd clambered over each other and over the white fencing to get to the track and to Beatrice and Two Socks. They had certainly entertained as Elizabeth had predicted.

Beatrice couldn't quite believe the reaction. It was overwhelming as the people came running up to them, they just wanted to touch Two Socks and the Highwaygirl. Today, her alter ego didn't disappoint, it enlivened. Beatrice trotted around the track enjoying the attention. She was celebrating her own glory, no more secrets, no more disguises, just Lady Beatrice Seymour-Barclay, the Highwaygirl, in all her glory. Beatrice could feel Two Socks also enjoying the attention. Her head was high, her victory pure.

Beatrice came down to a walk and then headed back to the tents. The crowds still hovered. With some just walking next to her. Beatrice's euphoria was absolute. All of her prior hardships just paled into insignificance, this was her crowning moment and she basked in its feeling.

Back at the stables, Christopher came running up to her.

"You did it, B, you did it!" Christopher picked up Beatrice and swirled her around.

"Kit, I did it!" Beatrice replied jumping up and down. "And no hiding, no disguises, no shame. Glory be."

Elizabeth came rushing into the stables.

"What a wonderful thing vindication is. What a triumph. What a tour de force. Lady Seymour, I think you have just won your freedom. I only wish the Duchess could have been here to have seen it. Come up to the house and celebrate, join us in the main hall."

After some time, the crowds finally started to dissipate. Christopher had work to get back to and had to leave. The adrenalin was gradually calming as Beatrice cleaned Two Socks.

"We did it, girl. The ladies did it. Lady Two Socks and Lady Seymour. You flew out of…"

"They are good listeners, horses," a tall slim man said interrupting Beatrice.

Beatrice turned around and dropped her horse brush. The gentleman bent to pick it up for her. "William Russell is the name, ma'am."

"Beatrice Seymour."

"Quite the rider, quite the Highwaygirl, quite the lady. You have a lot of strings to your young bow. I was wondering if you'd like to add some more?"

Beatrice was curious but dubious. The gentleman seemed nice enough. Was dressed elegantly. He had the manners and grace but also the informality of the Americans. Beatrice carried on with her grooming.

"I have a proposition. Myself and two of my associates are embarking on a new and exciting project and we need riders of your courage and calibre. It's called the Pony Express and we will be transporting mail from Missouri to Sacramento. It will be revolutionary. And having the Highwaygirl launch its maiden trip is good publicity, is good for business. It will also buy you your freedom. Today, I will buy your freedom if you join."

"I already have my freedom bought, thank you, but it could buy my cousin's freedom."

Russell frowned. Beatrice's mind instantly raced to Christopher. If Elizabeth was true to her word that I do have my freedom, then this proposal could buy Christopher's freedom, Beatrice thought.

"Christopher?"

"I'll only do it if my cousin, Christopher, rides," Beatrice bargained.

"But I need the fastest riders."

"You will get the fastest riders. I assure you." Russell went quiet as he thought.

"All right. It's a deal," Russell put out his hand for a handshake. Beatrice reciprocated.

"I want an official contract," Beatrice demanded.

"You will both get a contract," Russell emphasized 'both'. "I will arrange for my lawyer to meet with you both tomorrow. It's been an absolute pleasure, Lady Beatrice Seymour."

Russell tipped his hat as he made reference to her title and then left.

Beatrice went straight up to The White House. It was a flurry of celebration and excitement. Beatrice stayed in her riding clothes and proudly walked through the kitchens.

"Hurray!" the kitchen staff cheered as she entered.

Beatrice couldn't help but burst into a jubilant smile.

"Well done, lassy! I'm not yet a rich woman but you won me a fair bit, so I'm a happy one," said Mrs Watson.

Beatrice went straight to the grand hall. She walked in to a grand cheer. For the first time in her life, she stood tall and proud, comfortable in her own skin.

"The Highwaygirl rides again!" shouted a gentleman from the back of the hall. Elizabeth approached Beatrice and gave her a big and informal hug.

"Kentucky needs to start its own official derby. Let us celebrate," Elizabeth called over one of the waiters. "Champagne for the lady."

It had been a very long time since Beatrice had drunk champagne. As she sipped, she thought how incredible it was. Here she stood, in her breeches and shirt, sipping Champagne and smelling of sweat and horses. This I like. Maybe only this could happen in America. Or maybe only at The White House, Beatrice thought.

THE PONY EXPRESS

CHRISTOPHER was only too happy to leave The White House and happier still he was now a free man. He didn't like Barrow, of course, and it was not a very nice atmosphere between the grooms and the coach drivers.

Immediately after the race, Christopher had gone to check on Scout to see if he had woken or was dead. He held his breath as he entered the stables. He looked over his box door and he was not moving.

"Come on, boy, come round," Christopher said.

Christopher felt his pulse, he was alive but he wasn't waking up. Christopher was fuming at Barrow and with his accomplice; he was glad to be leaving tomorrow. What an opportunity, what a Godsend, he thought.

Later that day, Christopher went to check on Scout, and to his utter relief, he was on his feet. "Lucky. You are very lucky," Christopher said to Barrow as he approached him in the stables. Barrow suddenly threw him up against the wall.

"You're the lucky one, boy. Lucky, I didn't drug you. You can't prove anything. Horses go down with colic all the time so you'd best keep your mouth shut, boy!" Barrow unfortunately was right, Christopher didn't have anything that could prove his guilt.

The next day, as promised, Russell's lawyer arrived and was ready to escort Beatrice and Christopher to town where they would start their journey to St Joseph, Missouri.

"I'll miss yer. I never shared a room with a lady before and one that wears breeches too," Ann said holding back the tears as they both hugged their goodbyes.

"Shame, I won't be winning any more on the races now you're goin'," Mrs Watson said. "Now yer look after yourself, lass. It's lucky you got your cousin there with ya. It ain't safe for a woman on her own, even if she is wearing breeches," Mrs Watson gave Beatrice a big hug and was genuinely sad to see her go.

Christopher was mounted and Beatrice was collecting her bag when Elizabeth walked out.

"You better read that book or I'll be calling you back. I'll miss the fun of the ride, my dear. You are free now so, however disappointed I am that you are going, it's your freedom to do as you wish with it. You caused quite a pandemonium, what fun it was! Do write, my dear. Tell me about your adventures," Mrs Watson gave Beatrice two kisses, she too was touched to see her go.

Beatrice then mounted her horse and all three walked down the long and grand road with its beautiful white fencing. Beatrice looked back for a last look, Christopher didn't.

At Elizabethtown, the lawyer left and two other riders, Col and Jeremiah, joined them. As they started out on their new adventure, it started to rain. Was this an auspicious start, thought Beatrice.

"Thank you, B," Christopher said as they walked out of town.

"For what?"

"For my freedom. Your race to freedom."

"Well, I didn't want to go alone, to be truthful," Beatrice threw him a look and a smile acknowledging his thanks. "Well, I believe it's the least I could do considering I got you into this mess. Remember, I promised I got you into it so I'd get you out. And besides, I couldn't survive without you."

Christopher threw Beatrice a look and a smile acknowledging her thanks, but in truth, he knew she would survive by herself, she was a survivor. I don't know how she does it, but somehow, she does, thought Christopher.

The rain fell hard; their coats and hats were struggling to keep it out. They all decided to stop under a big old cypress tree to take some cover as the worst of it passed. It was an enormous tree, mammoth, and Beatrice thought it must be hundreds of years old. How many things and people and changes it had seen? Always standing, always growing, always watching. Finally, the summer rains softened and they carried on with their journey.

It was a funny thing to be a prisoner or held captive. You may be going about your day without the wearing of chains but you wore imaginary chains around you. It always hung around you, the smell and feeling of being captive, Beatrice thought as she walked.

Today, Christopher felt utterly free. He was beholden to no one. No one could hang him, imprison him and work him without pay. The feeling of not being owned fell from his shoulders like a dead weight. He felt physically lighter as he walked. Today was his first genuinely new day. New land, new adventure. No criminal life, no gangs, no guns, no jails. My books will have to wait, for now, Christopher thought.

The landscape was incredible. Both sweet and quaint and grand and foreboding, all at the same time. Christopher wondered about the native people. Where were they? Where did they live? Pushed from their homes and lands, I can understand that feeling, Christopher thought.

The nights camped out were safe enough; they always kept the fire alive in case of wolves and bears. Beatrice and Christopher both loved to camp out at night. Back in England at Lacey Manor, as children, they used to do just that. Make their makeshift tents on the manor grounds and eat a picnic for dinner, care of Betty's best. But that was a far cry from camping out in the wilderness of Kentucky. The sky at night was an explosion of stars and night light, a northern star guiding them, a full moon giving them light.

A week later, they all approached St Joseph, Missouri. They could see its size from the hilltops as they approached. It was a big town, its river wide and powerful.

They rode straight to the Pony Express office. This was a grand and monumental venture. The founders, William Russell, Alexander Majors and William Waddell, promised to deliver the mail in record-breaking time. If you sent your mail with the Pony Express, it would reach Sacramento ten days quicker than the mail coaches, it promised. They were greeted by Russell himself.

"Wonderful, you made it. Go leave your horses with Adam and feed yourselves at Wiley's Hotel, say you're from the Pony Express," Russell warmly welcomed the cousins.

Beatrice hadn't bothered to wear her skirts. She wore her breeches and was expecting to get a few looks of disapproval, which she did. Her short hair didn't go down too well either, but in general, most people weren't bothered and paid her no attention. She was, after all, a free woman; free from jail, from a hanging, from her father's expectations. I can wear what I want to wear, she thought. But on seeing posters stuck up around town promoting the Pony Express's grand opening with the Highwaygirl from England, she did wonder if those looks of disapproval were actually more of curiosity.

The Pony Express Grand Ceremony.
The Highwaygirl, all the way over from England, will lead the first expedition out. Do Not Miss the Party.

"If that is meant to look like me, it's not a very good impression. I don't look anything like that," Beatrice said to Christopher.

It was true, the posters had Beatrice with her long hair and rearing up on her horse. They looked nothing like her convict posters back in England.

The town was bustling. People and carriages and horses were all busy with their lives, going back and forth. The buildings were mostly brick but a lot were of wood. It was still a fascination for the cousins to see the colonial style of building and the simple layout of the towns compared to their English villages and cities.

They ate their lunch at the hotel. A pianist was on the piano, the dining room was busy, big red curtains hung from the windows, it was simple but ornate. It all felt so, so different. Alone together as free people in another land. Everything had happened so quickly that it would take some time to process it all. They returned to the offices, once finished.

"Here is your contract. Sign here," said Russell matter of factly.

"You haven't mentioned money," Beatrice enquired.

"One hundred-and-twenty-five dollars a month."

They both signed. This was a large amount indeed, Christopher thought, the average person he knew got forty dollars a month. Christopher instantly thought of his bookshop, his printer, he still had his highway money. Christopher felt very optimistic. He was excited.

"We have the press arriving. They are eager to see the official inauguration with the Highwaygirl at the helm. You have brought much publicity, my dear, publicity we need. There will be a band and a lavish send-off. Promotion, promotion, promotion. So, tonight and tomorrow, rest and the following day you depart."

Beatrice and Christopher listened attentively.

"Here is your map. This is your lifeline so don't lose it. You'll be by yourselves out there. It's going to be precarious and arduous but you have proved your metal so far. There are one hundred-and-eighty-six stations along the route, ten miles apart. Change horses at each station. At night, sleep in the home stations. And you die before letting the 'mochilla', that is the mailbag, out of your sight. On pain of death, you do not lose this bag. It not only holds important letters but also telegrams of the strictest of secrecy and importance.

Your leg of the journey will stop at Salt Lake City where another rider will take over. You wait there for another rider to return and then you make the journey back. And that, ladies and gentlemen, is it," Russell concluded his instructions with the emphasis and a raising of an eyebrow on the word 'ladies'.

"Oh, and the last thing. Keep a lookout for Indians, snakes and bandits. The last one you'll both be familiar with," Russell said wryly.

It did seem an overwhelmingly daunting task ahead. The America Beatrice now knew was vast and dangerous. Back in England, she had never travelled further than her two nearest villages and London. She was wondering if she had embarked on a venture too big. For the first time in her life, Beatrice was worried about her abilities but she kept her worries to herself. It was, after all, she who had agreed to do this.

"Each man for himself when you are out there," Russell added as if reading Beatrice's mind. "We will supply you both with a pistol. You are both already familiar with those, I believe."

The day after next, the town was buzzing with excitement. The grand opening of the Pony Express was imminent. The newspapers were waiting. The crowd were waiting. Russell was waiting.

Beatrice and Christopher had their breakfast and filled their stomachs as much as they could. It would need to last. They also took some food for along the way. They walked down to the stables and got their already-prepared horses from Adam.

"Now, you keep a good look out for them pesky Indians, ya hear. You can't be too careful. These two beauties are fast horses, they should outrun any dangers. Just as well you dressed as a man, eccentric, but practical," Adam said.

The two cousins walked to the Pony Express offices where all the fanfare was and where they would set off from. Once again, Beatrice was the star event. She wondered how this could be repeating itself. Do I attract such attention on purpose? Or does it just come to me? Beatrice thought.

"Ladies and gentlemen, we are proud to wave our brave riders off with their bags of mail on this tumultuous and monumental and historic event that will go down in American history."

The band started to play and Russell waved Beatrice and Christopher to come forward. He handed them the 'mochilas'. They tied them down on their saddles.

"With your lives!" Russell said quietly to them over the noise.

"The Highwaygirl from England takes her first steps into the frontier!" shouted Russell, he then walked to the ribbon and cut it. Beatrice and Christopher galloped off. The crowds cheered and the band played triumphantly.

And that was it. They were off into the wilds of the American interior. What were they going to find? Would they come back alive? Beatrice was confused with the theatrics of their departure. This venture, after all, was not a show, it was real and precarious. This was going to be nothing like her English cross-country rides, her Epsom Derby or even the fun Kentucky races, this was going to be life or death. It was going to be endurance and stamina as she and Christopher had never known.

The cousins slowed their galloping after their dramatic departure. They had to cross the river, so they rode onto the ferry and waited for its departure.

"You have your money still sewn into your lining, don't you?" Beatrice asked quietly. Christopher nodded.

The river was wide and powerful. The horses held themselves steady as they rocked and swayed their way across.

"Bètter a river than the sea, no?" Christopher said.

"Any day," Beatrice replied letting out a sigh of relief.

Once safely on the other side, they walked their horses off the ferry and leapt into a gallop. They followed the trails on the map. It wasn't complicated; they followed the same trails well-worn by many a hopeful immigrant. It was tough riding because it was relentless, there was no time to stop. Now, all they thought about was gaining time and making miles.

They kept the horses at a strong and steady gallop. It didn't take long to reach their first station but they had no time to stop.

"Good day, to you, sirs. Well, madams and sirs. Nobody told me there was gonna be a girl riding. Not safe out here, deary," said Shorman, the station master. "Here are your fresh horses," Shorman handed them their new horses and took their tired ones.

And that was it, no stopping, no talking, it was back on the trail. Their horses were tough horses. Born to this hardy land. Different from the thoroughbreds I rode back at home, Beatrice thought.

They stopped at another station house, and once again, changed their horses. This was gruelling. They were already tired but just kept going. Mile after mile after mile.

By nightfall, they had their tenth station, Marysville station, Kansas. They were making good and fast time. Christopher was enjoying this. He liked it. It was relentless but he liked it. Once again, they changed horses and set off again. By late evening, they reached their home station. Finally, they were going to rest, and more importantly, sleep. They were both bone-numbingly exhausted. Nothing came near to this before in their lives, nothing.

"I got some grub ready for ya. You both look like you've been through the mill," said Monroe.

"Because we have, that was a lot of riding. Good evening, good sir," said Christopher.

"Here, nothing like a hearty meal to give you some strength," Monroe was warm and hearty like his food, and like his cosy wooden step cabin.

Beatrice certainly felt bedraggled. Her hands and face were dirty and her hair untidy. They were both so grateful for their host's hospitality. They were starving and beyond any ability for holding a conversation, so they ate, said their goodnights and slept with their mailbags under their heads.

The next morning they rose early. The aches and the pains of the day before were running through their bodies.

"I never thought my legs could ache so much," said Beatrice.

"Or my rear!" answered Christopher.

"Now, Godspeed," said Monroe. He was on the portly side. Rough-faced from a life living outside but very genial.

The cousins bolted off. Once again, they had a lot of ground to cover. As they galloped along, Christopher felt the insignificance of his every step. The land was audaciously enormous and they audaciously small in comparison, even daring to travel across it. Their trail took them into wider and more open land. And soon, after changing their horses for the eighth time, they crossed the state border and into Nebraska. A mountain range outstretched to their right. Plains unfurled in front of them. There was nothing but them and the land; no villages, no towns, just land, lots and lots of land. They were completely alone. They thought of bandits. But they kept galloping. They thought of the natives but they kept galloping. Mile over mile over mile. The sky was bigger still, the sun hotter. It was undoubtedly beautiful. Green plains and endless miles to cover. The Little Blue River lay ahead.

"I need to stop, Christopher."

"Yes, me too, let's stop by the river."

They took shade under a tree. The sound of the full river gushing over its rocks was soothing to their aching bones.

"Not far to go now. Ten more stations and then we stop," Beatrice said. "England feels a long way away, doesn't it."

"This land is so vast, very different. Smells different too. Do you like it here?" Beatrice asked. "I can't believe it's taken me so long to ask you that."

"Yes, I do in a strange way. I like how big it is. I like how new it is. And you, B? Do you like it?"

"It's certainly beautiful. Breathtaking actually but I like England."

"But England has been cruel to you, why would you like it? Look at yourself now, wearing your breeches, being who you are, you can't do that in England."

"I know. I suppose I feel untethered here," Beatrice replied thoughtfully.

"I still dream of my printer and bookshop," Christopher said tapping his waistcoat with his loot still in it.

"We did well, didn't we, Kit? I gave some to Michael and to Lilly, to Betty and to her poor nephew who lost his hand."

"Seems so far away now. England, the highway robberies. I can't believe we actually did it!"

"Do you remember the look on Staunton's face, still makes me laugh," Beatrice laughed as she remembered. "I can't believe he would've happily seen me hang, knowing his sister steals from some of the homes they visit. Outrageous hypocrisy. Asta, I think of her much. I hope she is well."

"Me too, I dream of Moby sometimes. Such clever horses. I used to read poems to him, can you believe it? He either thought me crazy or wonderful," Christopher said laughing.

"Wonderful, I'm sure, even though it pains me to say," Beatrice said smiling back.

The cousins rested for a while longer. The horses continued to graze on the lush green grass by the river.

"Time to go," Beatrice jumped up revitalised.

"Time to go," Christopher agreed.

They went and got their horses, swung up on top and then galloped back on the trail. They kept their focus forward, riding towards the next station. Christopher took mental note of the sweeping open land for his writings. One day, I will write about all this, he vowed. Make it lasting, make it memorable. At the next station, they changed their horses and set off again. This was highly physical riding, the constant galloping was exhausting, was pounding. Beatrice was in awe of their horses, their resilience and their strength. They, more than her, kept them going. They kept the journey driving forward. So far, no sign of natives or bandits, Beatrice thought. Our 'mochillas' are still safe.

Beatrice looked at the countryside all around her. It was undeniably breathtaking. It was both grand and small. What was this place she was in, America! Beatrice was trying to understand it. It was both old and new. The old and new clashing. The old was too old and the new was too new. Beatrice thought of England. She missed it. It was small, quaint and familiar. Despite all her rebellion, Beatrice liked the familiar.

They made two more station stops. The journey just seemed to go on forever. The sun was sinking when they approached two big boulders.

"Beatrice!" Christopher shouted loudly to Beatrice who was in front.

Beatrice was in an almost hypnotised state, having locked herself and horse into a steady rhythm and didn't hear Christopher's shout.

"Beatrice!" Christopher shouted louder.

This woke her up from her hypnotised state and she looked back, slowing slightly. "What? Come on, let's keep going!" Beatrice shouted back.

"Stop!" Christopher said as he slowed his horse. Beatrice slowed gently, turned and cantered back. "Just look at these boulders. Aren't they incredible?"

"Christopher, you stopped us to admire these boulders, we don't have time for that," Beatrice was annoyed but had to agree they were mighty.

"Magnificent and towering. I just had to get up close to them."

Christopher then walked up close to them and put his hand out to touch them. Their stone was solid and comforting to him. He turned his horse and walked back to Beatrice.

"So? Felt anything different than rock? It's not quite Stonehenge." Christopher threw her a look in response to her sarcasm.

"Sorry. No, you are right, they are quite remarkable. It's true," Beatrice softened her tone.

And just as Beatrice said that, out charged natives on horses from the other side of the furthest rock. The natives raced directly to them. The cousins, in an instant, swung their horses around and ran. There began a chase, horsepower against horsepower.

"It's impossible to outrun them, our horses are too tired," Christopher shouted over the noise of the horses' pounding feet.

"Let's turn and face them," Beatrice shouted back.

And with that, they both abruptly turned their horses, and facing their pursuers, slowed to a canter, then a trot and rose their hands high up in the air. The bandits continued to charge towards them and came to an abrupt stop when only a metre apart. The cousins held their breaths. Silence. Just the horses snorting and shuffling. Everybody was thinking, judging, assessing. The moment was pregnant with anticipation. Fear ran up the spines of the cousins. They had never seen anything like this. The natives in front of them looked wild, wild like the land they lived on. Painted faces, feathers, bones and teeth hanging from their necks, their horses painted with bright reds and yellows. It was both terrifying and fascinating. Incredulous even and a universe away from England. What was going to be the next step? Who would make the next step?

Two of the young men circled them menacingly with their horses. They looked powerful and deadly. There were five natives in total but it felt like a hundred. Nobody spoke. The natives kept circling and only stopped when one of the men assertively walked up to the cousins. Beatrice was scared, truly scared. Christopher less so. Beatrice sat frozen. They both waited. Time suspended.

The air was charged, one wrong move could determine a disaster. But for who? Beatrice sat frozen in utter fear but her mind raced. Should I get my pistol? They look so menacing. I feel very white and very English. They do feel very connected with their land. Should I move my hands and get some coins from my pouch? They belong here. The man on the right has a very big scar, did he get that fighting? Beatrice's thoughts were in a whirl, they raced back and forth, scrambling over each other.

Beatrice's horse suddenly started to fret. He was picking up on the tension. Beatrice stayed with her arms held up high and tried to calm him with her legs.

"Ssshh," she said. "Sssh, boy, calm," Beatrice lowered her arms as he wasn't calming and took the reins, the natives did nothing. She then went to get her gun and held it up in the air as a gesture of peace.

"Ocantu. Trade," Christopher suddenly said in Lakota, he wasn't sure if he had said it right. Beatrice's horse was still fidgety, it was spooking from all the tension and fear and uncertainty.

Beatrice, holding the reins in one hand, managed to steady him but she instinctively and without thinking lowered the pistol which was in the other hand. The natives reacted instantly and picked up their bows but Beatrice, not wanting to let go of the reins and her restless horse, decided, in a moment of rash thinking, to put the gun on her head.

"Ocantu," Christopher repeated as he too was trying to calm his now nervous horse.

The leader, obviously a man of great reverence amongst his men as both the cousins noticed how the men reacted to him, suddenly smiled. From the outside, the scene looked both fearful and comical. Beatrice with a pistol on her head, the horses jittery, Christopher trying to talk Lakota. The unexpectedness of their meeting together appealed to the Leader. He watched amusingly as Beatrice managed amazingly to keep the pistol on her head as her horse nervously fidgeted.

"Ocantu," Christopher repeated and looked at Beatrice and was surprised to see her with her pistol on her head.

The leader then said something in his native tongue gesturing to Beatrice. Christopher understood this as being something about her and her pistol.

"Ocantu," the leader then said.

The leader was an impressive sight. He had presence and standing. He always preferred to trade rather than fight. Christopher had said the exact right word. And Beatrice had done the exact right action, lightening the situation, the leader found it amusing.

The leader spoke in his native tongue to his men. He then turned his attention to Christopher. "Ocantu?" he asked Christopher, what did he have to trade?

Christopher understood the leader's intentions and went to get his pistol. The men went for their bows, the leader put up his hand to tell them to stop. Christopher then politely turned his pistol with its handle forwards and handed it to the leader. The leader inspected it. Christopher then held up his little pouch of ammunition and gestured with his head if the leader wanted this too, the leader nodded. The leader then nodded to one of his men who gave Christopher his bow. Christopher took it and instantly got a feeling run through him. The wood felt alive and lived. This bow and its arrows had definitely hunted, had it killed? thought Christopher. It felt warm in his hands as he put it over his shoulder.

"Thank you," Christopher said nodding his head in appreciation.

There was an awkward pause. Nobody moved. The horses blew out, the sun was hot. What happens now? thought Christopher.

"Gift," Beatrice suddenly said breaking the silence and holding out a ring. Christopher thought, what is she doing now? That's her mother's crusaders ring.

The leader nodded for one of his men to come forward and take it. The man then gave it to the leader, who once again inspected it. After his inspection, he smiled and looked at his men to give another bow but Beatrice waved her head expressing a no,

"It is a gift," Beatrice said as she gestured the action of giving. "Gift," she repeated.

"Gift," the leader repeated.

"Gift," Beatrice repeated nodding her head.

"Ku," the leader repeated back to her. The Lakota word for gift.

"Ku," Beatrice said and smiled.

The leader asked in his language for the two men enclosing the cousins to step aside. The two men did and made space for them to leave. The leader then gestured with his arm to Beatrice and Christopher that they could pass.

"Gift," he said, their freedom was his gift.

"Thank you," both the cousins said in unison.

They were both somewhat humbled by the whole encounter. There was no arrogance in the leader's gesture. The cousins slowly walked off, no need for a fast escape. They were both shocked and mystified by the whole incident. Beatrice wanted to look back but thought it best not to, Christopher did. He saw the little band of natives still standing in their same positions looking at them walk away.

As the cousins walked back on the trail, they were a little lost for words. Christopher thought how they blended so completely with their surroundings, more so than the Europeans. It was definitely their land.

"Beatrice, what did you just do? You just gave away your mother's heirloom. You could have given them your pistol," Christopher was bemused rather angry. He had seen Beatrice do some spontaneous things before. But nothing like this.

"Better to be friends than enemies," Beatrice replied awkwardly.

"True but what got into you? And the pistol on the head. You were acting so strange."

"I was scared, Christopher, petrified, if the truth be known. I don't know, I panicked. "What about yourself? Where did you learn their native tongue?" Beatrice tried to turn the attention from her.

"Back in St Joseph at the Pony Express headquarters. I found a book and thought learning a couple of words would be useful."

"Well, it was, very useful indeed," Beatrice affirmed. "We best ride hard, to make up for lost time." They were both rattled by the whole incident; Beatrice because she was angry with herself for having been so fearful and Christopher because he was deeply touched by the connection he had made. Two different peoples completely divided yet completely united. They seemed so mysterious to him and totally intriguing.

The cousins galloped hard, instead of breaking gait to a canter they made up for lost time by staying in a gallop. It was getting dark. A sky full of stars lit up the sky. Skies in England are not this big, it's simply breathtaking, thought Christopher. They were nearing their home station, they kept their heads focused and their aches and pains hidden.

Finally, they arrived back at their last home station, Rock Creek station, it was very late when they arrived and they were both utterly exhausted. Bones, muscles, emotions were all completely shattered.

"Friends, come in, come in, you both look tired and saddle weary," the station master said welcomely; he was happy for the company.

The cousins put their horses away and then went back to the wooden cabin. It was simple and basic. It had a bed and food which was all the cousins could want for.

They both flopped into their chairs utterly exhausted. They looked tired and weather-beaten.

"I wasn't expecting a woman to be riding. That is not quite the normal thing. It's dangerous riding. I'm amazed you've come this far," John Baxter said as he handed them two big bowls of stew.

"The weaker sex?" Beatrice said sarcastically.

The cousins ate like starved people. John couldn't help but notice how refined their manners were. "I also weren't expecting no English folk either, come to think of it," John was in the need to talk but the cousins just couldn't muster the energy for polite conversation.

"What bought such folk like yourselves to these parts?" John pursued the conversation.

"Highway robbery," Beatrice replied dryly, too tired to elaborate.

"So, you were on the wrong side of the law. Well, everybody deserves a second chance. But what's a young lady like yourself doing with highway robbery? Seems mighty odd," John continued.

"Marriage," Beatrice replied.

"Yes, well, a marriage could do such a thing to a person. My wife…" John continued talking, just happy for the company.

The cousins let his voice fade into the distance as they ate. After food, they both collapsed into their humble beds.

Morning woke them early. Rested, Christopher and Beatrice met the new relief rider, Jack Thomas, and the station master for breakfast. The cousins handed over the mail bags to Thomas. It was like handing over the baton in a relay race. It was now over to Jack to continue the race. The cousins, for now, had done their bit.

Jack got his fresh horse, and at the crack of dawn, galloped off. The cousins now had to wait for his return and the new, returning mail bags, they would be returning them to St Joseph.

There was nothing much to do which was exactly what the cousins needed. Beatrice sat out on the verandah and looked around. She was a free woman. No marriage, no prison, no father. But what am I going to do with this freedom? Where do I live,? What do I do? Beatrice thought, she felt completely lost. She had fought hard for and risked much for this new-found freedom, but now that she had it, she didn't know what to do with it. All her life she was so used to rebelling against something that now that that something had gone, she felt lost without it. All Beatrice had ever had in her life was a reason for her to rebel and now, without it, everything felt strange. Being here in this new land only made her lost feelings feel all the more lost, all the more untethered.

For the first time, Beatrice had time on her hands. She went to her bag and got out the book Mrs Riley had given her and started to read.

Christopher started to write. He wrote down notes of the past events and drew rough sketches. His mind was abuzz with inspiration. Christopher, on the contrary, was not lost. He found inspiration wherever he looked and the thought of his bookshop seemed closer still. He felt motivated and driven. He felt excited for the first time in years. He had his freedom and he knew exactly what he wanted to do with it. Here, in this new land Christopher felt tethered.

The four days of waiting for their rider passed quickly. Jack arrived tired and weather-beaten but safe. He handed over the mail bags. They were heavy, too heavy for one rider. There were more on the way back taking advantage of the cousins being two riders. The cousins had gotten friendly with John over the last few days, but now, it was back to business. They had a schedule to keep and letters to deliver. The cousins readied their horses.

"Well, it's been a pleasure knowing you both. First time I met a lady who was a highway robber. Don't meet many of them," said John as the cousins mounted their horses.

"Thank you for your hospitality, John," Christopher said.

"Now, you both travel safe, do you hear, can't be too careful out there," John said.

And that was it. They both galloped off and back onto the trail. Their horses were fresh and fast, so were they. Their time resting had paid much dividend. They felt almost back to life, bones soothed, muscles relaxed, but now, it was back to the grind.

They were riding at a steady canter when they, once again, approached the two big rocks. No sign of the natives as they cantered past, they slowed a bit. They rode just past them when, from out of nowhere, Christopher's horse reared. It neighed and spooked and reared again. Christopher was thrown from his horse and fell to the ground.

"Argh!" Christopher shouted.

Beatrice turned back and went straight to him. She swung down from her horse. "Christopher! Are you okay?" Beatrice asked alarmed as she bent down.

"I'm not sure," Christopher said groaning.

Beatrice's horse started to get jittery. She stood up and tried to calm it. She had to try and calm her horse before helping Christopher. Once her horse was calm, she then went to go and get Christopher's horse which had spooked off towards the rocks. As Beatrice approached she was slightly tentative. Were the natives there? Would they be friendly today?

"Sssh," Beatrice calmly said to Christopher's horse as she got hold of its halter but then her horse got jittery again and started to circle and twist and turn which, then, set off Christopher's horse. They were banging into each other, and a few times, into Beatrice; it took her some time to get them to calm. Finally calmed, they all walked immediately back to Christopher.

"Christopher! What's wrong,? What's the matter? What's happened?" Beatrice said frantically as she approached; he had turned completely white.

"I feel terrible, B," Christopher said weakly. Beatrice stroked his forehead, he was very hot.

Looking very, very white and burning up with a fever, Christopher lay on his side on the ground.

Beatrice went white herself, she panicked inwardly, worry enveloping her. What can I possibly do out here? she thought. We are totally alone. I know nothing about what to do or what to give. Beatrice felt herself escalating as their situation became more dire.

Christopher was starting to shake. Beatrice couldn't bear seeing him like this. Could he die? She thought desperately. The thought of this brought on uncontrollable sobs.

"Christopher, I don't know what to do," she said through the tears. "I'll try and find you some shade at least."

Beatrice went and got the blanket from her horse, and with four sticks, made a makeshift shade. She sat next to him utterly helpless. I can't just watch him die, she thought. The tears came flooding back.

In the desperate need to do something, Beatrice went and pulled the heavy western saddle down of her horse and folded the saddle pad and put it under Christopher's head. At least he is comfortable. Beatrice thought.

"You absolutely cannot die, Christopher, I absolutely forbid it, you cannot leave me here alone. Do you hear me, Kit?" Beatrice spoke passionately through her tears to a semi-unconscious Christopher.

"After everything we've been through. The highway robberies, the escape, the capture, the jail, the death pardon, the journey across the Atlantic, the Americas, and through all of this, Christopher, you've never been ill or injured, always stoic and strong, steadfast and stable. And now here in the middle of nowhere, I forbid you to die, do you hear me!"

The tears just came streaming down her face. Beatrice held his hand, he looked positively terrible, white, shaking.

"What could have done this? I bet it was a bloody snake. This God-awful dangerous country. Russell said to be vigilant about the snakes." The very real thought of Christopher dying here in the middle of nowhere came flooding back to her thoughts and Beatrice couldn't contain herself and sobbed uncontrollably into his chest.

"I beg you, Christopher, don't die, I love you, cousin, you are all and everything I have, please don't die."

Beatrice was suddenly bolted out of her heartbreak when her horse startled and ran up behind the rocks. Beatrice got out her pistol and lay it next to her. She had to protect Christopher and herself. Adrenalin suddenly kicked in. But she also had to retrieve the horse, they needed it, so Beatrice got up calmly, wiped away her tears and walked towards the rocks to find her horse. Christopher's horse followed her. She walked around one of the rocks, and suddenly, saw two natives calmly approaching, then three, then the leader from the other day. She stood still. She then went and got hold of

Christopher's horse but it escaped from her grip and ran up to the native group approaching her. Beatrice stood facing them and waited. She watched them slowly approach. What mood are they in today? She thought. I need their help. Beatrice swung up on her horse to give herself better defence just in case she had to run.

They got closer and closer until, finally, they stood in front of her. One of the men held Christopher's horse and walked towards her, handing its reins to her.

"Thank you," Beatrice said cautiously.

Beatrice then took the next step. She needed their help. She said a quick and silent prayer that they would help her. Then she waved for them to follow her. She pointed in the direction of Christopher and then mimed he was sleeping. Beatrice led on. She hoped they would follow. They did. The whole gang walked tentatively back out from behind the rocks and towards Christopher. On seeing Christopher, the leader said something to his men. Beatrice looked around to them and pointed to Christopher.

"Ill, he is very ill," Beatrice said even though she knew they didn't understand her words.

They were walking very slowly Beatrice thought. Her heart was racing and she just wanted to run straight up to him but she walked slowly with the gang.

Once they reached Christopher, Beatrice urgently jumped down from her horse and kneeled next to Christopher. She waved for any one of them to kneel next to her.

"Ill, very ill," she said again. "Can you help us?"

The leader was the first to get down. He knelt next to Christopher and felt his forehead. He then said something in his language to his men who proceeded to dismount and go to Christopher. They lifted him up weightlessly. They heaved him up on the back of a horse behind another rider. The rider tied Christopher to himself. They have done this many times before, thought Beatrice.

The leader stood up. What he lacked in height, he certainly made up for in presence, thought Beatrice. He spoke to her in his language, gesturing for her to come with them to their village on the other side of the rocks. Beatrice nodded. She had nothing to lose, she trusted them.

Beatrice quickly gathered their possessions and saddled her horse, she checked the mail bag on her horse and gave it an extra tug for better security. Christopher's horse was now being held by one of the natives, Beatrice looked over at it and saw that Christopher's mail bag was also still tied on. Beatrice could hear Russell's words 'on pain of death, do not lose those bags', could his words actually be coming true? Beatrice thought. She swung up on her horse and nodded to the leader. Slowly, they all walked back towards the rocks. Beatrice walked a little behind. She was frightened and nervous but had no choice but to trust them.

Beatrice gradually caught up with the little gang. Would she be safe? Would they help Christopher? She walked next to one rider, his hair was black and long. He had armbands on and bones hanging and paint on his chest, he looked so different, he looked so wild, Beatrice kept thinking. He looked at her and smiled, she smiled back nervously. He said something to her, the words felt kind, his tone felt kind, he felt kind, she thought. But could they save Christopher? The little gang walked on slowly. Christopher slouched, lifeless behind his rider. Please save Christopher, she begged.

THE GIFT

THEY all entered the village. Tipis everywhere, people everywhere, the little village was busy full of life. Children running around. Animal skins drying, women cleaning by the river. It was a harmonious sight.

All the children ran up to them as they entered, smiling and cheering. The two strangers were obviously a surprise. They were greeted by a small group of men and women. The leader told them to take Christopher down from the horse. Christopher was untied and the two men held his dead weight and then carried him to a tipi.

Beatrice didn't wait for her instructions, she instantly got down from her horse and followed Christopher into the tipi.

The smell of the tipi hit her smack in the face the moment she entered. It wasn't horrible, it was different. Musky and intense. The air was smoky. Smelt totally new to her. Lacey Manor could be on a different planet compared to this, she thought.

Christopher was gently laid down and an old lady gestured for Beatrice to sit down.

The old lady must be their healer, Beatrice thought. She was small and rounded and wore lots of ornaments around her neck. Her hair was long, grey and braided. She was both warm and matter-of-fact. She was calm, didn't rush and Beatrice felt a humility run within her wisdom.

She felt Christopher's forehead, she asked the men to take off his shirt, and then with a cloth, wiped over his body. She lifted his arms and wiped them all over, his chest and his head. She then asked the men to take off his trousers. She was looking for something that she hadn't found in his top half. She then asked them to roll him over onto his front. She continued her inspection, she knew exactly what she was looking for but found nothing on his legs. She looked over his back and found exactly what she was looking for. She had done this a thousand times before, it seemed.

She then took some different leaves and ground them to a paste, adding some liquid periodically. This was all done in silence. Everybody in the tent just watched. Christopher was in her healing hands now. The healer then got out a knife. Beatrice took an inward gasp. Christopher was sweating, his back was covered in sweat. The healer then rubbed some of the ointment from the pestle and mortar onto two very distinct black marks. She rubbed the area and then, in a second with the knife, cut cut the black marks. Beatrice barely saw it, it happened so fast.

On the healer's instructions, the men rolled Christopher back on his back. Christopher was still white and still sweating, there was hardly any blood either, Beatrice thought.

The old lady took a cluster of leaves and lit them, blowing onto them until they smoked. Beatrice was spellbound with the whole process, but will it save Christopher? she thought. The healer then made circling motions with her bundle and started to chant a quiet and low song. She blew the smoke all over Christopher whilst singing her song. She kept her song rhythmic and repetitive. She went back again with her smoking bundle waving it all over Christopher. Beatrice found her eye lids getting heavy, she was being lulled and soothed herself.

The lady then poured some of the herbal liquid into a cup. She asked one of the men to raise Christopher up. He was so limp, it broke Beatrice's heart, in all her life she had never ever seen him like this. Please make him better, she begged.

The healer slowly gave as much as she could to Christopher who choked at first, but gradually and slowly, swallowed it. She also used a spoon to guide it into his mouth. The man lay Christopher gently back down. Beatrice's eyes were desperately trying to close, the whole healing was so relaxing, Beatrice felt drugged by it. She forced her eyes to stay awake. Christopher was safe but was she? Beatrice couldn't completely relax and trust these people.

The healer took a small round drum, and once again, sang a chant along to the beats of her drum. It was all Beatrice could do to stay awake. The chant went into a trance, the healer went into a trance, Beatrice herself went into a trance. She prayed whilst the healer sang.

The healer stopped and put down her drum, she once again touched Christopher's forehead. The Healer pulled out from under her deerskin a necklace. Beatrice gasped to herself, she couldn't believe it. She was instantly brought out of her relaxed and trance-like state. It sparkled in the dim light of the tipi. The Healer held up her mother's gold and emerald ring that now hung at the bottom of a chord, and with the smoking bundle of herbs, waved it slowly all over Christopher. She kept her eyes closed, and this time instead of singing, she spoke what seemed like a prayer to Christopher. She then looked directly at Beatrice for the first time and smiled. She spoke in her Lakota language to Beatrice, and with her gestures and tone, Beatrice understood it to mean that he was better. She then mimed with her hands a snake action. So, it was a snake bite, after all, Beatrice thought. It was the snake that had frightened the horses too.

Christopher seemed calmer. He was still unconscious and still white but the sweating and shaking had stopped so Beatrice felt a little hopeful.

The old lady gestured for Beatrice to leave. Beatrice shook her head. The Healer shook her head and gestured to the door. Beatrice shook her head. The Healer shook her head. They stood facing each other.

"Winyan napeyuze," said the Healer.

The old lady shrugged her shoulders and gestured for Beatrice to go sit next to Christopher.

"Thank you," Beatrice called after the Healer as she walked towards the door.

"Gift," the Healer said as she turned to Beatrice and smiled. She then turned and walked out. Beatrice sat down next to Christopher and let out a big sigh.

"The rest is up to you," Beatrice said quietly.

Beatrice then got a blanket, covered herself and lay down next to Christopher. She was utterly exhausted. Her body ached, her heart ached. Rebellion came at a high cost, her rebellion had come at a high cost.

The early morning movements of the village slowly began to wake Beatrice. At first, they were distant rumblings: children laughing, people talking, horses neighing. But as she became more awake, these noises got louder and so did the realisation of where she was. The first thing she did was sit bolt upright and check Christopher's forehead. He looked better. Some colour had returned, his fever had gone and his breathing was better. Beatrice closed her eyes and let out a long and slow sigh.

Beatrice was starving. Her stomach ached from hunger. It was time to face the world that was outside. She pushed open the deerskin door and was blasted by the sunlight. She covered her eyes from its impact. Once her eyes had adjusted, she looked upon this small and bustling village. A beautiful river lay ahead and its calming rhythms. To her right, were the horses in a makeshift corral.

"Oh, my goodness, the mail bags. I didn't take the mail bags off," Beatrice said to herself.

She walked quickly straight to the horses. Beatrice sighed an enormous sigh of relief as she saw both of them still tied on to their horses. But on looking closer, immediately gasped in panic. Christopher's mail bag had torn and some letters had fallen out.

Beatrice didn't have time to think as a group of children came running up to her. Laughing and touching her; totally uninhibited and talking to her in Lakota. Their joy was so contagious Beatrice couldn't help but be uplifted. I'll go back and find the dropped mail when I find a good moment, thought Beatrice. The children were so adorable, thought Beatrice. It brought a rush of love and warmth to her. I'd like to have children one day, she thought. Some women came over with their babies in carriers on their backs. They spoke to the children in Lakota and nodded to Beatrice but were more reserved than their children.

Beatrice smiled at them. She really didn't know what to say.

"Your babies are beautiful," she finally said pointing to the women's babies. The women smiled and nodded. The women spoke to their children.

"I dropped my letters," Beatrice mimed to them showing the mailbag.

One of the women pointed to a man to her left and spoke to him in Lakota. Beatrice understood it to be that he'll go with her to find the letters.

"Yes, that would be very good," Beatrice nodded and smiled.

It fell silent again. Beatrice was sure the women had come over, in part, to be with their children, but mostly, to come to see her. They were as intrigued about her as Beatrice was about them. They were beautiful, Beatrice thought. They had long dark braided hair with colourful ties running through them.

Their clothes were of deerskin and had beads sewn into their tops. They looked very feminine and very different from English women, they look comfortable, Beatrice thought.

"I better get back to my cousin," Beatrice said pointing to his tipi.

The women nodded and smiled, one of the little babies gurgled and put her chubby little arm out to touch Beatrice.

"You are very clever holding on so tightly to your mama," Beatrice smiled as she took the little baby's hand. It was so sweet it gave Beatrice a rush of love.

"What is its name?" Beatrice asked gesturing to the baby. "My name is Beatrice," Beatrice said patting her chest.

"Weeyaya," the mother said smiling broadly.

"Weeyaya," Beatrice replied returning the smile. "What a beautiful name for a beautiful baby. I better go back to my cousin, Christopher," Beatrice said again. "It was so lovely meeting you all," this seemed overly formal considering where she was but she didn't know what else to say. "Goodbye!" Beatrice said to the children. "I hope to see you later." This was true, Beatrice did hope to see them later. She enjoyed their company, enjoyed being around them, they made her feel relaxed and light hearted.

Beatrice walked back to Christopher's tipi holding the mail bags. She walked slowly trying to absorb her surroundings. Am I really here in such a foreign place. It was the complete polar opposite of Lacey Manor and of England. Life as a debutante, and even as a highway robber, seemed a million years ago. But although so drastically different, she thought this place, this village beautiful. It felt harmonious, natural. The river lay to the bottom of the village and Beatrice could just hear its trickling. I'd like to go down there later, she thought.

She walked into Christopher's tipi. It was warm and smelt musky. The incense and herbs hung in the air. Christopher was still asleep. He looked much better, Beatrice thought. She lay back down under her blanket next to him and looked at all the paintings on the tipi walls. There were horses and their riders, animals, the sun and the moon. She let the sounds of the village and the river in the distance lull her into a sweet doze.

A snake reared up and then another and another. Her father walked out with Staunton and they laughed and shook hands and Staunton got a rope and tried to put it round Asta's neck. Asta reared and bucked until finally free. Asta galloped across the fields free, a carriage with her mother and father lost a wheel and fell to one side. Beatrice then woke up in a startle and with a horrible feeling. Asta, she had just dreamt about Asta, riding free over the fields of Lacey but was she really there, was she really alive? And then seeing her parents together in a broken carriage. It left her with a very strange feeling.

"B?" Christopher said very faintly. "Beatrice, the mailbags, have you got the mailbags?"

"Christopher, you're alive. How do you feel? Oh, thank goodness, you're better, thank goodness," Beatrice said.

"The mail bags?"

"Yes I have them, everything is fine," Beatrice reassured Christopher.

"The horses?"

"Fine too. We are in the village of the native people. They are looking after you. You got bitten by a snake, Christopher. You are better now," Beatrice was so profoundly happy to hear Christopher's voice that tears welled up in her eyes.

"You go back to sleep. I'm right here next to you reading. I have to say this book Mrs Riley gave me is a bit boring. The equality of women is good but it's just a bit boring to read about, more fun doing it," Beatrice said, Christopher smiled.

Beatrice stayed a while with Christopher, he went back to sleep. Now she knew Christopher was better, she felt it was the right time to go and find the dropped mail. She was now worried about their journey back and getting the mail delivered safely. They would obviously be arriving late, missing their deadline by a few days. I bet they are getting worried about us though, thought Beatrice. Beatrice put her book down and ventured outside. She went to look for the kind-looking man whom she rode into the village with.

Everybody looked as she walked slowly around the village. Beatrice felt quite self-conscious, she smiled at whoever looked. She felt so unbelievably out of place. She walked past some women cooking. One was cooking in a big pot hung over a fire, they all looked at her warily. This made Beatrice think of Betty cooking her stews in her big pot over the fire. The same action but on completely different sides of the world. We are all the same really, thought Beatrice.

It was quite a big village, maybe perhaps eighty people. Beatrice couldn't find the young man anywhere and wasn't quite sure what to do, so she went straight to the horse corral.

Once at the corral, a beautiful paint horse rose its head and slowly walked straight to her. "Aren't you beautiful," Beatrice said as she stroked its soft nose over the wooden pole. Another horse became curious and came to say hello, then another.

"Sorry, I don't have any carrots. Do Native horses eat carrots? Of course you do, but I don't see any carrots around here." Beatrice spoke quietly to the horses.

Suddenly, they all turned their heads in the other direction, Beatrice followed where they were looking. They had seen the leader and the young man approaching on horseback. Beatrice turned to face them.

"You have beautiful horses," Beatrice found herself saying, she didn't really know what to say. They stood in silence and looked at her.

"Thank you for helping my cousin," Beatrice pointed to Christopher's tipi.

"My name is Beatrice," Beatrice said tapping her chest. They still sat silent. "I am from Surrey, England," Beatrice mimed a ship sailing on the sea.

Beatrice then climbed into the corral and went up to her horse.

"My mail bag, mochilla, I have to find some letters," she mimed her actions in the hope of them understanding.

The leader said something to the young man but didn't move.

"Wait a minute," Beatrice put her hands up to express for them to wait. She hoped it wasn't in any way disrespectful to them.

Beatrice ran to Christopher's tipi. When she entered he was awake and a young woman was sitting next to him with a pestle and mortar. Beatrice didn't have time to stop, she picked up the broken mailbag and ran back out. Thankfully, the men were still there at the corral.

"Mailbag," Beatrice showed the broken mailbag and mimed all the letters on the floor. "Letters lost. I need to find the letters."

The leader nodded and pointed to the paint horse Beatrice had been stroking. He then waved his head for her to come with them.

Beatrice threw the mail back over her shoulder. She had temporarily mended it with some string. She then climbed into the corral and swung up on top of the paint horse bareback. She stroked his neck. The young man went to the other side of the corral and brought back a crude rope halter. He got down from his horse and put it around Beatrice's horse's bottom lip and then over his head. This was the simplest form of a bridle Beatrice had ever seen. He swung back on his horse and the leader turned and walked away, everybody followed.

Once again, everybody looked as the trio slowly walked out of the village. Beatrice liked bareback but not enough to suffer its discomfort. Her horse's back was bony, Beatrice was bony; she was used to Asta's fuller, fatter back. She didn't complain, she was too grateful to be guided back to the accident. But am I safe? Can I trust them? Maybe they are leading me somewhere isolated? Beatrice's heart raced as fear started to envelop her.

The pair were in front and spoke at moments in their language. Maybe they are plotting my demise? Maybe they are plotting to steal from me? I can always gallop back to the village if I need to, Beatrice was trying to calm her racing heart.

They finally reached the two enormous rocks. They quietly and slowly walked past them. The bags must have fallen when the horses got spooked, Beatrice thought.

Once on the other side of the rocks, Beatrice slid down from her horse, held the reins in her hand and started to scour the ground. She walked slowly and methodically but there was nothing where Christopher's horse had reared. She went to the left, then the right but nothing. It was quite windy today, maybe the wind had blown them afar, thought Beatrice. The leader and the other man waited and watched her. Beatrice walked quite a bit further downward and more to the right. She walked towards some bushes and cacti when, suddenly, she saw some envelopes scattered in the cacti, caught by its thorns. The wind must have blown them there, Beatrice thought.

"Ahh, thank goodness!" Beatrice said quietly out loud as she collected them one by one. "To the governor of Boston," Beatrice read out.

Beatrice picked up another and another and another, five in total.

"Is that all? Five letters?" Beatrice said.

She looked at them all, curious as to their destinations. One was for a Mr Wainwright in Washington D.C. Another one for General Clover in Boston and another one was for, Beatrice's heart stopped. It couldn't possibly be. She was instantly catapulted back to Lacey Manor, the woodland, the Highwaygirl and her collision with the lone rider. She looked at the name in disbelief.

To J. Montifiorre, 2471 Beacon Hill, Boston, Massachusetts.

"Maybe it is another Montifiorre," Beatrice said. "It can't possibly be the same Montifiorre." The leader shouted out to her in his language. They hadn't moved from their original spot. "I've found them. I've found them," Beatrice called back waving the letters in the air.

She swung up on her horse and walked back to them.

"Thank you," she said as she arrived. She was thanking them more so for her safety than anything else.

The leader turned to return home, the young man and then Beatrice followed.

Beatrice couldn't believe what she had in her pocket. J. Montifiorre, could it be that same man? It is not a very common name so it must be him. What were the chances of finding his letter there? What were the chances of his letter even being in their mail bags. Was this destiny playing its part again? Why Boston? Does he live in Boston? I must go to Boston, Beatrice's mind and heart were in a flurry. So many questions.

It was a beautifully sunny and breezy day. The warm wind blew through Beatrice's short hair and through her linen shirt; it felt good. It was certainly beautiful here, Beatrice thought. The sun was hot on her back but not too hot. She watched the native men walking slowly in front of her. How they rode to the rhythm of their horses, swinging from side to side with their long hair and bright colours. She had never seen a man's bare chest before, it made her think of Montifiorre, her heart raced again and she became impossibly impatient to go straight away to Boston.

As they approached their village, some people spoke to them in their language and others went about with their work. A little girl and boy came running up to Beatrice. The little girl was smiling and jumping up and down asking Beatrice to lift her up on her horse. Beatrice looked at the leader to ask for permission, he nodded. Beatrice stopped her horse, lent down, and with a big heave, pulled the little girl up on the horse with her. What a beautiful little thing, Beatrice thought. She held her round the waist and a warm rush of love and happiness ran through her. She had never done anything like this before with a child. It felt nice. It felt playful and Beatrice loved it. Then the little boy was jumping up and down asking to get up. Beatrice looked at the leader, who nodded. Beatrice stopped again, and this time, a man helped the little boy up on the horse behind Beatrice. Beatrice laughed.

"What fun," Beatrice said to the children.

"Where shall we go?" Beatrice playfully said. "Shall we go to the castle or shall we go and find the lost treasure?

As if understanding her, the children laughed and waved. The little girl then pointed to the river. Beatrice followed her instructions. Once at the river, the little girl and boy shouted to the other children. They wanted to show all their friends them riding with the white girl. Beatrice waved and smiled.

"Do you want to get down?" Beatrice asked motioning for them to get down but they shook their heads, so Beatrice continued with her walk. She liked playing with the children. The people smiled and waved as she walked past. These people didn't seem to be as scary as they had been portrayed. The men looked a bit more threatening, this was true, but I suppose they had to protect their families.

She walked back up to the corral where she could see the other man and the leader. "Beautiful children," Beatrice said on arriving.

The men nodded and the leader gave a half smile. The children shouted at them excitedly. The little girl said something and the leader chuckled. Beatrice helped the little girl down first, then the boy. Beatrice slid down from her horse, tied him and told them to wait. She ran back to Christopher's tipi and ran inside. The young lady Beatrice saw before was still sitting next to Christopher. Beatrice thought, they've been sitting together for a long time.

"No, time to stop. I've got the letters. You'll never believe…" there was no time for Beatrice to finish her sentence, she dropped off her mail bag and picked up her personal bag and ran back out.

Beatrice ran down to the waiting children. The young man and leader were now standing with the horses and talking to the children.

"Here, these are for you," Beatrice said kneeling down to the children.

Beatrice handed the little girl a silver hair clip she used for her own hair when it was long and the boy her silk ribbon she used when she fashioned a man's queue. The children smiled and ran into her, giving her a big hug. Beatrice was completely taken aback with their show of such uninhibited affection. It was such a free and joyful hug she realised how she had never had such affection given to her, whether that be from adults or children. She vowed to herself there and then, as their hugs sank into her, that she would shower her own children with such affection. And there, in that beautiful moment, Beatrice's rebellion found a cause. Whatever the social expectations of being a mother would be, she would defy them all. She liked the warmth and cosiness, the sense of community that this village gave her. Mothers and their children, aunties and grandmothers, fathers, uncles and grandfathers, all living together. It was nothing like her austere upbringing.

The children went running off towards the river and their mothers shouting with joy. Beatrice turned to the men.

"Thank you for taking me to get the mail," she said.

"Mahkah," the leader said to her tapping his chest.

"Chaska," said the young man. He then pointed to the leader and explained they were father and son.

"Where am I?" Beatrice asked. "What is the name of your village, your people?" Beatrice motioned her hands to the village and to the people.

"Lakota," the leader said. "Lakota," he said again thumping his chest proudly.

"Thank you, Mahkah, thank you, Chaska," Beatrice said, she was genuinely touched by their exchange. "I better get back to my cousin," she said pointing to Christopher's tipi.

The leader nodded and took all the horses and walked past her. Beatrice walked back up and ran straight into Christopher's tipi.

"Hello," Beatrice said to the young lady sitting next to Christopher.

"Christopher, you never believe what I found. Look at this letter," Beatrice got out the letter from the bag. "It's addressed to J. Montefiore in Boston. Could it possibly be the same Montefiore?"

Catching herself she stopped.

"How are you, Christopher? You look much better. Who is your friend?" Beatrice asked.

"My name is Wichahpi," the young woman said. "Daughter of Healer."

"It means star. Isn't that beautiful? I've been teaching her English and she has been teaching me Lakota," Christopher said.

"Trade," Wichahpi said with a big smile.

"Ocantu," Christopher smiled back.

"You look much better, Christopher," Beatrice said. "I'm so relieved. You had me worried for a bit. Thank you, Wichahpi for looking after my cousin," Beatrice said to Wichahpi.

"Why don't you get some fresh air. Would you like to go to the river?"

"River," said Wichahpi proudly.

"Wakpa," Christopher replied also proudly. "Yes, I would like some fresh air. Beatrice, we should leave tomorrow morning," Christopher said whilst carefully putting away his pencil and paper.

"Are you well enough?"

"Yes," Christopher said determinedly.

Christopher then threw back his blanket, sat up and made his first steps to stand up. He took in some air as he stood.

"So far so good," Beatrice said. "So far so good."

Wichahpi opened the tipi door, Christopher and Beatrice stepped out. Christopher was instantly hit by the sun and the village life. The people bustling, the children running and playing.

"What a wonderful place," Christopher said.

"My village," Wichahpi said proudly.

"Beautiful village, Wichahpi, beautiful," Christopher genuinely thought it was beautiful.

They walked down to the river. The children came running up to Christopher. He sat at the river's edge. It was so clear and transparent. So healthy. He took a drink. The children splashed in it. Christopher smiled. What joy to see children playing. He threw a pebble. One little boy got out and came next to Christopher and threw another pebble. Then another child. Christopher threw a pebble and it bounced five times across the water, all the children cheered, Christopher laughed. The sun was so soothing, the laughter soothing with the breeze on his face. Christopher felt instantly energised. What a magical place, he thought. He looked up and took a quiet moment to absorb his surroundings. The soft trickling sounds of the river, the laughter of the children playing, the women's chatter in their language, the breeze blowing through the green grass, the perfectly placed rocks by the river's edge, the mountains in the distance. Christopher didn't want to leave. He liked it here. England seemed so stale and old and nothing called to him from there. He had nothing there anyway except, of course, Moby.

"Food," Wichahpi said as she offered him some meat. Christopher eagerly took it, he was starving. Beatrice as well.

"Thank you," they both said.

The cousins spent the afternoon in sheer bliss by the river. They chatted happily and peacefully, Wichahpi came back and forth as well. It was easy company, and for the first time, their spirits felt happy. Their bodies relaxed.

The next morning the cousins woke early. They packed their meagre belongings and stepped out of their tipi. The healer woman was standing there.

She spoke to them in Lakota and gave Christopher a little pouch, and with her gestures, explained to Christopher to drink the tincture and rub some on his snake bite. Christopher nodded obediently.

"Thank you for saving my life. I am truly grateful," Christopher said meaningfully, he was genuinely grateful to the woman who stood in front of him. He went forward and gave her a long and heartfelt embrace.

They went to the corral and hoped to see the men from the last two days. No sign of them so they waited. A little while later, the young man came walking up.

"We have to go back," Christopher said lifting the mailbags to explain why.

"Mahkah?" Beatrice asked.

The man said something but Beatrice didn't quite understand. They then went into the corral to get their horses. They too had had a long rest. As the cousins were saddling up their horses, the leader came to them. He nodded his head to say hello and said something to his son who went into the corral to get their horses.

"They are going to escort us out," Beatrice said.

The leader then shouted over to a woman at the other side of the corral. She walked away. "Wakanyeja," the leader said.

"Children," Wichahpi translated as she approached.

Beatrice and Christopher waited for the children. A woman came walking up the hill holding the hands of the little girl and boy Beatrice had gone riding with yesterday. They walked straight up to Beatrice. Beatrice bent down and put her arms out. She felt instantly maternal. The two children came walking up to her and gave a warm and very sweet hug. Christopher noticed their little hands as they wrapped them around Beatrice.

Beatrice noticed the silver hair grip she had given her in the girl's hair and the ribbon tied into the boy's braid.

"Goodbye," said Beatrice.

"Goodbye," said Christopher.

"Toksa akhe," the children said together smiling. Wichahpi didn't need to translate.

"Mother?" Wichahpi shrugged her shoulders wondering where her mother, the Healer was. Wichalpi went ahead and gave the cousins their parting gifts. An eagle's feather and a piece of deerskin each, each one with a painting of their spirit animal.

Christopher looked at his painting of a deer. It was simple and beautiful. Beatrice looked at her painting of a bull.

"Brave," Wichahpi said pointing to Beatrice. She then did an action to describe determined.

"Stubborn? Determined?" Christopher said wanting to clarify between the two.

"Determined," Wichahpi said.

"Kind," she then said pointing to Christopher and then pointed to his head, "clever," Christopher smiled in response. He was deeply moved by the moment.

Christopher folded his little piece of painted deerskin and knew he would keep it forever. A token of the gift they all had given him, the gift of life. Twice now, his life had been saved.

Beatrice too was touched, she folded hers and put it safely inside her waistcoat. She would never forget the children, how they had stirred in her a woman's call to be a mother.

"Toks akhe," Christopher said to Wichahpi and embraced her.

"Farewell," she said. "Safe journey."

Christopher was deeply touched, his throat got tight and he fought to hold back the tears. He really didn't want to leave. He vowed to return.

Beatrice and Christopher mounted their horses. They made sure their mailbags were tied on safely and then nodded to the leader, they were ready to leave. All four of them set off together. They walked past the tipis, some of the people waved, some just watched and then carried on walking. The women carrying their babies on their backs waved, Beatrice smiled and waved back. They then saw, standing on a grassy mound, the healer woman.

Christopher sat up on his horse and waved. Beatrice as well. The Healer waved back, quietly. She wanted to see them off from a distance, send them on their journey with a blessing. Christopher loved this feeling of unity, of community. He had never had this feeling before in his life, this togetherness. It felt healthy. It felt connected. Nature and people intertwined. He was sad to leave.

Beatrice was curious about the letter to Montifiorre and held it safely inside her coat. For now, they just had to get back to St Joseph then, once back, she could think about what to do next.

Once at the rocks, all four stopped. "Tosa akhe," the leader said.

"Goodbye and thank you for your kindness," Beatrice said first.

"Thank you, Mahkah," Christopher said, he wished he could speak their language, communicate better. He could already speak French, Spanish and Latin but Lakota he, unfortunately, didn't speak. He would make it his next language to learn.

The cousins walked off. They didn't look back, but after a few strides, Christopher couldn't help himself and turned and tipped his hat. The leader put his hand up in reply. Christopher then put his horse into a gallop. It was time to leave. He hated goodbyes.

THE WAGER

THEY found a fast and steady speed with their horses, they would all have to ride hard to make up for so much lost time. Both the cousins were lost in their thoughts. Christopher was genuinely moved by his whole experience at the village. He felt caught between two worlds and his heart felt heavy. Although something deeply resonated with him with the Lakota people, he didn't quite belong there but he also didn't quite belong in England. Where do I belong? Christopher thought. His strength still wasn't back to its optimum, he still felt slightly weak, he hoped he would be able to endure the journey.

Beatrice, on the other hand, was eager to get to St Joseph and find out more about the letter. She felt strong and revitalised. She had an innate stamina, built-in endurance, she thought of her painting of the bull. Bulls are brave and determined, she thought. I'm determined to deliver our mail. I'm determined to find out more about Montifiorre.

Christopher now relied on Beatrice's strength and durability to get them there. They stopped at their first station.

"What happened to you two? I thought you'd been killed, attacked, gone for good," said the station master. "Russell ain't gonna be too happy."

This they knew would be true. They also knew that they had to just keep going. Ride, ride, ride, it was exhausting.

They arrived at the next stop station, changed horses and rode on. They stopped again at the next station, and again, at the next, always changing horses. Christopher was feeling pretty wretched but he dug deep to find his strength. At the home station, they ate and went straight to bed. That day, they had made good time, and by tomorrow night they should arrive in St Joseph.

The next morning, Christopher felt better despite his hard day of riding yesterday. He had taken some of the herbs Wichahpi had given him just before bed and this morning. The cousins ate, mounted their horses and galloped back on the trail. By dusk, they arrived in St Joseph; they were dusty and thirsty. They were also thirsty for their well-earned wage. They cantered straight up to the offices in a flurry of dust.

"Where in darn name have you both been. Russell ain't happy, fuming like a banshee. Thought you'd been killed or something, lost his mail even," Jefferson the Pony Express clerk blurted out.

Beatrice dismounted her horse, tied him and threw her mailbag down on the table. "Water please," she said directly.

Christopher did the same.

"So anybody gonna tell me what happened?" Jefferson asked.

"Well, I got bitten by a snake and nearly died but was brought back to life by the people of some nearby Lakota village to whom I am most solemnly indebted," Christopher said matter-of-factly.

"Do you have that water? Please," he added.

The cousins sat and drank their waters. They took a few moments to catch their breaths. "Our wages. Please," Beatrice said.

"Ahh. Well, I think Russell is wanting to have a word about that, he ain't gonna pay riders who bring back the mail late," Jefferson said cautiously.

"Where is he?" Beatrice demanded, her blood instantly boiled. She hadn't been through all of that for nothing.

"In one of the taverns," Jefferson said sheepishly.

Christopher knew what was about to happen and this time decided to sit any confrontation out. He thought of Beatrice's deerskin painting off the bull. The Lakotas were very right.

Beatrice stormed out of the office. Her boots vibrating on its wooden floors. She went straight into the nearest tavern and stormed in. Her male attire garnered some looks of disdain but she neither cared nor reacted. Russell wasn't there so she stormed straight out. She then stormed into MacCreedy's tavern, scanned the room and found her target.

She looked sweaty, dirty and covered in dust, she looked exactly like she had crossed the American Plains.

"Sir. Good day to you. Lady Seymour-Barclay requires her wages for work completed," Beatrice stood defiant in front of Russell and his friends, all sitting at their table.

"Lady Seymour-Barclay, I correct you. For work not completed," Russell calmly replied.

"Mailbags delivered herewith at your office. Work completed."

Everybody in the room went quiet. This was an entertaining showdown. Beatrice didn't falter, she stood her ground. The silence in the room was held suspended.

"Young lady, the work may be completed but it wasn't completed on time. It specifically says in the contract, mail has to be delivered within its deadline and you were out of its deadline. If the mail arrives late, I don't pay, simple," Russell enjoyed saying that, he was deadly serious.

"My cousin nearly died for your deadline," Beatrice said just as Christopher walked into the tavern.

"Occupational hazard," Russell came back.

Beatrice was absolutely fuming. The stage was theirs. All eyes were on the Highwaygirl and Russell. Who was going to win? Who was going to lose face? Beatrice was determined not to walk out of the tavern without a deal. She thought of her painting from the Lakota, the bull. You could hear a pin drop. Everybody held their breath.

"A wager, sir. I challenge you to a wager," Beatrice came back with.

Russell was not expecting this and was caught off-guard. He felt his friends around the table suddenly gain an interest in this stand-off.

"I don't gamble," Russell replied sheepishly.

Beatrice raised an eyebrow as she looked at his cards on the table and then looked back up at Russell.

"What is your wager, Lady Seymour-Barclay?" Russell was a little cornered and he knew it.

"That my cousin and I ride again, and if we beat the deadline time and arrive earlier, even if only by a minute, we each get paid our normal wage plus the double and are freed from our contracts, no more deliveries. But if we don't, then we don't get paid at all and have to complete two more runs."

Beatrice was determined to walk out of that tavern with a deal. This way she walked out with her head held high and the sound of dollars in her pockets.

Russell thought. He felt his friends loving the deal, loving the game. He felt pressured. He had already paid high to buy Christopher's freedom and now this.

"Wager!" a gentleman shouted from the back of the tavern.

"Wager!" another shouted.

Some started to bang on their tables. The room was building. Russell felt cornered. "I accept your wager," he quietly replied. "But you have to leave immediately."

Beatrice put out her hand to seal the deal. Russell hesitated for a moment and then put his hand to hers. They shook a firm handshake.

"You are witnesses to this," Beatrice shouted to everybody in the tavern.

Inwardly, Beatrice was jubilant, triumphant. Like racing down the final lap at the Epsom Derby, all she had to do now was win the wager. She walked out of the tavern with her head held high. The bull had won, for now, at least. She walked towards the doors where Christopher was waiting.

"Cousin, what have you done?" Christopher said.

"I couldn't let him win!" Beatrice said as she continued to walk out of the tavern. Noticing Christopher didn't follow, she stopped. "Are you coming?"

"I need a drink, I'll see you back at the hotel," Christopher said and walked to the bar. "A whiskey," he said to the barman.

"You got yourself a tough deal there, son," said the barman.

Christopher didn't reply. He needed to think this over. It was a tough wager, the barman was right and he really didn't think he could go through the whole journey again so soon. They were obliged to do two more trips as stated in their contracts but not so close together. Leaving so soon would be a mammoth undertaking and he still didn't feel back to his full strength. He had followed his cousin dutifully in everything, trusted and believed in her but was this time one time too many? But at the same time, they stood to make a lot of money and avoid doing another two trips. Even though he was tired, he knew Beatrice had wagered well. They just have to win the wager and then Christopher will be three hundred-and-fifty dollars richer. His printer and shop seemed tantalisingly closer. It was a wager he felt he could not refuse.

The cousins rested for one day only. Their relay rider returned with the new mailbags early Tuesday morning, and without any fanfare, any speeches or a cheering crowd, the cousins galloped off. Beatrice's competitive streak was at the fore. She had to win this wager. A wager she had proposed. A thousand different variables could hamper their journey but Beatrice only focused on one, winning.

It didn't take long for Beatrice and Christopher to find the perfect pace for their canter, a pace that covered the most ground in the quickest time. It was steady and constant, and once the horses had settled into it, they really did move fast. The horses seemed to like the rhythm too and they pounded along the miles.

It was tough riding, relentless, but Beatrice's resolve didn't dent. Her determination was absolute. The Healer was right, she thought about her totem animal. Every now and then, Beatrice would move up into a gallop but then back to a canter. Christopher let her lead and followed her pace.

They stopped at their first stop station, changed horses and moved on. Then, the next station, fresh horses and back on the trail and the next station and then the next. They just kept going.

"Look!" Beatrice shouted to Christopher over their galloping. "A storm is approaching. I think we should keep moving."

"Maybe we should wait whilst it passes," Christopher shouted back.

"No, let's try and beat it. We will lose too much time if we wait for it to pass."

Christopher didn't answer. His silence was his agreement.

They both galloped on. The storm was getting closer. It looked big and powerful. Lightning in the open plains was very treacherous.

The storm approached. It looked nasty. The clouds looked dark and laden down with rain. They were just waiting to drop it all. The cousins kept going though. Beatrice just kept focusing on being on the other side of the storm, safe.

Low ominous rumbles shook to the left. The storm felt like it had some wrath in it. The air shook with every rumble.

"We can do it, Christopher," Beatrice shouted over the noise.

Suddenly, a bolt of lightning filled the sky. It lit up the dark clouds as it exploded across them, trying to earth itself. The cousins kept their focus forward. Nobody shuddered not even the horses. They just kept going. At the next stop station, they changed horses.

"Are you sure you don't want to wait out the storm?" the station master said. "You're mad to keep riding," he insisted.

They didn't stop to talk or to be persuaded, they just kept going.

The storm was rumbling loud now. It was getting closer. Was it actually chasing them? Testing them? Another bolt shattered through the sky, pure electricity in motion. They kept going. The storm was closing in fast. Then another streak of lightning lit up the clouds. It was the biggest storm both cousins had ever seen. Christopher flinched a bit. Beatrice didn't flinch, neither did her horse, they were both dogged in their determination.

They arrived at the next station.

"Don't think it's wise riding out in that," said the station master.

"We have got to keep going," Beatrice said.

Christopher had never quite seen her so deeply enraged and so deeply determined. It was contagious and he found himself digging deep and finding his. They changed horses and were back on the trail. They kept galloping, they pushed their horses more than ever. Christopher was riding next to Beatrice. They were in it together. We have to win that wager, Christopher thought.

"Let's not stop at the home station, we can sleep a few hours at the next stop station," Christopher shouted.

Beatrice nodded. She could feel tiredness seeping in but didn't allow it to take hold. They galloped on. Another bolt came frighteningly close.

"Argh!" Beatrice yelled out this time.

"We can outrun it, B," Christopher shouted.

The horses too found some extra power, it seemed they too wanted to outrun the storm. Both the cousins were in awe of their horses, incredible animals. Their stamina and strength didn't dent or waver for a single second. The sky rumbled low and menacing. It hung low, black and oppressive, constantly threatening them with every outburst. Then the thunder clap exploded so loudly and so close to their heads, that they both involuntarily ducked in response. It felt like it was on top of them, on top of their heads.

And then the rain came. It literally dropped from the sky. The thunder roared, the rain poured, the whole storm was of biblical proportions, with Beatrice and Christopher caught in the middle. It was like nothing they had ever experienced before. They were on their own. Nothing was out here to help them. The rain was cold and lashed at their bodies; they were soaked in a second. This was utterly terrifying; alone on this wide Wyoming open plain with nowhere to take shelter.

The mail was protected in their special wax-coated mailbags. Christopher checked his bag was still tied tightly. They just kept going, pushed on and on and on. Is Zeus himself testing us? Christopher thought. They eventually arrived at the night station.

"Quickly come in, get out of the rain," said Walker the station master.

"No, just give us fresh horses, we're moving on," said Christopher shouting over the rain.

"What! Are you insane! You both gone mad? You're lucky to have even reached this far."

"We'll stop at the next station," Beatrice said.

"Don't say I didn't warn you," Walker replied putting on his coat and going out into the rain to get the fresh horses.

They made the swap and the cousins galloped off. No time for conversation or ceremony. The rain came down hard and fast. The gaps in between the thunderclaps were getting longer, the storm was abating. They charged on at an incredible pace, their horses fresh and strong. Finally, they arrived at their next station, soaked to the bone and exhausted.

"I wasn't expecting anybody now," said Samuels. "You ran through the storm. Why such a rush?"

"Let us just say it's a matter of honour," said Beatrice.

"We just need a couple of blankets," Christopher asked.

"Right to it," Walker said as he sped off to get the blankets. The cousins slept a couple of hours. Beatrice woke first.

"Christopher, wake up. It's time to go," Beatrice whispered.

Christopher groaned as he slowly awoke. Every muscle ached but it was mind over matter now.

They put on their still-wet clothes and went to have breakfast. They filled their bellies with as much food as possible. They felt so uncomfortable with their wet clothes on aching bones but they shrugged any discomforts or negative thoughts off. Beatrice's resolve was unwavering; she had a job to do and she was going to do it. I can rest afterwards, she thought.

It was still dark but the sky was clearing when they stepped outside.

They thanked Samuels and galloped back onto the trail. Samuels made the sign of the cross as he watched them ride off.

Ahh, what glorious comfort, Beatrice thought as the sun slowly rose. It was an awe-inspiring sight that would normally demand them to stop and take the time to admire it but not this morning. This morning there was no time.

The sun gradually got hotter and it felt glorious. It warmed their cold backs, it warmed their tired bones and it dried their wet clothes. They travelled hard, station after station until, eventually, arriving at Salt Lake City. They galloped up to the stop station and handed over their bags.

"You both did that in record time. Not bad," said McBride at the station.

All there was to do now was wait an agonising wait for the other rider to do his leg of the route. The first thing they did do whilst they waited was have a hot bath. They were thick with grime and dirt and sweat. Beatrice slid down into the soothing water, closed her eyes and let the water wash away all the aches. She hadn't had any luxury for so long that she had almost forgotten what it was like. As she soaked, she thought of her bed back in Lacey Manor. Its soft mattress and soft cotton sheets. She thought of the sweet smell of lavender that filled her room. She thought of Betty's shortbread and the cosy fire in the kitchen. She thought of Asta, her beloved Asta. Her heart filled up and her throat clenched. "I miss you so much Asta. You would be proud of me," Beatrice whispered aloud, keeping her eyes shut. She envisioned their rides over the hills, and their rests together, sitting down together. Beatrice thought of the meadow. I miss England, she thought. The green fields of England called her.

The two days waiting were excruciating for Beatrice; she was impatient, biting at the bit just to get going again. All she wanted to do was get back on the trail and win her wager.

They were both sitting out on the verandah when they saw Edward Stevens loping towards the stop station. He rode straight up to them.

"Here you go. They're all yours," said Stevens as he flung the two mailbags onto the verandah by their feet.

Beatrice jumped immediately into action and saddled the horses. The big western saddles seemed heavy this morning, even though she was fired up and burning to get going. Despite her impulsion, she stopped for a second, rested her head on the side of her horse and breathed in its sweet horse smell. She breathed in its strength. Their strength always seemed to give her strength. She didn't know what it was about horses that meant so much to her, whatever it was, they had always, always been her refuge.

"Ride us to St Joseph safely. Ride us fast. Thank you for your strength," Beatrice whispered quietly into her horse's side. Beatrice gave the mailbags an extra tug to secure them and then walked out to Christopher who was talking to Stevens.

"Let's go," Beatrice said.

"Let's go," Christopher affirmed.

They both swung up on their horses and galloped off. Beatrice's resolve was steadfast. She bore down, she had a wager to win.

Wyoming was vast, flat and utterly enormous. It was the same as it had been on their way out. They changed their horses at every station, station after station after station, they didn't stop and they pushed their horses. The weather was sublime, warm and encouraging. A breeze blew a cool breeze over them as if subtly pushing them along from behind, giving them that extra needed speed.

They rode into Nebraska and just kept going, eating up the miles. Both had gone past all the aches, both had gone past any mental obstacles. Now their endurance had reached a rhythm of the highest stealth. Nightfall came and they kept on riding.

"Do you think you can ride through the night?" Beatrice asked Christopher as they cantered.

"Do you?" he replied.

"Yes."

"Then let us ride through the night."

With fresh horses, they didn't stop at the home station to sleep. They picked up some meat and ate it whilst they rode. They cantered and cantered and cantered. They didn't stop. They did catch a few hours of sleep on the side of the road, heads propped up on their saddles. By the first crack of dawn, they were approaching St Joseph. By early morning, they trotted into St Joseph.

Looking utterly bedraggled, the cousins trotted into the centre of town. The streets were wide and the urgency of their mission took them directly to the Pony Express building. Their weather-worn appearance and Beatrice's male attire, as always, attracted some looks. Beatrice's minor

Highwaygirl celebrity was still familiar and her wager with Russell only strengthened that.

They cantered straight up to the building in a whirl of emergency, the long wide street like the last lap of the Epsom Derby. Beatrice let out a breath, they had done it, glory soaked into her every bone. She knew they had arrived half a day ahead of time but she wasn't completely relieved yet. The real winner's cup was when she received the double pay. For all my wins in the past, I have won freedoms, this win, I will actually win money, Beatrice thought.

They tied their horses and Beatrice was the first to storm in, her boots resounding on the wooden floors, announcing her entrance. Two press men were already there, Beatrice didn't even notice them, she was on the warpath; she wanted their vindication.

"Where's Russell?" Beatrice demanded.

"Well, you ain't no shrinking violet, are ya?" said the clerk. "He's at the tavern."

"The same one, I suppose," Beatrice said as she made an instant turn and back out the door, not even bothering to wait for the answer.

Once again, her loud boots on the wooden floor marked her entrance. Russell was sitting in exactly the same place, at the same table with the same men. It was like a repeat of the day of the wager. Beatrice charged straight up to Russell with her horns pointing, the bull was back. The healer woman was certainly right. She plonked the mailbags on his table. The room went silent just as it did before.

"Your mochilas, sir. Delivered on time," Beatrice said.

"Lady Seymour-Barclay, you are indeed early. Congratulations," Russell said, he was galled and hated the fact that he had to hand over a lot of money. "Nothing ventured, nothing gained and today you gained."

"Yes, a deal is a deal, gentlewoman to gentleman," Beatrice put out her hand for a handshake, Russell took it.

Beatrice took one last look at the mailbags knowing that there was one letter that she didn't deliver. One very intriguing letter that lay safely in her inside pocket.

BOSTON

THE next few days, the cousins did nothing but rest, they had definitely earned it. Christopher read and Beatrice started a diary. The tensions and aches slowly fell away from their bodies. It was over. It was all over. They both had money in their pockets and freedom in their hearts. What with their Highway bounty and now their double earnings, Christopher had enough to start his bookshop, maybe even start to write? But where? he thought. England didn't call him back. He felt unwanted there. St Joseph too didn't feel much like it could be a home.

"Boston, cousin, do you want to come to Boston with me," Beatrice suddenly said over lunch as she put the Montifiorre's letter in front of him.

"Mmm, Boston," Christopher was pensive.

"Do you think it could be the same J. Montifiorre I galloped into back at Lacey?" Beatrice was excited.

"Well, there's only one way of finding out. That's where it all started, their independence, America's independence, maybe that's where ours will start?"

"Ever the romantic, cousin," Beatrice said, but as the word 'romantic' fell from her lips, her heart began to flutter. Maybe it is the same Montifiorre and maybe it will be romance for Beatrice.

"It's about time I became romantic," Beatrice said out loud almost by mistake.

"Why not. Let us go. There is nothing here for us in St Joseph," Christopher replied.

Christopher liked the idea of Boston, something rang right, rang true about it. He felt excited. "He may be married, B. I wouldn't want you to get your hopes up."

"Of course, of course," Beatrice said a bit bashfully. This was a side of herself that both she and Christopher hadn't seen much of, if at all.

Christopher, however, had had his lady loves. Both country girls and both in secret. Beatrice, of course, knew. His loves had completely stolen Christopher's heart. Mary was his first love, and when her father got suspicious of their secret rendezvous, he stopped them from seeing each other. Christopher's heart was quietly broken but nothing too painful to get over.

"Boston has a university and is cultured, so I hear," continued Beatrice.

"Maybe a city with its streak of independence would also appreciate some storytelling. A bookshop maybe?" Christopher was now the one thinking aloud.

Two days later, the cousins were ready to set off for Boston. They had both bought new cotton shirts and Beatrice some new breeches. The shop seller was aghast when the new breeches were for her and not for her cousin but he had seen so many strange and fanciful things in St Joseph that he actually wasn't too aghast. Beatrice packed her skirt in her bag. She wasn't quite ready to give it up totally.

They got the stagecoach back to Jamestown. This big new world here in America was actually becoming familiar. They had both traversed much of it already and even made friends with its original people.

They had to wait a week in Jamestown for a ship that was sailing to Boston. They bought their passage upon The Endeavour. Once again, they both thought the name of their ship was very appropriate for their next endeavour in life. It was a glorious feeling to be finally free. Making their own choices, carving out their own lives. That was, after all, all Beatrice ever wanted. To make her own choices, make her own mistakes.

"Good morning, ladies and gentlemen. Welcome aboard The Endeavour. Mr Lewindon will see you to your cabin," said Captain Ross, a big towering Scottish man.

Both Beatrice and Christopher felt safe in this Scot's experienced hands. He was an old sea dog who had grown up on the sea since he was twelve-years-old. Like all their captains so far, he was succinct, professional and direct. He minced his words for no one or suffered fools lightly.

"So, Lady Seymour-Barclay, yer that lady that fell from grace and fell into highway robbery. Well, you've fallen far and travelled far, ain't yer, lass. You should fit in perfectly good here," Ross gave a big bellowing laugh. "Keep your eye on Williams, I would," he said with a cheeky wink.

Christopher liked the man instantly, knowing too well that he wouldn't want to get on his wrong side.

Their journey north was plain sailing, literally so. No storms, no incidences. It seemed like a short journey compared to their traverse across the Atlantic and even Beatrice's seasickness was better this time round.

The port of Boston lay ahead. The boat and all its sailors leapt into action as all aboard prepared to sail into port.

Both Beatrice and Christopher were utterly intrigued. Their curiosities were piqued. It looked much like all ports. Crates and people and horses and mules all jostling and shouting and clambering.

"Port side!" shouted Ross.

Like a perfectly rehearsed theatre work, the men performed their arrival at the port of Boston. "So this is where it all started," Christopher said to Ross as the sailors tied the ropes.

"It most certainly was. I was here on The Endeavour. Bloody fools, the English. Lost the lot. Too arrogant. No wonder the colonists rebelled," Ross said.

"Well, thank you, good sir," Christopher said shaking Ross's hand.

"Good day. I've never travelled with a lady in breeches before. I've seen many things but not that one," Ross said. "Well, actually, there was a pirate once… crates over to the right!" Ross interrupted his own story distracted by the unloading of his merchant ship.

"Thank you, Captain," Beatrice said.

The cousins walked down the ramp and stepped onto the quayside. Here they were in Boston. Beatrice's heart was in a flutter. She couldn't quite believe she was here purely in the hope of discovering the truth about a lone stranger she bumped into all the way back in England.

Christopher was here in the hope of discovering culture and literature. They took their first steps forward and towards their new endeavours. Both apprehensive.

"We need to find our lodgings," Christopher said.

They had been given the name of a good lodgings by Ross and so they went straight there. Boston was an explosion of activity. It really felt like a city. It felt like a place closer to home.

They could feel some of England within its streets. It was very much American but with the flavour of old England.

As they walked, Christopher imagined the beginnings of the War of Independence taking place; small skirmishes along these narrow cobbled streets. Rioters and soldiers running up and down, in and out of the wood and brick buildings. Guns firing. The history felt very alive, very present, after all, it wasn't that long ago.

"Good day to you, sir and mademoiselle," the Landlord said. "Je m'appelle Pierre."

"Bonjour, monsieur. Avez-vous des chambres libres?" Christopher asked Pierre if they had any rooms in his perfect French.

"Follow me," replied Pierre.

Their lodgings were perfect. They had their separate rooms and each room had a wooden four-poster bed. It wasn't Lacey Manor but it wasn't a ship's cabin or a prison or a home station. Beatrice flopped on her bed and let out a big sigh.

After a little while, Beatrice knocked on Christopher's door. "Shall we pay him a visit?" Beatrice said holding up the letter.

"Why not," Christopher replied.

"But first, I need to repair my skirt," said Beatrice. "It's completely torn."

"I'm sure Pierre knows someone."

And as predicted, Pierre did know someone, his wife.

"Follow me," Pierre said again. "A dress would help," Pierre said sarcastically referring to Beatrice's trousers.

"They are both comfortable and practical," Beatrice replied in defence, she was totally unoffended. Pierre led Beatrice to the back of the building and to a conservatory at the back. It was very cosy; full of silks and crepes, haberdashery and mannequins, cottons and textiles; very feminine. There was colour everywhere.

"Mon Famme, Marie. My wife, Marie," Pierre said introducing his wife.

Marie was petite and wholesome. She was dressed simply but with a touch of glamour expressed in her sleeves. She gave Beatrice a big smile.

"Bonjour," she said. "How can I help?"

Marie was the seamstress to many of the rich women of Boston. Her Parisian fashions, especially her corsets were very much in demand.

"My skirt needs repairing," Beatrice said holding up her rather old skirt.

"Oh la la. You need a new skirt. And those trousers? Is this the new fashion from England. You are English? No?" Marie talked fast and was not shy to express her opinions.

"I have this skirt for you," Marie sat up from her chair and found a ready-made skirt and held it up to show Beatrice.

Beatrice hesitated. Should I wear a skirt to see Montifiorre or stay with my trousers? Beatrice thought.

"Mademoiselle, your trousers may be the nouvelle mode in England, but here in Boston, no, no, no!" Marie said sensing Beatrice's hesitation, she didn't approve of the trousers.

Beatrice was slightly annoyed by Marie's outspoken judgement of her attire but she did look down at them, and after so much wear and tear and having been across the plains of America on horseback, Beatrice had to agree that her old breeches she wore today, did look rather worse for wear. Beatrice succumbed and went to try on the skirt.

"Mademoiselle, it looks beautiful. I can repair your old skirt and you can buy this one to wear now. Now, a corset. I make the most favourable corsets in Boston," Marie boasted.

"No, thank you, Marie, just the skirt."

"But your shirt looks very untidy."

Beatrice had to concede to this too as she looked down upon her shirt. It too had travelled many hard miles. Marie held up another shirt. Beatrice smiled. She wasn't so annoying after all.

"Let me also repair your breeches," Marie sat down and picked up her needle. "The Highwaygirl from England can't be wearing trousers with a tear," Marie didn't look up when she said this but Beatrice felt her smile.

Silence fell between them. How does she know about my highway robberies? Beatrice thought "Well, mademoiselle, infamy travels fast. There are not many women in Boston wearing breeches, uh, you know," Marie said heartily as if reading Beatrice's mind.

Beatrice thought Marie's powers of deduction very good. She was quick-minded, but then, I suppose it was rather easy to figure out.

"Mademoiselle, I hear a lot of gossip. Everybody likes to tell me things in this room. This room is full of talk when I am pinning and measuring and sewing for my customers. There is a lot of talking, uh, you know."

Beatrice put on the clean shirt, she felt a lot better too, Marie was right. "Voila!" Marie said joyfully.

Beatrice gave Marie a few coins for her work. "Merci beaucoup!" Beatrice said.

"Avec plaisir, mademoiselle."

"You can call me Beatrice."

"Avec plaisir, Beatrice," Marie said charmingly.

Beatrice had to admit Marie was rather charming and could imagine a lot of gossip being shared in this room; all the gossip. Beatrice doubted much of it actually stayed in the room.

"Cousin, you look beautiful," Christopher was taken aback by Beatrice's new clothes. He hadn't seen her dressed this way for such a long time.

They both started walking towards Montifiorre's residence. The streets were busy; a hive of activity.

They turned a corner. The streets were cobbled and not comfortable to walk upon. The cousins heard a bit of a commotion coming from a livery yard. A horse was neighing and its hooves could be heard clomping on the cobbles. Just as they were approaching the livery, a big, black horse jolted out, nearly colliding into Beatrice. She instantly flew backwards getting out of its way and then tried to get hold of its reins. Christopher ran in front of the horse raising his arms to try and stop it from escaping up the street. The owner then ran out; it all happened so quickly. Beatrice holding the horse's reins, got the horse to calm, she then turned around to face the owner. The air stood still, hearts stopped beating and the chaos of the last ten seconds disappeared.

"I believe this horse belongs to you," Beatrice said in a daze.

Both Beatrice and the gentleman locked eyes. The last time they had done that was in England on a woodland path. She recognised him instantly but would he recognise her. The gentleman could never forget those eyes and could never forget the day he collided into them. The highway robbery only cementing his love. But now in Boston, he was so utterly shocked that he stood frozen, said nothing. Am I looking at a ghost? He thought. I thought they had hanged the Highwaygirl. He most definitely recognised those eyes but he didn't recognise how she was dressed. Today, the lady in front of him was dressed very differently. He had known back in March that the Highwaygirl was actually Lady Beatrice Seymour-Barclay but what he didn't know was what Lady Beatrice Seymour-Barclay had actually looked like. He had brazenly, and with much risk, left her that note in his pouch as a hope of opening up any courtship, a dangerous liaison indeed but one he was willing to take. But then, he heard of the Highwaygirl's hanging, and broken-hearted, let her go from his heart. So, the incredulity of this moment hung heavy. From the outside everything stood still, from the inside everything was racing. Heartbeats, minds, deductions and assumptions. The gentleman was convinced it was indeed the Highwaygirl he had ridden into all that time ago in March at Lacey Manor. But there was an element of doubt. Wasn't she meant to be dead? And if not, what possibly could she be doing here, in Boston? Maybe I am confusing her with someone else? The gentleman's mind played tricks on him but his heart knew exactly that the girl in front of him was indeed the Highwaygirl he fell in love with.

"Your horse had quite the stir. What startled it so?" Christopher said breaking the ice like a pick axe.

He instantly guessed this was Beatrice's romantic stranger she had bumped into back in England. "Excuse me but have we all already met?" Christopher tried to jump the formalities and go straight to the awkward truths.

"Quite possibly but under very different circumstances," said the gentleman cautiously. Should I ask if she is indeed the Highwaygirl? Maybe she doesn't want me to know. Maybe she doesn't want her past revealed. Maybe she is here in Boston in hiding? Thought the gentleman.

Should I tell him I'm the Highwaygirl? Beatrice thought. That it was me who had held up his carriage and that it was me who collided into him. And here we are colliding into each other again. He knows I am the highway robber, I know he knows but maybe I shouldn't reveal it all here and now in the middle of the street. Beatrice's mind was racing with thoughts. He is indeed extremely handsome. Very European. Not as tall as I had envisioned.

The gentleman quickly collected himself.

"How positively rude of me. My name is Joseph Montifiorre."

"Lady Beatrice Seymour-Barclay," Beatrice said knowing that the gentleman would then know that she was the Highwaygirl. Everybody knew Lady Seymour-Barclay was the Highwaygirl.

"Christopher Seymour-Barclay."

Everybody was a bit spellbound about the whole serendipity of this moment. Montifiorre was relieved to discover that the Highwaygirl standing before him hadn't been hanged. So, this is what the Highwaygirl really looks like, undisguised and in all her feminine glory.

"Get out of the way!" shouted a pedestrian.

"We better move," said Christopher. "We are in the way."

"Well, we should stop meeting like this, Lady Seymour-Barclay. Quite the coincidence!" said Montifiorre hinting at their prior meeting.

Beatrice smiled bashfully. Nobody wanted to reveal anything. Everybody was unsure of what or what not to say.

Christopher had never seen his cousin in this more awkward and mute light. He then lead the conversation.

"What an incredible coincidence, Mr Montifiorre we were only walking towards your residence."

"You were!" Montifiorre replied genuinely surprised. "For…"

His horse suddenly started to fret interrupting his sentence.

"Hey! You're blocking the way!" said a man trying to get by with his cart.

"Move out the way!" said another passer-by.

"Well, it's just as well we bumped into each other here as I'm on my way to a meeting and would not have been at home.

"Hey, mister! Move along!" said another pedestrian. Montifiorre's horse started to fret again.

"As you can see, Mystery here is keen to get going, we are already late. Would you both care to join me for tea this afternoon?"

"Tea would be lovely," Christopher enthused. "Say four o'clock?"

"Perfect,"

"I look forward to it," Montifiorre said.

"Likewise," Christopher said tipping his rather weathered-looking hat. Unlike Beatrice, Christopher hadn't had a makeover.

Montifiorre walked off both enthralled and bemused. He just couldn't believe what had just happened. He kept shaking his head in disbelief as he walked.

Beatrice and Christopher walked in silence for a while.

"So, now, I'm your chaperone?" Christopher finally said smiling and throwing a look at Beatrice whilst they walked.

Beatrice just thumped him playfully on the arm. "What were the chances of that?" Beatrice said. "Incredible!"

"Nobody spoke of our robbing his carriage. Of the Highwaygirl," Beatrice said.

"A bit strange, to say the least. Suddenly, having tea with the man I held a pistol to," Beatrice said suddenly doubting the incident. "Should we go?" Her mind was playing tricks on her but her heart, as was Montifiorres', knew exactly what to do.

"Of course, we should go. We haven't travelled this far for nothing. You can't get cold feet now, cousin. You always knew that there was going to be a robbery between you both," Christopher spurred her on.

"So, where to now. Shall we go and discover Boston?" Beatrice suggested changing the subject but not her feelings. "I still have his letter."

"He seemed pleasant, don't you think?" Christopher said looking forward as they walked. He had always been proud of his good judge of character and did feel Montifiorre was a nice man.

"We'll wait and see," Beatrice replied reservedly as she walked.

The cousins strolled around the city. It was big and prominent with tall and robust brick buildings. It was also small and quaint with alleys and windy streets with taverns and tea rooms. The more dangerous parts were downtown by the port but their lodgings where more uptown. They walked down Lawrence Street and noticed a board up in the window. For rent, it advertised. Both the cousins looked at each other.

"Could be perfect for my bookshop," said Christopher as he peered inside.

Beatrice looked through the window and it did indeed look perfect. It was certainly big enough and seemed to have a back room as well.

"I'll make contact tomorrow," Christopher said.

The cousins went for some lunch. Christopher did most of the talking. Beatrice was a bit nervous about meeting Montifiorre, she had built him up so much in her head over the last few months that maybe it was impossible for him to live up to her expectations. This was definitely unfamiliar territory for Beatrice.

"Should I tell him I am the highway robber? Maybe he'll be appalled? Maybe he'll hate me?" Beatrice asked.

"Let us just see how the tea goes. See what he is like. Let's measure the situation when we are there," this was the first time Christopher had ever seen an unconfident Beatrice.

"He may even be married with children," Beatrice said.

"Exactly. We deliver the letter and see what we make of the man."

It was time to leave. They left the restaurant and it wasn't long until they reached the address. They stood outside the gates of a large but not overly grand house. They were both expecting something with a lot more grandeur. They opened the tall iron gates and walked along a path lined with big and beautiful red Maple trees. It was October so their leaves had started to turn into their deep orange autumn colour. The path was a glow of rich colour.

They stood at the door. Beatrice took a breath. Christopher rang the bell. They waited. They heard footsteps approaching, then stop.

"Good afternoon," the butler said cheerfully as he opened the door. "Please do come in, Mr Joseph is expecting you."

Beatrice and Christopher were getting used to the informality here in America. "How are you both enjoying Boston?" the butler casually asked.

"Yes, it's a wonderful city," Christopher politely replied

They both followed the butler through a big but modest hall, its wood-panelling made it very cosy. They were led along a corridor and then into a conservatory at the back of the house. The butler didn't need to introduce the cousins as Montifiorre came forward immediately. He made them feel most welcome.

"Oh, I'm so pleased you both came. Please do come in and make yourselves welcome," Montifiorre said.

He was a lot more high-spirited than earlier, the shock of their meeting earlier having worn off. But Montifiorre was still not sure of whether to mention anything about the highway robberies, he was still of the thinking that maybe Lady Seymour was here in America to hide from her past. He went straight to Christopher, shook his hand and put his hand welcomingly on his shoulder.

"How may I address you both?"

"Christopher," Christopher liked the informality.

"Beatrice."

"So, Lady Beatrice Seymour-Barclay, please allow me the honour of giving you a proper and cordial greeting," Montificrre said as he gave Beatrice a warm and small bow.

They both smiled.

"Please let me show you my vegetables and herbs. My pride and joy," Montifiorre said excitedly and began to explain all about them.

Beatrice inwardly approved. She liked his mix of formal and informal. He seemed very European. She was heart-struck, if not still a bit taken aback, with how quick and how serendipitous the whole finding of Montifiorre was. But all she wanted to do was talk about their hold-up back in England, break the ice. She was feeling uncomfortable with all the secrets, having secrets now didn't feel right. She just wanted to blurt everything out.

As she watched him talk with Christopher, she liked his thick dark hair and hazel eyes, but most of all, she liked his big warm smile, it was positively contagious. He seemed very exotic. Very foreign, she thought. Her mother had said his family were of Jewish and Italian descent. She liked this. She liked his mix. Beatrice was heart-struck. There was little she could do to stop her heart from racing madly.

"Ahh, perfect timing," Montifiorre said as tea was brought into the conservatory. They sat amongst the plants. It was a perfect temperature inside.

"So I have to be honest that this morning I was completely taken aback by our meeting. It was an incredible shock, so do forgive me if I came across as somewhat reserved."

Montifiorre did seem a lot different now. Jovial, light of heart.

"I mean, what are the chances of meeting here in Boston. Incredible, don't you think? May I ask what brings you both to Boston?"

And there was the question Beatrice had been waiting for.

"I wanted to deliver this to you," Beatrice went straight to the truth. She got out the letter in her pocket and gave it to Montifiorre.

"My! You travelled far to give me this letter."

Beatrice was suddenly overcome with bashfulness. It was true she had travelled far in order to deliver a letter to someone she wasn't even sure was the person she hoped he would be. Her own forwardness now embarrassed her.

"Well, actually, it wasn't just to deliver your letter. I wanted to visit Boston with the interest of opening a bookshop. Buying my own printer. Early days, though, for my new enterprise," Christopher had felt Beatrice suddenly recoil and stepped in.

"A printer's shop. What a wonderful endeavour. Are you a man of books, Christopher?"

"My true passion. And yourself? What is your line of work?" Christopher asked.

"I'm here representing my father on some business and banking ventures."

Beatrice sat as their voices faded into the distance. Had she been a fool to have come so far to visit a man she had met momentarily? Maybe that was a meeting best left where it was? Back in England. He hadn't mentioned anything of that day or of her highway robber's disguise. Beatrice's mind raced, suddenly full of doubt. Her heart too raced, but fortunately, not with doubt. She listened to both Christopher and Montifiorre as they talked and laughed. They seemed to get on famously. They bantered well, thought Beatrice. Christopher was laughing too, something she hadn't heard him do in a while. Montifiorre was rather funny and brought out the funny side of Christopher.

"Where are you both staying?" Montifiorre enquired. Beatrice was suddenly brought back from her reverie.

"The lodgings on Blyth Street. Pierre is the Landlord," Christopher answered.

"Ahh, yes, yes. I know it well. My sisters have their dresses made by his wife, Marie."

"Horses. You seem like a lover of horses as I noticed this morning. Ah, forgive my manners, I never thanked you for grabbing Mystery and calming her. She took a liking to you," Montifiorre said.

"Yes, I most definitely am a lover of horses," Beatrice replied.

"Well, then, let us go for a ride."

Beatrice was overjoyed. She couldn't think of anything more wonderful and wanted to get some fresh air. It was getting a little stuffy as nobody was mentioning anything about their highway robbery.

"It's a beautiful afternoon," Christopher said.

They all walked to the fields. Beatrice's heart lifted. He kept his horses free to roam in the field. "Lovely to see your horses grazing free," Beatrice said as they walked past.

"Of course. I wouldn't have it any other way." Christopher felt Beatrice's happiness on hearing this. They walked into the stables.

"Would you like to ride Mystery?" Montifiorre asked walking straight up to his big black horse.

"Only if I can saddle her myself," Beatrice said.

"Of course," Montifiorre said.

Montifiorre was smitten with her. He loved her brazen attitude. She was bold. He loved her informality. Should I mention the highway robbery now? I don't want her to feel uncomfortable. Is this a good time to bring up the subject? Montifiorre thought. I'll wait and find the right moment, Montifiorre decided.

In a jiffy, they were all mounted. Montifiorre whistled and a border collie came pounding around the corner and jumped sky high over a tree trunk, they all laughed.

"His name is Chance and he likes nothing more than a run in the country."

Chance lead the way. They cantered along the fields at the back of the house and then slowed to a trot as they rode along a public path, in no time, they reached the woods.

"I know a beautiful spot to watch the sunset. Are you ready!" Montifiorre shouted.

There was nothing more exciting than riding cross-country through the woods, Beatrice thought. She felt better already. Any awkwardness from before lifted instantly. She didn't care what or what not should be said. Her mind instantly cleared.

The open plains of Nebraska were indeed beautiful but they were flat and repetitive, thought Beatrice as she cantered, feeling, finally, back in her element. Cross-country, however, is challenging and constantly changing.

Fallen trees to jump, streams to cross, up hills and down hills. The woods are nature's obstacle course.

The woods were also full of the explosion of autumn. Colour resounded everywhere. It was magical. An autumn song of colour and light. This ride was about fun. No race, no wager, no fear, no threats. Just a fun ride in the woods.

Chance was pounding ahead, and with energy to spare, he raced to the top of a hill. The others followed and stopped where Chance was standing.

"A beautiful spot for the sunset, don't you think?" Montifiorre said as they rode out of the woods and onto a look-out.

It was true, it was beautiful. The rich colours of autumn flowed out before them in a valley full of autumn trees. It was a carpet of colour as far as the eye could see. Virgin and pristine land. A big and orange sun sank low and fast behind the horizon, throwing out its abundant splash of colours. Its farewell gift until tomorrow.

They all sat in silence, the view demanded it. They watched the sun slip slowly down behind its horizon.

"I delivered the gold coin to the beggar lady and her child by the way." Beatrice couldn't contain herself and blurted out what everybody wanted to be said. "Apologies for the hold-up, by the way."

The silence that already was, now got longer. The truth, the identity, the secret was out. Everybody knew anyway. Everybody knew Lady Seymour-Barclay of Lacey Manor was the Highwaygirl. Nobody spoke. Who would make the first move?

"Apology accepted but no need. In truth, it was a pleasure to be stopped, have the carriage crash, have a pistol held to my head and then my money stolen from a highway robber such as yourself," Montifiorre said throwing Beatrice a big smile as he looked at her.

"I'm glad to say, you look nothing like your artist's impression on the wanted posters and a lot more like your portrait hanging in Lacey Manor. I saw it there after we had collided so dramatically on the woodland path, which led me to make my leaping assumption that the highway robber was indeed yourself, hence my note. I was also led to believe you had been hanged hence my utter shock at our earlier collision." Montifiorre was genuinely relieved to have the truth out in the open.

"Well, I'm glad that's out in the open," Christopher said. "Apologies for any discomforts."

"All's fair in love and war. And well, my lawyer associate that day was not the most principled of men," Montifiorre said.

"Mystery would make a fine getaway horse," Christopher said with a big smile.

"Asta, I'm afraid to say, gentlemen, is the queen of all highway horses," Beatrice defended. They all let out a sigh of relief. The curtain had been lifted.

One curtain had been lifted but another still lay closed. What are Montifiorre's true intentions towards me? Thought Beatrice. This is new territory for me and I'm not quite sure of what to do. Do I make my feelings known first? Does he make the first move?

"We'd best get back," said Montifiorre.

Chance, once again, lead the way. Beatrice went ahead and led up front with Chance, this gave Montifiorre his chance to admire her and admire her he did. He was utterly smitten. She is so brazen and exuberant, so different. Quite serious, he thought. And very athletic and agile much like the horse she rode. Montifiorre's thoughts raced. And of course, she is absolutely beautiful, especially now seeing her without her mask and scarf on. Her warm brown eyes stand out just as they had when they had been hidden behind the mask. Even her short hair is eccentric. Father and mother won't approve. Especially knowing that it was her who was the infamous Highwaygirl.

"Mystery is definitely an incredible horse. She is so athletic, both light and grounded. How did you come about such a horse?" Beatrice asked as she slowed so as to ride next to Christopher and Montifiorre.

"Actually, I won her in a bet," Montifiorre answered, amazed again as he remembered the night it happened.

"Yes, indeed! She is a fine horse. Do you know anything about her?" Christopher asked.

"Nothing. A bit of a mystery really, hence her name. The owner before me also came upon her in a bet."

It was twilight by the time they got back to the house.

"Can I invite you both in for a sherry?" Montifiorre asked merrily.

"We really should be getting back to our lodgings," Christopher said.

"Well, in that case, I will send for the buggy. George can take you both home," Montifiorre said.

George soon came round with the horse and buggy.

Montifiorre put his hand out to help Beatrice up into the buggy. The minute she took it and felt its warmth, a charge went through her. That was the first time they had touched and it felt nice. They kept their hold for a little longer than the norm.

"It's been an absolute pleasure, Beatrice," Montifiorre said warmly. Christopher climbed in afterwards.

"I'd like to invite you both for lunch next week."

"That would be wonderful," Christopher said accepting the offer.

Christopher genuinely liked the man. For the first time in a long time, he had laughed. He brought out his witty side.

"Tuesday at one p.m. I'll have my carriage send for you," Montifiorre said excitedly. "Oh, and please call me Monti."

They all waved goodbye, looking forward to next Tuesday. Any love that was, had been cemented in that horse ride and in that holding of hands, their first touch. He seemed perfect, thought Beatrice. He was amiable, funny and a lover of horses. What was not to like? Thought Beatrice.

The next morning, Beatrice woke early and with a skip in her step. Is this what love feels like? She thought. She knocked on Marie's door.

"Come in!" said Marie.

"Bonjour. I've come for my skirt," Beatrice asked. "I have a luncheon next week and I was wondering if you had a prettier shirt than this one?"

"Ahh! Mademoiselle! A luncheon, how charming! And so soon. You have only been in the city a few days. May I ask who with?"

"Joseph Montifiorre," Beatrice said breezily.

"Oh, no, mademoiselle! Not Joseph Montifiorre. No, no, no," Marie said strongly.

"What do you mean? No, no, no?" Beatrice's breezy mood was instantly shattered.

"Mademoiselle Joseph Montifiorre is a very bad man. He is a cad, a gambler, a womaniser," Marie was steadfast in her opinion.

Beatrice's mind raced. He did say he had won Mystery in a bet. But he seemed so genuine, I can't believe he is a cad.

"Are you sure you have the right gentleman?" Beatrice questioned.

"Oui, oui, oui! Joseph Montifiorre. Most certainly, mademoiselle. His sisters come to have their dresses made. I know them well. Even they talk badly of him," Marie said.

Beatrice was devastated. It was true, even he said himself that his sisters go to see Marie, Beatrice thought.

"Mademoiselle, if you continue to see him you will be considered nothing but a harlot. Don't be charmed by his charm. He is a cad of the highest order."

Beatrice's mouth went dry, words failed her, she went cold and fell silent. Of course, he was a cad, she thought. What was I thinking to think otherwise. Aren't all men cads? My father, Staunton, the Judge. Well, Christopher is not. I travelled so far to see him. I feel like a fool.

"Montifiorre has ruined many a man and woman. He tricks, cheats and is of ill repute," Marie continued, enjoying the gossip.

Beatrice couldn't bear to hear any more, she thought her heart would literally break in two. "Voila!" Marie said chirpily as if completely unaware of the damage she had created. She had, after all, thought she had done something good in warning Beatrice. Beatrice snatched the skirt and fled the room.

"Tut! I was only trying to help," Marie said offended at Beatrice's rude exit. Christopher, a little while later, knocked on Beatrice's door.

"Come in," she said.

"B! What's the matter?" Christopher said surprised to see Beatrice flopped on the bed, her face buried in the blankets.

"He's a cad, Christopher, a cad!" Beatrice said, her words muffled from the bedding.

"What? I didn't hear you. What did you say?" Christopher couldn't hear her muffled and tearful voice.

Beatrice sat up and turned around. Her eyes were red from crying. "Marie said he is a cad of the highest degree. Those were her exact words."

As Christopher sat next to Beatrice on her bed and looked at her, he thought that, despite all her experiences and all her confidence, she was really very young and innocent.

"You can't believe everything everybody says, B."

"She says he's a gambler and womaniser. His sisters say so as well when they go to see Marie. He said himself he had won Mystery in a bet, didn't he, and that his sisters go to see Marie! I feel like a fool. I've had my head in the clouds. What was I thinking? Ridiculous! I never want to see him again!"

"Yes, but still we have to find out a bit more before we cast such judgement."

Christopher was surprised too. He felt confident of his good judge of character. Montifiorre definitely did not seem like the character painted by Marie, but then, in his experience with all sorts of criminals, most often people are not what they seem.

"Let us find out a bit more before we lose heart," Christopher said warmly. This lifted Beatrice's spirits a little.

"Come on, we had arranged to see the shop for my printer," Christopher said chirpily, lifting the mood. "The fresh air will do you good."

And it was true, it did make Beatrice feel a little better. It was a sunny and crispy October day. Boston looked charming. As they walked, Christopher slowly fell in love with it. It felt cultured, it felt like a bookshop would be both needed and welcomed here. Christopher just liked the feel of the city. It felt new and full of possibilities, unlike England which felt stale and old and unwelcoming.

"Well, this looks like it," Christopher said as they both walked up to the building they saw the other day.

The owner was waiting outside for them.

"Good day to you, sir," the owner said shaking Christopher's hand. "Ma'am," he nodded his head at Beatrice.

They all walked in. The space was quite large and Christopher instantly imagined books in their shelves piled high, ceiling to floor. He felt a twinge of excitement run through him.

"And here we have the back rooms," the owner said.

He guided them to the rear of the room which was a perfect size to put his printer and any other machinery needed.

"And here?" Christopher pointed to a tiny courtyard at the very rear.

"Yes, this comes with the shop. I used it for my tools but it's good for anything," the owner said. Christopher instantly imagined building a conservatory here and this could be his writing room. It all felt too good to be true and Christopher wondered if there was a catch.

"Well, I like it a lot and I think it would be perfect for my bookshop and printer," said Christopher.

"I know where you can get a printer. I used to sell parts to a man. His workshop is on 44 Gallard Street. Not far from here," said the owner.

"Oh, that's rather convenient. Would you mind if I had a second, please?" Christopher asked.

"Of course, I'll wait outside."

"Do you like it, B?" Christopher asked looking at Beatrice excitedly. "I can build a mini library along this wall. Maybe it's better if I put the printer at the front of the shop for all to see?"

Christopher's joy was contagious and Beatrice couldn't help but be uplifted. "Kit, its perfect, absolutely perfect."

"I'll talk money and see if I can afford it all. I have to find out how much for the printer and how much for the renovations. I'll put in an offer," Christopher said thinking aloud more than anything.

They walked out and said their goodbyes to the owner. Christopher then raised his head up to the sky and let out a big and long sigh.

"This is a truly marvellous day, Beatrice," Christopher said quietly.

Beatrice could not help but realise the gravity of this moment for her cousin and she leant forward and gave him the biggest and warmest of hugs. He had put up with too much for too long. It was now his time for some glory.

"You deserve it, Kit," Beatrice said with all the love she had.

Beatrice was truly aware of all the devotion and protection he had given her. He had nearly died for her, he travelled the Atlantic for her, he had been a highway robber for her. This was now his reward for all his good deeds and Beatrice was profoundly happy for him.

"Thank you, B! If it wasn't for the lengths and depths of your adventures I would still be back in England, still a smuggler."

"My pleasure," Beatrice replied aware of the irony.

They both smiled. Today was a good day for Christopher. For Beatrice, not so much. "I still have to iron out the details. But for now, let's go celebrate. Champagne?"

Christopher held out his arm for Beatrice to hold and they walked arm in arm to a restaurant. They both feasted themselves on the finest Boston could offer and celebrated with Champagne. It was magical.

They arrived soon enough at their lodgings.

The next morning, they were both going to go and see the man with the printer. They got up late and went down for some breakfast.

"Mademoiselle," Pierre came straight out to meet them at the entrance. "A letter came for you this morning."

"Thank you, Pierre," Beatrice said looking at Christopher with a surprised and questioning look. It was indeed strange that a letter would find her here. How did it find her here? She thought.

She read the very beautiful handwriting on the front and recognised Radcliff's writing. How did he find me here? Beatrice thought. He knew I was doing the Pony Express so it must have come through that way. She felt it would reveal something ominous rather than joyful.

Beatrice curiously opened the envelope, unfolded the paper and began to read. Christopher noticed Beatrice's face change both in colour and expression. She went white. "What is it, B?" Christopher asked.

"My parents are dead," Beatrice said quietly.

"I never said goodbye," Beatrice fell into tears and into the arms of Christopher.

Christopher took the letter and read for himself about the horse and carriage accident that had killed them both.

"Oh, B, how shocking. I'm so, so, sorry," Christopher consoled.

"I will have to go back to England immediately," Beatrice said through her tears. "You go ahead Christopher. I want to be alone for a bit," Beatrice said.

Christopher nodded. He left Beatrice back at the lodgings and went to meet the man selling the printer. He may have not liked Lord and Lady Seymour but they were Beatrice's parents for all their faults and he knew full well what it was like to lose your parents. His heart wrenched for his cousin. So much had happened so quickly, Christopher felt that they had already both lived two lifetimes. Even being here and finding the shop, and now, the printer had happened so quickly, it was hard to catch one's breath, thought Christopher.

That night, Beatrice had time to think as she wallowed in her despair. I am finally free and I finally find love. But that turns out to be false, and then my parents have died. Am I doomed for forever? Is it all my wrongdoing? Have I cursed myself and others around me. Beatrice felt very,

very low. She wished she could undo everything that she had done. All the rebellion, all the defiance. All the turmoil and shame she had cast upon her family. Her heart bled for her mother. At least I said goodbye to Mama, Beatrice thought, as tears rolled down her eyes. I will get on the first ship to England. But what about Christopher? She thought.

The next morning, Beatrice rose solemnly. Everything had changed. Everything felt different. The joy, the light had gone. The only thing that did remain was Beatrice's joy for Christopher.

"You must stay, cousin. I absolutely refuse you coming with me. I will disown you for life if you disobey me." Beatrice, despite her sorrow, gave Christopher a wry smile. "Did they accept your offer?

"Yes."

"And you have enough? With all the highway loot and wager money?"

"Yes."

"Then, cousin, Boston is the place for you. And I am so exceedingly happy for you."

Christopher didn't know what to say. His heart wrenched at the thought of Beatrice returning to England and them separating. But he couldn't go back. Everything in his being was telling him not to go back and they both knew this. They also both knew he had done his duty to Beatrice, he had surpassed himself, over and above all normal expectations. It was time now for her to go. Lacey Manor had been left to her. No male heirs. Her father never got the heirs or the title he so wanted.

They went to the port and found a captain that would be leaving for England next week. Christopher felt confident of the integrity of the captain and that Beatrice would be kept safe.

"I can do this by myself," Beatrice said as if reading Christopher's thoughts. "And besides, it's probably for the best. I never want to see that cad again!"

They walked home in silence. Beatrice's heart was ragged and torn. She had lost the only man she had loved and lost her mother who, despite her weaknesses, Beatrice did love. The love for her father was turbulent, to say the least, but now that he had gone she did feel sorrow. He was after all her papa. And then, I'll be leaving Christopher, Beatrice thought. A thought that was too much to bear.

As the days went by, Beatrice had time to prepare her bag and fully absorb her new reality. She was going back to England, she was going home. She was also going home as a landed gentlewoman and a little, little part of her, albeit deeply hidden, was secretly happy about this.

I'm going home, she thought. It is going to be unbearable to leave Christopher, she thought. But his place is here, in the new world, creating his new life and his new identity.

Beatrice also secretly was looking forward to shocking society life with her return. 'The Highwaygirl returns,' she could hear them all talking and gossiping, aghast at her presence back in society. For Beatrice, this was going to be fun, it was going to spark her rebellious nature once again. Only this time, it would be better, she would be a landed gentlewoman and she would have power supporting her rebellion.

Beatrice had pushed the thoughts of Montifiorre out of her mind. Her heart was broken in two but it would mend, England and horses and meadows, and dare she think of it, Asta, would mend that. It was a stupid and childish fancy anyway, she thought. And I never want to see him again.

Asta, Beatrice thought. Her heart lifted. She imagined her running towards her as she always did. Imagined their rides. Imagined their dozes in the barn together. Had her father taken her from her hiding? Had he killed her? Took his revenge out on Asta? Could she ever forgive him? The thought of him doing such a thing and the thought of Asta not being there tore at her heart and tears rolled painfully down her face. Lacey Manor without her Asta would never be the same. Would Betty still be there? She wondered as she packed her highway robber's clothes into her suitcase. I'm going to hang the mask and scarf up on the wall. She packed her deerskin painting and thought of the healer woman. Her heart warmed with gratefulness. She thought of all those beautiful and happy children. Her mind was in a whirl. Her heart was tired from all its hurting. Christopher knocked on her door.

"Come in," Beatrice said.

"Do you want to come and see the printer? They are delivering today," Christopher said.

He was beside himself with joy but also sorrowful for their impending separation. Having such extreme feelings was hard to live with, he thought.

"I'd love to."

They walked along the bustling streets of Boston. Christopher offered his arm and Beatrice took it. They enjoyed each other's company. They arrived at his shop.

"So here it is. Ta da!" Christopher said lifting off the white sheet protecting it.

"Oh, Christopher, it's a beast of a machine. Like something from the future."

"Grand, isn't she? Actually this is only a part of it. The rest will be delivered at a later date." He was so excited he could hardly contain himself.

"Well, I want to see your first book published from the beast," Beatrice demanded. "Let's go celebrate!"

"What are you going to call your shop? Any ideas?" Beatrice asked.

"Meadow Books. What do you think?"

Beatrice went straight and embraced Christopher.

"What a wonderful achievement, Kit. Here we are in your bookshop. Your bookshop! You did it, Kit, you did it. I'm so very proud of you," Beatrice was gushing in praise, something she didn't usually do, but today, Christopher deserved all the praise and congratulations.

JOSEPH AND JOSHUA

JOSEPH'S excitement was overspilling. He just couldn't believe how fate had put himself and the Highwaygirl together. The minute he had locked eyes with her back at Lacey Manor he had fallen in love. It was only when her hat fell and her hair spilled out was he sure that he had actually locked eyes with a girl. And on seeing the portrait of Lady Beatrice Seymour-Barclay at Lacey later that day did he guess who that girl actually was. And then, to have actually had their carriage stopped and robbed by the Highwaygirl was too much of a delight. Joseph liked the scandal and embraced the clandestine affair of it all.

A few days later, however, Joseph was told to go to New York on business for his father. His father had been struck ill with a fever and couldn't go. So, Joseph, against all his protestations, had to go.

"But Joshua is already there. Surely he can sort it all out," Joseph had said to his father as he tried in vain to not go.

"And you know what a drunk and a bully and a buffoon he is. You have to! Otherwise, I stand to lose a lot of money. You cannot leave your mother destitute, Joseph," his father had said.

And it was true, his brother was all of the above. In fact, you couldn't get two brothers more different. Joshua was the eldest but the one with the inferiority complex. In contrast to his brother, Joseph chose reason and humour and loyalty as his modus operandi. Joseph was all those things and more. He was reliable, amiable, jolly and a lover of food. He also had a little mischievous streak which revealed itself with a practical joke here and there but that was the extent of his folly. So, when he was held up by the infamous highway robber, and knowing it was the same highway robber he had locked eyes with and that the highway robber was, in fact, a girl, instead of it enraging him, it did the opposite. It simply tickled him pink, he was in love with her.

But he had to give up any notion of meeting her when he was sent to New York. He adored his mother and the thought of her being left destitute was too much for him. Joseph, after all, was a very loyal son; he was also a very good businessman and would be able to broker a good deal.

Montifiorre was born into a family of business and finance. For generations, his family had been in business in Venice, Italy. They were merchants, property owners, money lenders. He neither liked nor disliked the world of business, it was just something he had only ever known. He actually didn't really know what else he would like to do. Cook maybe, he loved food.

So, it was with much trepidation, that he left for New York. After his time brokering a successful deal in New York, he then went to Boston to stay in their family residence and sort some of their merchant business. Joseph was not looking forward to rejoining his brother in Boston. Joshua was loud and overbearing. A bully and a drunk. He had always bullied Montifiorre, especially when they were both at Eton taking full advantage of his older brother status. Joseph often thought of Cain and Abel when he thought of himself and Joshua.

Joshua lacked all the grace and gentility that his brother, Joseph, had. Joshua used and abused money, he loved it and squandered it. As the eldest son, he had been spoilt and his sense of entitlement went with him everywhere.

"Ahh, Joseph! So father has sent you to come and save the day. Save his finances and his deals," Joshua said sarcastically as Joseph walked through the front door on his arrival.

"Come here and let me give you a hug," Joshua forcefully took Joseph into his arms. "You have put on weight. You look a bit portly. You have lost your glow. Father's been working you too hard in London. Come have a whiskey with me. A celebration of your success in New York."

Joshua poured them both a whiskey. Joseph, despite not much liking alcohol, drank some. "Oh, don't be such a light weight. Drink up, old boy!" Joshua pushed.

"So what's the latest gossip from England. I hear they hanged that Highwaygirl. What a disgrace. So she should have hanged. Can you imagine the humiliation, a girl of noble breeding becoming a robber. The daughter of our clients, the Seymour-Barclays. Yes, definitely a hanging for the girl. Anything else of interest?" Joshua went on.

Joseph stopped in his tracks. They had hanged the Highwaygirl? The girl he had locked eyes with. The girl who had held up his carriage. The girl he fell in love with. Joseph went cold. His mouth went dry and he felt his breathing waver. He was genuinely in shock. He let Joshua talk away in the distance as he fell silent.

"Joseph, are you listening?" said Joshua as he poured himself another whiskey. "We have to visit the Governor tomorrow and we have to sign the contracts. Have you read the contracts? Joseph, have you read the contracts!" Joshua shouted.

"Yes, yes, yes, I've read the contracts," said Joseph bringing himself back to the room.

"Whiskey, brother! I hate drinking alone," Joshua said.

This time, Joseph gladly drank it and drank it in one go. This time he needed it. He put his glass down, and with it, put all notions of the Highwaygirl away. When someone is alive, so lives the hope, however small. But when someone dies, then all hope dies too.

"It's nice to share a whiskey with you. Here, have another. I have some of my fellows coming around for a game of cards and a few bets, why don't you join us, we need another gentleman to make up the numbers and I would very much like to introduce you to them. You can't say no, I've already agreed with them that you would."

"Cards, brother, is not for me?" Joseph said.

"Don't let me down, brother. I need the extra player," Joshua insisted. "Here, have another." Joseph took the whiskey.

Joseph felt low and badgered. The whiskey felt good.

"So, the game starts at eleven o'clock. Don't disappoint. You only need to play one round."

"Eleven. I'll see you at eleven. But never, ever ask me to play cards again."

"Deal."

Later that night, Joshua's friends arrived. All on horseback and all a little bawdy. Joshua excelled in this kind of fun and was loud and obnoxious. Joseph was already regretting his decision to play. Joshua was already drunk and Joseph knew full well how aggressive he got when he was drunk. One game, he said to himself.

They all sat around the table and the cards were dealt. Bets were thrown and the drinks were poured. Joseph didn't much like the look of the men he was sitting with. Not his type of people. One game and I leave, he said to himself again. There were eight players in total. Joseph had absolutely no interest in knowing who any of them were.

The first hand was dealt. The money was put in the middle. A gentleman called Simons won the round.

"Simons, you sly old rogue," Joshua said slapping him hard on the back.

"Your majesty, I am solid gold," Simons said using Joshua's nickname.

"Well, it's time for me to make my leave. Gentlemen," Joseph stood up readying himself to leave.

"No, you don't! Joseph, you can't leave now," Joshua insisted.

"Don't let him leave, Joshua," said Bannerman.

Joseph knew it was hopeless and sat back down. He hated being there and longed for his bed, its warmth and its quiet.

The night went on. The gentlemen got drunker and the losses got higher.

"Gentleman, I have nothing left but I have one last arrow in my quiver before I give up," Mr Percy said bravely. "My Black Beauty, my most gallant mare."

"No, Percy, not Beauty," said one of the gentlemen.

Percy swallowed another whiskey. He was already very drunk, he was also very desperate. Inwardly, he was a pack of nerves. He owed so much money to so many people that he had to win this hand. Some of those people were not very nice people and they wanted their money back more than anything. Percy had to win and he bargained everything on the luck of his black mare.

The hand was dealt. Joseph put in just enough to stay in the game. Everybody wanted to win this round, everybody wanted to win Black Beauty, except, of course, Joseph. The atmosphere was tense. Any sweat that was shed was running underneath the gentlemen's well-groomed suits.

Percy thought his hand could win. The room for the first time became very tense, it sizzled with anticipation as, one by one, the players revealed their hands. Percy dropped his head when he knew he had lost. And Joseph raised his when he knew he had won. He was not expecting to or even wanting to win.

"Ahh, brother, you rogue, you did it. What a cad!" Joshua shouted as he jumped up in the air and then brutishly thumped Joseph on the back, Joseph fell slightly on the table.

Joseph hated it when his brother got so drunk.

Percy had lost. He hid his disappointment. He was distraught. How was he going to explain to his wife that he had lost her favourite mare in a card game. But worse still, how was he going to repay his debtors?

"Joseph, look after her;" Percy gallantly said as he stood up from the table. Joseph couldn't believe it. He had won the hand and the Black Beauty.

"Percy I don´t think…" Joseph was about to renounce his win when Percy interrupted.

"Good lord, man! You can't go back on a win," Percy drunkenly said. "It's not the gentlemanly thing to do." And then tipped his hat before he left.

And so, Joseph, a man neither of drink or gambling had won himself the finest horse of all of Boston. He couldn't believe it and promised that he would return the horse to Percy. Acquiring such a fine and glorious animal by means of gambling felt strange and not right.

"Good hand, brother, good hand, what a fine win!" Joshua said again, he was drunkenly thrilled with his brother's win.

"Well, gentleman, I think it's time for me to take my leave too," Joseph said and quickly made his escape.

As Joseph walked away, he could hear the men laughing and shouting. He wasn't ready for sleep so he thought he would go and visit Black beauty in the stables. I'll offer Percy the carriage to get home, Joseph thought.

Joseph couldn't see Percy anywhere. He seemed to have disappeared into the night. I hope he's all right, Joseph thought. As he entered the stables, Black Beauty raised her head. Joseph went straight up to her. The stables were warm and musky. She leant her head forward and put it into the cupped hands of Joseph.

"You are definitely a beautiful horse. A little mysterious I would say. Shall I change your name to Mystery?" Joseph said to the mare.

She had such an aura about her, a deeper look in her eyes, he thought.

It was late, Joseph was tired, and tomorrow, he had a long day so he went to bed.

Two days after the night of the gambling, Joseph had another meeting. He took Black Beauty. What a wonderful horse indeed. She seemed almost godly. Her walk glided and her trot more so. It was effortless to ride her.

After his meeting with the Governor, Joseph rode Black Beauty to Lord Percy's house with the intention of giving her back. He lived not far from his own home in the affluent uptown part of Boston. A big Georgian style house lay before him. Joseph rode up the long path and dismounted Beauty just as he reached the front door. Holding Black Beauty by the reins, he rang the door.

"Good afternoon. My name is Joseph Montifiorre from Beacon Hill. I am a friend of Sir Percy, we were dining the other night. I'd like to speak to Sir Percy," Joseph said to the rather stiff and old butler.

"Sir Percy isn't here. He has left on business," said the butler.

"When will he be back?"

"Not for a while, sir. He's gone back to New York for the winter."

"Oh dear," said Joseph, he was surprised and didn't want to leave Black Beauty without Percy being there.

"Well, thank you. I'll write to him instead then," Joseph said and turned to walk away.

"Well, I suppose you and I are now together," Joseph said to Black Beauty as he climbed up on top. Joseph looked a fine figure of a gentleman indeed on the back of the mare. His warm, sleek European looks matched her warm, sleek stature. They made a dashing pair.

"Well, then, maybe I will rename you Mystery. There is definitely something mysterious about you. I must find out more about you."

Business went on as usual. Joseph had meetings. Joshua got drunk. Joseph went to work in Boston. Joshua went out at night to the city taverns. Both brothers kept their distance from each other.

So, it was with an incredible shock that, on the morning whilst walking to another meeting, Joseph bumped into the Highwaygirl. So much so, he could hardly speak. He felt frozen and awkward in his speech. Words were coming out of his mouth but they all seemed totally detached from his body. He just couldn't believe it was her! Or was it really her? He believed it was, he knew it was her. The eyes were definitely the same but was it her? But then, she said her name and it was her and that she was actually alive and hadn't been hanged. I'm so glad I managed to ask her for tea, he had thought. I'm so glad she came.

After their tea all together, Joseph was on cloud nine. He liked her cousin, Christopher, instantly and hoped that they could even be friends. He didn't actually have many friends. But he had one thorn in his side, Joshua. He was lucky Joshua was out when they came for tea but he had to make sure he would be out for the entire time of their luncheon. He knew Joshua would try and disrupt the whole affair.

The day before their luncheon, Joshua walked into Joseph's study. He was on the warpath. "You have to go to New York tomorrow, not I," Joshua demanded.

"No, I can't possibly go. I have too much work. And besides, Father wants you to go."

Joseph panicked. Joshua can't stay and I can't go to New York. Joseph knew it was futile to argue with his brother so, instead, he had to concoct a plan so that Joshua actually did go. Joseph then stood up, signalling Joshua to leave, but instead, Joshua came threateningly up to Joseph. He took him by the lapels and slammed him up against the wall.

"You will go to New York instead of me!"

What was he up to? Thought Joseph as he stayed pinned against the wall. Finally, Joshua released him and stormed out.

Joseph was used to his brother's bullying, but this time, it wasn't going to ruin his chances at love. Joseph tried to continue working but he couldn't concentrate. So, he went to his favourite source of comfort, food and the kitchens. This time, I am not going to cower to my brother, Joseph thought as he walked.

"Good morning, Veronica. Do you have any of those little cakes left?" Joseph asked.

"Si, signore" said Veronica as she gleefully passed him a plate of her best Napolese cakes. Veronica was from Naples, Italy. She had travelled with the family to Boston. She had been their cook since Joseph was a boy.

"Il cafè," Veronica said as she gave him a cup of the finest Italian coffee.

Joseph felt better all ready. He had learnt a lot about food and cooking and baking from Veronica. She was big, hearty and was a lover of food herself. Pizzas, pastas, soups, fish, cakes. The best of Italian food. Joseph used to sit and watch her cook. Veronica used to let him sit on her lap and stir the ingredients in her big mixing bowl. She taught him to make dough and pizzas. She used to call him her 'little bambini' but now that he is older she calls him Signore Bambini.

So, Signore Bambini sat quietly in the kitchen. He didn't talk much. He just watched Veronica busy about her work.

"You all right, signore?" Veronica looked at Joseph with a quizzical eye.

"Yes, Veronica."

As he watched her pour some herbs in the bread dough and then crush some more in her pestle and mortar, the thought suddenly came to Joseph. What if I could take something that would make me ill for a few days. Some of Veronica's herbs maybe? Today is Friday, Joseph thought. If I take the herbs today, I will surely be better for Tuesday. His little plan was making him excited. Joseph waited for the kitchen staff to leave.

"Veronica, could you make me ill?" Joseph said in a hushed voice.

"Signore! What are you saying? Veronica only make better."

"I know, Veronica, you do always make me feel better. Your cakes today were especially wonderful. No, I mean could you make me ill that would then make me better?" Joseph knew he was talking in riddles and Veronica's bemused face expressed that.

"Could you make me have a bad stomach ache. I need to be sick for a few days. But I need to be better for my luncheon with Lady Beatrice and Christopher."

"You like the young lady, no?

"Yes, I do, Veronica, and I do not want to miss this wonderful chance of fate." Ever the romantic, the truth of Joseph's situation touched her.

"Joshua is trying to get me to go to New York instead of him, and Veronica, this time, I won't be bullied."

"Bravo, signore! Si, Veronica can make you sick. I will put a little of mushroom, only a little, in your lunch. But signore, please be careful!"

Veronica never liked Joshua and wanted to help Joseph. She hated the way he had bullied Joseph and the way he had been spoiled as the eldest son.

"Thank you, Veronica," Joseph said giving Veronica a big hug. "Now, don't put too many of those mushrooms in," he said with a little smile.

Joseph was joking but really he was a little nervous. But he knew he couldn't just pretend to be ill with his brother, he had to make it real. Joshua may not be talented in business but he was very talented at being cunning.

Joseph sat in his room which overlooked the house's beautiful grounds. They were awash with colour; oranges and reds, rusts and yellows, truly, a beautiful sight. Joseph rang the bell for his lunch to be brought up

Veronica placed the hot, wood-fired pizza on Joseph's tray and made the sign of the cross whilst saying a little prayer. She then handed the tray to Mary who took it up to Joseph.

"Here, sir, here's your lunch," Mary said as she came through the door.

"Thank you, Mary," Joseph said politely.

Joseph watched Mary bring the tray, upon it lay his surreptitious attempts at food poisoning. He looked down at the plate of food. He was nervous but adamant. It looked so tasty, no one could possibly think it had ominous intentions.

Joseph slowly and nervously began to eat Veronica's pizza. It tasted so delicious. More so today than any other day. Was this Joseph's imagination? It tasted better because it was going to deliver his success, success on a plate. Every mouthful held some trepidation. Joseph waited for any of the effects to start, but so far, nothing. He only hoped Veronica had put in the correct amount.

Immediately after finishing his lunch, the plan started to work. His stomach wrenched and his head pounded, the wild mushrooms were hard at work. He ran to the bathroom and vomited and vomited and vomited. He felt utterly terrible. Never again would he underestimate this little fungi. The colour drained from his face as he continued to vomit. He begged it would stop. This was utterly ghastly. He vomited some more. He begged for it to stop, and finally, it did. He rang the bell for Mary to come. He felt awful, truly awful. His stomach ached, his ribs pained. Joseph was never really very good at being ill.

"Mary, I don't feel very well. Can you inform Joshua."

Mary left and Joseph waited. He had never done anything like this before. It was easy for him to deal with the comings and goings of money but anything surreptitious was not easy.

A few minutes later, Joseph heard, as expected, Joshua's footsteps pounding down the corridor. Joseph could feel the anger vibrating with every step. He waited and prepared himself for the torrent that was about to enter his room.

Joshua slammed open the door with no regard for his ill brother behind it.

"What do you mean you are ill, you're not ill enough!" Joshua roared. He was infuriated.

"I cannot travel, let alone do any business in this state," Joseph said in his frailest of voices, a voice he actually didn't have to fake. He felt genuinely terrible. "I wouldn't want to lose money on the stocks because I was too busy vomiting."

And then, Joseph sat up and vomited straight into his bowl. The mushrooms performed perfectly as if they had timed their next vomit bang on cue. It was also the vomit that sealed the deal. Joshua had to concede. It was true and it was plain to see; Joseph was in no shape for New York's stock market. There was someone Joshua did fear and that was his father, so he knew he had to go to New York after all.

Joshua turned in a spin of rage and walked out. He slammed the door behind him, getting his dressing gown caught in it, and his trying to pull it loose only infuriated him more.

"Argh!" he yelled releasing himself and slamming the door shut.

Joseph held his breath. He listened for Joshua's pounding steps to disappear, and only when he could hear nothing, did he finally sink down into his bed, letting out a long and slow breath. It worked, he thought. Thank you, Veronica.

After a short while, Mary knocked on the door. "Come in," said Joseph.

Mary walked in holding a tray.

"Your herbs, sir, from the cook," said Mary.

"Thank you, Mary," Joseph replied.

"She said to drink it slowly, very slowly. They will make you feel better."

Over the day, Joseph did exactly as Veronica had said. He drank her herbs slowly and he did feel better. He lay in bed, something he hadn't done in years, he actually felt pleased with himself. This fight he had won. Most he had lost. Whether that be physical or verbal, Joshua had to win at all costs. He knew how to give the right punch in the place that would hurt the hardest. Joseph often thought his brother was wasted in the world of finance and business, he would have made a good Roman general or a medieval knight. Now, all Joseph had to do was get better in time for his luncheon with Lady Beatrice. He was very excited to be seeing them both again.

The next day, he heard the commotion of Joshua's leaving downstairs. He was shouting at staff and basically having a tantrum. Joseph watched from his window as his brother stormed about on the forecourt and then, finally, got in his carriage and rode away. Joseph watched him as he slowly rode down the driveway and finally out of sight.

Joseph let out a massive sigh. He's finally gone, he thought as relief flooded all over him. Joseph went back to bed, he still felt terrible, but at least, he had the day to rest. Tomorrow they will be coming and I have today to think about the menu, thought Joseph excitedly.

In the afternoon, Joseph sat up in bed. He was excited at the thought of them coming tomorrow. I must go down to Veronica and talk about the menu. He felt a bit wobbly. His stomach still had waves of nausea. Joseph got up and walked to the door, and suddenly, everything around him went blank.

"Sir, sir, wake up, sir!" Mary called worryingly, she was trying to push the door open.

Joseph had fainted just by the door. Mary couldn't open it as he was blocking it. His last moment of awareness was seeing his hand touching the door handle and then, bang, he went down like a dead weight.

Joseph got up, arranged himself and then opened the door for Mary. "Are you all right, sir?" Mary asked concerned.

"Yes, I must have fainted."

"Sir, you have cut your head. Are you sure you are all right?" Mary was a little worried.

"Yes, of course," Joseph touched the blood on his forehead and looked at it. "Goodness gracious me."

"You had quite a nasty bang, sir. Let me help you to your feet," said Mary. Mary bent to help Joseph but he put his hand up to stop her.

"Thank you, Mary, but I'm fine," Joseph politely said.

Joseph then went back to bed and rested some more. He just had to get better for tomorrow he thought. Whatever it would take.

Later that day, Joseph felt better and managed to go down to Veronica. "Signore, you are better," Veronica said giving him a wink.

"Yes, much better, thank you, Veronica," Joseph winked back. It was going to be their little secret together, now added to the long list of other secrets they shared,

They both arranged the menu, a light Sunday lunch of venison, vegetables and a pumpkin pie for dessert.

Joseph went back to bed. Tomorrow was nearly here. No disturbances, no Joshua, wonderful food and fine weather. What could go wrong? Joseph thought.

Sunday morning, Joseph woke early. He went to his study to finish some work and then at eleven-thirty he went to tell George to prepare the horses and carriage. At twelve twenty George set off to pick up Beatrice and Christopher. Joseph stood on the forecourt and watched him ride away.

Joseph was so excited for their day ahead. He was looking forward to getting to know Lady Beatrice, as he liked to call her to himself. He thought they could all go for a ride out once again and he could show them both another beautiful spot. He was also looking forward to seeing Christopher again. He found him charming, funny and easy company, a pleasure to spend time with. So, it was with bated breath that he waited to see George and the carriage return up the driveway.

He went briefly back to his study to drink some more of Veronica's herbs. His stomach still felt a little delicate and he still felt a little weak. But the excitement of the day would carry him through. Joseph was also looking forward to showing Beatrice more of his true self. Their first encounter was awkward and then, the second, less so but was hindered by time. What a delight not having Joshua here, Joseph thought as he sipped his herbs. The house literally feels calmer and happier.

At twelve-fifty, Joseph went down to the entrance to wait for their arrival. I wonder what she'll be wearing, Joseph thought. A dress, breeches or a skirt? I adore her short hair. This time, if the moment is right, I'll find an opportunity to hold her hand again. I will also try and find the opportunity to tell her how I feel about her. Make our courtship open. She must be interested in me otherwise she wouldn't be coming today. Joseph's mind was aflutter as was his stomach, full of butterflies and the residue of some very powerful mushrooms. He looked at his watch, it was ten-past-one.

"Where could they be? I hope everything is all right. Maybe it was difficult trying to leave the city?" Joseph was starting to get worried.

"Oh, thank goodness! Here they come," Joseph said out loud as he saw the horses of his carriage ride into the driveway.

Joseph waited. Excitedly he prepared himself. He chose a dapper dark blue coat and pulled it into place.

George approached. They are nearly here, what joy, he thought. George stopped the horses and climbed down.

"Sir, I'm terribly sorry to be the bearer of such news but Lady Seymour wasn't at her lodgings. The landlord was out so I couldn't ask for her whereabouts."

Joseph didn't even skip a beat. He ran down to the stables, saddled Mystery and bolted down the driveway. He was going to be asking Mystery to ride the fastest she had ever ridden. He rode at lightning speed to Beatrice's lodgings.

"Where is she! The young lady! The young English lady! My name is Joseph Montifiorre and we were to meet today," Joseph demanded as he stormed into the lodgings in a panic. Thankfully, Pierre was there.

"The Highwaygirl, you mean?" Pierre calmly responded.

"Yes, yes, yes, the Highwaygirl." Joseph urgently replied.

"Monsieur, she has left," Pierre replied calmly, which was in complete contrast to Joseph's panic.

"Left?" Joseph questioned. He felt his heart slowly breaking. "Left?" he asked again utterly bemused. "What do you mean, left? We have a luncheon today."

"Oui, monsieur, to the port for Angleterre," Pierre seemed absolutely oblivious to Joseph's plight. Joseph was completely shocked and felt his legs weakening from under him. He was already in a weakened state. "But why?"

"Monsieur, are you all right?" Pierre asked.

"To England you say?" still bemused.

"To England, yes. She received a telegram informing her of the deaths of her parents, an accident in England."

"An accident! Good lord."

"I must go see her immediately. I must go to the port," Joseph jumped into action.

"Oh, no, sir, you cannot go, she wants nothing of you, she told me so, well, my wife, Marie, told me so, Monsieur, I like to play the odd game of cards," Pierre said confidingly in his broken English and heavy French accent. "Don't worry, I understand, us men, we like the cards."

What on earth is he talking about? Thought Montifiorre frantically, I don't have time for this.

"My Marie, she don't like the poker but I still play. I am sorry but she told the English lady that you like the cards. I don't think the English lady like you playing the cards. My Marie is very good at sewing and très bien at gossiping."

"No, no, no!" Joseph said out loud but mostly to himself. "She thinks I'm Joshua. She thinks I'm the gambler and the cad. No, no, no, this is terrible!"

"No, no, no! My brother is the gambler and the cad. Tell your wife that if she likes to gossip then to get her gossip correct!"

Joseph flew out of the lodgings, swung up on Mystery and galloped directly to the port.

"But the ship has set sail, monsieur!" Joseph heard Pierre shouting after him as he rode as fast as he could.

He was absolutely beside himself. His heart and stomach were both in knots. My god-awful brother will not destroy my chance of happiness. Despite his urgency, Joseph feared he would fail in reaching the ship in time. He noted the wind which, unfortunately, seemed perfect for a midday departure

THE PORT

THE morning of her journey, Beatrice woke extremely early. She had hardly slept and her heart was heavy. Her one bag was packed, she hardly possessed anything anyway, her book from Mrs Riley, her deerskin painting, her mask and scarf, her jockey hat and a pouch with some of the robbery bounty.

Her feelings were mixed and torn. The thought of saying goodbye to Christopher was unbearable but they both knew it was the right thing to do. It felt hard to do but it felt right to do. Christopher had just found his printer's shop, his dream had come true. I'm so happy for him, thought Beatrice. It had all happened with such ease, it must have been fate at work, she thought.

Beatrice definitely liked this new world. It was staggeringly beautiful and her eccentric ways seemed more accepted here. But England was her home. She was an English girl at heart. The woodlands and meadows. England was small, America was big and Beatrice preferred the small.

So, with heavy hearts and much trepidation, the cousins started their walk towards the port.

"B, we will write. I will tell you all about my shop and my books," Christopher tried to lighten the mood but his heart was breaking.

Beatrice didn't reply.

"You must write too, B, and tell me all about Lacey and England," Christopher continued. Beatrice wanted to reply by saying something like, the meadow will never be the same again without you, but tears started to well so she held her words back. "You'll have so much to do at Lacey," Christopher continued.

Beatrice found herself going dumb. The words simply didn't leave her mouth.

Her mind jumped to Montifiorre and then her heart crumpled. Her one and only love had turned out to be nothing more than a cad, a cheat and a despot. He seemed so nice, she thought.

"He seemed so nice," Beatrice found those words spilling out.

"Yes, I know. I thought so too. He really didn't seem like a cad. I can't quite put the two together," Christopher said, he was genuinely surprised to find out about Joseph's secret life.

"But sometimes it is very hard to tell," Christopher consoled.

"The day of his robbery back in England, he was in the company of not a very nice man," Beatrice said still putting the pieces of information together. She still felt like a fool for having fallen so heavily for him.

The cousins walked on in silence.

"I will miss you terribly, Kit," Beatrice suddenly said.

Christopher felt his heart wrench, tears filled his eyes. Whenever she used Kit as her term of affection, it hit straight to the core of his sensibilities.

"A perfect day for a sail," Christopher said purposely changing the tone.

They both walked on in silence. Finally, they reached the heaving activity of the port. Their ship was easy to find. The Plymouth was a hive of activity as the sailors were up and down, loading up all the mercantile.

"Welcome aboard The Plymouth," said Captain Somerville warmly. "Best to say your goodbyes. We're about to set sail," Somerville said. "Below deck!" he shouted to a man loading up a box.

"Thank you, Captain, for my cousin's safe passage home," Christopher said sincerely. He shook the Captain's hand. Somerville then went back to work

"Write," Christopher said turning to Beatrice.

"Write," Beatrice said. "Your book, I mean. I also want letters."

Despite all his efforts, Christopher couldn't hold back the tears as they flowed to the surface. She looks so young and alone, he thought as he looked at her. But he had so much confidence in her strength and ability which gave him some peace of mind.

"Sir," the Captain said signalling for Christopher to leave.

The dreaded moment had finally arrived. All the emotion then took hold of Beatrice and she leant forward into Christopher's arms and cried quiet tears. She held on tight. She couldn't actually let him go.

"Sir, you have to leave the ship now. She will be looked after," Somerville said.

They finally let go of each other; there was nothing more to say. Christopher turned and walked down the plank to the quayside. Beatrice calmly walked to the side of the ship. The plank was lifted.

"All hands," Somerville shouted.

The ship was a flurry of activity as all the men were busy with ropes and sails. Beatrice stood frozen staring at Christopher, incredulous at this moment actually happening. Are we really separating? she thought. Is this really happening? The tears quietly rolled down her face, she just couldn't believe she was saying goodbye to Christopher. The wind filled the sails and The Plymouth pulled away from the port. She was sailing. This was it, the separation had started as the distance between them widened.

Beatrice was so absorbed in their departing moment that she barely noticed a commotion happening at the other side of the quayside. She saw Christopher turn to look. It had caught his attention as well. People were shouting and things were crashing. Beatrice could hear hooves. She knew the sound of a horse all too well.

As The Plymouth sailed further away, Beatrice could not believe the dramatic and chaotic sight of Mystery and Joseph cantering along the quayside.

What on earth, thought Beatrice. What was going on? She looked at Christopher whose face said the same as hers, what on earth was he doing? It was mayhem. People were running in flight, some were trying to get hold of the reins of Mystery. Joseph was shouting at them to let go of Mystery.

"Stop! Stop"! Joseph shouted.

He thought his heart would break in two. It was all too late. She had gone. She was sailing away. He had missed her by only minutes.

"Beatrice. Beatrice!" Joseph shouted in a blind panic.

A crowd of men had gathered around Joseph to try and stop him. He was causing a danger and a havoc. They tried grabbing the reins and tried blocking his way. Joseph pushed Mystery on. She knew the urgency of her owner's mission.

"No, no, Stop! Stop! Please! You don't understand!" he shouted at the men jumping at his horse. "Beatrice, Beatrice!" he shouted again. It was pandemonium.

"Beatrice, my brother..." Joseph continued in vain, he was desperate.

The men were gathering strength, they had turned now more into a mob and Joseph's efforts to get closer were being horribly thwarted.

"Beatrice, Beatrice, my brother is the cad, not me! Beatrice! Marie confused the brothers. I'm not..."

Once again, Joseph was interrupted as the men took a stronger hold of the reins. "Stop! Stop! I have to get to that ship!" he shouted to the small mob.

Beatrice couldn't believe what was happening. Christopher ran to Joseph's aid. Joseph, Joshua, yes, of course, the names and the brothers could easily be confused, Beatrice thought. Her mind was racing, her heart was lifting but panic soon set in as she was sailing further away. What do I do though?

Christopher reached Joseph and tried to pull some of the men off of him. "Get off him. Leave him alone!" Christopher shouted.

Mystery was rearing, trying to get the men away. It was chaos. She was being pushed towards the edge. Mystery was desperate to get free from the scrum. She reared some more but still the men held on. Joseph pushed Mystery closer to the water's edge. She made a half turn to the right and then another half turn to the left but the mob held on tightly, they were suffocating her and she was getting angry and panicky. Horse and rider both thought the same thing as the water's edge seemed their only way out. Joseph then, suddenly, made a dramatic turn around and darted Mystery forward, crashing her through the mob and leaping her sky-high into the water.

"Ahh!" Beatrice cried.

Christopher was not expecting that along with the rest of the mob. Everybody gasped in shock. Mystery and Joseph flew in the air as they both made their daring leap from land to sea, crashing into the waters.

Beatrice, along with everybody at the port, the Captain and sailors, the workers, the mob, Christopher, everybody, were utterly dumbfounded.

Everybody on the port ran to see if man and horse were all right. Joseph fell to the left of Mystery as they hit the water. They both rose to the surface in a gaggle and a splutter trying to catch their breaths.

Beatrice then, in an impulsive and spontaneous act of sheer emotion, ran to the stern of the boat and jumped overboard.

"Beatrice! No!" shouted Christopher.

"Man overboard!" Somerville shouted.

Everybody was aghast. The whole crowd of people let out an enormous cry, just as an already unbelievable moment got even more unbelievable.

Christopher held his breath as he waited to see Beatrice rise to the surface. He waited, he waited and he waited but she wasn't rising. In a panic, Christopher jumped into the water in an attempt to save Beatrice, who still hadn't surfaced.

Beatrice had worn her skirts to travel but they were now pulling her down, they were drowning her. Christopher saw her being pulled down and he frantically tried to get to her as fast as he could. Beatrice fought to swim to the surface but her skirts were strangling her legs and they kept pulling her back down. Beatrice tried to untie them, she was desperate to free herself from them. Their tight waist made it hard for her to breathe and she was losing her breath fast. Joseph also tried desperately to reach her. The mob now turned their attention from trying to stop them all to trying to save them all. Somebody threw in a buoy and then two other men jumped in, in an attempt to help. Mystery was tiring fast.

Beatrice was also tiring fast. Her skirts were too strong for her. Christopher dived down to try and swim to her, he couldn't even see her. He came up for another breath and to see if she had risen. She hadn't.

"Beatrice! Beatrice!" Christopher shouted.

The crowd of people were shouting for them all to swim to the other side where there was a mooring ramp.

"Beatrice! Beatrice!" Joseph shouted.

Beatrice's breath was shortening. Her skirts were too tight, she just couldn't get the waist free. In a last attempt, she gave a desperate tug at the clasp which finally broke open, releasing her from their death hold. They slipped away from around her legs and slowly fell to the bottom of the sea. Beatrice, in a manic last push and with her last breaths, swam to the surface taking in an almighty gasp of air when she got there.

The first thing Beatrice saw was Mystery. Beatrice took hold of her mane and guided her to the ramp. Christopher and Joseph caught up.

The crowd ran down to the water's edge on the ramp to help them all out. Mystery found her feet on the ramp and walked up to safety. Beatrice and the others likewise. Everybody was speechless, everybody was busy catching their breaths. Mystery shook off the water. They all sat there and watched The Plymouth sail past.

"You're not going to England today, are you, love?" said one of the men on the jetty with them.

"No, not today," Beatrice quietly repeated.

"Beatrice, I'm not the cad. Joshua, my brother, is the gambler," Joseph said breathlessly. Nobody spoke, everybody was still in shock and recovering from the incident.

Joseph stood up and held out his hand for Beatrice to take, she wholeheartedly took it. He helped her up from the ground and gave her his coat to wrap around her now skirtless body and then brought her in for a big and warm hug.

"The tavern, ladies and gentlemen, the tavern. You are all cordially invited for a round at the tavern," said Joseph.

The crowd exploded into cheer and walked straight to Murray's Tavern. Christopher took hold of Mystery and they all walked to have a beer themselves. Christopher took Mystery to the courtyard at the back of the building. The sun was hot and warm there and they all sat to dry off.

"What were you thinking, cousin? You nearly drowned."

"What were you thinking, cousin, jumping in the water like that?" Beatrice came back.

"Well, I wasn't thinking actually," answered Christopher quietly and honestly.

"Well, neither was I," agreed Beatrice. "So much for our goodbyes," they both gave each other enormous smiles and ran into each other for a hug.

As the cousins were talking, they heard a quiet but heavy thud and turned to see Joseph had fallen deadpan onto the ground.

"Monti, Monti!" Christopher called urgently.

Christopher and Beatrice shook Joseph trying to revive him.

"He's alive," Christopher said as he felt for his pulse.

"Monti, Monti" Beatrice said quietly in his ear. "Monti, wake up."

The sound of Beatrice's sweet voice filtered through the haze and blurb of his head. Monti, Monti, he could hear her voice calling him to wake. He was absolutely starving, he thought of all that food waiting for them back at home. "Monti, Monti!" Joseph could hear Beatrice's voice faintly in the background. He thought of Veronica's pumpkin pie and tiramisu, his mind was clearing. The thought of food and the sound of Beatrice's voice was clearing his mind, slowly, his eyes opened. I must have fainted because of my hunger and weakness, he thought. Thank goodness, she's here. Monti's mind was busy thinking but his body was slow to catch up. He could hear Beatrice and Christopher talking.

"Lunch?" Joseph said when he opened his eyes. All he could think about was food.

"Are you all right?" Christopher asked.

"I'll be better after some food," Monti replied, and slowly, with the help of Christopher sat himself up.

Beatrice ran off and got some water from the tavern and then gave it to Joseph who drank it slowly. He felt positively dreadful. His head pounded and his body felt so weak, he had used every inch of his strength in trying to get to Beatrice.

"Ouch, ouch!" Joseph said touching his head.

"Thankfully, you fell on the grassy part," Beatrice said. Beatrice touched his head in sympathy.

"You'll have a nasty bruise," she said.

"On top of another bruise I gave myself today," Joseph replied but he didn't care, he was just so happy Beatrice was here.

"We'll take you home, Monti. You can't ride like this," Beatrice said.

Beatrice went to get Mystery. Her saddle was still wet. The sun was warm on her black coat. Beatrice got up on Mystery in her bloomers and signalled for Christopher to help Joseph up.

"Up you get. I'll ride you home," Beatrice said warmly.

"Yes, ma'am. Yes, Lady B," Joseph weakly joked.

Joseph found the strength to heave himself up on the back of Mystery. He put his arms around Beatrice's waist, he had never been happier in his whole life. This moment, however ghastly he felt, was perfect.

"I like it," said Beatrice quietly as they walked off.

"What?" Joseph asked.

"Lady B," she replied. Beatrice too couldn't have been happier.

Joseph didn't have the strength to reply but squeezed her warmly around the waist in reply. Christopher walked alongside them. He was absorbing all that had just happened. He was readjusting to Beatrice being here again next to him. He looked up at her as he walked. Only a short while ago he had been so utterly full of sorrow at her leaving, but then suddenly, here she was, back again in Boston. Who would have thought such a thing was possible, he thought. Life truly throws some unexpected surprises.

As they walked, Joseph melted into Beatrice's back and lulled to the rhythm of Mystery's walk. The sun was on his back, warming him through. His heart was full and warmed through.

So, Marie had confused the brothers, Beatrice thought. The names Joseph and Joshua are very close in sound; it was an honest but terribly stupid mistake. Beatrice was happy, elated. A warm glow started to run through her as the dramatic events of the day began to slip away, the sun melting them away. The relief that Joseph wasn't the cad was insurmountable to her. The feeling of Joseph or rather Monti being exactly who she thought he was, was like the sweetest gift from heaven. Beatrice then thought of her native friends and their word 'ku' meaning 'gift'. Beatrice thought of all the gifts that got her to this point. The feeling of Monti's arms wrapped around her waist, tightly holding onto her was sublime. Mystery's slow and grounded gait gave rhythm to her contentment.

They finally arrived at Monti's home. Christopher helped Monti down from the horse and the butler came running up to help. Monti was taken by the staff straight up to bed. He took off his damp clothes and slithered under the warm blankets of his bed.

Beatrice and Christopher walked casually into his room. All formality now thrown to the wind. "I'll go and get some dry clothes," said the butler and ran off in a rush.

He soon came back with some new and dry clothes. "Here, Mr Joseph, some dry clothes," the butler said.

"James, could you bring lunch up here please. I'm famished," Monti requested.

"Of course, Mr Joseph," James said and instantly walked out.

"I can't stop thinking about all that food Veronica had prepared. Shame to waste it," Monti said, Beatrice went straight to sit on the bed next to Joseph, Christopher sat in a chair.

"I poisoned myself two days ago," Monti suddenly said.

"What!" Beatrice said.

"It was the only way to get my dastardly brother to leave. My brother, Joshua, to leave," Monti said putting the emphasis on Joshua. I'm so sorry, Lady B, about your parents. That part, I believe, is true," Monti said.

"Yes, that part is true," Beatrice replied.

"I raced to the port in an effort to stop you from sailing but you had already set sail, and well, the rest is history, so they say," Monti explained.

It was true it was going to be their history. The story of their rather unconventional courtship. Mary knocked on the door. Christopher opened it.

"Lunch, sir," she said.

Everybody was completely famished and the sight of the food couldn't have been more appreciated. They ate in silence, too hungry to speak.

"You must compliment the chef for me, Monti. The food is truly exceptional," Christopher said as he finished.

"Veronica is her name. All the way from Naples," Monti said proudly.

"Well, I'd like to thank her myself, if you both don't mind me leaving," Christopher thought this the best moment to leave Beatrice and Monti alone.

"I still have to return to England," Beatrice said jumping directly to the point once Christopher had left.

"Well, so do I. What a coincidence. We have been having quite a few of those," Monti said looking directly at Beatrice with a smile.

"You do?" Beatrice said suspiciously. "What for?"

"Firstly, as your escort, and secondly…" Joseph leant forward towards her.

Beatrice wondered what he was doing? As he leant forward, he leant too far to the side of the bed and fell off.

"Monti! Are you all right?" Beatrice said getting down to help him.

"And secondly, as your husband, if you'll have me?" Monti asked with a big smile. Monti then got out a little box and handed it to Beatrice.

"All the way from Italy. It was my mother's and my mother's mother's, and mother's mother's mother's, and my mother's, mother's, mother's, mother's ring," Monti found this very funny and so did Beatrice, they both laughed.

"Yes, I most certainly will but on one condition," Beatrice said with a big smile. Monti gave a questioning look.

"That you stop falling over," Beatrice said.

"Yes, it is true, this is the third time I've fallen today. I solemnly swear not to fall over again," Monti said with a smile. "I promise I haven't had a drop to drink, pure fungal intoxication," he found this extremely funny too, making himself laugh.

"And the second. That I run my estate as Lady Seymour-Barclay and not as Mrs Joseph Montifiorre."

"You said you only had one condition. If my calculations are correct you have just made two conditions. Lady B, are you trying to fox me? Well, I demand to have a condition too," Monti said.

"All right. I will allow you just one condition," Beatrice said with a smile.

"That you let me let you run your estate as Lady Seymour-Barclay," they both laughed and fell into an embrace.

"Oh, I have another condition," Beatrice said still laughing.

"That's three conditions and counting, Lady Seymour-Barclay. I'm not sure if I can allow it."

"That we marry under an arch of trees at Lacey Manor," Beatrice continued, ignoring Monti's comment.

"Sounds perfect," Monti said. "Do you think we should get up off this floor?" Monti said smiling.

"Absolutely."

The last thing Beatrice was expecting was a proposal of marriage. How things had turned so dramatically around. A few hours ago, she was leaving alone on a ship to England, miserable and broken-hearted. And now, her heart was in bloom and life was hopeful. How things can flip so quickly.

Christopher was elated with the news and extremely relieved. This time the goodbyes won't be as painful, he thought. Not only would Beatrice be off embarking on her new life, as landowner and wife, but most importantly, she would be escorted. Her safety was always Christopher's top priority.

The following days were spent organising the trip back to England. Monti had arranged a ship that was sailing to Plymouth in a week. It was his family's merchant ship so he knew the Captain.

"I want to show you something," Christopher said the morning before their departure.

Beatrice and Christopher walked to his new shop, Meadow Books. It was his, it was official. He had signed the papers, paid the money. It was all his. Christopher couldn't quite believe it. He was on a cloud of quiet euphoria. He kept pinching himself.

"Close your eyes," Christopher said to Beatrice.

Christopher took her hand and lead her inside the bookshop. He swept off the white sheet covering the monstrously big printer.

"Open your eyes,"

"Oh, Christopher. It's enormous. I thought it was big when I saw it last week, but now that it is complete, it truly is enormous. Do you know how to work it?" Beatrice was enthralled with the machine.

"No. But next week the man who sold it to me is going to explain everything. Beautiful, isn't she? All my books are going to be printed on this. B, I can't believe this is actually a reality. I thought my life was going to succumb to nothing, and again, I have you to thank. If it wasn't for your grandiose, cavalier and supremely risky venture of becoming highway robbers this would never have come true."

Christopher pulled Beatrice into his arms.

"Thank you for being the most annoyingly stubborn and persistent person I know. I love you for it. I will also miss it."

"You deserve it, Kit. Why don't we give this enormous machine of yours a name?"

"All right. Any ideas?" Christopher liked the idea.

"How about Boadicea?" Beatrice suggested.

"Yes, Boadicea, I like it. Boadicea it is," this appeased to Christopher's love of history. "I bought this to celebrate this occasion," Christopher held up a bottle of champagne. "I name this printer Boadicea and may God bless all that is printed by it." Christopher then ceremonial smashed a glass of champagne on it. They all cheered and drank to celebrate this monumental moment.

Beatrice was so genuinely happy for her cousin. He deserved all the success and happiness for his cultured soul. He had already and so quickly made a home for himself here in Boston. The printer arriving so quickly cementing that. It was all perfect really, Beatrice thought. Leaving a week later was so much kinder too.

The day of their goodbyes had finally arrived. Monti said his goodbyes to all the staff and left Veronica for the last.

"Goodbye, Veronica. I'm utterly indebted to you. If it wasn't for you, I wouldn't be going back to England with Lady B," Monti said to Veronica. "I will miss you." They both embraced, Veronica was in tears.

"Goodbye, Signore Bambini," Veronica said amongst her tears. She didn't like being at the Boston residence with only Joshua but she also took peace of mind that she would be returning to the Montefiorres' London residence in a few months and will be seeing Monti soon.

They all arrived at the port in good time. Mystery walked up the plank, confident of her new adventure ahead. Beatrice and Monti followed suit. It was only a week ago that their spectacle at the port had happened, and thanks to this spectacle, both Beatrice and Monti were returning to England together.

"Welcome aboard New Tides," Captain Wallace said.

Beatrice, once again, thought the name of their ship quite apt. She was, after all, now embarking on her new episode in life. *I'm going home. I'm going back to England*, Beatrice thought. She couldn't quite believe it.

Christopher too came on board for his goodbyes. Beatrice ran into his arms and they both embraced long and hard. They didn't dare think or let alone ask when they would ever see each again so they held on longer in their embrace.

"Goodbye, B, I will be thinking of you. Write," Christopher's voice cracked as he spoke.

"Goodbye, Kit. Write. You have no excuses now, you have Boadicea waiting back at the shop," Beatrice said, keeping her composure. She held back the tears.

"Look after her, Monti. You don't find many like her. She is the rarest of gems. No highway robber could steal this gem," Christopher said and gave Monti a farewell hug.

"Time to depart," Captain Wallace said gesturing Christopher to leave the ship.

Christopher walked down the plank and onto to the quayside and watched as New Tides slowly set sail.

They waved and waved and waved until, finally, they were both out of each other's sight, only then did Beatrice burst into a flood of tears.

ENGLAND

THE coast of England approached. It was a cold November day. The wind scratched her face, the grey clouds were heavy and the rain was imminent; Beatrice couldn't have been happier.

The journey had not been so bad. They had run into a storm halfway across the Atlantic. Beatrice and Monti sat it out as best as they could but the seasickness, finally, got the best of them both. Beatrice longed to reach land. She longed for England and longed for her feet to touch solid ground, but most of all, she longed for the sound of birds.

Land did arrive and it was the sweetest gift. It was green and solid and home. Beatrice was apprehensive though, she didn't know what to expect. Lacey, the staff, her reputation? She imagined herself driving up Lacey's beautiful driveway and seeing its stoic facade greeting her. She imagined riding its woodlands but her thoughts abruptly stopped there, she didn't allow herself to imagine Asta, would she or would she not be there?

"All hands on deck!" shouted Wallace.

New Tides slowly sailed into Plymouth. Plymouth was busy with the hubbub of all ports. "Ropes!" commanded Wallace.

And that was it, they were tied to land, they were tied to England. The sails came falling down along with the rain. As if it was England's welcome home greeting.

"Thank you, good sir," Monti said on deck as the rain poured.

"Thank you," Beatrice added. "It was a pleasure sailing with you."

"England's brought you its finest," Wallace said looking up to the sky and referring to the rain.

They had, after all, spent most evenings dining together. Wallace had enjoyed their company in his cabins.

Beatrice put her first foot on English soil, but this time, this step was different. It was infused with the experience of a changed girl, now a woman. She left England a girl and returned a woman. So much had happened and so quickly. Despite the rain, Beatrice stopped as she put her first footsteps on English soil. She took in a long and deep breath. It was the smell of England Beatrice breathed in; she loved it, she was home.

They were wet through by the time they arrived at a tavern. They dried in front of the fire, their rooms were cosy. And gradually they let everything sink in.

"Lacey tomorrow," Monti said.

"Lacey tomorrow," Beatrice repeated. "I wonder what to expect? It's going to be strange without mother and father. We will see."

The next day there was a carriage available. Mystery, tied on, followed from behind. The day was clear, their clothes were dry and the day ahead was a new one.

Beatrice was mostly silent throughout their bumpy journey. It was a lot to take in, an enormous amount. She looked at England's countryside, its rolling hills, its hedges, its order, it felt ordered compared to America's wildness. Beatrice already had the flow of wildness running through her so maybe that's why she needed some of England's order to balance her out.

Beatrice's heart raced as they came upon Shere village. She just couldn't believe it. Here she was in her home village. It was all the same; sweet, small and cosy. They continued on the short journey to Lacey. Then they turned left onto the main road that was once her highway robber's road. Beatrice looked at Monti. Her look said everything. She put her head out the window of the carriage as they slowly and noisily trundled along it. Oh, my goodness, she thought. It all started here. Look! There is the oak tree. It's true, one can hardly see anybody from behind it. I have never seen it from this perspective. I can't actually believe I did it, that I was the Highwaygirl, a highway robber. Beatrice's thoughts and emotions were racing, both trying to absorb it all. And then there she was Lacey Manor. Beatrice saw the tops of the beautiful chimneys over the tall trees, they had always been her beacons. And now, they still stood tall and constant, waiting for her return, The oak trees on the forecourt were still there, still growing, still observing. They had been there for hundreds of years. Her driveway drew them in, as if welcoming them both with open arms. Beatrice was both excited and nervous the closer she got.

As they got closer, Beatrice saw some of the kitchen staff running out, and then she saw, to her utter delight, Betty. Nobody, of course, knew who the inhabitants of the unknown carriage that was approaching were and they stood waiting, curious and transfixed.

"Who could it be?" said Betty. "We haven't had visitors for a long time."

The carriage finally turned and stopped. Beatrice couldn't contain herself and shouted from her carriage window.

"Betty! Betty! I'm home!"

Beatrice slammed her door open and ran into Betty's arms, she was truly, truly pleased to see her.

"Lady Seymour! You're back! You're back!" Betty let out a yell of delight on seeing Beatrice, abandoning all formalities.

Beatrice let out a long sigh of relief. She was home and Betty was here. Her embraces had always been there, having been steadfast in comfort for almost all of Beatrice's life.

"Ah, come here, lass, let me have another good look at ya." Betty pulled away from their embrace to look at Beatrice. "Ahh, Beatrice lassy, come here," and gave her another hug. "Are ya real? Are ya alive! In heaven's name, what glory, you've returned!"

"I am so pleased to see you, Betty, truly I am. I didn't know if anybody was even going to be here. Betty, I'd like you to meet Mr Montifiorre," Beatrice said introducing Monti.

"I've heard all about you, Mrs Crowley, especially about your famous shortbread," Monti was genuinely pleased to see Betty. "I am a lover of food so I would love to see your kitchens."

"Nice to meet you, sir," Betty curtsied.

"We thought we'd never see ya again. Ahh, I can hardly believe it!" Betty was still in shock. "Susan, go and put the kettle on. I'll go and bake up some shortbread now."

Betty curtsied to walk away, she was a flurry of emotion but turned on remembering something. "My dear, Mr Coombs is not here any more and we've lost a lot of staff, since the terrible accident. It's just me, a few of the kitchen girls and two grooms."

"Michael?" Beatrice asked nervously.

"No. Ma'am, he's not here. He went to the Knutley Estate down the road."

Beatrice's heart sank a bit but maybe she could bring him back to Lacey. That could wait for another day, she thought.

"Well, Monti, let me show you around. But first, I have to do something." Beatrice said, her nerves were settling but there was still something that tugged at them.

"Please, Mr Montifiorre, let me show you to the kitchens," Betty warmly said with a smile. Betty couldn't be happier. They were all on cloud nine. Firstly and most importantly, to see Beatrice but also because it meant they still had their jobs and could stay on at Lacey. Lacey, after all, was their home as well. They had only been kept on until the lawyers had sorted out the legal complications.

Beatrice made the tentative steps across the lawns. The gardens looked a bit unkept. Beatrice headed down towards the stables, crossed the little bridge over the stream. She never normally took this route as it was too exposing but now she didn't need to hide. It is impossibly quaint, she thought as her nerves twisted and turned. If Asta wasn't there she didn't know how she would react. She then walked past the stables and across a big muddy patch. Her shoes got caught in the mud so Beatrice bent to free them, and in doing so, she looked up and there, at the furthest part of the field, stood Asta. All Beatrice could do was drop her face into her hands and wept tears of sheer relief. Asta's head, of course, rose the minute she sensed Beatrice and came running up the hill. Still crouching, Beatrice stayed frozen. The relief was insurmountable and it took a hold on her, she froze, stuck in the mud. She watched Asta gallop up the hill to her. Beatrice then leapt up, and forgetting all about her shoes, ran barefoot towards Asta like she had done a million times before.

"Oh, girl, you're here! I can't believe it! I just can't believe it!"

Beatrice wrapped her arms around Asta's neck, sunk her head into it and stayed there. You are alive, you are alive, Beatrice kept repeating in her head. Tears rolled down her face. Nothing could replace the love she had for Asta, not even Christopher, not even Monti. Something ran so deep between them that no other horse and no other human could come close to.

Time stood still. They both stood still, lost in the moment. Asta too was struck by it. Without a word, Beatrice dropped her skirts, and as she had done a million times before, she swung up on her back. She was home. Beatrice took hold of her mane and they cantered off into the woodlands, up the fields and through the streams. It was November and the streams were high. What joy as they crashed through them. And then, they walked into the meadow. Beatrice stopped, lay back on Asta's back, and with her arms behind her head, looked up to the sky. She watched the clouds pass overhead, changing their shapes. Asta grazed. Did all of the past extraordinary events actually happen? Had it all been an unbelievable dream? Beatrice thought. Here I am, in the meadow at Lacey with Asta as if nothing had ever happened. Beatrice's thoughts obviously went to Christopher. But instead of pushing them away, she thought of his new bookshop, Meadow Books. He was now in his meadow, she in hers, it felt right, Beatrice thought. Beatrice daydreamed until she thought it best to go back to Monti. After all, I want to make him feel so welcome. And with a surge of optimism, Beatrice sat up and looked forward to her new life at Lacey with her husband.

"Come on, girl, we must get back."

Back in the field, Beatrice grabbed her skirt and ran back to the house. She was muddy as she always used to be; she was definitely back home. Instead of creeping back in through the kitchens, this time, Beatrice walked up to the big front door, opened it and walked proudly into her house. What fortune, she thought, how things have turned around. Beatrice thought of all the ships she had sailed on over this last tumultuous year; The Fortune, The Endeavour, New Tides and pondered on their relevance.

Beatrice took a moment and stood alone in the big entrance hall. It felt cold and lifeless. I'm going to make this a happy home, full of life, Beatrice thought. But most of all, I'm going to fill it with love and children and food. She suddenly missed her mother. Her mother would have loved to have had a home like that. So, in her honour, I will make it so, Beatrice thought. She went straight to the kitchens. There was a lot to absorb and take in.

"I see you've already been out on a ride?" Betty said seeing Beatrice enter covered in mud and in her bloomers. "Some things never change."

"She was still there. I can't believe it! She was still there, in the field," Beatrice was still overcome with emotion. "Asta was in the field."

"She fought tooth and nail with the Lord not to have her put down or sold. Tooth and nail," Betty said, speaking proudly of her mistress.

Tears filled Beatrice's eyes and her heart wrenched when she heard this. Her mother's legacy was now solidified. Thank you, Mother, Beatrice said to herself, wherever you are in heaven.

"Lady Seymour got her back from her place in hiding after the trial. A terrible time, mi'lady, a terrible time and put her back in the field. Paul, the other groom's been looking after her," Betty explained.

"So, you have made yourself perfectly at home, I see. I am exceedingly pleased to see that. So, how do our kitchens fare?" Beatrice quickly changed the subject to a lighter tone.

"I approve," Monti said with a very big smile. "Especially with these! Betty, your shortbread is exceptional," Monti was genuinely impressed.

"It's his favourite place to be, Betty. You'll never get rid of him," Beatrice said as she put her trousers on.

"Mrs Crowley's already made me feel very welcome. Care for one?" Monti said offering Beatrice a shortbread.

Beatrice flopped in the armchair that was still by the fire and ate her shortbread. She was so glad to be home. She had mud on her feet, it was crispy cold outside and cosy inside, the fire was warm and Asta was in her field, Beatrice could not think of anything more she could possibly want. Later that day Monti and Beatrice chose their new rooms. They needed to be made cosy and lived-in but that would come in no time. Beatrice was in a rush to do just that. And the first thing she did to set this in motion was open her precious linen bag that held all her belongings. She got out her highwaygirl mask and her red scarf. She took down from the wall an old frame and then carefully pinned the scarf and mask behind its glass. She held up the frame to admire its contents. Her highwaygirl memories rushed through her like a current, like a living flashback. She then placed the frame with its proud contents on a hook on a small wall by her dressing screen. A gallant reminder of her time as an outlaw. A gallant reminder never to forget her courage. She then lit a fire to warm up her new rooms, warm up her new life. Beatrice was excited.

The next few days Beatrice leapt into action. Her determination was absolute. Lacey Manor would be a working and profitable manor. She was going to make Lacey vibrant again. Monti, after all, was a business man although he considered himself a lover of food first so his input would, of course, be invaluable.

Beatrice's father had bred horses, not many, but it had been a part of his businesses so Beatrice planned to expand on this with Asta. Still young, she would be the mother of Beatrice's first siring. She also planned to turn some of its ten thousand acres of land into farmland. She had lots to do and even more to learn.

Thanks to Betty, Beatrice knew where Michael was living. On a chilly late Sunday November morning, Beatrice swung up on Asta, and in her skirts but riding astride, Beatrice headed down to Michael's village and quickly found his street, Oakly Street.

Beatrice knocked on the door. She heard the commotion of the life inside; children, adults, dogs barking. Beatrice heard Michael as he walked towards the door, shouting to one of the dogs to stop barking. Michael opened the door. He froze cold. He went white. He couldn't believe what he was seeing.

"I thoughts you were dead, ma'am. Or gone to America," Michael stuttered in a daze. Beatrice couldn't help herself and went straight for an embrace. He looked older, of course, she thought. More weathered.

"Call me, Beatrice," said Beatrice, after all, they were friends.

"Would you be interested in returning to Lacey? I need you there. Sorry, I mean, I would like you to be there to help with the horses, with Asta," Beatrice threw Michael a look, expressing her amazement at having Asta again.

"The Lady fought tooth and nail to save her, you know!"

"I know. My gratitude is unmeasurable. I couldn't believe it when I saw her in her field. So what do you think? Or do you already have other commitments?"

"Well, ma'am, uh, Beatrice, sorry, ma'am, but I can't call you Beatrice, it feels strange," Michael was still in shock.

"All right ma'am."

"I do have other work, ma'am, but nothing I can't rearrange."

"Michael, I also need farmers and another head gardener. Do you know of anybody?"

"Yes, I do, in fact."

"So, when can you start? As soon as possible, I hope."

"I'll let you know, ma'am."

Beatrice went and gave Michael another hug. "I'm so glad to see you, Michael, truly."

Michael felt her sincerity. He too was utterly joyous to see her although a little shocked and reserved in his reaction.

As Beatrice rode back slowly to Lacey she thought she'd walk past the old oak tree. Once there she stopped in front of it and mulled over her first escapades as the Highwaygirl. She went over those past events in her mind. Her coat and mask, Christopher's nods on seeing the carriages, the anticipation, the rain, the pistol held outstretched, Monti, so many moments, moments she couldn't believe she was the centre character of. "I can't believe what we all did. Partners in crime we were. We were all partners in crime," Beatrice said aloud to Asta. "I have to find your partner in crime, my girl. I must write to Radcliff and find Moby. For you, for Kit, for Moby." Once back at home Beatrice wrote a letter immediately to Radcliff in the hope of finding Moby.

The following week, Beatrice had a meeting with her lawyer. She didn't much like the man but he was her father's lawyer and had to inform her of all the recent details of the estate. Monti joined them for the meeting and agreed a new lawyer, a fresh lawyer would be a good idea. But the good news was that Beatrice had been left with a large inheritance and she had more than enough money to start her business ventures. What her father lacked in love he made up for in business. So, it was with great excitement that she planned to make a surprise visit to Lord Derby.

Both Beatrice and Monti turned their journey north to see Derby into a mini holiday. They didn't rush, they stopped at Stratford-upon-Avon and visited Shakespeare's house. Beatrice had never done anything like that before and with her husband-to-be. She was, they both were, on cloud nine. The weather was dismal but they were both so in love, they were oblivious. It actually made their trip all the cosier. Long dinners by the fire, long morning rests in bed. It was magical.

Ten days later, they arrived in Merseyside. Beatrice had taken the enormous risk of arriving unannounced. Lord Derby may not even be at home but Beatrice wanted, more than anything, the element of surprise.

"I come unannounced. Is Lord Derby at home?" Beatrice asked the butler, holding her breath and crossing her fingers behind her back.

"Yes, ma'am. Who should I say is calling?" the butler asked. Beatrice let out an inward sigh.

"Can you tell him it is someone who likes winning as much as he does." The butler went off and soon came back.

"Follow me."

Monti stayed back and waited in the entrance hall. Beatrice followed the butler down the corridor and was looking forward to making her surprise. She was getting used to this and liked the impact it created.

The butler opened Lord Derby's door and Lady Beatrice Seymour-Barclay walked in. She looked a fine figure of a woman as she walked into Lord Derby's study. She had grown into herself and made the impact she so desired.

"Lord Derby. I believe we are already acquainted," Beatrice looked commanding in her burgundy dress.

Lord Derby was rarely lost for words. Today at this moment, he was completely dumbfounded. He could not believe who was standing before him. It was the last person in the whole world he would ever expect to see.

"Well, you certainly like making an entrance, Lady Seymour. I would expect to see the King more than I'd expect to see you," Derby said collecting himself.

"I come on business. I am now the owner of Lacey Manor and I'd like to sire horses, and I believe, you have one that I would be greatly interested in. Stormboy."

"I feel a sherry is in order. Do you partake?" Lord Derby asked hesitantly.

"No, not for me," Beatrice replied.

The pair talked for a while and a deal was made. Derby and Seymour, after all, shared a secret. A very big secret. And Beatrice, after all, had made Derby a lot of money last June so he owed her a favour. Beatrice was here to claim his favour. Beatrice, once again, shook Derby's hand. The second time she had done so and it felt good.

"Before you leave, Lady Seymour, I'd…"

"Call me Miss Seymour now that we're in business together."

"Miss Seymour, I'd like to show you something."

Lord Derby guided Beatrice over to a cabinet and he opened its dainty glass door. "Grand, isn't she?" Derby said as he held up the Epsom Derby gold cup.

"She is indeed. Congratulations on your deserved win on a marvel of a horse and a wizard of a jockey." Beatrice gave Derby a cheeky smile.

"A fine win, Miss Seymour. A very fine win," Derby proudly put the cup back in its place.

Beatrice left happy with her new business plan. After Christmas, she hoped Asta would be pregnant with Stormboy. Their bonding would be Lacey's first siring. It couldn't be more perfect or more meaningful.

But before any fillies were born, Beatrice and Monti had a wedding to arrange.

Christmas was approaching. It was cold, the mornings were frosty and bitter. One bright morning, Beatrice, dressed in her breeches, went to Monti who was already in the kitchens.

"I want to show you something. I'll saddle the horses. Meet you at the stables," Beatrice said. Beatrice was already sitting on Asta when Monti arrived. He then climbed up on Mystery and they both walked off into the woodland.

"So, what do you think of December twenty-second for our wedding day?" Beatrice said.

"Sounds good," Monti replied.

"Do you remember one of my many conditions I gave when we were back in Boston?" Beatrice questioned.

"Yes. Yes, I do."

"Well, here it is."

Beatrice turned the bend where the tunnel of arched trees started. She led them down under it.

"It has its charm and beauty in the winter. I can ask the vicar if he'll perform the ceremony here. What do you think?"

Beatrice was excited and so was Monti.

"It's beautiful. Magical even," Monti replied. "We can adorn it with winter flowers and ribbons."

"What a lovely idea," Beatrice was genuinely enthused, that was a lovely idea and something she would never have thought of, Monti being the more creative of the two.

Beatrice stopped in the middle. The birds were full of song. It was a peaceful and heavenly spot. Their horses were side by side. Beatrice leant across to Monti and gave him a kiss.

"I love you, Monti," she said with all the love in her heart.

"I love you, Lady B," Monti replied.

Monti couldn't quite believe this was all happening. Beatrice couldn't quite believe this was all happening. She had made a vow many months ago in this very spot and here she was about to fulfil it. Even though it had taken robbery, arrests, servitude and America to get her here. Life truly casts its windy roads.

The wedding was a simple one. The leafless winter arch had been decorated with red ribbon and some wild winter flowers, it looked beautiful. Beatrice wore an indigo blue silk dress and a cream wool cape, it was cold. Her hair was just long enough to be worn up, and as she had done so many times before in the past, she sprayed it with lavender. Beatrice had thought of Lilly as she had dressed and missed her. She had been her friend, her confidant. The whole highway robber idea was, after all, hers. If it wasn't for Lilly, Beatrice wouldn't be back here at Lacey, marrying the man she loved. I will try to find her, Beatrice thought.

Beatrice on Asta, Monti on Mystery walked through the decorated arch with birdsong as their chorus. When they reached the vicar, they both dismounted and handed their horses to Michael who was also their witness.

"Do you Joseph Abraham Montifiorre Solinni take this Lady Beatrice Clementine Seymour-Barclay to be your wife?"

"I do," Monti said smiling.

He had never really seen Beatrice looking so beautiful. She looked dashing in her highway robber's clothes and breeches, but today, as she stood in all her feminine glory, she looked beautiful, Monti thought as he said those all-important words.

"Do you Lady Beatrice Clementine Seymour-Barclay take Joseph Abraham Montifiorre Solinni to be your husband," the vicar continued.

"I do," said Beatrice smiling.

"I now pronounce you both, man and wife," said the vicar.

And that was it. It was simple, beautiful, but most of all, it was full of love. Beatrice stood under the arch and took in a deep breath, absorbing the moment. The moment that so nearly didn't happen.

Food, plenty of food, was laid out for the guests to eat. Betty had gone to all lengths to put on a feast. Monti was very proud. A few of Monti's London and Cambridge friends were invited and a debutante friend of Beatrice's came, escorted by her brother and aunt. All the staff were invited to join in with the dancing once all the food had been served. It was all very joyous, exactly how a wedding should be.

January 1st 1800, Beatrice and Monti celebrated with a horse ride in the country. It was cold and sunny. The January air scratched at their faces and Beatrice adored it. It was bracing and it made her feel utterly alive. The streams were full of ice and there was nothing more pleasurable than crashing into them.

Beatrice lead Monti to the meadow. It held all its beauty and secrecy even in the winter. It was subdued but full of life. Monti had to admit it was a beautiful spot and held something quite magical.

"I'm pregnant," Beatrice blurted out, she was never one for subtly. "I thought this would be a beautiful place to tell you."

Monti was so shocked he couldn't say a word. He thought he was being shown Beatrice's secret meadow for the first time not being told he was going to be a father for the first time.

"Amore!" was all Monti could say, his joy stealing his words. "Amore, this is so wonderful!"

"I have to get down. I have to be sick," Beatrice said changing the tone immediately. Beatrice got down, throwing her legs over the neck of Asta and then ran to the tree to vomit. "Anybody would think I was back on the ship," Beatrice said walking back to Monti.

"I thought it was something I said," Monti said smiling.

Beatrice smiled back and got back up on Mystery, deciding to swap horses without asking Monti. "I'm hungry!" Beatrice enthused. "Especially for some of Betty's apple pies."

Monti, still in shock, did as he was told. He climbed up on Asta, lagging behind Beatrice. A baby, he kept thinking, a baby! He trotted up to Beatrice so they walked side by side.

"Amore, a baby! A baby, amore!" Monti said.

Beatrice put out her hand to take his and gave Monti a warm and beautiful smile. "Yes, darling, a baby. We are having a baby."

"You will have to stop riding," Monti said kindly but unknowingly touched a nerve.

"I will most certainly not!" Beatrice withdrew her hand instantly and gave Monti a sharp look. Monti didn't say a word more. He would bring this delicate topic up another day.

They walked back slowly. And still glowing in the news of their baby-to-be, ate a hearty lunch by the fire. That afternoon Beatrice told Betty.

"Well, look at you," Betty said to Beatrice. "I can hardly believe it. One minute, you're a girl running havoc up and down the country, and the next, you're going to be a mother."

Betty really couldn't believe all that had happened in such a short time.

"That girl's already lived three lifetimes and she's still only eighteen. And you know what? I don't think motherhood is going to stop her. She's still going to cause some stir or another," Betty said to Florence as she was plucking a chicken. She was going to feed Beatrice like it was Christmas all over again.

"She's too skinny anyway," Betty said, murmuring to herself as she continued plucking. "Got to fatten her up."

Beatrice did fatten up too. Her tummy grew and grew and grew. It was all the talk around the house, everybody predicting that it would probably be a girl.

"You are big all the way round. It's a girl, for sure," Betty said to Beatrice one spring morning as Beatrice came down for yet more shortbread.

"All my girls were big and round too," Matilda said.

Matilda was one of the new staff taken on along with two more grooms, gardeners and two footmen. The house, as Beatrice had promised, was coming back to life. Spring was in the air, hope was fluttering with the butterflies and the daffodils were blooming.

"Is it not best to rest, darling. Riding may not be the best of activities to do now," Monti said cautiously, he had lost that fight a long time ago.

"Monti, dear. A pregnancy is not going to stop me from riding. I'll know when it's time to stop." And it was true. By her fifth month, it was too uncomfortable to ride. Beatrice had ridden Asta gently all over the estate up until then. Watched the winter turn to spring. Watched the bluebells come up in the meadow. She would sit amongst the flowers, holding her belly, embracing her first pregnancy. She thought how all the years prior to this had been so endlessly turbulent. It felt like one fight, one struggle after another, and now for the first time, everything just seemed to flow. Anything could change like the flip of a coin, but for now, everything was blissful and Beatrice intended to embrace that.

There was also some other exciting news at this time.

"I think she's pregnant," said Beatrice in disbelief to Michael. "I do believe my Asta is pregnant."

"Yes, ma'am. You are right. She's pregnant," said the new head groom, Marlow. A warm man and lover of horses. A far cry from the other groom.

"Asta! You are going to be a mother like me," Beatrice whispered into her ear. "We're going to be mothers together," Beatrice was ecstatic.

This wonderful news, made her last months, more bearable.

By the seventh month, Beatrice's romantic pregnancy had turned into discomfort and impatience. She was not used to being hindered or slowed down. But despite the discomfort, Beatrice went about the business of the estate as much as she could. Thanks to Michael, who had found her the head farmer and helpers, the first crops had been planted. Everything felt like new beginnings. Beatrice enjoyed going to see the farmers working. She would bring down water for them. It was a massive endeavour she was undertaking and a scary one. Would the seeds bear good crops? Would she even be able to sell the crops? It was a new world to her and she depended wholeheartedly on the head farmer, Wilkinson. Beatrice was a sponge, taking in as much information as she could about farming. She wanted to learn.

"Well, you've got good soil, ma'am. I don't see why your first yielding won't be good," said Wilkinson, from Lancashire originally.

Mid-September was her due date. August the crops had to be harvested. And Asta was due in January. So much was going on.

Beatrice happened to be looking out of her window and onto the front grounds of Lacey when she saw a horse and rider enter the driveway. Who could that be? Beatrice thought quizzically as she lovingly stroked her belly and her wriggling baby. As horse and rider came closer Beatrice turned instantly and ran down the stairs and out the front door. What a surprise, what an apparition, Beatrice thought gleefully as she waved.

Radcliff and Moby trotted right up to Beatrice. Radcliff jumped down in a whirl of glee and ran straight into the arms of Beatrice.

"What a wonder, my dear. You are a marvel and a woman in bloom," Radcliff was overflowing with joy.

"I am back. I am home. And it is all thanks to you, my friend. You brought Moby! Oh Christopher will be so joyous and Asta too," Beatrice embraced Moby who instantly rubbed his nose in her hands, he too was happy to be here. "You look well, boy. My faithful friend has been looking after you. Radcliff you are truly a gentleman. Come, let us have tea, we have much to talk about. What a truly wonderful surprise. I must introduce you to my husband, Monti. Now where do I start." Beatrice was a flurry of excitement

Beatrice and Radcliff took tea together and talked about everything. Radcliff could not believe what a fine woman this young girl had evolved into. Courageous, stoic, an adventurer. Just as her name bequeaths her. He adored her and couldn't wait to tell his mother, the Duchess, all about their meeting.

They talked for hours, about America, Meadow Books, The Lakota, The Wager, all the highs and all the lows. It was all so adventurous thought Radcliff. They laughed and gossiped, it was wonderful. Life had given Beatrice a true friend. Finally it was time to leave and they both walked to the entrance where Radcliff's carriage was waiting.

"Tell your mother the book is an inspiration," Beatrice said smiling.

"I will indeed. You are a triumph, my dear," Radcliff said giving Beatrice a hug.

"Come visit soon. Come see the baby," Beatrice said as Radcliff got into the carriage.

"I will indeed," Radcliff said.

Radcliff's carriage rode away leaving Beatrice waving it goodbye. She stood for a while on the driveway letting the moment settle and then walked across to the field where she looked upon Asta, Mystery and now Moby, all grazing. I can't wait to tell Christopher, Beatrice happily thought.

With a bulging belly and the hot August English sun shining down, Beatrice sat under a tree with the water and watched the farmers bringing in the harvest. It was back-breaking work and it didn't stop. If it wasn't for her pregnancy Beatrice would be helping the workers. She too now knew about back-breaking work, she had lived it. The hay, the barley and the oats all had to be cut and divided and rolled before any rains. So, the farmers sometimes worked well into the night. Beatrice had employed more farmers especially for the harvest. She fed them well and she also didn't let her pregnancy stop her from helping whenever she could. After all, she enjoyed it, she needed it. Sitting still was something Beatrice just couldn't do.

"Sheep," Beatrice said to Monti one day as they sat under a tree. "I'd like to have some sheep next year. I want Lacey full of life."

"Why stop at sheep? We could get some goats," Monti joked.

"Goats. I would like to have some goats," Beatrice said seriously, she wasn't joking.

August rolled into September. Everybody at Lacey was excited about the newcomer's arrival, none more so than Beatrice herself, who was happy for her pregnancy to end and her motherhood to begin. Monti too was excited but was nervous too, scared even. Many a woman's life had been sacrificed in the endeavour of bringing new life into this world. Monti prayed that Beatrice's life wouldn't be. He just wished that Beatrice would do less. But there was no telling her, she was stubborn to the core. He still had his business to run and had to go to London frequently. His father was none too pleased with his son having left Boston but Monti had salvaged his father's finances so there wasn't actually much need for him to stay there. His mother and father didn't approve at all of his choice of wife. An ex-criminal and a famous one at that. It was totally scandalous and utterly unconventional, but once they found out about the imminent birth of their first grandchild, their hearts softened. They planned to visit after the birth.

Beatrice wrote avidly to Christopher. She told him all about Moby and Radcliff. Christopher was so utterly happy that Moby was safe. With this news his heart finally felt at peace. Beatrice poured out her heart in every letter. She explained with excitement all her ideas for the future and all the ones that were now in motion. She missed him. He missed her. She would have loved to have shared the farming and Asta's pregnancy with him. He would have loved to have shared the opening of his bookshop with her. But they were grateful for their letters.

It was when she sealed one of those letters that her baby made its first stirrings. Beatrice stood up, looked out of the window to admire the three horses that were now in the field nearest to the house. She watched Mystery stroll over to Asta when, suddenly, her waters broke.

It happened so quickly that Beatrice didn't even have time to ring the bell. The contractions came hard and fast and she bore down under their force. Beatrice could hardly think. She was completely taken by surprise and in agony. How could anything be so forceful? Beatrice surrendered to its will, she had no other choice and did her best to hone in all her strengths. A strength now greater and more profound than all the others. Beatrice managed to get to the bell and rang it hard before another almighty push came pounding down. It was gruelling and all-encompassing like nothing she could compare it to. It was childbirth, its own unique entity of the power of giving life. And like everything in Beatrice's life, it was happening quickly.

Florence opened the door and was instantly taken aback. She was expecting to deliver her tray, not deliver a baby. But that is exactly what she had to do.

"Ma'am. It's nearly here. Ma'am, I can see the baby's head." Florence leapt into action. She had three of her own children and knew quite a bit about giving birth but not about delivering.

"Ah, here it comes, here it comes!" Florence said encouragingly.

Beatrice let out one last push and then a sigh as her baby came into the world. She was exhausted but elated. Florence took hold of the baby girl and instantly gave it to Beatrice.

"A baby girl," Beatrice said giving her daughter a smile. A smile only a mother can give when having just given the gift of life. Baby and mother looked at each other, both spellbound, both in love.

"A baby girl," Beatrice repeated. Her heart swelled with an all-encompassing love. She held her baby daughter in her arms and just kept staring at her, she was overcome with maternal love.

"A baby girl," Beatrice said again.

"I'll get some water. Let's get you both clean and in bed," Florence said. Tears welled up in her eyes. Tears of pure emotion, of love. Tears when seeing the miracle of life being born.

Florence cut the cord and poured alcohol over it. Beatrice and baby got into bed and instinctively she fed her baby.

Monti arrived home and the new butler, Withers, gave him a big smile and looked upstairs. Monti dropped his bag and pounded up the stairs and then quietly opened their bedroom door.

"It's a girl, Monti," Beatrice beamed.

"Oh, Lady B! It's a girl. Oh, she's so beautiful. What the most incredible thing," Monti was completely overcome with emotion. He burst into tears. "It is a girl!"

"Are you all right?" he asked taking Beatrice's hand.

"The hardest fifteen minutes of my life. It happened so quickly."

Monti just couldn't believe there was a whole new life now in their lives, in their room. It was an incredible thing. Words simply failed him and he let the emotion take over.

"What shall we call her?" Monti asked.

"I'm going to feed her myself," Beatrice said.

"Of course! My mother fed us."

"Well, I thought of Esmerelda Ku. In honour of my mother and her crusaders emerald ring and Ku in honour of my Lakota friends for saving Christopher. Ku means gift and this little thing is the most beautiful gift of all," Beatrice said.

"Esme for short. I think that's a lovely name," Monti loved it.

Lacey Manor had truly come alive. A whole new zest flowed through it and its walls. The cries of a baby. The busy feet of staff. Beatrice had adopted two dogs, two border collies, and they ran about the place. Horses in the field, crops in the barn. Beatrice became even busier whether with the baby or the horses. Esme went everywhere with her, to the fields, to the stables, to the town, she even went riding with her.

It was only a few months later that Michael came running at night to get Beatrice. "She's started, ma'am. Asta is in labour."

Beatrice ran down to the stables and saw the birth of Asta's beautiful baby boy. His long scrawny legs struggled to hold his body up. Asta was a caring and doting mother to her new foal. How strange and amazing that both herself and her mare both became mothers at the same time, Beatrice thought.

That Christmas came and went. It was a hard winter. They had lost much of their barley crop and Esme was very ill with a cough. Florence too was ill and couldn't work for a while. Betty kept everyone going with her warm fires and warm food.

Beatrice hadn't had a letter from Christopher for a while and hoped he was all right. She wondered how he was in Boston. Had he found a wife or a sweetheart? Beatrice wondered. I hope he isn't ill.

Beatrice was sitting in her chair by the fire feeding Esme on a cold February morning, when Florence knocked on the door.

"Ma'am, this came for you," Florence said.

Florence handed Beatrice a little package and a letter. It was Christopher's handwriting. Beatrice, as always, got excited when one of Christopher's letters arrived, but this time, it came with a package.

Beatrice was overflowing with excitement and tore off the string and wrapping to reveal a box. With Esme wriggling in her arms, she eagerly tore open the very well-wrapped box and opened it. Beatrice burst into an enormous smile. Her heart was overjoyed.

"Oh, my goodness, Esme, he's done it. Your Uncle Kit has done it!"

Beatrice lifted the book out of its box and gently glided her hand over its beautiful cover and chuckled to herself as she read the title.

"The Highwaygirl by Christopher Seymour-Barclay."

THE END